THE GOD
IN THE MOUNTAIN

THE GOD IN THE MOUNTAIN

a novel

Colin Thubron

W • W • NORTON & COMPANY • INC •
New York

For my Mother and Father

Printed in the United States of America.

Library of Congress Cataloging in Publication Data
Thubron, Colin, 1939–
The god in the mountain.
I. Title.
PZ4.T554Go 1977 [PR6070.H77] 823′.9′14 77-13906
ISBN 0–393–08785–9

1 2 3 4 5 6 7 8 9 0

PART 1

Chapter One

The oars lifted and fell with a desolate splashing. In the night the harbour lamps lit up an empty wharf, and reproduced themselves in derelict vanity against the water. Behind, with no noise of parting waves, the two-decked *Artemisia* was moving southward.

The young man felt as if he was returning home. Nothing he could see had altered, except that the lighter must have broken down and they had sent the fisherman to take him off the boat. He dangled his fingers in the warm sea and leaned against the suitcases, letting his head fall back and closing his eyes. He could hear, faintly, the hum of a car along the wharf, then somebody slamming a door, and a woman's voice. They passed the beacon on the harbour arm; the winking lantern floated by quite close above his head. From time to time the old fisherman leaned his elbows against the oars in his lap, while the water dripped from the blades with a sad, metallic distinctness. He had waited for his passenger to speak, but instead the young man continued to sprawl in this untidy attitude of rest, with his head tilted back and his eyes closed.

Even on this mirror of a sea the boat was leaking and the fisherman's feet squelched on the boards. He was rowing more slowly now. After a while the young man opened his eyes and looked behind him. The *Artemisia* had dwindled to a tarnished star on the sea. He watched the fisherman's face, which looked solid and pleasant under its white hair, and asked: "How are things at Kalepia?"

The fisherman grunted: "Much the same." He was starting to wheeze. "Where've you been then?"

"America, England."

"Emigrated?"

"Sort of."

"You don't hear about the Republic there?"

"No." The man's head fell back against the suitcases again. "You hear about Greece, even Albania. But nothing about here."

The old man pulled more vigorously on the oars. He was thinking of his wife and grandchildren now. He wanted to get back. "Nobody comes here," he said.

The other man did not answer. He was wondering whether to ask the fisherman something particular. His hands had tightened on the sides of the boat. He stared up at the sky. The stars seemed not so much to glitter, as to shine with an immaculate vacancy. If he stared at them they began to hurt his eyes, as though the light was penetrating his brain. Keeping his gaze on the sky he asked: "Is Andreas Alastos dead?"

The water plashed again around the oars. His hands clasped one another to keep from shaking. How long the silence was!

"He was ill," the fisherman said, "the last I heard. But not dead."

When he heard these words, that his father was alive, it seemed to the other man as if a whole world, an integral part of him, had formed itself again. Kalepia, the harbour, the sea—everything which had contained his childhood—were resurrected with his father. Six years had passed since he had last been back, but suddenly all these elements—even the lighthouse and the crawling coastline—were running again in his veins.

He reached forward and laid his hands on the fisherman's knees. "Thank you."

The old man stared at him in surprise. "You must be Alastos' son?"

"Yes."

"I remember you now, your mother too. Wasn't she the handsome woman, English? And how long ago did she leave?"

"Seventeen years."

"But you've been back since. I recognize you."

"A few times."

The fisherman frowned. "People still remember your mother in the town." He added in the rough way of poor men in the Republic: "They thought it strange. Andreas Alastos was a good man."

Already, the other man thought, they are speaking of my father in the past. "He married again."

The wharf lights shone above them. The lights of the town itself showed only here and there as rectangles in disembodied windows. A soft, May wind had sprung up and was spreading ripples over the harbour.

A policeman strolled across to them, but when he heard who it was he waved him away, and the light in the customs shed flickered out. The fisherman glanced at the fifty drachmas which the man offered him, then grinned and saluted him.

"Are there any taxis?"

"Not at this time."

Alastos was left alone on the wharf with the two suitcases. Rats were dragging something along a gutter. There was a smell of rotted seaweed. He picked up the cases, walked along the quay and took the main street in a long, measured stride. It was empty. Its lamps were white and intermittent. After six years, he had forgotten how at night the faintest breeze shifted dust and rubbish along these streets and tugged the torn posters from the walls. A few of the shop windows were still lit, but most were barred with iron meshing.

Although Alastos was a big man, the suitcases began to pull unbearably on his arms. He dropped them in front of a restaurant and sat on them, wiping the sweat off his neck. He had not slept on the ship from Patras; he had barely slept since leaving England.

Music came from the restaurant radio. He could see into the room where two men were playing backgammon. They threw the dice with a childish bravado. Ten or twelve other men stood round watching them, their hands in their pockets. There was nothing else for them to do, as far as they knew. Alastos felt his shoulders buckle. This scene returned to him with the remembrance of others; all his youth he seemed to have watched the men at their backgammon, shovelling counters into spaces as if their lives were staked on it. But this time the restaurant window cut him off immeasurably from them. He breathed on the glass and drew a rude face in the condensation.

Five minutes later he passed beneath an iron arch over the road. The town had been proud of that, he remembered, when he was a boy. Its extinguished neon lights read 'Welcome to Kalepia', but pointed the other way. He turned down a smaller road, walking between low-built houses. He smelt jasmine. His arms ached so hard that he played a game, walking the distance between five street lamps before he rested. He watched his shadow stride grotesquely in front, shorten, vanish, leap on. He reached the path by the stream and rested again. The lights of the Lythrangomi copper mines covered the opposite side of the valley, and even from this distance he could hear the throbbing of the ventilation unit behind the hill. He could not tell if anything had changed. Tomorrow, he promised himself, the daylight would bring the town to life and it would glow with purpose, as it had once seemed to do. If it looked lost tonight, like a town which had borrowed itself from a hundred better towns, it could only be because he was tired and obsessed by his father's illness.

He started to walk along the path by the river, which was almost dry. There was no more light. The giant eucalyptus trees hung above him. On the far side of the stream the myrtles had been turned all in one direction by years of winter storm. He passed a woman asleep under the trees, her legs doubled to her chin for warmth. Her withered face—its wrinkles showed quite clearly in the starlight—was tied up in a heavy scarf, and her head rested on a reed bag. He remembered that the fruit of the olive trees on this side of the valley, which belonged to the Church, was given to the poor and that in the summer people slept here. Sometimes as a child he had stumbled with a start of fear upon their lean shapes under the trees.

He set down the cases for the last time. He could see more houses where the town's farthest outskirts touched the stream. He still tried not to think of his father. He stared about him for a distraction: a memory, anything; but felt only the tightening of his throat and a gap which had opened in his stomach. He wrenched up the luggage and half ran along the path. His heart was beating. He ran faster. The house sprang up between the trees; its shutters showed pale against the darker stone.

The first thing he noticed was the pallor of the old man's face on the pillow. The skin stretched thin as paper over its bones and was sucked in so tightly at the cheeks that it looked as if a needle had punctured them on either side. For a moment he thought that it was not his father who lay there at all but some withered peasant who had been placed in his father's bed.

He stood by the doorway for several seconds searching for some feature by which he could recognize the face. He fixed his gaze on the white hair, whose curls were still tough and small, and said softly: "It's me." The words had come in a whisper. He said again louder: "It's me. Julian."

The old man did not move. His lips were drawn back from his teeth as though they grinned perpetually at a joke written over the ceiling. One hand rested loosely on the coverlet. The young man repeated "It's me, I'm back," but this time, after there was no reply, he did not know what to do. He had to silence the booming of his heart which was a physical pain; he was afraid to speak again. But he felt that if he waited there much longer he would start to weep.

The door on to the verandah stood open and let in the warm night. Through it shone the lights of the mining company on the opposite hill. The whole valley-side was ablaze with them. But there was no noise of cars, only the drilling of the cicadas in the shrubs, a sound which he had forgotten. In his father's room even the armchairs were unchanged, standing in their semi-circle, and still propped in one corner he saw the striped pole on which, when he was a boy, they used to hang out a banner during the municipal elections.

He walked to the bed. His boots thumped on the carpet. His ungainly frame blocked the light from the bedside lamp. He tried to smooth down his hair with his hands. "It's Julian," he said. "I would have come before if I'd known."

His father's eyes opened without expression, but merely through their being open his features seemed to fall into place. He became recognizable. His face was intelligent and steady. And watching him, his son felt the emptiness of his stomach contracting and filling up. He wanted to take his father's head in his hands, yet was afraid to do even this, the old man looked so frail. So he stood by the bedside, clenching and unclenching his fingers in uncertainty and knocking against the table whose litter of medicine bottles tinkled.

But now his father had seen him, for he was slowly turning his head. In the silence his voice came diamond-clear: "Is it you?"

"Yes, father." He took the hand which lay on the coverlet. Its fingers felt like bones. He crouched down so that his face was on a level with the hand. "I came as quickly as I could. We were delayed in Athens."

His father's brows puckered. He seemed to be trying to remember something, but Julian could not guess what it was. Perhaps he was trying to remember where Athens was, or to recall from where his son had come, or to fit anything together at all. His lips rubbed faintly against one another. "Let me look at you. Turn on the light."

"It is on."

The old man held his hand against his eyes. Then he said louder, as if to hold himself: "I didn't know you would be here so soon. Somehow the time ... When you lie like this, time disappears. Now stand up and let me look at you."

Julian stood up and leaned towards him. The old man twisted round, compressed his lips as if to prevent their groaning, and stared. Now he clearly saw his son's heavy-boned features; the whole man looked more formidable than he remembered—a gangling tree of a man, he seemed.

His father asked: "Did you get the train to the Capital?"

"No. The boat from Patras."

"That wasn't needed." His eyes were perfectly alive now, for they looked irritated. "What has Zena been telling you?"

"Just that you were ... ill."

The old man looked down at his son's hand enclosing his own, at the swelling of its veins. These hands too, with their clumsy sensitivity, were larger than he remembered. 'Well, I'm not dying yet," he said sharply.

Suddenly the young man stooped and embraced him, gathering the frail shoulders in his arms. How terrifyingly light he was! He might have been made of grass.

"Father!"

A spasm of relief passed through the sick man's body, and was breathed out again through the shrunken chest. Julian laid him back against the pillows, still holding him. His father was like a child in his arms. For a while the young man remained stooping above him, his hands behind the narrow back. So this was his father now: a man who could weigh no more than seven stone, with a voice as thin as a flute. Looking at the eyes, now closed, Julian felt as if some huge ship was moving from under him in the dark. He let his father's hand drop back on the pillow, and remained a moment staring beyond it at the wall, waiting for his fear to pass. He was still kneeling like that when Zena came and whispered: "The thing has a cycle. Two hours ago he was sweating and coughing. But by early morning, you'll see, he'll be quite different. He ought to sleep now."

Julian sat down at the far side of the room and remained there with his knees bunched up, facing the woman. He barely knew his stepmother. Her face, even in stress, kept a Mediterranean softness, but he noticed a worn look which was new. Her black hair was filled with grey, and the corners of her mouth were depressed by little creased jowls. She was very Greek, and warmer to him than ever his own mother had been. "Your mother", she used to ask, "Am I like her? Not at all?" Once, when Julian was nineteen and had returned to see his father for three months, she had pulled out the old, foolish-looking photographs of his mother as a bride with his father standing beside her—a shy, thirty-two-year-old immigrant to Britain looking, in his formal clothes, like an animal tamed for the occasion. "And wasn't she lovely?" Zena had asked unaffectedly, "And is she so still?" Then she put questions to him—questions which she had never dared to ask his father. Why had his mother returned to England? Had she tired of Andreas? Or had she found the Republic unendurable? But to half these questions Julian could only guess the answers, because his mother hated to talk of her past. She had tired of his father, yes, just as she tired of everything. She was wilful and self-sufficient, and Kalepia had been a prison to her.

Recently Andreas had talked of the past in his delirium, Zena said. "And all the time he talked of you"—she laughed brokenly—"never of your mother, always of you. And at last he said, 'Bring him back.' But it was like a defeat for him. It was always a defeat to ask things of other people."

"You should have told me before." Julian felt irrationally angry. "He's got to the stage of delirium!"

"He didn't want you to lose your job. That's another thing he kept saying: jobs were hard to get in England now." She looked straight at him. "Did you lose it?"

Always practical, Zena, even now. Just as he remembered. "Yes, of course I lost it," he said harshly. "I'm staying here." This became a fact to him only as he said it.

"Where will you get work?"

He nodded towards the window. The copper mines were still lit up on the darkness of the hill. "Over there," he answered, "if they'll have me. There's nothing much else a man can do here." His record would sound all right—a degree in mining engineering; five years in Utah in open-cast; three in London with the Copper Foundation. Not many people could have that sort of experience. He spoke to convince her. But in fact he had no real experience of underground mining. His work in Utah had come to an end with the closing of the pit, and in London he had been little more than a clerk in a consultancy office.

She recognized that roughness in his voice. She knew that he was never as sure of himself as that, unless he had changed. At the same time he detected her scepticism, and added: "Father's reputation must count for something. Seven years as a pit superintendent!—That must count for something."

"That was five years ago," she said dourly. "And now there's going to be trouble up there."

"What trouble?"

"Your father will tell you."

The young man glanced at the shape in the bed. At once he forgot the mines. His gaze returned to the woman's face and pleaded with it in silence, and the silence lengthened between them. He thrust his clenched fists between his knees. He was asking her to give him hope, to say "The doctors seem more cheerful" or "They mean to try a new drug on him" or simply "I think he was a little better today".

But she did not offer any of these. She only said distinctly: "At least the brain does not suffer. That will stay clear until he dies."

His head felt heavy like a boulder in his hands. But of course she was right. They must remember that. Andreas would die sane. That was how anyone would want to go, his mind lucid and himself the same man to the people he loved.

Julian reached for some question with which to breach their silence. There had been so much he had wanted to know, and now there was nothing. He managed to ask: "What did he say in this delirium?"

"He talked about the sea." The woman grimaced. "He went on about his trip to the East Indies and the others round the coasts here. He wasn't always distinct, but I could tell which way he was going by the names of the ports." She gave a dry laugh. "He always spoke those as if he had just sighted them and was shouting them to the quartermaster ... Izmir, Latakia, Limassol ... and a whole lot more which meant nothing to me. I dare say he spoke about things which he wouldn't normally remember. They say you do, in delirium. And then about his year in England working at Southampton. He even mentioned Lily ... you remember Lily, that I used to tease him about? He even mentioned her ... what a frightful name!" She laughed, then steadied herself, as if the laughter might turn into something else. "And he talked of your mother's father. He was afraid of him—did he ever tell you?—because he was a priest. He felt that in England people of Greek extraction weren't thought to be quite Christian. He began to laugh then, but coughed up so much phlegm—it was a terrible dark yellow that night—that I was alarmed. But then he was quiet again and ... and oh, he said good things about me." There was weeping in her voice, which she kept purposely light. "The doctor said it wasn't usual to have such long deliriums in tuberculosis."

Julian nodded. He thought with a bitter astonishment of what he had been doing while his father lay dying—living in London with a job he didn't like, girls he didn't love. And all the time his father's life was fading. Why hadn't something told him?

In the silence, from the far corner of the room, the old man called out.

Zena answered: "You should be asleep. What do you want?"

"I want my son. I haven't seen my son for six years. I'm feeling better." It was true. He was able to lever his back upright against the pillows, then rest his hands over his stomach. "And I'd like soup," he said.

She left the room gratefully. Pulmonary tuberculosis, she had heard, withers a patient away until he no longer wishes to eat anything. So long as he asked to eat, he would live.

Julian sat on the edge of the bed. He was beginning to hate his own clumsy movements; the very size and health of his limbs seemed indecent. "It will please her to cook the soup," his father said in the fluting voice which his son accepted now. "I couldn't drink it—but when she's not looking, you take it."

"I won't touch it." He was surprised at the hardness in his own voice; he had never used to question his father. "Tell me how this started. Your letter ... you spoke only about colds, chronic colds. Was that true?"

"There's nothing to tell you," the old man said brusquely. "My tuberculosis is no different from anyone else's. Yes, you keep getting colds. You get dejected. Your appetite goes. You're less use than a dog." Julian was glad to hear that acidity; the old vigour was not quite gone. "I started coughing as soon as I lay down at night—coughing on and on like an engine which can't get started. I was thin by then, and the doctor's prescriptions weren't doing any good. Then one day I woke up with phlegm on my chest, streaked with blood. Zena took me to the hospital to get proper treatment. But you know, when a man is old ... They sent me back."

Julian tried to keep the anger out of his face. So the hospitals had given his father up. They didn't want his death statistic on their records. A death at the age of twenty was a medical failure; but a death at seventy-one was acceptable. They could give up the old without conscience.

"You should have come to England!"

"That would be worse than the Capital," he said testily. "It's the humidity that's bad. I'm better off here . . ." his cough returned ". . . here where it's dry . . . and there is the sea. We had a cold winter, this last one. Good and cold. In the day I sat out with rugs on the verandah, and at night Zena left all the doors and windows open—so. Like she still does."

"But you should be in the mountains now. It's already May."

He jerked back his head. "I've always hated mountains. Zena thinks I'm obstinate. She wanted to take me to a Swiss sanatorium and ruin us all. But I won't die in those places. Next she wanted to have this room air-conditioned. Air-conditioned! What is it that makes a dying man a sort of idol? Zena—she of all people I would have expected to keep a sense of proportion."

His coughing increased, then faded in spasms. Julian longed for anything rather than those puffs of sound which the lungs emitted when they were too weak to do more. But his father went on talking. He even appeared stronger. "I'm sick of this disease. Why must we talk about it? It's you I must talk about. You see, I'd like you to be with Zena for a while afterwards. She has nobody, now that Panayota is dead." He suddenly laughed to himself at some recollection—a weak laugh, but low, like the one Julian remembered; and his voice was touched with humour. "You heard about that? Zena's sister Panayota died last year in a ridiculous way. She never did anything sensibly. I don't suppose there's more than one venomous snake in the country, and Panayota goes and treads on it. Instead of sending somebody to the doctor she walks a kilometre to his house. By that time her circulation has rushed the poison round her and the doctor finds her on his doorstep blown up like a rubber doll. If I don't want to die, it's because Panayota will be there."

He laughed again, and Julian found himself laughing too at the thought of Zena's sister fussing his father in the afterlife, and was astonished that he should be sitting here enjoying this joke. It filled him with relief that it was possible. Even if the joke was not a joke at all, but a nervous necessity, as if to say "Yes, Panayota will be there." As if to say that "there" existed at all.

But his father was laughing only with his lips; his chest lifted in pain, and the hacking cough began. Zena came instantly with a bowl and a flannel, and tilted him forward. Within two or three minutes his lips and chin were covered in dark yellow phlegm; a strand of blood curled in the basin.

Julian said bitterly: "I shouldn't have excited him."

But she answered: "It was so fine to hear him laugh. God knows when I last heard him laugh. You'll do him good. But don't let him talk on." She wiped Andreas' mouth and eased him back on to the pillow, where his coughing died away. "Lie still. Don't talk."

"I want to talk," he said distantly. "I will talk in this whisper. Can you hear this?"

Julian edged closer. "Yes."

"Then we'll talk sensibly," he whispered, when Zena had left the room. "Tell me. Will you stay with her for a while after I've gone?"

"Yes."

"You did not give up your job?"

Julian could discover no expression in the weakness of that voice. "I'd decided to give it up before."

Andreas was silent, but his son could guess what he was feeling. Thirty years ago he too had cut short a job in England and had returned to Kalepia, his home town, giving up thoughts of a career on the sea, because he was married. Then he had gone into the mines. Mining was all there was to do in Kalepia. It gave a life which his countrymen considered too menial for a man of education, but jobs in those years were scarce in the Republic. A man had to take what he could get.

Julian bitterly observed the aimlessness of this career, and knew that his own was no better. In theory he believed that a person could always carve out his life as he willed it; in practice he had never done so.

His father breathed: "And what will you do now?"

"I'll go into the mines," he said. "It's the obvious thing." Some irony in the phrase struck him faintly. But his father was not answering him any more. He seemed to rest.

Julian felt that he himself had been led into mining only by naïvety—a childhood memory of miners as heroes—and by a lack of anything better to do. He had quarrelled with his mother over this—he had quarrelled with her over most things—and had finally taken a mining engineer's degree at an English university. But now, at the age of thirty, he had no more direction than then. Sometimes, when he thought about it, he became hot with his own unfulfilment, like a painter groaning with shapes and colours just behind the retina of his eye. But this frustration could not be shaped. He imagined that it would lessen only as he grew older and reconciled to his meaninglessness. Sometimes he felt violent. It was hard to know what was least futile to do. The best thing was to work at something simple and physical. He would go back into mining.

"They pay well enough," he said at last. "Don't they still?"

"Yes, they pay," his father said.

"Well then, what do you think?" He watched his father's lips tauten back from his teeth. He wanted to tell him not to do that, it made him look already dead. And he wanted to know that his father approved of his going into the mines. Something about them was troubling the old man.

But Andreas merely said: "The miners aren't a bad lot." He ran his tongue around his teeth and resumed his stare at the ceiling until Julian thought that he had given up speaking because of the hurt in his lungs.

All the time that Julian watched him, his father's face was reviving in his memory—not this shrunken mask, but the face as he had known it as a boy, as a younger man. However much he tried to stop recalling it, these memories erupted in his mind—and in them his father was always capable, laughing and cruelly healthy. Julian's love for his father now appalled him. Watching the pared face, he felt as if a part of himself was dying. He belonged to his father more nearly than he ever had to his mother. Yet now, with the man grown old and unrecognizable, linked to him only by this weak voice, he wondered if he had ever really known him at all. It suddenly seemed there had been so much more to know than he had ever known. And now it was too late. With a vague panic he felt that he himself was dying here, all that was closest to him, all that was Greek in him, all that the years in England had driven out. It was being irrecoverably lost. This father, this beloved, emptied frame, was sinking with it into the dark. He felt this with a distinctness and horror which grew minute by minute as he sat by his father's side: that his father was carrying into the grave the secret of himself.

After a while he took his father's hand, stooped down and rested his cheek against it. He said simply: "I love you."

The tears were starting under his eyes, and he pulled himself upright. Zena came in softly. It was after midnight, she said. She drew up a chair by her husband and patiently, in teaspoonfuls, fed him with clear soup. Without turning round she said to Julian: "I don't want to hear about this mining business any more."

He thought how tired she sounded, and her shoulders, now that she had turned her back to him, looked heavy and rounded. He put his hands on them and kissed her. A few minutes later his father was in pain again, rolling his tongue about his lips and trying to arch his back. But he was angry if either of them took any notice. He went on in that extraordinary, expressionless tone, as though nothing was wrong: "The mines ... all right ... we'll say nothing more ... but if you want the job you'd better see Oldenburg ... he's still the General Manager ... a hard man, but a good boss. . . ."

His voice tailed away. Julian listened from the verandah entrance. The lights of the mines were shining on the opposite hill. His gangling figure in its threadbare cardigan almost filled the doorway. He had taken off his boots and tucked them under his arm, and his stockinged feet had left their footprints in sweat on the floorboards. He was wondering why he had not come home before.

Chapter Two

Kalepia is the smallest district town in the Republic. Until copper was discovered there forty years ago, it was important only as a depot for the export of grain and a little salt. Its people were mainly small tradesmen, with a community of dockers and fishermen spread round the harbour. This port was never enlarged, because the crushed ore from the mines was taken by lorries to the larger harbour of Nikitari thirty miles along the coast.

It was these lorries, moving up the road on the opposite side of the valley, which woke up Julian Alastos next morning. He noticed from the verandah steps how hugely the mine had grown. On this, his first morning for years in the town which he used to call his home, he wanted to go into Kalepia and see if that too had changed. His father's house, with its cream-coloured shutters and wide balconies, was one of several properties which stood upstream on the outskirts. He had always thought it the grandest of them. But he was reminded now that it was rather plain; the paint was peeling off its shutters and the stucco wall round the garden was crumbling.

It did not seem smaller, but poorer, oddly rudimentary. His father's library, which had fascinated him as a child, consisted of two shelves of history books and encyclopaedias. The garden was a tangle of hibiscus and oleanders. The things which he had thought beautiful were now only sentimental. But he had never wanted, or imagined, that he was returning to the childhood of seventeen years before. Nobody ever returned anywhere. Simply he was surprised at how much he, and not these surroundings, must have changed.

He could not remember who had lived in any of the houses which he passed along the road, but he could see the whole valley where the sunken river ran. On his own side, above the harbour and the town, the hill climbed under olive and eucalyptus trees to the whitewashed shrine of St Vichinos. On the other, the houses of the miners had been built by the Cômpany in neat white squares. They looked wealthy, with their television aerials and their cars parked under awnings. Above them hung scarps of slag in the weird pastel shades of andesitic lava—rosy pinks and pale, synthetic greens, with a glinting iron waste which crowded down almost into their gardens. Above this again the open-cast mine was scooped from the head of the mountain.

Alastos could hear the friendly grumble of the excavator along its rim. Shading his eyes, he tried to discern how much ore was left to mine. But he could not, and now he was already walking past the town's public buildings: the municipal hall, the post office, the law court, all built in a jaded Doric style. They had weathered badly. Almost before he knew it, he was in the main street, going between the concrete-built shops with their metal signs and flaking balconies. He was stared at. In his habitually untidy clothes—even a simple shirt and trousers managed to look complicated on him—and with his hair standing from the back of his head in tufts, he seemed to have sunk his Greek heritage entirely.

The street was lined with cars imported from Germany and England, and mostly old. A bus and a lorry carrying "Kostis Orange Drinks" blocked the thoroughfare. On the shady side of the street the shopkeepers and tradesmen sat in their cheap, dark suits and stared in front of them. Now and then they talked and argued together or raised little cups of coffee fastidiously to their lips; then they retracted into torpor again, all staring in the same direction, at the road, as if waiting for something. They smoked ten or twelve cigarettes without stopping, lighting them from one another and flicking the stubs into the gutters. The noise from transistor radios gave a travesty of life. The men twirled their finger-beads. They were deeply, almost professionally bored.

Alastos was unconsciously walking more slowly. Everything was quite as he had known it, if only he could remember. But he was seeing it with other eyes. He was a stranger. He was hoping, now almost desperately, to glimpse something which would make him think "Ah! I remember that! That is what I loved!" He wanted this thing so badly that he was sure it existed, althought still nameless, somewhere very close. Turn the corner, and there it would be.

But nobody hailed him. He recognized nobody. He began to wonder how he had ever thought this place his home. He passed empty restaurants, the cinema, and the hotel, whose shutters were closed. At the far end of the street were the "smart" shops, as he had once thought them. There was nobody near them except a pair of country women gazing at shoes they would never buy. He stared at the windows. The tawdry goods were ridiculously expensive. He wondered who could either afford or want them. What was it, then, that he had seen in the windows before? He could remember only an aura of richness and inaccessibility.

Once a group of boys shouted at him in English, thinking him a foreigner. And so he was. He was separated for ever from what he saw. He had left it all at the age of thirteen. He was his mother's child, an English Midlander. He even moved in a different way from these people—in a long, graceless lope with his weight on the balls of his feet. He had never had the silken walk of the Mediterranean.

In the harbour a crane was landing boxes of fruit on to two rusted barges. Alastos watched it, and the sun beating out gold ripples on the bay. The harbour looked smaller than it had the night before, cramped and pretty. Along its rim wide-bottomed fishing-boats idled on their ropes. The fishermen were not there, but had left inside their tackle and little pronged anchors; and the paraffin lamps were set in their sockets near the prows. The wharf sent up smells of seaweed mixed with those of charcoal-cooking from the restaurant whose chairs stood along the quay.

The dockers—there were twelve of them—were dressed in nothing but bathing pants, helmets and gauntlets which reached to their elbows. They bellowed at one another from wharf to barge. The only person Alastos recognized was an imbecile fisherman whom the dockers called God-Asleep, because God—they said—must have created him while He slept. The madman seemed to recognize Alastos too, for as he passed by he grabbed his hand and cried: "Eh? Twenty-two in one day! The saint have mercy! Tell you now, give you seven for eleven, eh? Eight for twelve, then? *Po-po-po-po.* Eight for twelve, eh?"

Alastos sidestepped him and went into the bank. He opened an account. He had forgotten how people with nothing else to do lounged against the counters and watched the money passing back and forth, their eyes filled with a sordid and hopeless dreaming. They craned their heads at his English pounds, and peered over one another's shoulders. He wanted to shake himself free of their gaze. One of them asked how much he had paid for his watch and where he had bought it. He pretended not to understand. He had half forgotten the fetish for money in the Republic. If a man was going to Nikitari or the Capital, three or four different people would as likely as not ask him to buy some commodity there, which was a drachma or two cheaper than at Kalepia. Even among the better off, nobody could bear to pay more than his neighbour had.

He found a coffee-shop and sat down to a bowl of the local yoghourt. Its cold sourness refreshed him. The shop's owner watched narrowly. Alastos asked him what had become of the old woman, the lamp-seller.

She had died last winter, the man had said; it was the will of God; the last winter had been hard.

The will of God was beginning to depress Alastos. He asked sharply, nodding at the street: "Are those men out of work?"

"There's no work to be out of." The man went behind his counter; he thought the stranger a fool. "If you're looking for work, go to the Capital. Those men live here. They work sometimes."

"There seem to be more of them than there used to be."

"Just the same."

He walked back up the main street through the avenues of bored shopkeepers. Little by little this human waste was filling him with sullenness. He felt like shouting: "If you don't need your lives, why bother to live them? Why don't you die now?" He wanted to pluck them up and show them something extraordinary, magnificent, beyond themselves, something which would make them say "So that is how it is! I never knew!" Yet he felt, too, the stupidity of his indignation. He could show nothing to anybody, nothing to himself. Perhaps it was only this inarticulate rage which separated him from them at all. He told himself: do not forget, you are a foreigner. There was nothing more contemptible than the returned emigrant who boasted how things were better elsewhere. And it was absurd to feel disgust for other people when all they were doing was sleeping in the shade.

From the garden of the primary school a yellow-haired dog barked sombrely at him. He looked inside the school hall. How old and dark it was! A group of girls, in their green and white uniforms, filed out into the sun. Their faces and limbs had the rounded Levantine softness. They examined him through hazel eyes, and giggled. He searched for his schoolmaster, Sofroniou—it was many years since they had last met—and found the old man perched behind his desk in an empty classroom as if the years were of no account. Sofroniou could not at first distinguish him, but swayed his head back and forth on its frail neck.

Then he exclaimed: "Alastos! Julian Alastos!"

When they embraced, Sofroniou's head barely reached to his pupil's collar-bone. Alastos saw that this head was now bald except for two white wisps on either side of his temples. "So you're still here."

"For a little longer," Sofroniou said. His voice shook with a habitual querulousness. "But next year I shall be taking up a job in the Capital." Every year, Alastos remembered, Sofroniou threatened to take a job in the Capital, threatened the school council, the municipality, his pupils, his wife. "And you? What of you? You are back to ... to ..."

"To see my father."

Sofroniou coughed awkwardly. "He is an excellent man, your father, really excellent. I had once hoped he would teach here. His knowledge of history is extensive, surprisingly extensive." Sofroniou often repeated a part of what he said, as if for the benefit of slower pupils. "But they pay us so little here ... when you think what an ordinary official gets ... an ordinary customs official.... But you have come back for a long time?"

By now he had seated himself at the raised desk again and Alastos was left standing beneath him in the subdued unease which adults still feel in front of their teachers. He expected Sofroniou at any moment to mew: "Take one black mark, Alastos." But instead he had asked about his father.

"Yes, I'm back for a long time."

"And what will you do?" Sofroniou asked. He was leaning forward with something like sympathy. It made Alastos uncomfortable.

The young man shifted from one foot to another. That question, he supposed, was inevitable. "I think I'm going into the mines. That's my qualification."

In the gloom Sofroniou's glasses glinted like two orbs of independent light; the white wisps touched his head with goblin fantasy. He hesitated. Then he said: "Yes, you may be right. You may be. Qualifications, yes. You have a mining engineer's degree. Mining. I suppose that is ... the future." Sofroniou felt sorry. He watched his big, sensitive pupil clasping and unclasping his hands in that characteristic way: a pair of hands which could not find their work. "You've heard the Company means to take the Mountain? Yes of course you would have. Yes." His voice rose thinner and higher. "To you we must seem very ... unprogressive."

Alastos stared at him in amazement. "The Company take the Mountain?" He was trying to realize precisely what Sofroniou meant. He thought he had not understood him properly. "You're saying that they want to buy the Mountain of St Vichinos?"

Sofroniou went on: "Yes, yes. But an American-run company ought to go delicately. The people still don't trust it. Everyone's known for years that there was copper on this side of the valley. You can see the *gossan* for two hundred metres up the hillside. But now there's trouble between the Company and the town. Even the Church is involved."

Julian was speechless. So they were trying to buy the saint's mountain. How long, he wondered, could he have been abroad? Surely not six years but fifty, a century! Things could not have moved so fast. People could not have changed just like that. He laughed in disbelief, shrugging his heavy shoulders. A mine in exchange for a saint! The idea was grotesque. He could remember from his childhood the yearly pilgrimage up the great hillside to the shrine of St Vichinos on the summit, the golden icon from the episcopal church carried in front and Bishop Fantousis censing the pilgrims, the olive trees, even the flowers all the way up.

Sofroniou must have got that wrong, he thought. "They'll never sell. Not a hope. Never. Oldenburg will have the whole town against him."

"But the Mountain does not belong to the town," Sofroniou said. "It belongs to the Church."

"Well then, they'll never sell. Fantousis would ..."

"Fantousis is dead," Sonfroniou went on in his high-pitched voice, which Alastos could still not believe. "We no longer have a bishop. Last year the town was demoted. Our population is dwindling ... yes, seriously dwindling."

Julian asked: "So who takes the decision?"

"It rests with our archimandrite. We are now a part of the See of Nikitari, but the bishop there is senile, I've been told. You know how one hears these things ... positively senile. The archimandrite can do as he likes."

All the same, Julian thought, they were playing with the people's saints. Things could not have so transformed themselves in his absence. Six years was not long in the life of a saint; the saints were all but eternal.

"The people would go mad at the thought of it!" he broke out. "Even if the Church wanted to sell, it wouldn't dare. Who's the archimandrite now?"

"A new man from the Capital. He is not much liked."

"And the General Manager has made himself pleasant to him?"

"Pleasant? Well ... I wouldn't say so, no I wouldn't. Oldenburg doesn't know what it is to be pleasant. I expect he had made him an offer."

Julian did not know what to say. Perhaps, he thought, some balance had after all silently altered. That must be how things happened. A century, a millennium went by and everything remained as before. Then one day a crack appeared in a wall. For a while nobody noticed, and after they had it was a long time before they dared to speak of it. But there was nothing they could do, because underneath some gigantic settlement was taking place in the earth, some stratum shifting irrecoverably, until soon the whole surface would be in turmoil and people forced to adapt as best they could.

So copper had overtaken the saint in the esteem of the people. The idea was no longer preposterous. And it was perhaps a good thing.

Sofroniou said again: "But you mean to go into the mines?"

The question made Alastos still more uncomfortable. He had a terrible compulsion to start calling his old schoolteacher "Sir". "I only returned yesterday." He began pounding the palm of one hand with his fist. "It's hard to accommodate." The desks behind him were filling up with pupils for the next lesson, but Alastos was thinking of the dead-seeming men on their chairs in the street. He said gruffly: "I don't even want to accommodate to people's poverty or anything which ... which narrows them." The words worried him as soon as he had spoken them. He had returned only a few hours before, and already he felt this superficial—it must be superficial—desire to redeem everything.

Sofroniou smiled weakly. Watching Alastos, he clearly saw the boy in the man—the face of young intensity. But there was something uncouth about him too. He went wrangling at the world, like a dog worrying a bone. If he continued like that, the old teacher thought, the world would break him one day.

Alastos walked back along the river. It was choked with rubbish, with heaps of fallen building stone, oil cans, old motor tyres, gas cylinders. It ran among them with a degraded whisper. That too he hated: the loss of pride. From where he walked the town's skyline showed little but rusted pipe-chimneys and electric cables which jumped from house to house on makeshift struts. Some buildings were left for years with only a layer of concrete for a roof, stuck with iron prongs so that their owners could claim that they were unfinished and be exempt from house tax. Along every street were posters which nobody bothered to strip, so that they tattered whole walls: advertisements for drink, agricultural equipment, women's deodorants, last year's municipal elections, and the elections before that. He wanted to tear them down with his own hands. Because these people were a good people, at heart intelligent and proud. The people of Pericles. One day something would happen and they would be restored. They simply needed money, education. Education would transform them. Now their pleasures and dreams were nothing but noisy bursts on a sea of lassitude. But once plant a question-mark in their brains, and they would struggle for an answer. It was a matter of time, just a little time.

At the summit of the ridge, where the trees thinned out, the shrine of St Vichinos was no more than a white point against the sky. Alastos, walking along the pathway three hundred feet below, could scarcely see it. He was looking instead into the upper part of the valley where the river came down from the hills. As a child he had fished there, and gathered its bright silicate rocks to build dams.

He crossed the stream on the stepping-stones which his family had placed—his father used to carry the small boy over them when he took him to see the mines. Now, noticing a child asleep under the trees, he felt momentarily as if it was his own body, as if he were gazing across at himself, a sleeping boy, looking into the valley from another time. He shaded his eyes and stared: a goatherd stretched under the dwarf-oaks.

He reached the other side and found the path home, which led between the myrtle and eucalyptus trees. He associated these with his youth too—with the few months, at the age of nineteen, when he had returned to see his father. The long, fragrant summer, he thought, must have been responsible for the stupidity of falling in love—the last act of childhood. She also had been half English, and they had drawn naturally together, mocking one another for their split personalities.

The eucalyptus trees stood as huge as he remembered. The ground was vaguely scented. Deceit of memory! Had he really been so happy? He could not tell for sure. His father had written to give him Ekaterina's married name, but Julian could not imagine her married. The more passionately a man had loved somebody, it seemed, the less real became her memory.

He rubbed his fingers hard over his forehead. His eyes were unused to this glare. That, too, made him feel a foreigner. Now the sun hit the river's arc in a blinding sickle of light, and the goatherd was up and throwing stones at his flock with harsh cries.

Chapter Three

Alexander Drosinis, archimandrite of Kalepia, had been unhappy at his transference from the Capital. While living there for twenty years he had maintained the sentimental regard for country values which city people may profess when they have no possibility of adopting them. Now that he had been sent to the provinces, he pined bitterly for the city.

It was true that the appointment represented promotion for him. He would be responsible to the Metropolitan of Nikitari for a district of more than fifteen thousand souls. But most of these were farmers in hill country to the north and east, and when he saw their uncouth faces in the streets, or in the old metropolitan court-house, he was ill at ease. Even the celibate priests with whom he had to share his residence were, like the married ones, an ignorant lot. Moreover he suffered periodically from a stomach ulcer, to which the hard local water would do no good. And the district wines were acid.

So on his arrival in Kalepia six months before, he had felt homesick. But his brother had been a priest in the town for many years, and had left behind his widow and a teenage daughter. The archimandrite had taken to visiting them almost every day, at first for his own consolation, but more lately to air his views in safety, for he could trust nobody. The widow was a swarthy, uneducated woman (his brother had not 'married well') but she always listened attentively—she was rather awed by her august relative—and greeted whatever he said with noises of assent or sympathy. Her own position in the town had improved since the archimandrite's arrival. People were more deferential to her. Shopkeepers offered her credit (which she never accepted) and her daughter Helen had several times been asked to the house of Mr Oldenburg, the General Manager of the mining company.

Today the archimandrite looked more sombre than usual. He paced up and down her small sitting-room, one moment pulling at his fingers behind his back, the next attentively stroking his pectoral cross. His walk was sleek and measured. The widow waited for him to speak, but instead heard only the rasp of his robes and the cracking of his finger-joints. To indicate the importance of the occasion, he had not removed his *kamelaukion*, which hid a thinness of grey hair twisted in a knot behind. The head-dress added six inches to his stature, and this, with his broad stomach and pearly gush of beard, lent him superficially an imposing appearance. But a pale, soft skin blurred his features together, and under his colourless eyes the lids drooped to show a watery redness.

He continued walking up and down without looking at the widow or at her nineteen-year-old daughter, who sat reading in a chair with her legs hooked under her like a cat. Even when he addressed the woman he kept his gaze in front of him. "I suppose you get to hear the town gossip, don't you? Well, what are they saying? Are they saying I'll sell?" He noticed how abrupt, even bullying, he sounded, and quickly spoke again before she could answer, using his public voice; this was a tone of habitual moderation—as if he were addressing a synod—but now through the pompous words some strain was showing. "I've noticed that everybody here seems to know what I should do, except me. Yesterday a garage mechanic told me flatly that I should refuse the Company's offer."

The widow exclaimed: "How dare he!"

Her outrage established the archimandrite's dignity sufficiently for him to say: "We can't ignore the opinion of our fellow men. After all, the Mountain of St Vichinos is important to the more simple people of the district; it has belonged to the Metropolis for as long as our records go back; and as we well know, even the humblest of saints is an intercessor before God. However—" He cleared his throat. The widow watched him pleasantly. "It would be irresponsible to neglect the possibility of this land being put to a use which may, in the long term, be more beneficial to the faithful in Christ."

"Irresponsible," murmured the widow. "Yes. . . ."

The archimandrite ceased his pacing up and down and remained squarely in the centre of the room. He said for the hundredth time since the Company's offer: "This involves a great deal of money, Maria." He tapped the letter inside the pocket of his soutane. He had never told her precisely how much; but then he was debating aloud rather than talking to her. "And there's a great deal which needs doing with it. We have the new seminary to be built at Nikitari, and there is the Church of Ayios Charalambos here which is in urgent need. My own residence is not all that it should be, not at all, and we cannot even afford a properly trained tutor for Byzantine singing."

"Not even a tutor," repeated the widow.

These repetitions increased the archimandrite's feeling that he was talking to himself. "Now if there's copper on the Mountain of St Vichinos it's there for a reason. Nobody can afford to sleep on God's gifts."

The widow vestigially crossed herself. Her daughter Helen, who was dark and coarse like her, paid no attention but went on reading. She had finished her first term at university, and had decided that God—at least her uncle's God—did not exist. The archimandrite was permanently peeved by her indifference, but he did not show it.

He began to pace the room again. The minutes went by. It was as if his eloquence had been contrived to convince himself, and it had not succeeded. He started to twist a strand of his beard slowly round and round in one hand. Twice he touched the letter in his pocket. Eight hundred thousand dollars. He stopped in the middle of the room again and said in a different voice: "The trouble is that I can't gauge the temper of the people! If I had been here longer . . ."

The widow ventured: "The people love the saint."

"But at the pilgrimage last month the *ikonomos* said the numbers were down on last year," said the archimandrite sharply. "A dying cult is unhealthy."

Helen looked up from her book as if to say something, but did not. "Unhealthy," her mother repeated.

"All the same," added the archimandrite slowly—and a genuine distress sharpened his words—"the Church is the instrument of God on earth and His saints are a part of that glory. If we neglect the saints, we neglect God." He looked down at the widow. "Now the mining company is not popular in the town, is it? There's too much jealousy in people." His eyes were beginning to water.

"There's no knowing how the people would react. It would be terrible if . . . if . . ."

He tucked his hands into his sleeves, and resumed walking up and down. The letter was not all that the Company had conveyed to him. In private conversation the Company Secretary had mentioned that as intermediary between themselves and the metropolitan, the archimandrite should accept an unofficial gift.

"The third course open to me," he said bleakly, "is to place the matter in the hand of the metropolitan without advising him either way."

Helen closed her book. "The metropolitan's senile," she laughed.

The archimandrite thought: So that's what education does. "The metropolitan is the servant of the All-seeing," he said importantly. "It is true that he's recently been ill. But though the body is broken, the spirit continues from God."

Helen uncurled her legs from the chair. "You said yourself that at the episcopal elections he fell asleep across the lap of the Higoumenos of Peyia."

Now that she was sitting conventionally, the archimandrite saw that she was wearing jeans. This provoked him beyond endurance. He had specifically told her that he did not approve of jeans. "Not tomorrow!" he cried in warning, pointing at them. "I won't abide it. Not on a Sunday. At the university, all right. You may all look like pigs. But this is a country district. They need example." She did not answer. "I cannot remember what I was saying. . . ."

Helen grieved him. As a young girl she had been the most respectful of his brother's children, and he had grown fond of her, sometimes bringing her trinkets from the Capital on his visits to Kalepia. Now the devil had climbed into the girl. She would not listen to anybody.

"This has been a difficult time," he began again querulously. "The rumour is everywhere that the Church is going to sell. I have had a lot to bear." He stood by the window, his hands spread over his stomach as if it ached. "Now whatever happens, most people will do nothing. One may always be sure of that. But the active few, if they represent the feelings of the rest . . . they are a kind of antenna. And as the antennae advance, the body follows." He looked a little alarmed. He was recalling the hard faces of the country people. His imagination sometimes ran away with him.

"The Church has a great deal to gain in this affair," he continued, "and also a great deal to lose. She must pray for wisdom and proceed with caution. This decision is heavier than a single man's conscience can support." Even in his exasperation he could not rid his speech of its pomposity. "But the Church does not ask us to stand alone. We may appeal to other authority." He looked at the widow. She had never seen him less sure of himself. The weakness in his face was suddenly emphasized; his lower eyelids were now like stoops of water. He dabbed at them with a handkerchief, then said wearily, almost as if it were of no consequence: "Today I will lay the matter in the hands of the metropolitan—and advise him nothing at all."

"So you've decided," whispered the widow.

"Yes, I've decided." The archimandrite did not know whether to feel martyred or beaten. He was merely surprised at himself; the decision had dropped from his mouth almost of its own accord; but now it was here, it seemed the only answer.

Chapter Four

Julian Alastos had come back too late. In a few weeks all that would be left of his father would be Kalepia, the place which had enclosed him, and for the moment it seemed to Julian to be the only place which existed. Yet he could barely remember a soul here. And Kalepia, unquestionably, was mean. It was a backwater town in a backwater country. Even the beauty of its setting was defaced by the shoddiness of its buildings.

In fact he loved only his idea of the town. Kalepia itself he almost hated, and could measure his attachment by his rage at the place's squalor. Moreover he wanted to change it, to make it conform to himself.

The time which he did not pass at his father's bedside was spent searching for the few childhood friends who might have remained. Every year dozens of young men left for Canada, South America, West Africa, while the old town, drained of its youth, stagnated. He knew that his first love, Ekaterina, had stayed, married to the Company Secretary of the Lythrangomi Mines. But he recoiled from seeing her. In some obscure region of him, which he despised, he did not want to encounter the reality of her, to disturb his memory of that liberated summer—the only thing a man could know of self-forgetting. Moreover he was ashamed. Those years ago, when she had been violently emotional and certain, he had been boyish and confused. And the months which he remembered—of rendezvous in the eucalyptus woods, of kisses and passionate longings—had ended in a knowledge that he did not want to marry her, that marriage was too solid and final; had ended, in fact, by revealing only his own adolescent loneliness, his rootless sexuality and an idealism unadapted to real life. All that, he felt, was behind him; but he did not want reminding of it. He wanted a job to do in the world.

As for his other friends, almost all had either emigrated or were working in other parts of the country. By the end of a week his quests had acquired a chilling sameness. The elderly face at the door would say, "Nicos? You mean Nicos Stylianou? He went to Canada...." "You want Alexia? Well, you know she is married now ... in the Capital." "You must be Andreas Alastos' son? Spyros? No...."

He visited the girl who used to help in his home with the laundry. Even so frail a shred of his past seemed significant. Now she was living with her husband near the harbour: Zena had written down her address. It was a narrow, two-roomed house, one of the ones which the fishermen used to build with their own hands. The paint had flaked from its walls. But when he rapped on the door he heard inside, quite distinctly, the mewling of a woman when there is a death in the family. That was another noise he had forgotten. He stood undecided on the doorstep, feeling no strength to face a bereavement other than his own. To him ritualized lament robbed sorrow of its dignity, it robbed the dead. Such wailing had frightened him as a child. His mother would hurry him past the graveyards. She too would be disgusted. Sorrow to her was of the tight-lipped, Nordic kind.

The noises on the other side of the door were not those piercing dirges yet, but a low, quavering complaint: the hushed misery which precedes the end. Alastos turned from the house, but the woman must have seen his silhouette through the glass door, and before he could leave she had opened it. She fell on his hands, kissing them. He barely recognized her. She looked old. Now her cries and sobs were scarcely articulate. It was her child which was dying. She seized Alastos' wrists and pulled him in. Her eyes implored him. A terrible hope had sprung up in them, that he—after all he was a man who had travelled, who understood things—could give her child life. These eyes were emptied of everything but an animal protectiveness. She was silent while he looked at the infant, which lay in a coma among blankets—no more than a baby, his face a spotted rash. A brown fluid dribbled from his lips, and his tongue sticking through was black and dry as if he had died from thirst. It was typhus.

Was that the name, the woman asked? Infectious? She did not mind. She did not want to live, she said. And she would not go to a doctor. A doctor would take the child to hospital, where people died. He'd give injections and liquids—he would steal the child's blood.

The smell in the room was nauseous. It came from the baby's lips. Alastos did not want to look at him. Propped among the blankets, his arms outstretched from the elbow, he appeared like a decaying waxwork of the Holy Infant. Alastos glared round the narrow room, at its clutter of chairs, clothes and the bed whose mattress rested on the stone floor. Typhus probably meant lice. A child should not die of it. The boy must have been undernourished.

But his anger at the mother was drowned in pity. Now she wept uncontrollably. Was it God's will? It must be God's will since he had not answered her prayers, and the blessed St Vichinos had not interceded for her. She kept touching his hands. Was there no hope? In her home village there had been a woman who used to sell crushed roots which would cure almost anything. Did he know this root? It grew in river beds. Had he heard of it?

Alastos could not face the woman's stare. It seemed to beg him, to expect him, to solve death. At this moment he would have exchanged his own body for that of the blotched infant. He found himself prowling round and round as though there was something he might do if only he could lay his hands on the right instrument. He threw open the door into the next room, which was as dark as this. Two other children were playing there. In its far corner the grandmother rocked herself, but her misery was a polite gibbering. He came back to the woman, avoiding her gaze. Above the child's head an icon of St Vichinos was lit up by a red bulb. She accused it with a whispered stream of prayer. She had given money and candles to his shrine on the Mountain. Was his voice not heard in heaven? Did he not have the ear of the Almighty? Why then, why . . . ?

The saint's eyes were small and sterile.

"Open the windows," Alastos said. "Give the child air."

The woman opened them. Finally she asked him: "Light a candle for me in the cathedral. Pray for his soul."

She had gone quiet. She was beyond weeping. She rested against one wall. The hair tangled her head like a wild beast's. He could not comfort her. What was the use of sympathy? She was defenceless. No saint would hear her, not the Virgin, not the Almighty.

He went back up the main street where the men waited for nothing on their chairs. Death! Most of these poor seemed dead in a part of them. Only the rich called them content. He rang the hospital and reported a case of typhus.

In the cathedral there was no one. It was so silent that he walked with a cautious lightness. The epitaphion glinted from its case on the wall. He gazed around, waiting for something inside him: waiting to feel a presence. But he knew already that it would not happen. The great processions and feast days were a distant memory. He had left all that behind seventeen years ago, when he and his mother sailed for England. It had grown superfluous. He looked up at the dome, where as a child he had thought that God lived. Out of its gloom the once-terrible Pantocrator stared back at him with poorly frescoed eyes. This cathedral, this casket which had enclosed his boy's faith, was hollow.

He fumbled for a candle to fulfil the woman's wish, but he could not bring himself to light it, and pushed it back into the box. St Vichinos, he had read somewhere, had probably never existed. But the woman's child had existed. And her grief and her bewilderment. He lumbered up to the iconostasis, where the saints spread in glimmering order: mediators before God. He set his jaw at them. Ridiculous nursery-rhyme figures! He wanted to kick in their panels. They waved their books and swords at him. On one wall was the same picture of the Last Judgment that had terrified him as a child, and he found himself looking at it with disgust—the cruelly meticulous Damnation, the absurd Heaven.

From the lady-chapel came the noise of a singing-master and two choristers. *"Let all mortal flesh keep silence. . . ."*

"Stop, stop. Again—"

"Let all mortal flesh keep silence. . . ."

But things would grow better for these people, Alastos thought. This God and his Church would not extract their sacrifice much longer. And as for reward, where was that? Justice was created by men, not by God. What, in her life, had the illiterate laundry girl done, except wash other people's linen and fail to wash her own? It was better not to believe in God, than to believe him cruel.

He stopped in front of the icon of St Vichinos, where the expired tapers bent like suppliant worms. He wanted to take that icon and crack it over his knee like the rotted piece of wood it was. That would be his prayer for the dying child! As for the shrine on the saint's mountain, the only salvation it offered was under its soil. Copper would not make all the people rich—it did not matter to be rich—but it would give them a basis from which they might free themselves.

Alastos strode across the nave, as if treading on his childhood.

No, St Vichinos did not answer prayers; his whole existence was probably a lie. But drill fifty or a hundred metres into the mountain, and there would be copper pyrites. They were not a lie. They could be held in the hand, smelted, hammered. A mine geologist could draw a map of their extent and a feasibility study give their weight within the nearest hundred thousand tons. And they would ensure the living-conditions of the laundry girl's children.

On the way home he went by the house of Oldenburg, the General Manager of the Lythrangomi mines—the most handsome house in the town, near the edge of the mining community. But before he had reached it someone ran up behind him and placed her hands over his eyes. "Guess who?"

Just to look at Caroline Oldenburg was like throwing off some weight of clothes which had been suffocating him all day. She wore a sleeveless cotton dress and her almost golden hair was tied back at her neck, which emphasized the impertinence of her nose. A year ago somebody had given her his address in London—she had been a student there—and they had seen one another occasionally. But she looked happier and freer than he recalled her in England.

"Oh Julian, you do look funny."

He tried to smooth down his hair, which continued to stand in tufts. "I've been walking."

"I can tell. You're covered in dust. When did you get back?"

"A week ago."

"I knew you'd come. Your stepmother told me. She said they hadn't seen you for—how long was it?—four years? Six. Jesus!"

He was not listening much to what she was saying. He was watching the way her eyes flickered while she spoke, with a perpetual, amused existence of their own. He was a little surprised with his pleasure at seeing her again.

"I'm sorry that you've had to come back, because I know the reason." She tried to look unhappy, but her vitality did not allow it. "When do you return?"

Return? Everybody talked about returning, he thought. Everybody knew that things were better "there" than "here". People only came back to Kalepia to die among their roots. Their children did not come back at all.

"I'm staying."

"You're staying!" she exclaimed. "Come inside and tell me. We can't stand out in the street."

He shook his head. "I mustn't." He was genuinely regretful. He wanted to walk into the big, cool house with her. "It's late—I've been away hours ... my father ..."

"Of course." She touched his shoulder in a gesture of sympathy. "Only tell me, what will you do here now?"

He did not want to answer the question. Caroline might help him find a job with Oldenburg, but now that he had the opportunity to ask her, he did not use it. He had already decided to apply to the General Manager himself. But suddenly she pressed the palms of her hands on his chest and breathed: "I understand. Of course. You are going to join the Company."

"I don't know."

"You do know," she laughed. "What else could you do here? You were with the Copper Foundation in London. And before that with the Utah Federal Mining Corporation. You see, I remember. Have you been in touch with papa already?"

He began to laugh too. "No, I haven't. I haven't done anything."

She looked at him happily. He was not a handsome man at all, she thought, but she was glad to see him. In London he had been a friend, although he had never done more than kiss her for a few minutes after driving her home from some party or other; and even this he had done in a solemn, deliberate way, and she had thought him a little drunk. He was certainly strange, at once headstrong and susceptible.

She leant against the wall of her parents' garden, with her arms behind her, and asked without looking at him: "Did you hear the rumour?"

"You mean about the St Vichinos Mountain? Is it only a rumour?" He would not have been surprised if she had said "You didn't believe *that*, did you? The Company buy the Mountain? We'd be torn in pieces." But instead she bit her lip and stared down at the pavement between them.

"No, it's not a rumour. The Company's made an offer. Is that why you're waiting before you see my father? Don't you approve?"

"I approve?" he said. "I approve entirely! A new mine could be this town's salvation! Wealth means education. The next generation might be another people altogether. What sort of life is it for a man here?" His answer came out slowly. It was as if the words themselves were forming his thoughts, and he listening to them for the first time. Only now that he had spoken them did he know what he believed, and he wondered how he could not have known before.

Babies did not die in a wealthy town, not like that.

Caroline impulsively kissed him. "I'm so glad you say that! That's how we all feel!—I mean the Company does. That's how everybody feels who wants this town to live. I thought you would say that, but I wasn't sure."

"Why weren't you sure?"

"I don't know." She smiled and shrugged her shoulders. She was slightly embarrassed. "I don't really know."

"Well, that is what I think," he said, to himself as well as to her.

"So can I tell my father you'll write to him?"

She was hugging her arms. Dimples appeared in her shoulders. He wanted to place his fingers there. But instead he said: "No, you can't tell your father anything. I'll write myself."

"I can't even say you're back?" She was mocking him a little. The eyes, with their light, iridescent irises, were playing a game, a game which he did not mind.

"I know you," he pretended to grumble. "You'll say anything you like. I've got to go now." He leaned forward and momentarily held her arms. "Good-bye."

"These people," Zena said—she still called them "these people" after more than fifteen years among them, for she was from the Capital—"these people will not be changed. They don't want to change. How much does that matter? Typhus is a rarity here."

He appealed to her. "Children don't die of typhus in England."

"In England," she said, "they're probably run over instead." She even wanted him to delay going into the mines. She was anxious about the mood of the town. She had not known it like this. "It's not your nature to go meddling in fights. Your father says that as a child, when other boys started fighting, you went into a corner and played on your own. That must be your nature."

He said that he was not a child any more. He was looking heavy and stubborn, and she knew it was no good arguing. But when he spoke to his father that night the old man was disgusted at a case of typhus in his home-town. "We've been among all this too long, we've grown used to it." Julian, by now, could interpret the moods in that weak, flat voice, and this was one of self-reproach. "It's like going into a badly lit house," Andreas said, as if he had felt the same as Julian a long time ago. "The eyes grow accustomed. People grow accustomed to anything. That's the trouble. Anything."

Chapter Five

In the evenings, before the hour for mullet fishing and after the dockers had finished work, the wharfside restaurants filled up quickly. Although the dockers frequented one and the fishermen another, their chairs and tables were set so closely together that the customers mingled. These restaurants were also frequented by workers from the nearby flour mill, and usually a priest or a policeman was to be seen sitting with them, or the customs official from Nikitari. In conversation the dockers shouted loudest but the fishermen showed greater stamina; after a while they wore the dockers down; and by the end of an evening it was the unemphatic tones of the older men which commanded attention, discussing the advantages of nylon netting or last year's shipwreck.

In October a small cargo-boat had hit the headland to the west of the bay during the night, and had gone down in an almost tideless sea leaving her hull above the surface. Now the fishermen, cruising round the headland where this stern glistened, could clearly see the rest of the boat tilted on its prow under the waves, and they said the place was good for cuttle-fish. The ship's cargo was thought to have been olives and colocassia, but local rumour claimed that it had been carrying wine. The fisherman Philippou, who enjoyed a joke more than anybody else, swore that he had seen red mullet dancing under the waves, and that later they had floated to the surface, quite drunk, and he had caught them easily.

"Now there's something! Vintage mullet!" He clapped his fat arm round the shoulders of a doltish-looking docker beside him. "And did you hear what happened at Cape Mosphiloti last week? You did not? Listen. A ship went down—a Swedish ship—with a cargo of ... Guess!—Contraceptives. No, I don't joke! This is true. Ask anybody."

The docker stared heavily round the table, but before he could ask, Philippou grabbed his elbow. "Listen," he whispered fiercely. "This could be very serious for us. This is the mating time for mullet and there are few enough in these waters as it is without ... Believe me, we could claim damages. Somebody should dive on that ship and see precisely what is going on down there. He might find ... Holy Virgin forbid it!" Philippou settled his stomach under the lip of the table. "But this is not all. Last Monday a big freighter—Italian it was ..."

"Enough of that!" a fisherman interrupted. "Do you want to make him seasick?"

A gravelly voice, pitted deep in a man's stomach, said cruelly: "The sea can have *him*." This was Marangos, the dockers' foreman, who was generally silent. His frame spread over two chairs, and his shoulders sloped so powerfully from his neck that he used to be able to load a fruit-barge single-handed. Now he was old. He watched people in silence; and his rare sign of pleasure was a soft whistling through yellowed teeth. Most of the dockers stood in awe of him.

"The grandfather rumbles!" said Philippou rudely. "But listen! I will tell you something true! Every day I say something true! Today it is this." He suppressed his chuckling. "I've just caught a most crafty sea-creature. You will not guess!"

"A dog-fish," said one fisherman.

"Craftier."

"A bream."

"No." He stood up portentously. All the lines of his body flowed down to the genial stomach, from which his trousers seemed on the point of slipping. "Today I caught the Lythrangomi Mining Company! Look!" He flung something on to the table. They all looked. It was an enormous octopus. "See," he laughed, rearranging the tentacles and convulsed by his own joke. "Many hands and no heart!"—he punched its fluid out—"And a great producer of ink!"

The fishermen shook with laughter. Only Marangos stayed quiet, watching them through slightly narrowed eyes, and the cadaverous priest at a far table never even looked up from a meal of chick-peas which he was spooning rudely into his mouth.

A slight, colourless man came over from the cranes; his smile was only perfunctory. "What's this, Philippou? You've caught the Company?"

"It's worth forty-five drachma." Philippou held it up. "Will you buy the Company for forty-five drachma, Kallis?"

The sallow man sat down among them. His hands on the table were delicate, almost hairless. "The Company will buy you," he said, "next year."

"Why only next year?" demanded Philippou. "What's wrong with me now?"

"Dear Philippou," said Kallis seriously, "nothing's wrong with you. You're a fine fellow. That's why you may hold out a year."

Everybody else at the table had stopped talking, and men at other tables had turned round to listen. This was partly at the mention of the Company, but partly because of Kallis. He was thirty-seven years old and at first sight might have been mistaken for a businessman or a bank clerk. His father, in fact, had worked fifteen years in a bank, but had died early and had left his children with their schooling half completed. The family had gone downhill. Kallis worked one of the cranes on the wharf. His self-contained manner set him apart, and although he was younger than most of the dockers, his intelligence was respected and they thought of him as an educated man. Everything he did seemed premeditated. Apart from his pallor, the first thing you noticed about him was the smoothness of his skin and the discreet, precise mouth.

This would have set his companions on their guard, but the man was quick in his sympathy. Sometimes it seemed as if he listened to them almost with compassion, as an adult to children. But after he had begun talking himself—and he only talked about what interested him—it was his eyes which attracted attention. They appeared to become hot and to darken. You expected them to sweat.

"It's being talked about all over the mines," he said in his quiet voice. "The Company has formally approached the archimandrite. They think it's a foregone conclusion now. They plan to start clearing the Mountain next spring."

This announcement, confirming what all had expected, had an oddly numbing effect. The voices which answered were still too bewildered for anger. *"Panaghia!"* The older fishermen crossed themselves. "God have mercy!"

"I don't believe it," murmured one. "The archimandrite would never . . . No. It's not to be thought of."

Kallis' voice became still sourer. "The archimandrite might do anything. He's not one of our people. The Company could twist him. Can we know what's going on up there?"

"Oh," hooted Philippou, "we're not important! As far as the Company's concerned, we can eat dust! We'll spend our old age on a slag-heap! I tell you, I was speaking to a man from the mining offices the other day—that slimy Lerides, got up in a new suit—and he says you find copper in coral and molluscs and seaweed-ash too. So look out! They'll be stealing the sea next."

Kallis cut him short. His words had grown tense. "This won't be a town any longer, it'll be a pit. Look at that mountain!" They stared up at the tree-covered ridge. The valley was almost in darkness. "The present open-cast mine is a baby to what that'll be! And its slag will go into the sea—sulphur and all. Then you'll see fish floating to the surface all right, Philippou. Poisoned and inedible! The whole shore polluted!"

One of the younger fishermen drummed the table with his fists. "Not this shore. They'll have to pay compensation."

Several men gave sickly laughs. "Compensation!" bellowed a docker. "Who can compensate you for ruining your occupation?"

Kallis said: "What compensation did they pay last year? The whole town complained because of the noise of blasting. There were two claims for miscarriage. And what did they pay? They only have to pay the government. If they pay the government they do as they like."

One of the flour-mill workers leaned over them and said: "It won't reach that far. The municipality will stop it. You'll see."

"Why should they?" demanded the docker. "We don't put enough in the municipality's pocket. Are they going to support us? What sort of fools are they meant to be then? No. They'll back the Company."

A number of the men by now were clenching their hands restlessly, especially the fishermen. They did not know how much to believe of what they heard. But they were self-reliant men and could believe anything of authority. Because they were not its servants, it might sweep them away. You never knew what was happening in your own town, let alone the Capital. For years you might run a business or own a piece of land; then one day a law was passed or a municipal council decided something. And that was the end of you.

The feverish look was in Kallis' eyes. He could not stop it; he could feel them stinging. "As for the port," he said, "do you think that will escape? They won't be taking the ore to Nikitari any more. It's the whole mountain they'll be moving! They'll build a maritime ropeway or a conveyor belt loading installation."

"Words," Marangos muttered. The passive spread of his shoulders and the inscrutability of his face were a sterile island in the agitation. "How do you know what the Company will do? And what are you worried about? Are you going to lose your job? So. This harbour will be in the fist of the Company. What's that to you?"

Marangos knew perfectly well. He and Kallis were too much alike not to understand one another. Marangos was old. He felt the world sliding away from him, leaving him redundant. As a younger man he had tried to follow the world's current, to exploit it; but he had long ago given that up. His vigour had deserted him and his ambition, once considerable, had darkened to bitterness. He wanted Kallis to fail, just as he had. He watched all the younger men now, waiting for the tide to recede from them also, and leave them dried. Instinctively he knew what Kallis felt. Kallis was still young. He still fought. He still believed that his life must bear some recognizable fruit. But already the sight of others' achievement left a hollowness in his stomach. Opportunities were no longer to be welcomed; they were invitations to failure. He was afraid of them. He could not bear much failure. That was what Marangos understood about Kallis.

Kallis said hotly: "Make no mistake, this will affect everyone. The Company will hold the port like this"—he cupped his hand—"and they'll have their own people here, just as they will in the mines. The Capital's seething with out-of-work personnel since the closure of the iron pits. As for us, the older ones"—he was looking straight at Marangos—"will be pensioned off, while the younger ones can adapt or be damned under a crowd of new bosses and specialists." He turned to the other dockers. "Can't you just hear it: 'Have you a degree in this, have you experience in that? No? Then we regret that since our ceiling for unskilled labour has now been reached . . .'" Something exploded inside him. "May God rot them! Americans and Germans! Why are they in our country? Let them leave us to run our own affairs!"

A shout of assent went up from several tables of dockers, who had become as tense as the rest. One of them banged the hilt of his knife on the table. "Let them try! Let them try! The Devil will wipe his feet on them!"

In the tumult Kallis heard Marangos say to him: "The Company won't eat you, it'll just forget you."

The flour-mill workers were caught up with the rest. Some of the shopkeepers on the quay were swearing and gesticulating too. A general unspoken feeling had taken root that already they were all being exploited. The Capitalist creature was manoeuvring under them, sucking from some secret gland which they themselves had not discovered, could not shut off. All their lives they had passed in a bent toil, by the sea, round the headlands, behind dark counters, along the wharf. Yet they had nothing to show for it. They could not even afford to send their sons to high school, let alone university. They did not drive cars. They did not even let the barber shave them.

Even Philippou's round face had turned plaintively angry. He jumped on to a chair and cocked his leg in the direction of the Company: "I revile you! I shit on you! May God forsake you!"

But nobody was listening. For five or ten minutes they had bristled and fumed. Now they turned to staring morosely into their coffee-cups. Their fury was dribbling away. It was being replaced by anxiety.

The priest had finished his meal and stood up: a dark man, remarkably tall. He was not like the priests with whom the people were familiar. He was without humour; he did not drink or play cards. He did not even carry on a part-time business. Only he read a great deal, and in summer he might be seen working in the carob groves of the poor, beating the branches with a twenty-foot stick as if his arms were made of iron.

Now he suddenly said: "Isn't that enough? Can you have forgotten?" His voice was hollow, as if his gullet were malformed. It might not have been his voice at all.

They stared at him, exhausted by their own talking, fidgeting with their beads. He was standing in front of the tables where they sat, the only one standing. This increased his authority, together with the peculiar voice, like a sound-box for somebody else's.

"You talk about your position, do you? What is that? Listen, I'll tell you. Your position is that of suppliants before God. Keep that position pure, and you may lose any other. Destroy it and you destroy your souls! You seem to have forgotten that the saints are your embassy to God." He spoke as if reading and preaching were his total occupation. Already several of his listeners were muttering pieties as a safeguard. They were not used to him. It was difficult to imagine him even talking as an ordinary man. You could not gossip with a voice like the Almighty's.

"St Vichinos of Blessed Memory," he went on, "has a single shrine in our country. It's here. Over the years it's worked miracles. It's become a place of pilgrimage for the entire province, even beyond. Our ancestors took comfort from it. The whole Mountain's been consecrated by tradition to the saint." When he tilted back his head a great blackness of beard accentuated his cheeks' gauntness. "The saint is a manifestation of God's mercy to His people. The Mountain is in trust to the people. The Church cannot dispose of it."

"That's true," Kallis said. "The Church would betray its trust."

The priest looked at him. His eyes, like his voice, were introverted and disturbing. They held not the faintest sparkle. "The Church is the servant of God," he said. "That is her trust. If a priest or an archimandrite betrays it, he's no longer of the body of the Church. The angels have deserted him, and he is cast forth." One of the dockers knocked over an ash-tray. The noise in the silence was like a clash of alarm. "The blessed St Vichinos is mediator for our souls. If we forsake him, we do more than refuse our salvation—we mock the Almighty."

The priest turned round, hitching his robes in one hand, and started to walk away. It was as if he had said what he wished to say, and had too much else to do to pursue the matter. But he left most of the men filled with a sense both of alarm and responsibility: a certain pride. They had been placed under obedience. Although they were exposed and uneasy, they were somehow stronger than before. But the fire had gone out of them, and after a while, one by one, they began to drift home or to the boats. Several went into the church.

Now you could hear the sea flopping on the sand. Marangos eased himself out of his chair and thrust away his coffee-cup, jerking his head in the direction which the priest had taken. "His family were from the Mani," he scowled. "They're a different lot there.... They love trouble."

Kallis and Philippou were left sitting alone. The fisherman yawned. It was his private opinion that all priests ought to be hanged. He looked at Kallis, whose lips were pinched together. They both reached across the table to find some coffee, but the little cups were all cold.

Chapter Six

The offices of the Lythrangomi Copper Mining Company were situated at the foot of immense waste heaps. These andesitic mounds appeared to have coated the whole premises in grey. Most of the employees—clerks and assistants from the drafting and planning rooms—went about in shirtsleeves and heavy boots. Nobody stood on dignity. An incompetent employee would find nothing to shield him here. Above all, paperwork had been reduced to a minimum. There were no such things in the Company as inter-departmental notes. Problems were solved by confrontation, or dealt with in impromptu committees which pored over statistics or pit progress maps until a decision had been reached. Nevertheless the filing cabinets in Oldenburg's office touched the ceiling. Time was wasted in correspondence with the government, which had demanded altered terms for land-lease and higher redundancy pay for the open-cast miners. The Company was engaged in running disputes with the Ministry of Commerce and the Department of Industry, as well as with the Inspector of Mines. None of this was new—the Company had wrangled with the authorities almost since its inception forty years ago—but it wasted energy.

Oldenburg prided himself as a General Manager who spared himself less than he did his workers. At seven o'clock in the morning, when the second shift was going underground, he would be standing with the Mine Superintendent at the tunnel, checking the men as they climbed into the wagons. Already by then he would have inspected the compressor unit, looked over the ventilation plant and resolved any problems raised during the night shift. By the time his executive staff had arrived at the offices, he would have been studying reports or dictating letters into a tape recorder for a full hour. Frequently the Chief Engineer and the Company Secretary would be called into his room before they had reached their own. Oldenburg shared his office with his personal assistant; its door was always open and he was accessible to anyone. He sat in his shirtsleeves with open collar and a tie pulled free of his neck. His gloves and helmet were hung up behind him.

Alastos was encouraged by this. He was also glad that he had dressed casually for the interview. If he had worn a suit, he thought, it might look as if he hoped for an executive job. He knew that he would not get one, and he was not going to hint at the pretension.

But interviews drew out his pride, and although he fervently wanted a post with them, he had already decided that he was not going to crawl to the Lythrangomi Mines. Mining was the only profession for which he was qualified, and Oldenburg would know this; but Alastos would say that he was also considering a job in the chrome mines at Chakistra. If the Company wanted him, he would like a prompt decision.

But Oldenburg did not invite this approach. He scrutinized Alastos' references in detail, then checked them against his letter with a thoroughness which the younger man found offensive. Alastos, in his turn, took the opportunity to observe Oldenburg, but failed to see anything of Caroline in the stocky figure and bald head. The Managing Director looked younger than his fifty-five years, but forceful and impersonal as a bullet. "Bullet" was the image which kept recurring to Alastos as he watched him. Oldenburg gave precisely that impression of compact, undeviating energy. It was difficult to conceive of him laughing or sleeping or lying on a beach. The tightness of his face and manner, suggested deep inhibition, something stunted in the man.

But he was good at his job; that was certain. Now he collected Alastos' references in a sheaf and thrust them back at him. The gesture was depressing. He asked in a jarring Mid-West accent: "What were you doing with the Anglo-American Copper Foundation? Principally." He had planted his forearms heavily on the desk. Alastos hoped that this at least indicated willingness to spare him time.

"I was assistant to one of the consultants. We gathered information on the latest excavating machinery, specializing in East German equipment."

"For open-cast mining, then?" Oldenburg was staring hard at him.

"Yes." It was a poor start. He knew the Company's present open-cast mine would soon close, and that the new one was still in question. If he was to make an impression on Oldenburg, it must be for mining underground.

But he had no more leisure to think. The questions came at him like hammer-strokes. Oldenburg obviously had something definite in mind, but Alastos could not for the moment tell what it was. The questions had no connection with underground mining nor any relevance to working the Company's exhausted pit. He thought he understood, but he had no time to speculate.

"At the Federal Mining Corporation, when you were working as assistant to the Pit Super, did you get experience of Ammo-Nitrate oil mix?"

"Yes. For six-inch blast holes."

"And the host rock?"

"Porphyry, a little schist."

"What height excavation bench did you cut?"

"Twenty-seven feet."

"And you used shovel ropes or large-diameter cables?"

"Both. We made the transition while I was there."

The telephone interrupted them. While Oldenburg answered it, Alastos observed the production chart on the wall behind him. The forecast graph was drawn in red, the production in grey. Both of them climbed consistently until in the last few months the grey line bumped against the red. He next noticed Oldenburg's assistant. The youth looked like an Armenian, he thought, and the contrast to Oldenburg was ridiculous. Of an extraordinarily delicate build, this man moved with the susceptivity of a woman, and his skin held that sensitized glow which can light the gauntest features. He was like a nervous and beautiful snake. Alastos, who looked himself as if he had been put together from three or four different sources, found this mysterious and slightly unnerving. But Oldenburg now replaced the receiver and continued his questions.

"Did you ever have experience of stockpiling low-grade non-sulphide ore?"

"For leaching, yes."

"Did you deal with Copper Precipitate?"

"No."

And so on and on. It was practical experience that Oldenburg was after. He did not ask about Alastos' degree and did not seem to care about his office work in London. He wanted a man who understood the placing of blast holes, could plan bench wall slopes and dump areas, build access ramps. He wanted an assistant engineer. He must place his chances of buying the Mountain very high.

The questions stopped as suddenly as they had begun. Oldenburg continued to stare at Alastos, but leaned back in his chair. "You'll appreciate," he said (Alastos hated to hear that phrase—it preceded excuses), "that with the closing of the iron pits near the Capital there is a swarm of trained personnel about. I have a file full of applications here"—he knocked on his desk. "As you may know, we're a small company. This whole operation works on three hundred and thirty men. In addition, your experience is only in open-cast, and our pit is all but finished." He paused a second. "I regret I can't possibly employ you underground."

Alastos nodded curtly. So that was that. But he knew that he had failed on personal grounds, not on his qualifications, which Oldenburg had seen before. He felt profoundly depressed. He instinctively respected Oldenburg. And now that the chance was gone, he felt again, bitterly, how much he wanted to work on these mines. It was perhaps the only significant thing he could have done. If the Company bought the other side of the valley, he would live to see his town transformed and he wanted—desperately now—to be part of the instrument which would transform it. If the rumours were true, the mine on the Mountain of St Vichinos could employ half Kalepia. And a mining town nowadays was a rich town, a developing town, where men would see their children educated and their women fed.

But if Oldenburg did not want him, that was the end of it. He was not going to kneel. Perhaps, ironically, he would apply to the Chakistra chrome mines after all.

He had already half stood up when Oldenburg said: "However—". For five seconds, while the General Manager lit a cigarette, Alastos savoured the beautiful and harmonious word "however". No "however" had pleased him half as much as this strident Mid-Western one. He waited for Oldenburg to inhale and lay the cigarette on a paper-weight. "However," repeated Oldenburg, "we are hoping to resume open-cast operations in the near future—on a very big scale—and we'll need many more experienced men than we have here. For the past three years we've been gradually laying off our pit workers. Now we may be going to need them again. But this is the future. For the moment all I can offer you is a job as a foreman in the open-cast. You're lucky. Our junior foreman's gone down with silicosis. You'll supervise one two-and-a-half-yard shovel excavator and two thirty-ton dump trucks. We use the toe blast hole drill here with delay ignition. That's work you're familiar with. We pay three thousand drachma a week."

It did not seem to have occurred to Oldenburg that anybody could refuse work with the Company. But Alastos was too pleased, even with the job of a pit foreman, to make a show of deliberating. He grinned broadly, although it was ridiculous to smile at Oldenburg, and said: "Fine." But in a moment he had recovered and added: "I'd like to know what the Company's future is."

There was no change of expression in Oldenburg, and no delicacy about his reply. (Only faintly now did Alastos receive the impression that the man was not whole.) "We're negotiating to buy the St Vichinos Mountain. We haven't been able to make a full investigation, but primary drilling in surrounding property has shown that the extent of the ore is enormous: probably some five million tons. We start to hit it sixty feet below the pillow lava. As for time, if our overture to the See of Nikitari goes through, we hope to begin before the end of the year."

"And it's a high-grade ore body?" Alastos did not know if he should have asked. It seemed equivalent to demanding what a man's salary was. The English in him recoiled, but the Greek wanted to know. Besides, it was probably impossible to embarrass Oldenburg.

"Yes," the General Manager said. "We haven't exact figures—but it's a dream ore."

It was good to work in the open again. His back and shoulders, he felt sure, had straightened, and his hands had become capable hands once more, neither too big, nor too violent, for their job. Had he noticed how differently he used to walk when indoors? A feeling of being too large had constricted all his movements, even his step. But now, along the curves of the excavated hill, the same walk released itself in a long, invigorated stride. His body and motions seemed to have reached proportion and harmony.

The Company had cut their arc wide in this smooth skull of a hill and neatly picked out its brains. The loaded dump trucks went down to the primary crusher by zigzagging earth ramps, which had been capably engineered. Where the waste poured in strange flesh tints for hundreds of feet down, he found the lighter silicate rocks which were familiar from his childhood. They belonged to a limestone country. When he stooped to examine them he saw tiny zeolites glinting in the lava.

From here, on a clear day, it seemed as if half the world must lie in sight. Hills and mountains crowded to the horizon, until the farthest became no more than an illusion, a cloud perhaps, or the shadow of some other mountain thrown into space. The light on these June mornings was sometimes so transparent that he could pick out the red tongues of the goats in valleys half a mile away. All these near pastures were scarred and trodden into harshness; like the valleys of Greece, they had been too much loved. The farmers clung to them, shoring up the meanest slope for olives, and the goatherds led their destructive flocks by tracks which striated half the country. It was a violated land, with which only a part of him felt familiar. The signs of its endurance were always on it. That gave it a fierce sincerity. So it was to these ridges that his eye always returned—not to the sea, where toy boats moved to Nikitari, nor to the volcanic uplands—but to this core of glittering hills.

The mine was cut in benches thirty feet high. As the copper pyrites failed so the stone grew paler, and now, almost scraped clean of riches, went down by steps to a pool of green water impregnated with copper sulphates. The single power shovel moved along its wall like a fly on a carcass.

Alastos enjoyed supervising this machine's work. A good shovel-operator could make or mar an open-cast operation. To crowd with the shovel, trying to scoop too much, was to break your ropes. If you gathered clumsily you could crack the dump truck with a falling rock. If you swung too low you could smash it with the shovel teeth. But work with co-ordination, as his man did now, and the mountain was chipped away before your eyes.

Day after day, in the blinding dust and heat, the excavator picked off the layers loosened by blasting, and swung them in its claw, while the trucks moaned and roared on their double wheels as they carried the stuff away. Then the blasting would begin again. You sent the drill down thirty-six feet, deeper than the height of each bench, and fired fourteen charges one after another by primer cord. The noise set the dogs barking all through Kalepia.

Today the Chief Engineer came to check the positions of the new holes, and where his Land Rover turned back down the ramp Alastos saw the Company Secretary, Lerides, walking with another man along the edge of the excavation. He knew it was the Company Secretary because he recognized the car parked by the incline. The other man looked like a government official. Alastos shielded his eyes and briefly looked at them. Lerides appeared pale and thickset. So that was Ekaterina's husband. Alastos did not much want to meet him. But he imagined either that Lerides would not know who he was, or that she would not have talked of him. As for Ekaterina, the thought of seeing her again disquieted him. So when he saw the two men walking towards him he continued to work on the blast holes with his back turned. They passed a few metres away.

"We had a lot of overburden here," Lerides was saying, "nearly thirteen million tons. . . ." But he was looking sideways all the time, and Alastos was sure that he knew who he was. He even suspected that Lerides had walked along the excavation specially to look at him. Neither he nor the government official was dressed for the place. Lerides, in particular, in a suit and light shoes, was constantly trying to avoid treading in trickles of azurite. He was a little too carefully groomed for Alastos' liking, and was beginning to run to fat. But he was a handsome man, no doubt about that, with a healthy head of dark, crinkled hair and a thin moustache. Now he had detached himself from his visitor and was walking close.

"Excuse me," he said courteously. "Are you Julian Alastos?"

"Yes." Alastos raised himself to his full height. It was about his only advantage, he thought. He must look bizarre, chalky grey from head to foot. But it was the Company's chalk.

"I'm Michael Lerides, the Company Secretary. When I saw your name on our lists, I thought I must have a word with you. I believe you knew my wife at one time."

Alastos nodded. The "at one time" made the thing easier. "Yes," he said. He took off his helmet—it was the least he could do—and cradled it in one hand. "One summer. I came back to see my father." Lerides, he thought, was very suave, a glossy veneer of a man. He must be about thirty-eight years old.

"I mentioned you were back," Lerides said. "I'm sure she'd like to see you."

Alastos suddenly did not want to see Ekaterina at all. Not only must she have changed, but so must he. She had spent most of the years of his absence as a married woman. She had a child. She would have matured. Whereas he had passed more than half that time in the copper mines of Utah. He looked down instinctively at his coarsened hands. Those of Lerides were square and white; he wore a heavy gold ring.

Alastos thought he should speak, and so said: "And how is she?"

"She's very well, very busy," Lerides answered. "With her qualification as a nurse she works part-time for one of the doctors now. She's seen your father several times. I was sorry to hear about him." Alastos thought that Lerides was trying to be too charming. The effort dissipated the result. But he supposed he should be grateful for the effort at all. He was starting to feel irritable. Lerides, in spite of his tone, was observing him with a faintly guarded expression, and perhaps he, in his turn, was studying Lerides too frankly. His gaze kept reverting to the man's vestigial double chin.

They remained staring at one another for several seconds before either spoke again, staring in the vaguely puzzled manner with which two men may regard one another when both have been loved by the same woman. Alastos found his gaze returning, a little mystified, to the heavy neck and mouth of Lerides. But it all seemed too long ago to concern him.

Lerides smiled in a formal but ambivalent way and said: "It must be a long time...." Then he slapped the dust from his trousers. "You'll excuse me. I must return to my visitor."

Alastos went back to his work not much pleased. He would rather Ekaterina had not mentioned him; but he sensed by the man's tone that she had done so a long time ago, and that Lerides had remembered.

The sun's heat was now intense; but the work revived him. By the time he had gone down to the service depot and had returned to the site, he was singing to himself in a silly falsetto voice which he adopted to amuse children. The excavator was still at work. He was sorry that in this expiring mine the machines must soon be idle. Here he could not experience the excitement of a new site, of discovering that the ore went a little deeper than had been supposed, or had produced a richer vein. He was merely plucking the last ligaments from a skeleton.

But when he looked over the valley at the Mountain of St Vichinos, he saw the tell-tale iron stains everywhere. It would be magnificent to excavate. A single-track railway could run the ore down to the sea of its own volition. Then the port would be expanded. Everything would be expanded. This would be one of the richest district towns in the Republic. After that, Alastos thought, the young men might not find any cause to leave the land where they should properly be. After all, wasn't this their core, their tradition?

Alastos was over-conscious of this tradition, because by blood he only half belonged to it. He saw it, he knew, with the envy of not quite possessing. This disappointment at his people was the disappointment of the foreigner.

He looked over the blasting arrangement. He inspected it almost affectionately, as if it would detonate them all into a better world. New schools, television, books—it took an effort for an outsider to conceive what the flood of these would mean to a community which ever since its inception had heard only its own voice, century after century, like a monk's prayer.

This prayer had numbed the ears of so many that it did not do to count their centuries. Not another generation, he thought, must die like that. Not a single one more! They were born half-nourished. In school they barely learnt to read and write, or even to memorize a waste patch of history. They married the people their parents chose, followed their father's trade. After that they lived the lives of the men on the chairs by the street pavements. Their thoughts were childish dreams of money and prestige, and their refuge was any chance stimulus—a bargain or an accident. This they would dispute for hours and days, because there was nothing else to do. Old age, which might add forgetfulness to ignorance, was often a release, although the men grumbled, believing that things were not as good as they had been in their youth. But things were exactly as they had been. And when death came, the people were buried by the rites of a decayed Church, preaching a time-dishonoured legend. "They shall rise again," said the writing on the gravestones. "They only sleep." But what would rise again? What was so precious to this God that he must resurrect it?

Alastos could have wept for them—Greeks, whose ancestors first gave pride to man. They slept in the shade.

The sun glared from the rocks, dazzling his eyes. He watched the excavator clawing at the ridge. It took away its mouthfuls like crumbled cake. That was fine to see. He respected these machines. He had observed them often and they were worthy of their job. All day they shovelled and roared. Their caterpillar feet could manoeuvre with unexpected agility. Now they would not only heave up sulphurous rock and copper pyrite, but would mine for human development, pulling Kalepia into the day.

All the same, Julian could not discover any charity in his passion for this progress—he could not love a whole people, only one or two. It was more like bending things to his will. Nor did he know why mindlessness and waste angered him so: the men on their chairs in the street. Sometimes he felt as if he saw his nightmare self in them. Was he too close to their condition? If life was senseless, then they were the truth he refused to face. They were saying: "After our ancestors, after all philosophy and beauty, it is still only this. This is what it is. Nothing." In the end, he did not understand.

Chapter Seven

The archimandrite looked at the priest with misgiving. On the few occasions when this man had spoken at the monthly convocations, the archimandrite considered that he had shown an almost primitive mind. He represented precisely the kind of backwardness which the Church was trying to eradicate in its laity. Nowadays the Church was too sophisticated, its methods and organization too complex, to accommodate clergy who failed to recognize changed circumstances. Nor did he like the way the priest stood in front of his desk waiting for permission to speak, so that when this was granted he could continue to stand, over six feet tall, as if he were a preaching abbot.

So the archimandrite nodded at him with an air of preoccupation, as though he had a great deal of business, and said: "Please sit down, Reverend."

The priest did so, but his body looked so lank and hard that there was no relaxation in the movement and his stare was as disturbing as before.

The archimandrite folded his hands on the desk in front of him; he kept his movements easy and deliberate. "Yes?"

"Most Reverend," the priest said, "I want to ask whether the conscience of our Church is still pure."

The archimandrite drew back his chair, as though in mild reproof; his beard rustled over his soutane. "The Church is the body of Christ, Reverend. It is without stain."

"I meant the conscience of her servants." The priest placed his calloused hands on his knees and leaned further forward. "I'm anxious in particular for the shrine on the Mountain of St Vichinos."

The archimandrite smoothed the papers which lay under his hands. His movements, in their judicious slowness, suggested that the matter was confidential. He disliked the sonority of the priest's speech, as if he was sermonizing. It was close to impertinent. So was this "wish for assurance". He stared up very coldly at the priest. His pale eyes and pale skin gave the feeling of a man seen behind gauze. "The conscience of our fellow-clergy," he said, "you had better leave to them. As for the shrine of St Vichinos, its affairs, you may be sure, will be ordered for the glory of God." He smiled perfunctorily, took a pile of letters from a side-table with one hand, and a pen in the other. It was the equivalent of dismissal. But the priest did not stir and his expression did not change. He simply remained seated, awaiting the archimandrite's attention. The only unmistakable quality in his face was superiority—a withdrawn, impersonal superiority. The archimandrite glanced up with feigned surprise that he had remained.

"Most Reverend," the priest said at once—his remote boom extinguished any humility in the words—"the glory of God cannot be served by the impoverishment of His saints."

The archimandrite's lips tightened at once. He leaned back stiffly and stared straight at the other man. His patience had been tried enough. It was time this crude priest be taught a lesson, and the best lesson for the uneducated was to expose their ignorance. To discipline the man now would save trouble later. It was important to secure respect. The archimandrite whetted his voice: "The whole Church, Reverend, is a living expression of the glory of God. There are many ways of service open to her. The veneration of the saints is only one. St John Damascene stated the case clearly. The saints are our oldest brothers, but they are not in themselves objects of worship. They are only exemplars."

"But an exemplar, most Reverend, is one who reflects the Almighty."

"Certainly, Reverend, but he is not himself the Almighty." Two angry points of colour had appeared in the archimandrite's cheeks. "Even man may sometimes reflect God. He nevertheless remains man, and falls within the jurisdiction of the Church. 'A person cannot have God as his father if he does not have the Church as his Mother.' So spoke the blessed Cyprian. And so it is with the saints."

The priest's face, he thought, had darkened; but it was so dark already that he was not sure. The man still held his body exactly as he had when he had first sat down. His eyes remained without glitter. They were indecipherable, even dead. And when he spoke again his voice was more than ever like the loud but far-off beating of a drum. It reverberated most uncomfortably in the archimandrite's ears. "It is true that the saints are only a part of the Celestial Church. But this means that the Church cannot diminish them without paradox, for she would be diminishing herself."

"Precisely," snapped the archimandrite. "The saints and the Church are incorporate. The one cannot act without the other. Therefore if the Church decides to remove and re-dedicate the shrine of St Vichinos elsewhere, the decision is not only that of the Church. It is that of St Vichinos." The archimandrite felt rather proud of this dialectic, but he was now angry. This priest had overstepped himself. Would he lecture his superior on the status of the saints? An ordinary priest—not even a *protopresvyteros*! The archimandrite noticed that his own hands were clenching the edge of the desk. He checked himself and folded them in his lap.

The priest was speaking again. For the first time he made a sound of emotion. "Remove and re-dedicate?" A subdued horror clanged in the vault of his voice. The archimandrite found this more discomfiting than the expressionless tone of before. It was rather as if he had surprised an oracle, and it had groaned. "Remove and re-dedicate the shrine? Most Reverend, it is not only the building but the land which is holy. The relics of the saint are buried beneath the sanctuary. That is an ancient tradition here. Hundreds have been healed by faith in them."

The archimandrite was genuinely surprised. He had not heard of these relics. They complicated the matter a little. It would be embarrassing if an attempt was made to recover them, and nothing was found. People would say the saint had deserted his shrine in anger, or some such nonsense. The country people thought of anything. He wondered if this had occurred to the priest. But no.... The priest perfectly believed in the relics. All the same, the position was basically unchanged. Folk tradition did not count as dogma. Therefore the saint was a part of truth, but his relics were not. "Remember the Council of Carthage," he warned the priest. "'The Lord said, I am truth. He did not say, I am custom.'" The archimandrite was stepping back into the field of dialectic; he felt easier there.

But the priest ignored that fine thread. "St Vichinos is the people's saint," he answered. "However you would spend the money which—may God forbid it!—the sale would bring, you couldn't make reparation to them for the loss of their intercessor before God. You can't replace the glorious tradition of the saints. They are beyond price. *And the people would die for them.*"

Deep inside him the archimandrite felt as if something gave way. It did not yet show in his face, and if it had the harsh priest would not have noticed, but he felt its weariness seeping up his body. The people, that was the crux. Sometimes it even seemed as if the matter had nothing to do with God at all. He sat back in his chair to prop himself in an attitude of dignity. He began: "You must realize . . ."

But the priest was now quoting from Symeon: "'The saints in each generation, joined to those who have gone before, and filled like them with light, become a golden chain, in which each saint is a separate link, united to the next by faith, works, and love. So in the One God they form a single chain which cannot quickly be broken.' 'If a person deceives his conscience by false arguments, he will sleep the bitter death of forgetfulness.'"

The archimandrite fumbled with the pectoral cross on his chest. He had stopped being outraged by the priest. He felt very tired. He was even glad the man went on talking, because he no longer wanted to answer. All the time the priest's voice echoed more and more impersonally, until eventually the archimandrite received the impression that the voice was not inside the priest at all, but inside himself, as if the drum was beating far back in the base of his skull. "Take away this shrine," it continued, "and you'll destroy a means of faith. *You will damn souls.*"

Neither of them moved or spoke. The archimandrite remained propped up by the back of his chair. His hands rested along its arms. The priest appeared, if anything, still more taut. They could hear, quite distinctly, the noise of an electric fan two rooms away. The archimandrite had never noticed it before: it sounded like the pant of a heart which is reaching its end. He sensed the water collecting under the lids of his eyes. He was not thinking any more about the relationship between God, His Church and the saints. These remained always of a perfect, mystical beauty. But they changed. Every time you turned the kaleidoscope of logic a little, they burst into a new pattern. He did not check himself in this heresy. It would be orthodox only to say that they revealed themselves layer by layer to the heart. But that was not what he felt. At the moment they were simply a mathematical iridescence, which helped him not at all. He was not used to these decisions. His six months in Kalepia had tried him more than twenty years at the Capital. It was as if during those twenty years some faculty in him had corroded. He had not even noticed. And now that he needed it, it was no longer there. He moved a finger along his watering eyes. A quotation reached his mind—was it from the *Contrite Discourses*?—he thought it was: "When God created man, He implanted in him a certain divine power with a spark, like a warm and luminous thought, to illumine the mind and show it what is good and what evil. This is called conscience, and is natural law."

The Fathers had taught that conscience was only silent in the saint, or in the man fallen so low that it had been frozen to death in him. But no! He was not such a man! This natural law was speaking in him. Why, if it was not, did he tolerate this bigoted priest? The voice of this law was muffled. That was all. It did not direct him. Only the saint, or the frozen sinner, would know his direction in this affair. What would it mean if he were able to sell the Mountain and to send eight hundred thousand dollars to the Metropolitan of Nikitari? In what ratio did he want prestige, gratitude, a more comfortable residence (he was sure he could elicit that) and the other "gift" which the Company had promised? There was no telling. How much was for the glory of God? How much for the Church? How much for the people? How much for himself? He listened for the warm spark inside him, for this conscience which was natural law. He literally listened, during the few seconds which elapsed before either man spoke again. But he heard only a confused murmur, like country people chattering in church before the Liturgy.

From their photographs framed along the wall, the seven last bishops of Kalepia gazed at him through sepia eyes. He thought: I must wait. Perhaps the metropolitan would refuse his consent. It was unlikely, but it was possible. Meanwhile he must examine himself.

His hands, without his noticing, were clasped against his stomach. He appeared to be holding himself together. Now the water dribbled freely from his eyelids. He straightened himself in the chair, but he could not revive his own presence. His face looked as if it was dripping away through his beard. And still there was this priest. He was still staring with those filmy-dark eyes, in which the pupil and the iris ran together. Maybe, the archimandrite thought, he should thank him. Or thank God for him. But instead he felt a sullen hurt. He put up his hand to his forehead.

The silence had prolonged itself. He must say something. With an effort he focused the priest. "Now understand, Reverend,"—his tone was conciliatory, a little confidential—"we must not be hasty. You forget how complicated this is. We must indeed consider the interests of the people. The priest is the servant of the people."

"The priest is the servant of God."

The archimandrite faltered at this interruption. Would this man concede nothing? Did he want to humiliate him completely? But he continued: "It is for this reason that I've laid the whole matter in the hands of the metropolitan, who is the people's representative—and God's."

The priest answered: "You had it in your power to choke this at its birth—you, who understand what this means. The bishop is unwell. And does he know how many pilgrims come here? Is he aware of the traditions? Does he know that the fruit of the olive trees which will be destroyed on the Mountain is customarily a gift to the poor?"

The archimandrite himself had not known this. Why had nobody told him? He mumbled: "The Company would make reparation to the poor. And if not, I myself own a small olive grove. . . ." But no! This was intolerable! What was he saying? Who was this priest to persecute his superiors, to arrogate conscience to himself? He would be warning the bishops next, interrupting the Holy Synod! The archimandrite felt his strength flood back in anger. "It is not for you," he cried, "to question the ability of the metropolitan to make decisions! The metropolitan is the elect of the Church, the living image of God on earth!"

He might never have spoken. The priest got to his feet. "If this sale is permitted," he said, "I shall preach against it in my church."

The archimandrite's thoughts were now sleek and rapid again. "That will be your responsibility." If I complain of him, he thought, it will only draw attention to the affair. I will have to outlast whatever trouble he causes. But it might not come to that. There was first the metropolitan's decision, then he must think. He had time to think, to explore the labyrinth of conscience within himself which he had barely trodden since leaving theological school forty-eight years ago. That was what it was, he thought. Not a spark, but a labyrinth.

The priest had reached the door. Ever since he had entered the room, the archimandrite had been wishing he would go. But now that he was at last leaving, the archimandrite felt an inexplicable desire to call him back. It was almost as if the priest were taking reality away with him, so that after he had left, the room and its occupant would revert to whatever dream they had been inhabiting before. The archimandrite could not account for this sensation, but it was perfectly definite. It seemed to be contained in the man's mouth as he turned in the doorway. Only ten minutes had elapsed since he had come in and stood in front of the desk. But the archimandrite, glancing at his watch, could not believe that; he stared and shook it, thinking it must have stopped. Strange how whole days, whole years, could go by and nothing appeared to happen. . . .

The priest hesitated a moment. He did not know how to take leave of the archimandrite. He would not kiss his hand. His cheeks had darkened—that was noticeable in the clearer light. He was angry. The archimandrite was also angry, but his anger was now subdued. He was beginning to think less about the priest and more about himself. "You may go," he said shortly. "I cannot dictate what you preach. But beware you do not injure our mother Church."

"That has always been my care." The priest's shoulders stooped forward with a hint of physical threat. "The Church is not with you," he said. "You fall alone."

Chapter Eight

There was a feel of celebration about the party which the Oldenburgs gave to their employees and to the notables of Kalepia. It was tacitly felt that the sale of the Mountain of St Vichinos would be realized. The archimandrite, it was true, had said that it had been necessary to lay the matter before the metropolitan bishop, but this was considered a formality. When the bishop returned his assent, it would only remain for the archimandrite to deal with the Company, and perhaps with his conscience.

But the party also had a conciliatory flavour. It was as if the town had been invited specifically to meet the Company, to see that its executives were human as well as efficient, and that they would be comfortable neighbours. Although this had been Oldenburg's idea, he did not himself present a diplomatic figure. His wife had pinned an encouraging rose in the button-hole of his tuxedo, but it gave the same impression as the flower-beds which are sometimes planted round factories by a well-meaning management.

Oldenburg had organized the party six weeks before, but he left his wife to supply all human touches. That was their marriage. Claudia Oldenburg was delicately made. She walked with a slightly self-conscious poise and talked in the same way, in a soft, clipped voice. Her features were striking and spare, the eyes very pale blue. It was with these eyes that she appeared to be extending welcome, not with her formal handshake.

A servant-boy in white stood at the foot of the verandah steps and ushered the guests up to the drawing-room. All the larger houses in Kalepia were built to this pattern, with the living-rooms on the first floor. The verandah was fringed with potted shrubs—

not the usual stale-looking palms and grasses, but oleanders and a pair of datura trees, not yet in bloom. A second servant snaked among the guests with glasses of champagne; a buffet-table was spread with cold hams and chicken, three or four salads and, as a concession to Levantine taste, some plates of *zalatina* with several dishes full of *tiropites*. Some of the minor civil servants would have liked to indulge in these, but felt that they should toy with the ham.

The party looked precisely what it was. Apart from Oldenburg, two or three American executives stood noticeably tall in their white tuxedos, and were genial and expansive. Several of their Greek colleagues wore the same dress, but with grace and a touch of narcissism. They moved about the Americans with the ease and adaptability of water round stones, while the officials, in their best suits and shining shoes, looked no more consequential than they were.

The Oldenburgs worried that their guests were not going to mix, but while Claudia passed among them with smiling introductions, Oldenburg started to look grim, and stood isolated in the centre of the room, impotently tapping his champagne-glass. While at the mines he was all-sufficient, here he resembled some finely-tuned engine divorced from its body. He himself was aware of this, and ill at ease. Every time Claudia passed him she whispered, "Don't scowl, Frank", but his expression remained.

Yet slowly, as more people arrived, the party gained momentum, and half an hour later it was safe in the roar of its own volition. Oldenburg watched the guests with mingled envy and contempt; they were so warm together, and so trivial. All this energy, he thought, leading nowhere, wasting time, achieving nothing. Yet people poured themselves into these social activities as if they were the only thing on earth.

One of the few people who remained ill at ease was the archimandrite, but because of his heavy, concealing beard and natural pallor, this was not noticed. He ate well, and later Oldenburg was pleased to see that Caroline's conversation was charming him, and occasionally drawing his laughter. It was more than anything important that the archimandrite be kept amenable. Oldenburg also noticed that his son Howard had attached himself to the archimandrite's coarse-looking niece; he considered this an excellent thing for the time being.

Julian Alastos arrived late. He wore a suit which fitted his body as well as a suit could, and he was dark from the sun. With his heavy-boned features and wide-set eyes, he might have passed for a pure Englishman. But then, when a conversation excited him, his arm movements would begin. They owed nothing to the blunt English manner, nor to the Greek flourish, but were a frustrated necessity of his own. Caroline interrupted one of these gestures to place a glass of champagne in his hand. Her close, cream-coloured dress accentuated the roundness of her hips and breasts; she wore a girlish brooch. Her fair hair was tied back at her neck.

She seemed nervous about his job; she was not sure if he would like it; but when he even used the word "enjoy" she relaxed into a half-smile which remained all the time he was speaking.

"Did you know you can see half the country from that mine?" he asked enthusiastically. "Yes, really, on the north the whole Asproyia range—it looks quite green on some afternoons, like china—and the river shows in the hills behind for a good ten miles." He dug into his pocket. "And have you seen anything like this?—Look."

She peered inside his palm; it cradled a rock crystal: not the usual jagged crystal, but an almost perfect oval which shone brilliantly. "I polished it," he said. "How it got that shape, I don't know. But take it. It shows that nature includes the unexpected." He laughed at her and dropped it in her hand, thrusting his own back in his pockets. He was thinking how natural and young she looked: she made him feel as if too much of life had troubled him. He supposed that it showed in his face.

They moved a little away from the rest. He was embarrassed by being here, he said: a foreman among executives. He supposed he was there because of her. She shrugged. She noticed how his jaw had slightly tightened. It was the sort of look which implied that although he had mentioned the oddity of his position, that was a prerogative which belonged only to him.

"My father doesn't regard you as a foreman," she said, lowering her voice. "You see, when the new mine is opened, there'll be positions vacant on the engineering side; that's what you want, isn't it?"

"You're very sure that the mine will open."

She was sipping her champagne, but made eager noises at him over the lip of the glass. "Yes, I'm sure. It's going to be all right now." She spoke as blithely as a schoolgirl. "You see the man like Father Christmas over there, the archimandrite? He's the one to decide, and Daddy says he's just delaying a bit because he likes to feel important."

Alastos glanced at "Daddy", who was talking to the Mayor with his feet planted pugnaciously apart. "So he doesn't think there'll be any trouble?"

"Oh no, you see he's got the municipality on his side, and there's nobody else to make a fuss, and ..."

Alastos found again that he was not listening to what she was saying, but was watching her amber-flecked eyes which amused themselves all on their own. Was she nineteen or was she twenty-one? She must have told him, but he had forgotten. She acted on him like a poultice; she dispelled his darker moods. He wondered why he had not seen her more in England. Or perhaps he was simply depressed by his father's illness, and now needed her happiness to replenish his own. But she was speaking seriously. "... just like you were saying: this town's stone dead. Did I tell you I got a job with Sofroniou, teaching? I'm in charge of the six-year-olds. I can't tell you what *they're* like. I do believe that over half of them have got threadworms. They're always shifting about on their seats and scratching. I had to mention this to one of the mothers on Thursday—her child was so uncomfortable—and really, she was quite angry. Another child ... Why are you laughing?"

Alastos did not know why he was laughing either. He simply found that he was smiling into her face. He looked like a genial ogre. He told her, "You're right. Of course you're right"—but his laughter kept rolling out at her. Of course, he entirely agreed. It was disgusting, threadworms. It must have been the way she talked about it that made him laugh. She looked so clean, with her pale dress and child's brooch and her face with its missionary innocence.

She looked cross. "I don't see what's funny. You say yourself that the town needs education. You get passionate about it. Then when I say the same thing, you laugh. Why do you take your own opinions seriously and not mine?"

It was, he admitted, rather peculiar and unfair. But he did take her opinions seriously, he said. And he really did. "Perhaps it's the champagne—or maybe I enjoy being with you too much to be serious." She did not answer. Or maybe, he thought, it is this way my mind detaches itself from your words and attends to your face. It always seemed to be her face to which he wanted to listen. But he did not tell her so.

She was not pleased with him. She tossed back a curl of hair and began to look around, avoiding his gaze, as if she wanted to go away. He touched her arm with the back of his hand, then enclosed it in the big, rough circle of his thumb and forefinger. She looked at him. "I may give you back your crystal," she said drily. "Just to show you that nature contains the unexpected."

He smiled so affectionately that she began to smile too. She let him lead her on to the verandah where several of the guests were viewing the sunset. Between the valley-sides it covered the sea in a dense, pink glow. They leaned against the balustrade among the shrubs and watched the lights appearing in the houses of Kalepia. The town looked like a shabby model.

"They had a case of typhus down there a few weeks ago," he said. "Did you know?"

"Yes, I heard." She rested her elbows on the railing and her brown face in her hands. "Look at the sea!" she said excitedly. "We have such air here! It ought to be the healthiest town in the world, oughtn't it? How long will it take to be that? Five years? Ten?"

This time Alastos tamed his laughter into a smile. "What do you mean to do? You can't fumigate them all. You must teach them to want it. The next generation ..."

"You and your next generation! What about this one? We'll be forty before the next generation comes ..."

"I shall be fifty."

"... and by that time we won't care any more. We'll be dried up! Will you have any energy left at fifty?"

Alastos could not imagine fifty, but he also could not imagine losing this restlessness, this dissatisfaction, inside him. So he thumped the balustrade vigorously—his hair was starting to stand in its tufts—and said, "Yes! Yes! Certainly I shall! What's age got to do with it?" He looked down at the town and added more quietly: "When I'm fifty I'll still be fond enough to hate this place sometimes."

"It'll be changed by then. Everything will be changed by then. We will have changed it."

He wanted to believe her. She made him feel almost unhealthy if he doubted. Everything could be transformed by the will to transform it—he would see! "Look at the Mountain," she said. "What a size! Imagine what is in there!"

"I've already imagined," he answered. He moved against her warm lightness. She smelt of something fragrant and early, a girl's scent. "I suppose there are worse towns than Kalepia about, but this is like nurturing your own child, isn't it?" He added seriously:

"Up there in your father's mine I'm destroying my own aimlessness. I can't explain what it's like. Sometimes, honestly, I feel I'm repairing every trivial thing I've ever done."

He looked so warm and self-assured, she nudged his shoulder with her head. Her hair stroked his mouth. They were alone on the verandah. Her face was level with his shoulder. She was smiling at him as she had been for several minutes, her head tilted back a little. He found her wrist, and held it. She wriggled against him. He sensed that she was defying all the boring people in the nearby room. Her arms, as he felt his way up them, were firm and satin. He managed to be gentle. He found her lips in an experimental kiss. The kiss prolonged itself, deepened. He had forgotten what a young kiss felt like, a kiss which was not quite sure of itself, but which was ardent, almost grateful. When he opened his eyes, it seemed a long time later, she was bent among the oleanders against him. For a second she clung to him. "I've no more breath," she laughed. "You're a bear."

She looked buoyant and her eyes clear, perfectly controlled. He stared at her in a faint confusion, still holding her arms.

The next moment Oldenburg had come out on to the terrace. She stepped back and straightened her dress. Her father looked exasperated, and finished his whisky in a heavy gulp before he noticed them. Then he said, "There you are!" and stumped up to Caroline. "Do go and talk to the archimandrite. He's standing alone again. He won't get settled." Caroline followed him indoors but turned back to Julian before she vanished, and shrugged her soft shoulders, smiling regret.

He watched her go. For a moment she had made him feel adolescent. Kissing in the bushes again! He looked over the balcony. Down the valleyside the miners' houses were starting to show lights, solitary points in the thickening dusk, and car headlights were shifting through the main town. On a house roof below, oblivious of the world, sat a white cat licking its belly with thrusts of its head. Behind it the sun had set in a solemn glow, and the sea and sky were folding together.

Across the verandah Caroline's mother walked over to him, and the delicate Armenian assistant followed her, but remained a pace behind. Alastos felt sorry for Claudia Oldenburg: the party was so flagrantly a business tactic, and he did not imagine this would appeal to a sensitive woman. So he found himself telling her how successful the occasion was and what a beautiful evening she had for it—forgetting that the summers were always fine here—and remarked on her attractive daughter. He added with such friendly matter-of-factness "I see now—she looks like you," that she smiled at him without embarrassment and opened her blue eyes a fraction wider. Her features, Alastos could see, had lent themselves to Caroline. But they were more remarkable. They turned her face into a delicately-boned landscape, very pale. He thought she must be at least ten years younger than Oldenburg. Her stilted way of speech made it difficult to know what she was thinking; but she appeared to be interested in how he had met Caroline and in his job with the Company. Yet the mines too she neutralized by her formal tone.

All the time they spoke, the Armenian watched them, caressing a champagne glass in his long, graceful hands. After she had left, he nervously introduced himself—"Jon Adourian"—and Alastos tried to put him at his ease by asking him about those guests who were visible through the doorway. Who was the dark, coarse-haired girl in the yellow dress? Oh, she. She was the archimandrite's niece.

And the long-haired young man flirting with her? That was Oldenburg's son Howard. He had just finished college in the States. Nobody knew what he was going to do for a job. Adourian went on: "The thick-set man talking to the Mayor is the Mine Superintendent Muller. And the man next door is Lerides, the Company Secretary."

"Yes, I've met him."

"And the woman with her back turned is Ekaterina Lerides."

The words struck Alastos most oddly. The presence of that unfamiliar surname—a Cypriot name—was a reminder that Ekaterina herself was no longer known to him. Beyond the Mayor and the Mine Superintendent, the shining fall of dark hair was perfectly familiar. He felt a coldness, a lightness fanning up inside him; it surprised him; it was like fear. He turned his back on the party, as if this would render him invisible, and stared over the verandah balustrade. The Armenian also turned. "You don't like Lerides?" he murmured.

"No," Alastos answered. It was true, he did not care for what he knew of Lerides.

"I think he's all right," Adourian answered—his voice sounded adolescent, uncertain. "But at parties he's not at his best. You see, he drinks. There's nothing else wrong with him. He has an excellent brain."

"Nobody just drinks," Alastos said roughly. "You drink for a reason." Then he thought he had hurt the Armenian, who was silent, and added: "At least that's what I feel. It's usually an evasion." I ought to know, he thought. He had drunk himself sick in Utah for a while. Half the miners did. You drank out of boredom or unhappiness. If your boss was putting the screws on you, you drank. If your girl was cooling off, you drank. If you wanted somebody else's, you drank. But it was surprising how little a man needed it when his life was happy. Then, he remembered, after work you took the path which skirted the cinema and the bar—it led through a cathedral of beech trees, you made no sound —and caught the bus into the main town, feeling that the day had only started. Or in winter the Company's Land Rover collected the miners at the gates in the dark—all so heavily clothed, the men looked twice the size they were—and back in your cabin you drank no more than a pint of beer, waiting for your feet to thaw.

"Evasion? I suppose so, yes," the Armenian said hesitantly. "Drinking, one way or another ... it's a terrible thing."

"Yes," said Alastos.

"Now the Oldenburgs don't drink at all, barely at all. I think that's very good." Adourian appeared to want to defend his employers. "You would think that for such a hard-working man ... but no. And Howard too, I've never seen him even happy from drinking. He is very nice, Howard, very intellectual. I think you would like him."

Alastos turned to face the door—Ekaterina was gone. "I dare say," he said vaguely, but he did not like the word "intellectual"; it implied an absence. Oldenburg's son and the archimandrite's niece, he thought, made an incongruous couple. Howard was explaining something to her. His earnest expression and keen, small eyes were bent on impressing. The sentences left his mouth in chunks of argument and vanished without trace against the supine head of the girl. She was out of her depth. She merely stared at him with a look of bovine admiration. The archimandrite was standing near them. Some jelly from the *zalatina* was mixed into his beard. He looked as if he wanted to leave.

"Claudia Oldenburg is a handsome woman," Alastos said.

Adourian visibly jumped. His fingers massaged the stem of his glass. "Yes. Very." His voice was almost a whisper. "She's beautiful."

Alastos stared at him, then looked away. He did not want to

intrude on anybody's feelings. He tried to think of something to give the man his balance, and said in his too forceful voice: "But we were talking about drinking. Now a good bout, sometimes, never hurts. This is what I think: only drink when you're happy. Once you start using it as therapy—that's the end of you! What do you say?" He placed his burly hand on the Armenian's shoulder, but before the other man could answer he went on: "We can't drink away our feelings, can we? Feelings are responsibilities. We owe them to ourselves. They express us. Don't they? Don't they?"

"Yes ... yes," said Adourian.

Alastos vigorously nodded approval, as if this had been the Armenian's idea. "Of course they do! Everything's a balance. Remember that old platitude 'you can't love without suffering'?"

"Yes," agreed Adourian.

"Yes." Alastos grasped the balustrade behind him. "Every time we escape a feeling, we reduce ourselves."

The Armenian's face had grown crestfallen. He looked like a devotional painting, a saint, without any real qualities at all. "But what happens," he asked plaintively, "if the suffering just goes on and on?"

Alastos was feeling a bit ashamed of himself. He had talked too much, and had blundered on the man's susceptibilities. He said more quietly: "You just have to go on facing it, I suppose. On and on." He explored the bottom of the champagne glass with his finger.

The Armenian looked utterly depressed. His face had gone paler. "But doesn't suffering sometimes ... sometimes...?"

"Yes," said Alastos quickly. This was like talking to a woman. "It grinds you down. In a way it's a myth that it strengthens." Now he was contradicting himself. He shrugged his shoulders, and scratched his neck. "But it helps you understand. Is that a kind of strength? Not really. That's another myth. Nothing but myths!" He tried to encourage Adourian and said good-humouredly: "We'll believe anything, won't we—human beings! Did anyone tell you that moles were blind? Well, it's not true; they have perfectly good eyes, set rather deep, but perfectly good for their purpose—which is, admittedly, to see hardly at all." He reminded himself not to accept any more champagne. Was the young man cheering up? "And did you know that bulls were colour-blind? All that about seeing red—nonsense! A recent American study on the retina of a grown bull ..."

He was not himself conscious any more of what he was saying. His voice tailed away. He was watching Ekaterina's face, which had appeared beyond the doorway, talking to Sofroniou. At first he thought that she had changed a great deal. Then he realized that his imagination had changed her. As he looked at her, he remembered. Her face showed clearly over the old man's shoulder. It was lit up by a pair of beautiful grey-green eyes, which tilted backwards in her head, as if she might see sideways like a bird.

The Armenian had left him, and he stood heavy and isolated in the verandah doorway. The champagne, he suspected, had drained the colour out of his face. His mind did not feel agile. The party was splitting up. The archimandrite and the Mayor had left. Lerides was still drinking and looked, it was true, rather flushed and dishevelled. Caroline had been trapped in a corner by two young civil servants who were making her laugh.

Ekaterina had noticed him and was talking to Sofroniou in a more abstracted manner. In the end she asked to be excused and came over to him. It seemed absurd to shake hands and neither of them made any move to kiss. So they stood in front of one another, she apparently composed, he holding the sides of his trousers and wavering a smile. For a second they stared at each other. She looked, as he had thought she would, more mature and poised. You would not call her a girl now, not at all. Some adolescent fullness was gone. But the change rather suited her. Her face was not so much altered as emphasized. Beside her he felt almost threateningly uncouth. He wondered what she was seeing through those vivid eyes. That he was a man and not a youth, certainly. But a man who had discarded such youthful charm as he had possessed. It was humiliating to stand there and to imagine her thinking "How could I ever have. . . ?" But he could not actually tell what she was thinking. His arms and hands had never seemed so superfluous. They hung at his sides like sledgehammers.

"Julian," she said—when he grew used to her voice, he thought, he would realize it was unaltered—"I'm sorry you've come home for such a sad reason." She touched his hand in sympathy. He looked older, she thought, stronger. Yet he did not look happy. Her gaze travelled back and forth over his face. She wanted some sign of recognition from him; she would have liked him to joke or banter as he used, or simply to smile at her. She felt vaguely upset. She wanted his unhappy look to go; but it was a little like wanting the happiness of a total stranger.

She said: "I've been seeing your father from time to time. In some ways he's been contented."

Julian warmed to her. He remembered she was always sincere. He said: "I heard you'd seen him. Your husband told me you'd become a nurse." He squeezed his hands into his pockets. He had forgotten how Greek she looked, despite her mixed parentage. The contrast between her black hair and that almost translucent skin was most striking. She was certainly a handsome woman. "I forget how far your training had gone when we ... when ... I quite forget."

"I'd finished my first year."

Yes, that must be right. He used to wait for her at the outpatients door of Kalepia hospital. Once he had slipped inside the ward and surprised her looking starched and formal, pushing a trolley of medicines down the corridor between beds. She had been angry with him, and he had not done that again. He remembered too that the conditions in the hospital had been criminal. They probably still were. Several of the patients were lying on mattresses over the floor, and apparently there was not a capable surgeon in the building.

Ekaterina was wondering what he was thinking. She wanted to recall him properly. "Michael tells me you've joined the Company," she said.

"Michael" sounded odd to Alastos. So that was Lerides' Christian name. He did not feel he could absorb all these new things at once. She was Mrs Michael Lerides. He put his champagne glass on a table. He thought that she was staring at him in a puzzled way. Was he slightly drunk? The idea made him place one arm against the wall. He leaned on it, to reduce his stature.

"Yes, I'm working the open-cast mine," he said. "I'm a foreman." He did not see why he should be ashamed. But he heard himself adding: "It's as much a foothold as an employment. If we open up the St Vichinos Mountain, I hope to get another post."

Ekaterina was looking at him with a quiet inquisitiveness. The bracelet she was wearing was one which he had given her: a thin, gold circlet which had cost him more than he could afford. Now it slid a little up and down her arm. Because she still wore it, it seemed to indicate "Forgiven". "The new mine ..." she was saying, "there's a delegation coming to see Oldenburg tomorrow, isn't there?"

"Delegation?" he said. "What sort of delegation?" He was looking at her eyebrows: two light wings.

"Mostly from the port, and the small tradesmen. They've heard rumours about the sale; they want reassurance."

"Reassurance?" repeated Alastos in surprise. "What have they to lose? If the mines flourish, the small tradesmen flourish."

He thought he noticed a faint disappointment in her face. And he was right. It was not like him to look at things so materially, Ekaterina thought. It did not suit him. "The townsmen are nervous of change," she said, "and I imagine they're concerned about their saint." This new mine alarmed her. It seemed to leave nobody untouched; it antagonized some, brutalized others. She wished it had never been planned. And she felt a sadness that Julian, who ten years ago would have hated such a project, was now a part of its machinery.

The look of disappointment remained on her face. Alastos pouted and made an expression of doubt. "Nobody seems worried about the delegation here."

"No," she flashed out. "The people here have their own saint. They worship efficiency."

Alastos recognized the anger glinting through her poise. This was the woman who had once spat in his face then burst into tears and covered it in kisses. He did not answer. He did not want to grow sentimental about her. He found himself looking over her shoulder. The room had almost emptied. Caroline was still hemmed in her corner, and Lerides was talking truculently—he had lost his suavity—to a submissive-looking post office official against the buffet table. It was growing late and Alastos had to be home. It was at this time that the cycle of his father's fever reached its danger-point. Two nights before, the old man's temperature had risen to a hundred and four, and although he looked as if no drop of fat or moisture could survive in his skin, he had sweated hard.

"Is that normal," he asked Ekaterina, "in this kind of tuberculosis?"

"Yes. His temperature may go up to a hundred and five." She spoke as if unsure how much truth he could bear.

Alastos felt this harsh depression returning, or rather was reminded of its perpetual presence. "I think I'll leave," he said.

She saw the strain in his face. "If you'd like me to come back with you, I will."

It seemed unfair of him to accept. But he said: "I'd like that. Yes.

I would." He dreaded these bouts of sweating when his father, a man of iron restraint, croaked and whined like a baby.

He went over to Caroline to say good-bye. He wished he could have stayed with her. He knew now why people could call death a release, even for those left behind. Already he longed to end this grief which refused to fall in a blow but harrowed on and on and was carried about week after week as an ache in his own body. Yet he dreaded the end.

Caroline grasped his hand. "Do you have to go?"

Yes, he said, he must. He longed to sit with her, just to sit in her radiance, her life.

She exclaimed: "What about tomorrow? You heard about this delegation? I think it would be fascinating to know what they say, don't you? Daddy wants me to come and take it down in shorthand for him. I asked him if you could be there, and he said yes."

Alastos frowned. He did not like taking advantage of her to secure privileges. She squeezed his hand still harder. "Please come. Don't scowl like that."

He kissed her. She made him feel he was too complicated. "Of course I'll come."

He joined Ekaterina outside—she looked self-contained and quiet—and they took the road over the stream and up through the suburbs. The street lamps strung out white orbs all the way. They even made the trees look sordid. He did not know what to say to her. He watched his surroundings instead. The houses in this part of the town were supposed to be rich, but most of them looked ordinary. Their pink roof tiles were all dishevelled, and the shrubs in their compounds had been planted in rusted tins so that they could be moved between garden and verandah. The prowling dogs were a yellow mongrel breed, like stunted wolves, which flinched and growled from habitual maltreatment. And the radios were another blight; from almost every house sounded the synthetic songs which had grown so popular in the Republic. They were a way of filling out silence. They set up a curtain of noise half the day and all the evening. The enemy was always silence, thought, self.

Ekaterina walked briskly, hugging her arms although it was warm. Still neither of them knew what to talk about. It was like preparing to write a letter after a gap of many years. What was important enough to say? From the surrounding gardens the cats were howling like lost babies. Ekaterina began to walk faster.

To Alastos their past happiness had for years seemed like a vivid dream. In him the only real residue of their love seemed to be a sense of failure, of self-disgust, the knowledge that a total passion was not in his nature. He had even grown to despise that part of him which wished for such a passion: that futile longing in a man to transcend his own nature.

The change in Ekaterina made this compromise easier, because her maturity cut off the past from the present. She was a woman. He had known a girl. Yet as he looked at her, he was not sure whether she had really changed so much, or whether over the past years he had distorted her. In either case, it did not matter. He had never regretted the summer they had devoted to one another. But he was glad that such a time could never come again. That intensity, that single string plucked in the heart's darkness, was not to be relied upon. It was without sense, without proportion, deeply sexual. It was struck, and all your faculties worshipped it. Balance, intelligence—these could only be heard when its resonance had faded. Yet it was in these clearer sounds of reason that life had to continue. Find a good character, a pleasing body, a responsive mind, he thought, and marry that. Ignore the other. Block the ears. Forget. Maturity should compromise.

Ekaterina, certainly, had matured. A woman, he thought, grew up more quickly and totally than a man. He supposed that nursing must have made a difference too: this endless witnessing of pain, of humiliation. Disease was usually degrading. It could turn even his father into a puling infant — a thimbleful of grey tubercles destroying the courage of a lifetime.

He looked at Ekaterina. He thought they had been silent too long. "I don't understand," he said morosely. "These tubercles, or whatever they are ... they form ... where? What are they?"

"They're a kind of cell," she said, "a mass of round cells." She tried to speak with professional detachment, but her voice was sad. "I wish I knew more about it. It needs a skilled diagnosis. But you don't often get cases in a dry climate."

"These cells, then, don't they ever disperse of their own accord?"

"Not often, not at his age. They consolidate." She longed for him to talk of something else. She was remembering how much in him could be hurt by any kind of loss. "Healthy lungs keep a spongy texture. But these cells irritate and produce inflammation. That's how the lung grows hard."

"But if it had been treated earlier ..."

"They did all they could. He was even given streptomycin."

Alastos was walking so fast in his graceless lope that she was finding it hard to keep up with him. They passed the municipal gardens and the length of a dead-looking road where a cat wrangled at a sheep's rib. The street lamps whited out the stars. "This hardness of the lung, then," he said suddenly, "once that has happened, there's no way to reverse the process?"

She longed to tell him a lie. But she said: "The process reverses itself. The tubercles soften of their own accord. They break down. But by then they have impregnated the lung and so they start to take its tissue with them."

"You mean ... you mean he's virtually sicking up lung tissue?"

"Partly, yes."

He scrutinized her face, then tensed his hands in a characteristic gesture, as if he could restore that pitted lung by the force of his will or of his arms. They had reached the street which led to his house. "I'm glad you told me honestly." He realized that he could have done nothing but depress her for the length of their walk. "You haven't drowned me with clichés. What is it the mountain people say—'a hard-fought death is a privilege'? God save us from that! Anyway," he teased her (could he still tease her? He'd try.) "Perhaps the medical profession has renounced cliché as unscientific."

Her turned-up mouth completed its smile. "Yes, they disperse it at a yearly conference," she said. They smiled at one another, the sort of smile which says "That's broken the ice." He felt he was close to friendship with her. It would be fine, he thought, if they could manage that. And why not? Of all the bitterness in their parting ten years ago, nothing of what they had said or felt was relevant any more. Looking at her now, he was reminded of her intelligence and emotional fullness. Those, as far as he could tell, had not altered. Now that they must both be able to look back self-critically, they could understand, and—if there was anything left to be forgiven—forgive. Yes, they could even laugh a little and make confession! They could be frank with one another; they would discover that friendship was more solid than love. How good to pick out what was genuine from this timeworn mess!

Ekaterina was still walking fast to keep up with him. He noticed this, and shortened his pace, feeling weary with himself. But they were approaching the house, and by the time they saw the light in the bedroom window, he had forgotten his desire for friendship. He was drained of everything but the consciousness of his father's irreversible decay: this pointless but somehow necessary struggle.

His walk grew slower. He kept throwing back his shoulders as if to rid himself of a physical weight. Then he said: "This lung tissue, how far has it deteriorated?"

Ekaterina thought she could not bear this much longer. Already she was feeling like his executioner. She said: "I'm sorry. I don't know. I haven't enough experience."

"But it will just go on and on until . . . ?"

"Eventually it will leave cavities in the lung. They generally appear in the upper parts of the left lung. A patient can't survive that."

He hung his head and breathed: "You'd think by now they might have discovered something. . . ." But who "they" were he had no idea. He envisaged only some sterilized labyrinth in Sweden or Switzerland, where high-domed men watched through microscopes the flux of cells which could restore or condemn a man. And he imagined the grey tubercular nodule, the flesh-eater, resting invulnerable among microbes and anti-bodies. How many years before anybody found its conqueror? The domed men could not answer. In a sense they might not care. They did not know his father. Scientists, they were devoted only to the parasite and the anti-body. The parasite and the anti-body were natural law. Everywhere, in every drop of liquid or gleam of matter, this soundless warfare was going on. Something attacked. Something repelled. Something died.

Chapter Nine

The prospect of the delegation thoroughly displeased Oldenburg. Kalepia, as far as he was concerned, was represented by its municipality, whose mayor was democratically elected. These so-called delegates presumably only wanted to attract attention to themselves. It was a waste of time; and an awkward precedent would be created if the Company were to entertain any stray gang of townsmen or dockers. Lerides, on the other hand, had been in favour of receiving them, and Oldenburg respected his judgment when dealing with his countrymen. Lerides had said that they must be made to feel important, while at the same time giving them no loophole for agitation. To reject them would be to heighten bitterness; to humour them would help diffuse ill-feeling.

All the same, the idea irritated Oldenburg, who had kept the petition on his desk for the past week and now picked it up and scrutinized the signatures of these nonentities, several of whom were not even known to Lerides. In this country it seemed impossible to negotiate anything simply. The most straightforward business deal grew as complex as a wrangle in a bazaar. Everybody wanted to partake of the excitement, to inflate his dignity, fan his views or elicit a bribe. The archimandrite had to refer to the metropolitan, who would doubtless have held a six-month confabulation with the Patriarch, if he had not been senile. And probably the archimandrite himself would have fobbed off the Company with tales of monthly convocations if Lerides had not intimated a gift.

Now it was the tradesmen and the port making trouble. No doubt they would all want absurd guarantees. And next week some goatherd would discover that he had enjoyed grazing rights on the Mountain since the reign of the Emperor Comnenus, or a nosey judiciary would resurrect a forgotten law of the Ottoman *mutesefariyet.* It would then only remain for the Church to realize that it owned the Mountain but not the copper in it—that sort of thing, said Lerides, was customary—for the Company to withdraw in despair.

It was this feeling that the delegation might only represent a beginning, which had stung Oldenburg all week with the urge to reject it. Yet here he was, half an hour before its arrival, calculating how much time it would waste. He felt as if a blanket of dust had descended on him, his energies cloyed. "Who's this Marangos?" he demanded again. "The man can hardly write his name."

"He's the head docker," said Lerides. "An old hand—spent a month in prison a few years ago for roughing up one of the other men. Woman trouble."

"And Matheopoulos?"

"He owns the flour mill."

Oldenburg grunted. "Why the hell's he worrying? Miners eat bread, don't they? What's wrong with these people?"

"He's religious," said Lerides.

Oldenburg scribbled something against the name. "And Kallis? Who's Kallis?"

Lerides stared at the ceiling through narrowed eyes. "Kallis ... Kallis. I'm not sure. I think he's one of the dockers ... a small man, articulate. I think so."

Oldenburg had almost crumpled the petition in his fingers. The offices did not even contain a room large enough to properly accommodate this meeting. It would have to be held in the Chief Engineer's department. He was half in mind to cancel the whole affair. But it was too late for that.

After a few minutes Alastos arrived to sit in on the meeting, his overalls covered in stone dust. While the cables of his power excavator were being refitted, he had taken advantage of a three-hour break to look at the underground mine. The experience had sobered him. He had spent all his working life on open-cast workings, and until now the only underground mines which he had seen were in America, mines where the cage glided down as smoothly as a hotel elevator, and the concrete-lined galleries were cleaner than drawing-rooms. But this Lythrangomi mine was different. For half an hour he had marched through tunnels without light, while the air grew thin and stale. All around him had loomed empty caves which had been mined thirty, forty years before. The steps between gallery levels were sunk under oozing clay and over the years had been pushed against the skip-rails where the timbers bent inward from the weight of the mountain. He realized now how miners could become obsessed by these long-dead galleries behind and above them, their adits sealed up, their shafts shut off. For the men worked only on the rim of a labyrinth. It was these spaces in between, and the solid mountain—the black, threatening mass itself—which were the heart of the place. He imagined his father, and a whole generation, sucked into the maw of this leviathan, creeping along its arteries with their drills and lamps, tapping within at its sinews, growing weaker, suffocated, pulled up broken and old. He had never truly envisaged where those men went, who descended joking into the earth and emerged eight hours later like toilworn livestock.

After an hour he had found himself deep in the warm stomach of the creature. For a while the only sound was the noise of compressed air leaking from its pipe-joints. Under his feet a thick fur of silicate crystals lisped and glinted. Then something growled in the mountain, and was joined by other sounds, muffled roarings and hums, and he entered a maze of workings. Suddenly the mountain had turned into a fantasy of hell, where the naked arms and trunks of the damned were lit up in gleams of dissociated light. The men seemed to creep about directionless, muted by the mass which imprisoned them. The air shook with the roar and clash of the drills.

These men, he noticed, had not gained muscle like Northern miners, but were loose-limbed and sallow. The bones pressed under their skin. He passed a tiny, grizzled mucker striking sparks from a rock with a pick. Farther on, to his astonishment, a teenage youth stood up in front of him and complained of lack of air. His slack shoulders and defensive eyes expected nothing, but he said: "There's not enough air. I can't breathe."

This kind of work, Alastos thought, had no more relation to open-cast mining than a prison had to the open air. Then he had flickered his lamp over the walls. That also was something he had never seen before. The whole surface shimmered with a haze of sparks. They arched in a bowl of light above him—silver and russet constellations woken in their millions, like an astronomer's dream of the firmament. But the copper itself, he knew, was a dull grey-green colour, the greener the purer. These were only crystals, next to worthless, glistening in substitute for a real sky.

He was rude enough now, standing in the mining engineer's office, to ask Oldenburg if he was not worried about the men's health. The General Manager did not even notice his offensive tone, but answered bluntly: "Most of these people are unhealthy. When you see them dirty and half-naked like that, you notice. But put a mob of shopkeepers and restaurateurs down there, and they'll look the same, only flabby. However well they're paid, you can't make up for their having been undernourished as children. No underground mine is a healthy business. Not even the best of them. The ventilation plant's new here—we can't do more at present."

"You get much silicosis?"

"Some. But you can't help that. And we're not going to throw good money after bad. The capital expenditure on the Vichinos mine will prohibit modernizing this one. In five years it'll be exhausted anyway. So we'd best let it die."

Yes, Alastos thought, let it die. Soon all this generation of miners would die. Alastos respected Oldenburg. The General Manager seemed not so much callous as stoical: and he did what he could within the limits of his common sense. He was probably right about the miners' health too. They had no stamina; they cracked under the least strain. It was the business of their children, he thought, to make something of the sacrifice. And the reasonable upshot would be another kind of mine, not a dungeon for dwarfs but something like a theatre on a mountain, a thousand times more healthy and efficient.

By now the delegation had passed the compound gates and was walking up the slope in single file, looking disconsolate and slightly ridiculous in best suits. The trestle table in the Chief Engineer's department had been cleared of its drawings. Oldenburg and Alastos found the German superintendent Muller there, talking to the Chief Engineer and the Mine Geologist. Oldenburg waved them away. "This delegation isn't going to waste the time of the whole Company." He nodded at Caroline, as if she were any other secretary; she was perched in a corner with a note-pad. Then he sat down at the head of the table and waited, his overall sleeves pulled up above the elbow and the crumpled petition fidgeting in his hands.

Alastos seized the opportunity of sitting by Caroline. She looked him up and down and started to laugh. "You look like a black bear. Where have you been?"

"Underground. Have you ever been down?"

She wrinkled her nose. "Yes. Daddy took me."

Alastos could never associate Oldenburg with "Daddy". Whenever she used this name he found he was thinking of somebody else, whom he had invented to take Oldenburg's place. "I thought the men's health depressing." He crossed his legs, his boots thick with clay. "In the States the mines give a feeling of being properly air-conditioned. There's a running current all the time. You can sense it. But down in that place it drags on your lungs, makes you want to vomit."

"They must get used to it," Caroline said.

He sensed an offended family pride. He stared at the floor, rubbing the back of his neck. He had hoped that she, who cared about people's condition, would have agreed with him. He did not like "They must get used to it." That was what people said when they were walking round zoos.

"It's no excuse for not improving conditions," he said, but realized how boorish he sounded and added immediately: "Trouble is, the mine's been worked so long that it's uneconomic to do anything about it."

By now the delegates had reached the door and Alastos could hear them muttering and shuffling outside. Then a face peered round. Later he was to think of this moment as a turning-point in his idea of Kalepia—but that was far in the future. For the moment he simply saw the face, the face of a fisherman which resembled that of no townsman. Lean, uncomplicated, the wind had hewn it in furrows, and as if it had been forced to outstare this wind, and the sun too, the eyes were wide open and direct, and the chin lifted high on the neck. In a moment it vanished, and was replaced by the head of the chief docker, grizzled, cruel and running to fat. Then the men began to dribble into the room.

"Come in, sit down," Oldenburg said impatiently.

Lerides stood up. "Please take a seat, gentlemen ... Mr Marangos, isn't it? ... Mr Matheopoulos...."

The eight men grouped themselves round the table, scraping their chairs and coughing. Their suits looked newly pressed and their shoes showed a deep black polish above the Company's mud. Yet they managed to appear drab. Most of them leaned towards Oldenburg in expectation, but one or two looked at a slight, sallow man as if he was their spokesman. They had barely sat down before

Oldenburg planted his elbows on the table. Glancing at the petition which lay between them, he said: "Well, you express concern over the recent rumour about the sale, etcetera etcetera ..." then his voice hardened, "and you ask for certain *indications* as to the Company's plans." His head jerked up. "What indications had you in mind?"

The delegates hesitated. Most of them looked overawed. Their hands played in their laps or on the table. Then one of the younger men answered: "We'd like to know about employment, Mr Oldenburg—whether you'll offer jobs to people here or whether you'll call in workers from outside."

"If experienced workers for skilled jobs could only be found outside," said Oldenburg firmly, "we would employ them. We're a limited company. It's our business to run as efficiently as we can in the interests of our shareholders. However, for most of the jobs we'd be prepared to offer a short, intensive training, and the town would be the obvious place to recruit."

The sallow man had listened to this with his lips sharply compressed. He said in a quiet voice: "Is it true, Mr Oldenburg, that open-cast mines employ fewer men than underground ones—that instead, say, of a hundred underground miners you would need only ten pit workers?"

"Yes, that is true."

He went on: "Would you say then that there would be many jobs for the people here at all?"

"I've already said so. The mine itself isn't the only factor. We'd need maintenance personnel—ordinary mechanics; we'd need men to operate the new crusher plant, more caretakers, office workers, truck-drivers. And we'd need workers on a conveyor-belt loading installation at the port."

"Ah," the sallow man began, "now the port ..."

But Lerides interrupted him, opening the palms of his hands in a quieting gesture, smoothing back his cuffs. "Now Mr Kallis—it is Mr Kallis, isn't it?—I think we ought to make one thing perfectly clear before we go any further." He looked round at the others, smiling. "You are asking to know the plans of a company before any negotiations have been finalized. This is entirely unusual. We do not ourselves know how our offer is being treated, and our plans are still in the most preliminary phase. Nothing we say to you at this moment can be taken as definite. Of course we feel that your anxiety is natural, although I think you will come to see it as unfounded; but we ask that you honour the confidence placed in you today, and that you will regard what we say not only as tentative," he smiled around him—"but as entirely confidential."

The delegates, whose faces had grown increasingly serious and responsible while he spoke, nodded, sitting up in their chairs and straightening their ties and jackets. Only Kallis appeared to stare out the speech as if he was not hearing it; and Marangos remained sprawled at the far end of the table picking his teeth with his nails.

No sooner had Lerides finished, than Kallis said: "We are concerned about sea-pollution. One of the best fishing areas is where the Mountain of St Vichinos adjoins the sea. We'd like guarantees that this area won't be poisoned by waste."

An apparent look of regret arrived on Lerides' face. His slight moustache curled in another smile. "I'm sorry, Mr Kallis. Your petition asked for indications, not for guarantees. It's too early for us to give guarantees. When we do so, we wish to be entirely sure of our means of honouring them. Until then we must wait."

Another delegate, the old fisherman in a patched brown suit, seemed not to have heard, and wheezed: "Yes, that's right—the best fishing. If you pour waste in there, sir, that's the end of it."

Oldenburg broke in tersely. "The mine can be engineered ten different ways. We have only provisional diagrams. We await a Chief Engineer's report, and that can't be given until the sale is effected."

Kallis drew his hands to his mouth as if he were praying. His fingers were thin, like pencils. He said in his civil tone, which yet meant nothing: "The Company would naturally give compensation. Drainage of chemicals into the sea could be computed."

"I'm afraid I can't help you on such a thing," said Lerides, adding elaborately, "but we have an open-cast engineer sitting behind us. Mr Alastos, what would you say?"

Alastos, who did not like the look of Kallis, addressed his answer to the old fisherman. "I don't know about waste, but we'll keep chemicals out of the sea, I can promise you. The danger would be from water impregnated with copper sulphate, and no company wastes copper sulphates. I assure you that any well-engineered mine is constructed to channel this water where it can be collected."

The fisherman, who had turned with his hands on the back of the chair, said, "Thank you—yes ... thank you."

Alastos could see the game which Kallis and Lerides were

playing between them. They instinctively knew one another's minds. Whenever Lerides answered Kallis, his words were not really for him at all. Kallis, he knew, had gauged him. His answers were intended for the others, who were the marionettes in the show, and the day would be won by whoever could set them dancing. Lerides spoke a little confidentially. Only his smooth smile, with its echo of moustache, gave definition to his face. Alastos tried to discover in him what Ekaterina loved. The man's good looks were a little fleshy now and his blandness did not enhance them. But his expression in repose betrayed something which Alastos thought he understood: a residual softness, mainly about the mouth, a sag of disappointment which in this man would count as a likeable quality.

Kallis was delicate and sharp. While Lerides sent up a cloud of assurance and goodwill, Kallis pierced it. That was the game. Under his velvet manner, this small man was finely-strung. He looked as though he fed on nothing but thoughts.

But Matheopoulos was speaking now. He was a portly old man with glasses and a silver watch-chain linked across his waistcoat, which he wore even in summer. Every week, after inspecting the production at his mill, he gave out small bags of flour to the poorer families round the harbour.

"It's the question of the olive trees," he said, as if everybody must know what he meant.

Oldenburg looked at Lerides and muttered: "Olive trees . . . ?"

Lerides momentarily frowned, then turned to Matheopoulos. "I'm sorry," he said. "Yes. The olive trees. Please go on."

"It would be a matter of restitution, I imagine," the old man said, in a thin, rather mellow voice, "unless they can be saved. The tradition has always been that the poor people harvest them in September, although personally I think that is too early. But still, if it is left until later they get pilfered and . . ."

Oldenburg cut him short. "I'm sorry, Mr Marangos, I don't . . ."

"Matheopoulos," murmured Lerides.

"I'm sorry, Mr Matheopoulos, but could you explain the position? We're not clear about it." Oldenburg was tapping his pen against the table-top with a dry irritation.

"The position?" The old man lifted himself upright in the chair. His voice was courteous but held a faint edge of severity; it was used to people attending to it. "The position is simply that it is usual for the olives on the Mountain to be gathered by certain of the less wealthy families. It is a custom here."

Oldenburg's pen stopped tapping. "I gather that this is not a matter of law, then, only of charity."

Lerides said rather quickly: "I think restitution will be up to the Church, Mr Matheopoulos. I'm sure the archimandrite is aware of the problem. But in case he is not, I shall personally mention to him that the Company's offer was made in the hope that the See would indemnify."

Matheopoulos frowned slightly; but he went on: "The more important question still remains. Mr Oldenburg, Mr Lerides ..." He took off his glasses and wiped them methodically on his handkerchief; he even polished the rims a little. Then he replaced them very slowly on his head, bending their gold hooks behind his ears. "This is of course the question of the saint's shrine. I wish, we all wish, to know what measures would be taken to safeguard it."

There was a silence, punctuated by the renewed tap of Oldenburg's pencil. The gaze of all the delegates moved between him and Lerides. "It will be up to the Church," said Oldenburg, "if it wishes to rededicate the shrine elsewhere."

The old man appeared not to understand. "But can there be any problem about maintaining access to the shrine? Surely from some point or other ..."

"Mr Matheopoulos." Lerides' smile was one of sympathetic regret. It was becoming worn. "You must understand that an open-cast operation is something massive. Millions of tons of earth have to be moved. We have to lay the whole mountain-top bare. Under such circumstances the shrine would be irreparably damaged. To be frank, it would be swept away."

Matheopoulos stared at him with lowered head. "Oh no, Mr Lerides. I am not hearing you rightly." He looked like a bull which is too old to charge, but which nevertheless stoops its horns in token of its feelings. "You're treading on holy ground."

"The See is aware of the problem," Lerides said, "and would make efforts either to reconstitute the shrine or, more probably, to dedicate a new one."

"But such a place," answered Matheopoulos darkly, "is *theobadiston*, it is trodden by God."

"Precisely." Kallis pointed his forefinger at Lerides. "If you build a new shrine, does that deconsecrate the old? No, it doesn't."

"I'm not familiar with ecclesiastical law," Lerides said.

"But Mr Matheopoulos is right." The old fisherman half stood up, not in anger but in reverence. "Holy ground is holy ground."

"These matters aren't our province," Lerides went on. "The archimandrite ..."

"If Christ did not permit money-changers in the Temple of the Lord," said Matheopoulos, his voice bitterly severe, "would he then allow a copper mine to oust the sanctuary of his saint? No, no, no. I'm sorry Mr Lerides, Mr Oldenburg, but I ... really ..." He wagged his finger at them as if he was reproving a baby. "No, no, no!"

Caroline, who had been scribbling feverishly beside Alastos, started to giggle.

Three of the other delegates began talking at once in support of Matheopoulos. The gabble suddenly stopped, and one of them found himself speaking alone and went on nervously to ask if the Company could not make an underground mine and leave the sanctuary untouched. Oldenburg glanced at Lerides with pursed lips, as if to say "I told you this would be a waste of time," and answered intolerantly: "Quite impractical!"

There was silence again, a long silence in which the Company's siren puled and faded in requiem. Marangos was sprawled still further back in his chair, and seemed to be sneering at all of them. Then someone asked: "But what about the relics?"

Oldenburg gave an exasperated sigh, clasped his forehead, then visibly controlled himself and turned with a neutral expression to Lerides. "What about the relics?"

Caroline crammed her hands over her mouth. Lerides answered that the relics would be the affair of the Church. The Company had no right to interfere in matters of such importance.

"You understand," said Matheopoulos magisterially—but he, like Marangos, was sinking lower in his chair—"that you are planning to destroy not just a building, sirs, but a site consecrated to a cherished intercessor. A site cannot be transplanted. No. No. You can't deflect pilgrimages as if they were gutters." He looked back and forth between Oldenburg and Lerides, as if seeking for some sign in them. His voice was not only bitter but profoundly disappointed, because these two men had fallen short in his eyes. "Mr Oldenburg, Mr Lerides, it is simply a matter of values. By demolishing this shrine you will say, in effect, that copper must take precedence over devotion, that industry is more important than faith."

Almost everybody in the room looked embarrassed. Most of

them did not peer up from contemplating their hands. Everybody could feel that the old man was deeply wounded, not by abstractions—the Church, the Company—but by the two men facing him, who had failed pitifully as human beings.

Alastos thought Matheopoulos fine. He wanted to call out even now "Well said!" For such a man he could forgive even this tomfoolery about a saint. He felt like shouting "Your ideas may be wrong, but your heart is right! Bravo for your heart!" Yet how painful that this man too was suffocated by dogma! Alastos looked at him miserably. Couldn't he realize that he was withdrawing into mummery?

But the old man seemed to realize nothing of the kind. He remained sitting very still in his chair, and for the rest of the conference he did not speak a word. Alastos badly wanted to cheer him up. But why did these people fight against themselves? Couldn't they see a better future? Wouldn't they ever see? Even the miners knew what fresh air was when it was blown at them. But these eight men, these delegates—no. They did not even pace their cages. That was like an animal which Alastos had seen in the zoo at the Capital: a tiny, exquisite marmoset. "It just stayed there," the keeper had laughed. "I left the cage open by mistake—and it just stayed there." That to Alastos (he was a boy then) was more pathetic than anything he had heard. The animal was not only a prisoner physically, but mentally too.... It did not understand freedom.

The wind was now drained from the sails of the conference, but it continued to talk, becalmed on civility and evasion. It touched on ten or twelve more contingencies, from the siting of a powder magazine to the route of ore-carriers through fishing waters. But almost everyone took the same course unless Oldenburg refused to discuss it, ending with Lerides' suave tones, more thinly-oiled now: "That will be a matter for the See of Nikitari to decide" or "These things will have to be negotiated with the Municipality" or simply, once or twice, "That is a matter for law." Kallis' air of cold politesse had changed to cynicism. He remained as before with his finger caressing his jaw and his mouth as if perpetually sampling something bitter. But his eyes were growing heated.

The one subject which he did not let go was the question of the Company's installations at the port. Where would they be accommodated? There was no room on the wharf, and there was no other suitable site for miles. The mountains sloped straight into the sea.

"Your only solution could be to demolish houses round the quay. Wouldn't that be so?"

"We have not had time to look into that," Lerides said.

Kallis asked: "Well then, Mr Lerides, perhaps you could tell me the average area of a conveyor-belt loading installation?"

Lerides shrugged and smiled as disarmingly as he was still able. "I'm a Company Secretary, Mr Kallis, not an engineer."

Kallis turned to the General Manager. "Mr Oldenburg, then, would you tell me the minimum area of such an installation?"

Oldenburg snapped: "I don't know off-hand. Perhaps five thousand square metres."

"Five thousand," said Kallis almost to himself, dreamily. "So if we take into account the narrow space of the empty quay and the small frontage of dockside shops and houses, I imagine you would have to demolish a minimum of thirty. Would I be right?" Neither of the men answered. Oldenburg wore a look of almost pugnacious boredom. Lerides was steadying his arms over the back of his chair; he flinched. So Kallis went on in the same voice: "Yes, I think so. Now I feel that the people living round the dock would be grateful for due warning. . . ."

There was silence again. Possibly only Lerides knew exactly what he meant. The other delegates had a slackened look. Eventually the old fisherman in the brown suit piped: "But those houses have been occupied by the same families for years, even centuries." His mouth opened like a tiny fissure under a lichen of moustache. He looked isolated and lost. "Now my own house there was built by my grandfather's very hands. Yes, the date is still over the doorway. . . . Two rooms only, but solid as a fort. . . ."

Kallis edged in. "No doubt the Company will talk of rehousing; but how can you rehouse this man?" His tone had lost its cut. He was smiling at the fisherman, a smile which took place in the creases round his eyes. All at once it became apparent that whatever other motives he nurtured, his sympathy for victims was real and warm. He felt a victim himself. The flush had spread to his face. "A house, you see, Mr Lerides, is not the same as a home."

Without stirring his slumped posture, Marangos grated: "Most people want new houses. I can tell you that. Most people 'd be grateful."

Kallis darted at him: "No fisherman can be removed from the sea!"

The fisherman wiped his nose with his hand. "Now I didn't mean to criticize." His brown face held no grudge at all. He was ludicrously vulnerable. "I was only saying my people built the place strong, see, not like houses get built now. Which is no small matter, granted everything. Fishermen are not architects, you know, but all the same, I don't want to appear critical ..."

"Gentlemen," said Lerides briskly. "I'm afraid our time is running out. If you haven't any further questions ..."

Kallis squinted at him half-mockingly, half in anger. He was the first to get to his feet. The rest shuffled and pushed back their chairs, then drifted one by one to the door, where they waited as if something must be left to say. They wore such apathetic faces that they might have been emerging from a coma instead of a conference. In varying degrees they all felt as if they had been fighting a fog. Whenever they hit out, it gently retreated, and when they withdrew it returned gently to its place. They had merely exhausted themselves. Lerides opened the door for them. "Well, gentlemen, it has been a useful talk I think ... good-night, Mr Matheopoulos ... yes, good-night." Outside, the evening sunlight leaked over the slag-hills. The delegates filed out, shielding their eyes. "Good-night, Mr Marangos ... delighted ... yes ... Mr Kallis, good-night...."

They wound down the track to the compound gates. Alastos watched them through the window. As they went, their crumpled look seemed to dissipate. They started to gesticulate forcefully and to fling words backwards and forwards along their column. He saw their shoulders straighten, as if they were beginning to wake and stretch themselves.

Alastos said nothing because Caroline was busy checking and correcting her shorthand notes. The pencil in her fingers went flickering over the pages. She was laughing to herself a little. "Oh God, what a disaster ... that awful Kallis...." He could pick out the separate brown and gold strands in her hair; every one looked different. Oldenburg and Lerides had walked off down the passage, talking. He could hear their footsteps tap on the corridor tiles, then soft again in the General Manager's office. Neither of them sounded pleased. Beyond the window the delegation had passed the compound gates. He watched it crawl away like a disjointed centipede until the hump of the powder magazine obscured it. The light had grown stale.

He found that he was feeling sympathy for them. They had treated the Company as if at any time it might destroy them. No doubt it was mysterious, this great worm gorging and excreting the soil under their valley. But what guarantees could it have given?

"I feel quite exhausted," Caroline said. "How do you spell 'precedence'? '... take precedence over devotion ...'?" Her pencil poised over the note-pad. "That old Matheopoulos ... fancy getting metaphysical with Daddy...." She placed her hand on his arm. "What are you doing staring out of the window?"

He had pressed his forehead against the pane. "I was thinking about the fisherman. But it's no good, is it? It's impossible to move, to do anything, without causing damage somewhere." He was scraping his boots against one another, to remove the clay, but was not thinking about the action. He gazed through the window, noticing nothing. "It's simply a matter of degree, of whether you do more good than hurt." When he turned to her, his face looked red and exasperated. "There's always this feeling, Caroline, that if you stay still you'll do no harm." She looked at him uncertainly; he replaced his forehead against the cool glass. "But it's not true. Because everything is decaying unless we restore it. To stay still is to decay." He closed his eyes. "That's why tomorrow we may have to sacrifice that old man, his house. What happens if we get sentimental about it and say No? Something else is lost—something still unformed in the future. In this case it's whatever the conveyor installation brings—employment for thirty men, let's say, education for sixty children; God knows—nobody knows. We only know that to avoid ruining our future, we have to give up a bit of the present. And the old man has to go." He eased his forehead from the pane, and began to knock with his fists gently, frustratedly against its frame. "Perhaps that's why things change so little here. You can always feel for the present because it's staring you in the face. But you can kill the future in advance, and nobody will realize."

"But they must realize now," Caroline said. She had finished correcting the note-pad and was tucking the pencil into its spine. "In a few months the Company will be able to assess employment, rehousing, everything. And you said yourself that more wealth will make for more developed people. Those were your words."

"I know, I know." He breathed on the glass. "All I meant was that it's still a gamble. We can't yet see these developed people. You lay down your stake—let's say it's thirty uprooted families and an olive grove—"

"But ..."

"No, I'm just taking an example. Let's say it is that. You lay down your stake. And you wait for it to be trebled, quadrupled—in our case, multiplied by hundreds. You instinctively realize when you've recovered your stake." His rhythmic breathing stopped "Or perhaps you wouldn't."

"You're changing your mind."

"I'm just exploring it. I don't know." He felt her standing behind him. "I suppose the truth is you don't ever recover your stake. Not in this game. You may multiply it by a million, but that individual thing—that fisherman's house or old Matheopoulos' trust—that's gone for ever. It's not a gamble at all really, is it?" He half turned to her. "It's a sacrifice."

Standing behind him, she linked her arms over his chest. "You can't help that."

He stared down at her hands. They looked capable, the fingernails manicured to pearly tips, and her forearms were covered in a down of tiny golden hairs; he ran his finger along them. "I know. But when it's other people's sacrifice, it's sobering." He squeezed her wrists. "That's all I meant."

She rustled her hair over the back of his neck. "That's what you were saying before," she said. "A few things have to be destroyed. That was true. So don't get miserable about it. Look on the better side. Think of the future. That's the remedy."

He gently broke her grip and turned round to face her, laying his hands on her shoulders. "You're always full of remedies. How do you come to be so cheerful always?"

She smiled into his eyes. "I didn't know I was."

"Even when you're saying serious things. . . ."

She stepped inside his arms, pressed her lips quickly to his and danced back again. "You and your sacrifices and unavoidable destruction!"

He started to laugh. At the same time he felt sheepish, standing in front of her in his blackened overalls, with tousled hair. "It was those two old delegates who did it," he said. "I want everything for nothing. Not a flea harmed!" He squeezed the softness of her forearms. "Have you ever heard of the Jain?"

She shook her head.

"The Jain are an Indian sect," he said. "I used to admire them no end. In fact—don't laugh—I had a Jain phase at university. They believe that no living creature should be harmed. They dust their benches before sitting down, and walk with veiled mouths in case they swallow an insect." He thought she would laugh, but she remained looking at him seriously. "But isn't it crazy? We crush a host of organisms when we walk from one room to another. We kill them inside us every second by the chemistry of our bodies." He dropped her hands. "Compromise—what a terrible word to a twenty-year-old student! But now ... Have you noticed how the sound of a word alters with your fondness for it? Listen: Com-pro-mise ... that's more musical than it used to be." His hands lifted to her waist, resting on its small rounded hip-bones, and he repeated the word several times to himself in a self-mocking, exploratory way. "Com-pro-mise...."

Chapter Ten

The piano was out of tune, but there was nobody in the town to tune it. The notes sounded so stale that Claudia Oldenburg swore aloud and once even left the song in mid-air, gazing disheartened at the music sheet and resting her head in her hands. Her voice was low and pleasantly flexible, but there was no one in the house to hear it. She decided to apply the muffle pedal to several of the notes—it couldn't be helped. She straightened the song sheet and cleared her throat.

"... and they who never laughed at the sun
Kept watch on thorns under the moon...."

No, that was terrible. That was meant to be a D flat; but it made a noise like a biscuit falling on to an oven-tray. And Frank had said that the piano "seemed in tune to him"! Her voice did not sound right to her either; it lay too much in her throat. She tapped a note and sang it, moving the noise out of her gullet and into her mouth, pressing it forward to her lips. That was better. Perhaps, after all, she could have made a singer.

But she hated to think so. It was a comfort to think that she had no talent. If there was no talent there could be no waste. But when she heard the note jump full-formed from her mouth like that, she put her hands to her throat and quickly warned herself: "No, no, you fool. You could never have sung properly. Not with a throat like this—you're like an emu." Then she recalled the night she had sat in the upper tier of the Chicago Opera House and heard Lily Pons sing *Lakmé*—a tiny-throated woman whose voice had reached her with a resonance so bell-like and effortless that she had barely dared to breath.

But all this was childish, she told herself, for a woman in middle age. The past twenty years were littered with the remains of half-enthusiasms; that was the sort of person she was. Real talent imposed itself—at least she had always read so. Whereas hers was merely evasion; it simply meant: I can't bear to be like all these other women, locked in the circle of their homes and children. That was the trouble with this place. There was not enough to think about. The same faces haunted the same parties year after year, with less and less to say. People even began to look the same, crack the same jokes. Until eventually the trivial became important. Socially, it was death.

For years, she thought, she had been waiting for her life to alter, yet here she was at forty-two (forty-two!) and nothing had changed. How childish she still was! Forty-two seemed an age that only other people were. If she looked in a mirror she did not see forty-two there, only herself, which had no age. Her face was mature, but scarcely lined, and her small, high breasts were just as firm, or almost, as when she was a girl.

Years ago, walking along Lake Michigan, Frank had asked her if she minded marrying a man so much older than herself. She had laughed at him then. Now those years by Michigan, she supposed, were what people called "the best of your life".

She spread her fingers over the keys again.

> "... kept watch on thorns under the moon,
> To see God in the pure light of heaven
> Face to face one day...."

She stopped in frustration. One day she ought to find work, she thought, something to commit her; although what she could do she did not know. Everything here was done by servants, and her duties had long ago dwindled to thinking up recipes and playing hostess. Nothing else was supposed to be compatible with her dignity. It made her feel like a spayed cat. Next year, for all she knew, she might be a grandmother—at the age of forty-three! She stroked the corners of her mouth, along her chin, and the little slackness beneath it. Her elbow hit a note on the piano. She remembered. Schubert. Try again. Muffle the D sharp and the F.

> "To see God in the pure light of heaven...."

But it was no good. Her fingers refused to strike ugly notes. She got up, went to the sofa and picked up a newspaper. The *New York Times* sometimes took ten days to reach here; *Le Monde* came in six. News of wars and crises only seemed to penetrate to Kalepia after they had been resolved, and this isolation deepened the place's self-obsession.

The hum and squeak of a car sounded outside. Everybody arrived together: Howard on foot with a book sticking out of each pocket, Frank and Caroline bursting in, he saying nothing, she laughing; and Frank's assistant, Adourian. Claudia had closed the lid of the piano before they had reached the verandah, and had tucked the music sheet into the record cabinet. Absurd to feel guilty for singing....

"Oh Mummy," Caroline laughed, "you should have heard Daddy saying 'What about the relics?'" She went off into another spasm of laughter, hugging her arms as if she might fall apart. "He sounded like a—Oh Lord—like a colonel enquiring about cosmetics...."

Oldenburg did not smile. He threw off his jacket and sat in an armchair—he even sat down vigorously—accepting a glass of whisky from his wife without looking at her.

"Well?" she asked.

"Well nothing," he said. "Absolutely nothing—just as I thought—a delegation of nobodies expecting idiotic assurances and interpreting our refusal to give them as evidence that we want to sink the whole town. I can't tell you what it was like, with Michael Lerides being charming and calling them Mr This and Mr That when we should have kicked the whole lot out."

Claudia sat down beside him. "I'm glad you didn't." She crossed her legs—the cotton dress made her feel light—and lit a cigarette. "I dare say you did more good than if you'd refused them."

"We certainly did not." He finished the whisky and started to rummage through the brief-case. He could see no danger in the failure of the meeting, but it had thoroughly irritated him. "I don't understand these people. You offer them prosperity on a plate and they spit at you. Yet they go grabbing for half a drachma in their shops as if their lives depended on it."

Claudia had never shared this expectation that people be logical. If you gave up expecting logic, you could understand most things. "Perhaps they can't envisage the future," she said.

"That's precisely it," he answered morosely. "They've no logical imagination. Visual imagination, yes—too much of it. Logical imagination, no. It's the same thing over and over. They'll add up their small change all right, but think big, think at all, and—" He slapped down his hands on to the chair arms. The gesture dismissed the Eastern Mediterranean. "They're beyond patience."

It was strange, Claudia thought, how she wished for an expression of weakness from him. Once or twice, when he had come in exhausted from a day underground—not with that cold vigour at all—and had slumped sighing into a chair, she had felt almost as if she still loved him. She said curtly: "I'm beginning to wonder whether it's all worth it." She examined the carpet through the cigarette smoke. She did not want to see the expression on his face. "The whole town is starting to take sides. You can feel it."

"How can you say that, mother?" Caroline exclaimed. "You can't mean that."

Oldenburg snapped: "Worth it? Worth it? Just because some people don't like it? Argument is the spice of life here. A man only has to get up and say 'It is so' for half a dozen others to say 'It is not so'—before they even know what 'it' is."

"Yes, yes, I suppose." She stubbed out her cigarette half smoked. "I didn't mean give it up, but find a new site. You said you thought there were several in this district." Softly she added: "Does it really matter so much?"

She heard his jaw graze his collar as he jerked to stare at her. She did not look up. She knew precisely how he appeared: the blue eyes small and direct, with a hint of the temper which he never lost; chin thrust forward; lips hardened. "This is childish, Claudia." (Yes, I know.) "I hope you're not being serious." (I am.) "There are no indications anywhere of an ore deposit as rich as this one. To accept an inferior site would be a betrayal of our shareholders."

There they were again, she thought, that panel of shadows. As far as she was concerned the shareholders might as well have been a pantheon of Egyptian gods with tufts and snouts. She could not remember what a single one looked like. She had long ago given up the journey to Los Angeles with him for that annual meeting ("Waste of the Company's money," he had said.) All she knew was that every time she suggested he relax more, or delegate work, or that they take a longer vacation, the incense would start to rise up to the shareholders. It was rather terrible, when she thought how once she had wanted to partake in her husband's business, to support him. Such years between then and now! Now she hated the mines. Yet she knew that they had only been his escape. He could not make a personal, a family life, and so avoided it by negating its importance. Once or twice, in the middle of arguments and in the face of her prolonged and pleading stare, he had been deeply unsettled, so that he had refused to look at her and had become very angry.

She continued to gaze at the carpet—a Persian carpet from Tabriz, very expensive. Green, she remembered, stood for sanctity; blue was the symbol of heaven. "Do the shareholders matter so much?" Her voice was abstracted, without offence. "You've always said they're so confident they don't even enquire what's going on here. Whatever happens, they'll be rich." She waited for his answer with a dissociated interest which surprised her. She had never before so blatantly attacked the Egyptian pantheon, and now she had done so almost casually.

After a silence he did not answer her directly, but said: "If you feel no responsibility to the shareholders, what about our own security?"

"We don't want any more, do we? There's nothing to spend it on here."

"Shareholders", "financial security", "the Company". She knew that it was no good fighting these ghost reasons for his life. It was idiotic of her to try. Nobody could lift a man's self-inflicted burdens. And he talked of logic! Sometimes it seemed to her as if all spoken reasons were only curtseys to civilization. Necessary, but not true. Real reasons, almost by definition, were unknown or lay beyond the reach of language. They were like those ruins which snuggled here and there along the coasts of the Republic. You guessed their presence by the shape of the ground above them.

Yet she went on fighting the surface motives, because there was nothing else to do: except surrender.

"I will not talk to you when you're in these moods, Claudia," he said. "Business isn't a game. Once you slacken, you're finished."

She sighed audibly. This habitual gritting of his teeth at the difficulties of his job! Evidently the only way for a man to dignify his passion for work was to regard it as continually hard and important. So he always behaved as if to say "It's tough," "I can't relax," (he couldn't relax) "I have to fight on."

The Armenian assistant had been sitting all this while passing his hands over his face as if this would obscure him. Now Oldenburg noticed him. "Go and sort out the flotation pyrite figures, Jon," he said. "You'll find them in my study on top of the desk. You can work in there."

Adourian left.

"I thought you'd asked him for dinner," Claudia said, "not for work."

"I did; but it's not time for dinner," Oldenburg said tightly. "And I don't want Company employees here when you're talking like that."

He spared his wife a rare look of appraisal. She was conscious of it, it burnt the side of her face, but she kept her eyes on the Persian carpet, as if its convolutions, so much like a riddle, might contain an answer: orange, she remembered, for piety; white the colour of grief.

Once or twice Oldenburg had felt as if he was seeing Claudia quite newly, rather as he had first found her, during a lakeside vacation in Michigan, sitting in a deck-chair with her legs crossed, as they were now, and the same look of inhabiting some other stratum; perhaps it was simply her peculiar pallor. He remembered how her father, a Norwegian immigrant, used to play chess with himself by the lake, while she had sat in that deck chair browning herself, her high breasts cupped in a white bikini, and a book in her hands.

"I think you should be more discreet," he said.

She noticed the faint softening of his tone, and looked up. "I always forget about Jon. He seems like one of the family now."

"I know. All the same."

Caroline suddenly said: "I don't understand you, mother—" (all this not understanding—yet people used the words like an accusation) "—how can you not want the best for this town? You know what it's like."

Claudia did not want to argue any more. Caroline reminded her of herself at that age—so much enthusiasm for what was good and seemed simple. She was anxious to preserve that in her daughter; so she said non-commitally: "I know the townspeople don't follow our way of life."

"It's not a way of life at all," Caroline pursued. "It's a waste, a nothing."

Howard had been reading, and the concentration of his eyes behind their spectacles had seemed to exclude him from the conversation. But now he looked up and said: "How do you know it's a nothing? You don't live it. Do you know what Niedermeyer said about your so-called waste? No, you wouldn't. He said the only true-living human beings are primitives. *Civilized man is by definition in revolt against the truth of his nature*."

"I don't care what whoever-it-was said," Caroline answered blithely. She sat on the floor with her back to the sofa. "I disagree."

"That's because you refuse to reason," Howard said. "You just say 'I disagree'. A conviction's only decent as a hypothesis, when it subjects itself to the criteria of truth."

Caroline made a "Pooh!" into his face. She became so irritated when he adopted this tone that she did not listen to what he was saying. His words did not belong to him, they belonged to his curriculum.

Caroline's disdain always piqued Howard. He took it as personal jealousy—he regarded himself as more intelligent. Sometimes the whole family maddened him; they seemed not to think, or question, or believe anything. It was as if they had no proper identity. They used other people's thoughts, other people's convictions. They seemed, in fact, dead. "All this about resurrecting Kalepia," he went on. "Why should the townsmen want to exchange their barbarity for yours? Any study of comparative sociology shows . . ."

She rested her chin on her knees, not looking at him. "I don't need comparative sociology," she said. "I've got my own eyes."

"You're ridiculous," he said with satisfaction. "It appeals to your moralism, does it, to redeem Kalepia? Kalepia, I suppose, is dirty and decadent?" His eyes needled her from behind their glasses. "You're just a mess of sloppy feelings."

"Oh lay off."

"Tell me, then, what you feel for Kalepia if you don't feel morality. Pity?"

Caroline glared at him. "Maybe."

He shrugged his shoulders. He felt irritated and contemptuous. "Pity and love both idealize their object. Neither can be true."

Claudia said suddenly: "That's enough. That's enough from both of you." She hated the cynicism in Howard; it was like a symptom of disease.

But he went on: "So you have a duty to change Kalepia, do you? What about *Natur-recht*?"

Caroline realized that when he bent his thin face to her in that infuriating way he was not asking a question at all. He was demanding a confession of ignorance.

She had no intention of giving one. "What about it?"

But before Howard could answer, Oldenburg had turned on him. Howard's dilettantism angered his father. "Who's talking about rights to change anything? Kalepia wants to change itself. That's the point. I have approval for the mine not only from the government, but from the Mayor and municipality in writing. That's a hard fact for you."

A flush had appeared on Howard's cheeks. He touched his spectacles and for a moment looked as if he would return to his book, but instead he remarked tensely: "The Mayor and the municipality aren't Kalepia, are they?"

Oldenburg snapped: "They're elected."

Howard answered, with a dangerous amount of emotion—he was afraid of his father: "That doesn't mean anything."

Oldenburg stared at him: the rigid stare with its look of force and suggestion of temper. It was a stare which had always frightened Howard and it frightened him again. It never failed. His heart all at once seemed delicate in his chest. It was as if this stare was reminding him of all those times when as a child he had been guilty. It was difficult now to dissociate it from guilt, to stand up for himself. He heard the tremble in his voice as it went on: "Electoral choice only means freedom to vote for the least unsuitable...." Who had said that? "I don't see that a majority means anything ..." Who would defend him against that stare? Nietzsche, Marcuse ... ? "Nobody would accept a majority decision on what he should wear or eat ... so I don't see why he should accept one on how he's to develop." The threat of temper seemed literally to burn his father's eyes. "Society depends on the individual...."

"Society!" barked Oldenburg. "I didn't ask for a garble about society! Are you telling me my job? Development and the individual! We're going to excavate a mine, not a university. If people alter because of it, that's up to them."

Howard twisted his spectacles in his hands. He had a feeling of being physically strangled. His resentment was matched by his fear. "Environmental factors ..."

"Environmental factors!" Oldenburg watched his son's eyes drop from his stare and look for the protection of the book, which he did not dare reopen. "We've got a job to do and we're going to do it. And it won't get complicated by intellectual fairytales." The boy needed hard experience, Oldenburg thought; he'd never so much as studied a geological report, let alone lifted a pick-axe; yet he talked in that fatuous way as if his education (which had been expensive) gave him free access to the truth.

Howard went on looking at the floor; his curtain of lank hair concealed his face. He realized with sudden alarm that one day he would stand against his father; he could not endure this for ever.

Claudia said wearily: "Let Howard have his opinion, Frank."

"I would if his opinion was relevant," said Oldenburg.

Claudia saw Howard's mouth quiver to reply, and quickly said: "His opinions are relevant to him. We can't see everything the same." Why wouldn't he let the boy breathe, she wondered? He was always complaining that Howard had no guts.

Oldenburg gave one of his snorting sighs and sat back in his chair. Howard picked up the book and walked out of the room. "Is that what we sent him to college for?" Oldenburg demanded. "Where does all this rubbish come from? What's he been reading?"

Claudia wanted to explain. She looked into her husband's face, then glanced away again, afraid that she would despair even before she had started. "Does it matter what Howard's been reading? At the moment he may be full of Hegel or somebody-or-other, but aren't young men bound to be like that? Don't you remember?"

As soon as she had asked, it sounded a ridiculous question. But she maintained the silence which followed.

He said curtly: "I never had time for that sort of thing."

She nodded, and let herself relapse farther into the cushions of the sofa. Of course, she thought, he must always have been the same. Absurd of her ever to have doubted. That closed determination had fascinated her. To a girl newly out of college, where the boys were still immature, this direct, forceful man (he was already thirty-four) had been compelling. The mines too had intrigued her in those days. She had envisaged him going down with a pick and winkling out diamonds. She had found his gravity, his lack of humour, a little comical; but to laugh at it seemed somehow to annul it. It had not struck her as formidable. "Miss Nielsen," he had said, "don't hold the reel so high—and use your thumb." Trolling along the lake in afternoon sunlight—he kept his elbow on the handle of the outboard motor, but the rest of his body turned to her. He had a head of thick black hair then. "You must leave more play or you will snap the line, Miss Nielsen. Some of the pike are quite strong." He leaned over, his hand on hers. "That's better." This constant interchange of arms and brushing of shoulders in the interests of catching bass! And why always "Miss Nielsen"? Was he waiting for her to say "Please call me—and may I call you—?" It was beautiful there, with the pine-woods folding to the water. No doubt that had had something to do with it. "That is a sun-fish, Miss Nielsen, but too small. You must put it back." Her first fish! And he was going to put it back! She watched it swim away, as if he had dropped a medal in the water.

"The best thing for Howard would be to choose a profession at once," Oldenburg said.

She remembered that in spite of all this touching of hands and arms, they had not slept together before their marriage. She had liked this. And he had not mangled her as the undergraduates did, who treated pieces of your body as if they did not belong to you. But his energies flowed into his work. He was not a very sexual man. For several years now they had slept apart. She had never complained about this, but she could perfectly imagine him answering: "We have two children; one of each. Isn't that enough?"

"Howard should find work back in the States," said Oldenburg. "There's nothing for him here. What the hell use is a history degree?" Howard's future made him profoundly uneasy. He could find no advice or guidance for the boy; he did not understand him.

"Give him time, Frank." Claudia's voice sounded weak to her. "He hasn't left college a month." She did not add any of the platitudes about choosing a career, although most of them crawled into her mind.

"He doesn't take work seriously. He affects to despise it. You've heard him yourself. He's got a lot of adjusting to do before he buckles down, and the sooner he adjusts the better."

Claudia was only half listening. She murmured: "... Adjust ... well, yes ... I suppose." His voice seemed farther away. It was almost a physical sensation, and it often happened now: this cold mist in her. It was what she most disliked about the person she was becoming—the detachment, even sometimes from her children. She felt sure that if someone were to touch her hands or her face during these half-dreams, he would say "You're freezing. Are you well?" Occasionally she wondered if the house had not something to do with it. It was too big, and when the children were away it seemed nearly uninhabited. But the malaise was not self-pity, nor anything so warm. She was a little afraid of it—the proverbial despair of her ancestral Norway, a mental twilight. And it was increasing. There was a time when she had hoped that Frank would notice, when her whole mood seemed to be saying "Don't you see? Can't you see what's happening to me?" But she no longer did that. As a girl, she remembered, she had courted these deep breathings in which to listen to herself. She had valued them. Now they came of their own accord, too many, and when she listened this greyness, this isolation, answered her.

Oldenburg stopped talking. He realized that his wife was not hearing him; but he was growing used to that. Of his family only Caroline seemed to respond like a rational human being. Claudia and Howard inhabited separate and incomprehensible worlds.

He felt them ungrateful. "Sacrifice" was a word which he used to describe a lifetime of hard work in relation to his family. It did not strike him as peculiar to expect gratitude for a gift which they had never desired. And because he had become successful in his business, he obscurely felt that his values were vindicated and that his wife should now have the humility to be pleased.

Yet paradoxically he sensed that he had failed them. He met this failure in Claudia's stare sometimes, and in Howard's way of never meeting his eye. Was he afraid of their love? That was what Claudia had asked in desperation, years ago. And why did he never touch his children? Occasionally still, remembering these accusations, he felt an unsettling of himself, as if the whole structure of his life was being faintly shaken from inside. He did not understand it. He set it apart. Yet he continued to think of Howard's failure as a little his own.

Claudia stood up now with that look of abstraction, and said: "It's time for dinner. I'll call Jon."

Adourian had sat down at Oldenburg's desk half an hour before. He thought he must concentrate as hard as he could on the figures and indulge his own thoughts later, otherwise he would not finish the work in time. The desk was an enormous, leather-topped one, with a gold design tooled along the border. It was heaped with particulars of mining machinery, particulars of the copper market, particulars of particulars. Carefully positioning himself so that he would not disturb them, he perched on Oldenburg's chair, his light arms resting on the edge of the desk. Then he began to work at the flotation pyrite figures. All he had to do was to read the numbers in one column, compare them with those in another and note down the difference in a third. He had often done it before while sitting at a small table in Oldenburg's drawing-room.

For a while he worked steadily. Then he noticed that he was

making mistakes. By the time he had completed the first sheet he had crossed out so many figures that he began to use rough paper instead of transferring calculations straight from his head, as he usually did. It was as if he had lost a childhood talent.

He blamed this on the unfamiliar room. After completing a second sheet in the same way he left the chair and started to walk about, examining the aquatints on the walls and the ornaments along the mantelpiece. Looking at people's houses was as personal as scrutinizing their faces; but this was more an office than a living-room. Only the pictures and the mantelpiece spoke at all. He stroked the back of a porcelain horse. Whose taste: his or hers? Hers, of course.

He returned to the chair, but after filling in five more figures and miscalculating another, he dropped the pen. His gaze travelled over two piles of correspondence, tied with green string. The frame of a photograph showed behind. He stretched forward and picked it up. It showed Oldenburg and Claudia on holiday; he was incongruously dressed in shorts, his thinning hair flattened on either side of his head in two dark bands; she was smiling at him; the snapshot must have been at least ten years old. Adourian took a piece of paper and placed it so that it obscured Oldenburg and left Claudia smiling at nothing. He listened to the door in case anybody should come. Then he leaned down to the photograph of Claudia and kissed her lips.

Could Oldenburg really have meant that, he wondered: *"I will not talk to you when you're in these moods, Claudia"*? Her only moods were those withdrawals which were a part of her fascination, when her eyelids grew heavy and you noticed the concave smoothness of her cheeks. *"I will not talk to you . . ."* What sort of man said that, as if his talking could be a gift to her? And she had sat there accepting it as normal!

Claudia: he had not liked the name at first. It had seemed masculine: Claude with an -ia. But now, now it had weight and beauty. Clau-di-a: what sound was that? A 'cello, or a heavy silk dress trailing over a floor. "Claudia Nielsen" he had read in the fly-leaf of one of her books. It sounded, for some reason, like the name of a woman who had died. When he thought of it, he imagined it spoken in her voice, with that clipped softness. She often spoke as if she did not quite belong to wherever she was. There was some distance round her, he thought, even when she was happy. He loved the way she preceded her remarks by a little syllable, as if reconnecting herself: an "Ah" or an "Oh". Did other people do that? He was sure they did not.

Every few weeks, when a blue envelope arrived from the Nikitari mill with lists of flotation figures, he felt unsteady, because the next evening Oldenburg would be sure to say: "The office closes at seven as usual, but if you want to earn overtime you can come home and check the flotation figures for me." Earn overtime! He would have given a month's wages to walk through a room where she was sitting. As it was, she generally said: "You will stay for dinner, won't you?"

"Thank you, Mrs Oldenburg, I'd love to." And after several of these suppers, she had said—he remembered distinctly, she tilted her head to one side—"Don't call me 'Mrs Oldenburg', Jon. It makes me feel a hundred." She had not said what he might call her, but one day, he knew, her Christian name was going to slip out of him, and he would be horribly, deliciously confused, and she would say "Yes, please call me Claudia." He had envisaged this occasion several times. Each time she had spoken it differently, sometimes with greater sweetness, sometimes more humorously; but always with her eyes darting over his face saying to themselves "He's so confused. Can he ... could he be ...?"

He did not understand why he so much wanted her to know that he loved her.

He rubbed his knuckles over his eyes. He must continue with the figures, which meant nothing to him (they meant nothing to her either, which was worse). *"I'm beginning to wonder whether it's all worth it."* She had said that so hopelessly, he had felt that to her this "all" was not only the new mine, not even the Company, but everything, all feeling and being. Then he had had a furious compulsion to kneel and cup her head in his hands, his fingers round her cheeks, and to tell her that Yes, it all, all life, even suffering was worth it. If she had asked him why, he could not have told her, but that was what he knew. Hadn't she felt his adoration? He had almost been there, kneeling ... but Caroline had interrupted and Oldenburg had bludgeoned "Worth it? Worth it?" and she had been left alone again.

Adourian's face had tensed and his thin hands sweated round the pen. His body was crooked in the chair, twisted sideways by its dreaming. He returned hurriedly to the figures. He had still completed only two sheets. He decided to take the rest home after dinner. The photograph he carefully picked up and placed back behind the correspondence. Oldenburg, he thought, looked obscene beside her.

Only once had the General Manager ever mentioned her in the office. It was the day before Adourian's eighteenth birthday; he had wrenched his elbow on the way to work, and by ten o'clock it had grown so painful that he had felt faint and had asked to go home.

"You're white as a sheet, man." Oldenburg stared at him with concern. "You'd better look in at the hospital. Check that nothing's broken." He had picked up the telephone. "We can't spare anyone from the office, but I'll get my wife to drive you."

His wife! "Oh no, sir, no, no." That was unthinkable. "You can't get her to come all the way up here just for ... just for ..."

"What do you mean *all the way*? It's two minutes' drive."

"... and then take me all the way to the hospital. ..."

"The hospital's *five minutes* away." Barking into the telephone. "Hullo? Hullo?"

So she came. She was wearing a white cotton dress with birds printed on it. Her rather short hair, like a soft enclosure for her face, had taken blond streaks and lights from the summer. She walked in front of him to the car: her particular walk, delicate and a little stilted, as if she wore new shoes. Now they were sitting together. How long were those five minutes to the hospital? Time had nothing to do with clocks or with the sun. Five minutes were a universe; or nothing. But she did not start at once. "Let me see it, Jon. Roll up your sleeve."

She placed one hand beneath his elbow, and began to feel its joint with her long, cool fingers. These fingers mesmerized him. He felt as if his skin was violating them. They were feeling his arm. Exquisite they were, like hands in a painting. They set his heart fanning air all through his body. He wondered what they did all day. He tried to reconstruct her day from what he knew, but it remained unimaginable.

"Does that hurt?" she said.

"No." (How could she hurt?)

The fingers continued to probe—each so tender!—pressing along the swollen veins, into the pit of the elbow. He had never noticed before how each finger of a hand has a distinct character. "Does that hurt?"

"No." Please go on. Two rings: the gold band of marriage, the little diamond of engagement (did she have to wear that?).

"Does this hurt?"

"No." It did, but he was watching her face.

She laughed. "What does hurt then? It must have gone numb!"

So after this minute, this aeon, she had started the car, and the terrible thing was that he did not know what to say to her. He simply bathed in her nearness. He was sure that nobody else touched a gear-handle precisely as she did. She held it in the tips of her fingers, as if it was alive, and moved it so respectfully across—up—down, that the decisions might partly have been its own. The little gold-strapped watch which circled her wrist told him that two minutes had passed since they had started.

She asked him was she going too fast? No, he said, but thought at once "Of course you are." The road went by so cruelly that he could not look at it. She asked him about his job in the office and about his father's jewellery shop. Did her husband overwork him, she was afraid he was rather a slavedriver? No, said Adourian, he enjoyed it. Might his father have any of those attractive mounted amethysts left, not too expensive? Adourian had no idea, but said that he was sure his father had some. Do come and see them. Sometimes she glanced at him when she spoke, taking her eyes from the road. Those blue eyes and pale features, he thought, gave her an almost frightening strangeness, at once beautiful and remote.

"How is the elbow behaving? We're nearly there."

"It's marvellous. . . . It doesn't hurt much." (He would forgive it even if the doctor wanted to amputate.) Her watch showed their five minutes already gone.

This time, after she had leaned back from applying the hand-brake, the unbuttoned collar of her frock remained fractionally open and he saw, very smooth above her bra, the curve of her left breast. He glanced away and stared in agitation through the window at the passing houses, the cars, the people. He began to blush. Yet haltingly, in a surreptitious fever, his gaze returned to her collar, and moved down. He thought he had seen nothing so beautiful, so perfect, as that rounded glow of flesh which rose above her heart. He blushed so deeply that he had to look away again. Surely she had noticed? But no, she was watching the road. This beauty was simply a part of her.

"We're here."

They went into the out-patients department. It was empty. An orderly said that the doctor could see him immediately. He turned round to thank Claudia (how could he thank her really?) but she had sat down.

"I'll wait for you," she said. "You shouldn't walk home. You may still feel faint."

He glanced round the room, the out-patients room, with its bare tiles and single table. The walls were discoloured with damp, the windows curtainless. "But you can't stay here!"

She looked surprised. "Why ever not?"

"It's . . . it's horrible."

She stood up and took a step towards him. She was smiling. He had not seen her smile like that. She looked happy, and faintly embarrassed. She touched his waist. "It's perfectly all right here," she said. "Now you see the doctor."

All the time he was with the doctor he was making calculations. It was now sixteen minutes since they had left the Company offices. The doctor, who was absurdly slow, would take another ten minutes to bandage him while she waited in the bare room; and they would take another five minutes to reach his home. So she had given him more than half an hour of her life. It was inexplicable. Even if she lived to be eighty, she would have spent over a millionth of her existence with him.

He winced at the doctor's clumsiness. The arm throbbed now. After a while he began to feel sick, and nothing seemed so good. When he went out again, she would only smile her polite, friendly smile. He could not so much as kiss her cheek. Now, far more forcefully than before, he realized that not only could he never receive from her—he could not give to her either. Never. He felt appalled. That, he realized, must be the misery of loving the forbidden. Love the disinterested, and you could still pour out your affection for refusal. But love the forbidden and you would have to remain discreet, disciplined, living in the suburbs of her life. It was against all the nature of love. Meanwhile, you wonder. You twist her words, as he was already doing, repeat and repeat them. Were they meant to entice or to repel? Surely one or the other. It is impossible to believe that they mean nothing, that the beloved is scarcely concerned at all. He felt tears behind his eyes.

"You can get up," the doctor said. "You do feel all right, don't you?"

The arm was bandaged, crooked in a sling. He hoped he looked heroic. He stood up. The doctor was going to open the door. Would she be there or would she have gone? It was impossible that she could have remained, after fourteen minutes—waiting for him.

Yet there she was.

Chapter Eleven

For six weeks the archimandrite had received no reply to his letter to the metropolitan bishop about the sale of St Vichinos Mountain, and he was beginning to imagine that this silence concealed some important activity. Perhaps the metropolitan was considering the convocation of the See to discuss the matter; or maybe he had approached the Patriarch himself and it would be placed before the Holy Synod.

Meanwhile the archimandrite, self-pledged to explore his conscience, had grown exhausted. The business of exploration never ended. It was simple mentally to discard his own wishes and to consider the matter theoretically. But then the labyrinth appeared to have numberless dead-ends, and no heart at all; for a heart, it seemed, could only be created by a conviction.

Yet this cold-blooded probing was the only path left to him; he was too old to redevelop feelings. So he wandered about the maze of his dialectic, and emerged unscathed and unrewarded whenever he chose, thinking "Well that doesn't lead anywhere".

He was afraid, of course, that his personal interests might not be served by this process. But he comforted himself with two contingencies. First, he might honestly discover that the Church was, after all, best served by the sale of the shrine land. Secondly, there was the bishop's letter; the letter might remove the burden of decision from him altogether, and by now he almost hoped that it would. Occasionally he caught himself thinking it unfair of God to have prepared such a situation at all. But then the world was not paradise, came back the practised theological riposte, the world was the arena of man's trial. And even the unbelieving must admit that for this purpose it was subtly organized.

One thing, at least, the archimandrite had discovered. He had realized it while walking up and down the empty hall of the residence, whose windows overlooked a pleasant garden. The attraction of the eight hundred thousand dollars was not connected with comfort, but with pride. He had no real interest in renovating this building at all; it was perfectly adequate and he had grown used to it. Even here the only item which piqued him was a plaque which had been delivered by an official from the Holy Synod two days after his induction. Above the doorway the double-headed Byzantine eagle still clasped its sceptres; but the plaque, instead of reading "Palace of the Metropolitan Bishop, See of Kalepia", simply said "See of Nikitari: archimandrite's residence".

But the archimandrite thought his responsibilities equivalent to those of a bishop, especially since his superior was almost unable to carry on his job or even, it seemed, to write a letter. He knew, of course, that a bishop was chosen by God through the inspired voice of the Synod, and no man could consider himself worthy of such a calling. Yet the archimandrite, after forty years' experience of the Church, felt that the poverty of God's servants must greatly restrict His choice. And within this more limited and human category—as ranking among the least unworthy—the archimandrite could not help feeling he might sit with his masters.

Indirectly the sale of the St Vichinos Mountain could realize this ambition. He was sure that most of the money would be devoted to building the new seminary at Nikitari, and from years of acquaintance with the episcopal palaces of the Republic, he knew that the question would immediately be asked: "How did the See suddenly become so rich?"

The answer—and every ear would be bent to catch it: "The See negotiated the sale of some land with the Lythrangomi Copper Mining Company."

"Ah, I didn't know that." (It was the ear of the Patriarch himself which he conjured now.) "That must have been done in the time of Fantousis."

"No, no. Since then, Holiness."

"But, well ... you know the state of health of our bishop ... Surely, such strenuous negotiations ..."

"No, Holiness, the sale was negotiated by the archimandrite of Kalepia."

"I see. Good. Alexander Drosinis, you mean?"

"Yes, Alexander Drosinis."

"Alexander Drosinis. . . ."

This much the archimandrite's reflections had revealed to him. The sin was pride, not cupidity. Even the Company's bribe did not entice him greatly, otherwise he might have rejected it and felt his conscience shriven.

But what could he do about his pride now? He was sixty-nine years old, and for years he had unconsciously considered that the correction of personal faults was a pastime for the immature. By the time a man was middle-aged, faults were built into his structure. No doubt they weakened it, like the tombs those Latin prelates built into the walls of their cathedrals. But after a while it became difficult to know what would happen if they were removed. A man might be even weaker then. Better, perhaps, to possess a fault than a vacuum. Sometimes the archimandrite felt that he *was* his faults, and in any case, he had no idea how to set about eradicating pride. It would be easier to pick out his breastbone. With a great weariness he concluded that the best he could do was not to change himself, which lay beyond his power, but to see in clear logic what was good, and to try to implement it, this one time, almost as a parting gift of his failing character. So he returned to the labyrinth of pure reason, and hoped again that it might yield up an honest decision to sell.

Then the letter came. He knew at once that it was important because the deacon who brought it to his desk on a little silver tray remained in the room, pretending to check the bookshelves. No doubt he was waiting for his superior to open it, before rubbing his chubby hands together and enquiring "Good news, Most Reverend?" So the archimandrite put the letter to one side with a look of abstraction—although he could clearly see "Metropolitan Bishop of Nikitari" inscribed in the left-hand corner—and continued his work.

Even after the deacon had left, he remained staring at it for a full minute. He was tired enough to hope that the metropolitan had made a decision, but ambitious enough to be afraid of it. While he was cutting open the letter, he did not know what he wanted. But his fingers trembled. He read a single sentence:

'Very Reverend: your letter reaches us at a time most trying for our health, so that we cannot personally undertake the issue of the Mountain of St Vichinos; but confident that you reside in the wisdom of Christ and in our prayers, we empower and command you to do as God will guide you, to the benefit of our Mother Church—with love in Christ, Dimitrios Velissaropoulos, Metropolitan Bishop of Nikitari.'

The archimandrite returned the letter to its envelope and tucked it into his inside pocket along with the Company's letter. He walked into the garden where the hibiscus were in flower and sat down in a chair under the portico. His boots—an old-fashioned pair, black and very worn—were pinching his ankles, and he slowly unlaced them and slid them under the seat. Then his back seemed to be aching against the wooden chair-frame and he returned indoors for a cushion, finally pillowing his body on three sides before sitting down.

The bishop's letter did not surprise him. All the same, he felt as if he had been deserted. The old man had sent him no hint, no gleam of advice, nothing. Now he felt hot as well as frail. He let his chin fall on to his chest and rested his shoulders forward, noticing the whiteness of his hands. Better to be done with it all quickly, he thought: compute the number of souls which might suffer from the shrine's demoliton, and set them against those which would benefit from priests better educated in a new seminary. Draw graphs, make equations! Tote up salvation!

Impossible, of course.

Yet he was still obsessed by the thought that there must lie to hand some solution which would be as simple and perfect as turning a key in a lock. What would Christ have done? That was the cardinal question for the faithful in trial. Would Christ have demolished a shrine to build a seminary?

But Christ never seemed to be faced with that sort of thing.

The archimandrite laced up his boots again and walked up and down the portico. Walking helped him to concentrate. The garden was pleasant on July evenings, he thought, with a light wind in the coloured banks of shrubs. He folded his hands behind him as he went, cracking his finger-joints. The traditions of the saints, he conceded, were pardonable, even healthy, expressions of faith on the part of the simple. But their time was almost over. Just as the ministry of Christ superseded the older prophets, so the Church must lead her children to an enhanced understanding.

He strolled into the garden itself, but the scrape of his boots on the path was less reassuring than their tap in the portico had been. He sounded less steady. He wished to make clear to himself that this superseding of the past was not a matter of sophisticating belief. Religions had been sophisticated out of existence before now (he crossed himself).

He walked out of the gate and into the street. The evening sun was cool and threw mild shadows. At first he had taken a furtive pleasure in being the hub of the town's speculation. But now there was a tension abroad. It alarmed him. It would not die until something had been decided. And only a quick decision would kill it. If only his conscience would point a finger and say "There!" He twisted a strand of his beard around his forefinger. Momentarily he wondered if the whole issue was not a matter of simple absolutes: shrine or seminary—faith or understanding? Which was more important? Faith, surely. For the meanest priest could minister at the altar as drunk as David's sow, yet the sacrament was a mystery and the angels would hold up the chalice inviolate in his hands. Faith was more important than education. Always. So a shrine was more important than a seminary.

Now he was walking by the river; but not a drop of water flowed. Only a ghostly crease split the earth. He put no more trust in the last argument than he had in any other. When would this end?

"Hullo, uncle!" He stared round. He knew the voice but he could not glimpse the person. "Hullo, uncle!" Then he saw her, Helen, walking on the other side of the gully with Howard Oldenburg. They were both wearing jeans and looked, he thought, as disgusting as one another. "The Devil dressed me again this morning!" she shouted. "I couldn't stop him!"

If the archimandrite failed to smother a smile, he hoped that it was too far away for her to see. She was always disarming him like this. It was undignified; but today, for some reason, it soothed him. He watched her wandering away with the lean youth, then turned round and started to stroll back. He looked at his watch. It was later than he had thought, and he had to dine with the schoolmaster, Sofroniou. He walked quickly along the dried stream.

Sofroniou enjoyed some private means. At least this was the opinion of everybody in Kalepia, because a schoolmaster's salary could not have bought him his large house or allowed him to dress as expensively as he did. His dinner parties also were generous and frequent.

The archimandrite knew that he should not drink too much—it troubled his ulcer—but Sofroniou was one of the few people who bought his wines in Nikitari, and it was always a relief to escape the acid local product. The Nikitari wines were firm and slightly sweet, suiting the archimandrite's taste, and six or seven years discreetly mellowed them. At his end of the dining-table he was able to confine himself to a small circle of faces which seemed to glow very pleasantly. At one stage he even laid his hand on Ekaterina Lerides' arm—she had not immediately withdrawn it—and it was a comfort to feel his mind lucid while his body was suffused by this heavy, agreeable fire. In fact he must resemble—and he enjoyed the idea—a certain other wine which you could buy at the Capital: a pleasantly ripe flavour, with a full, underlying body.

It was a relief, this evening, to see his problems less urgently, and to speak of them almost as he felt. Lerides in particular was responding to him, and although it was obvious where the Company Secretary's interests must lie, the archimandrite noticed that he was sensitive enough to preserve a token impartiality. Lerides even suggested a site for a new shrine, near the present open-cast mine, and said that the Company would sell the plot of land cheaply to the See. The archimandrite warmed to that. The other side of the valley would suit very well. To build high on its ridge would enhance the mystique and prestige of the sanctuary, as well as demanding a steep climb from pilgrims—hardship was the essence of pilgrimage.

Lerides' face was pressed close to the archimandrite's. His eyes and elegant moustache gave an impression of confidence; the rest of his face was white. "I imagine the new shrine would cut away these superstitions which concern you." He was swirling a glass of brandy. "There'll be no more talk of martyrdoms and relics."

The archimandrite was pleased to hear this, although he did not believe it. "Yes, let us hope so." He wanted, all the same, to be charitable to the people, and added, smiling: "St Vichinos, you know, is one of the lesser figures of the Church, and where so little is known about a saint, the people will fill in the gaps. It is a time-honoured practice. Recently I've been discovering the local peasants' view of him, and the results are, to put it shortly, ridiculous. Even those with a sprinkling of historical knowledge are hopelessly at variance as to when he lived. Some say he was martyred in the reign of Diocletian, some say of the emperor Julian." Sofroniou's brandy, he thought, was excellent. "Oh yes! Everything has happened to this saint! He has been torn to bits by Gnostics and stoned by Turks. He was eaten by an asp sent from Satan. He even lived as a stylite, and died of exposure while chanting the *cherubikon*."

Lerides' laughter, which was discreet, nevertheless recalled the archimandrite to his station. He added rather pompously: "But isolate this saint in a new shrine and we would honour his real person and return his worshippers to truth. Faith without truth is superstition."

He met Ekaterina's gaze on his left. The contrasting black hair and creamy skin of this woman struck him forcefully. "Can you separate a saint and his legends like chemicals, archimandrite?" He did not like that, but her voice was sympathetic. "I imagine the people will transfer their legends to the new site."

The archimandrite imagined so too, but he had not admitted it to himself. He answered in a tone which was unhappy, yet grateful for this honesty: "Yes, Mrs Lerides, I think you are right. Yes, I do . . . I do."

Lerides looked annoyed. "It couldn't do any harm," he said.

The archimandrite stared into his brandy glass, but put it down without drinking. An island had appeared in his mind. The river of sophistry separated on either side. It created a momentary stillness. He found himself saying to her in a faint accent of enquiry: "But even superstition, if it is devoted to a worthy object, may carry merit?"

"I'm sorry, archimandrite," she said. "I don't understand these things." "Merit", "Sin"—she did not like such concepts, but she was feeling sorry for him and said nothing more.

But the old man would not let her go. He suddenly saw firm ground: the possibility of an answer from a disinterested intelligence. He sat himself very upright in his chair and kept his voice as impersonal as he could; but it was humbling to say: "The problem is this, Mrs Lerides. If one single soul should perish because of my removal of the shrine, nothing I can do or say would justify it. So you see the extent of my responsibility." He fixed his stare as sternly as he could on this attractive woman and considered that his tone required an answer.

"Souls perish? Can an archimandrite mete out damnation?" She returned his stare with mock solemnity. "I knew you were an important personage."

He suppressed his smile. If she put it like that, of course, it did sound ridiculous, even heretical. "But listen," he said. He still wanted to find this firm ground. He opened the palms of his hands. "Let us say I have a shrine in one hand and a religious university in the other. Now which is more important—faith in a thing, or wisdom about it?" Then, fearing he had lost dignity, he added: "It is always interesting to have a woman's point of view. That is something we churchmen are often deprived of."

"Well then," she teased, "women would probably like the shrine; but men, with their well-known objectivity, the university."

"You are mocking me, Mrs Lerides." He sounded suddenly querulous and tired. His hands had fallen limp on the table. "But I have to find a solution."

She wanted to help him, but knew she could not. There was no translation between their separate languages. She leaned quickly towards him. "But it won't be a perfect solution, will it? That would be impossible." She laid her fingers lightly on his arm. "The country people here say that solutions are only for the one-eyed. I like that."

The archimandrite looked back at her. "Yes," he said. He started to nod a little, pleased. "Yes, oh, that's good. I like that too, I like that very much."

He went on smiling in his mind. That made indecision positively civilized. It made it—yes—conscientious. He felt quite restored, but not to the kind of dignity which he was used to defending. Really, he thought, the senior churchmen should be allowed to marry. Women were so ... so ... ha-ha! ... whatever women were.

Lerides, for some reason, had lost his sang-froid, and interrupted brusquely: "You need seminaries these days, there are quite enough shrines. You only have to drive between here and the Capital, and there's a dome to St Somebody on every hillock. The Church must move with the times."

The archimandrite stiffened. "The Church is beyond Time," he said.

Lerides checked himself at once. "But superstitions must move with the times," he said. "The people must."

"Yes," replied the archimandrite, "I know." The people. It was not God, but the people who made him afraid—their new way of looking. Only yesterday he had seen a picture of the saint in a shop window, and written underneath: "God will be the Judge". Those notices had a habit of multiplying. They went up side by side with photographs of the President of the Republic and heroes of the War of Liberation. "I'm looking for a way to reassure the people."

Lerides was biting his thumbnail, and gazing to the other end of the table, where Sofroniou talked with his old pupil, Alastos. "It may be possible to reassure the people," he said. He left the words alone for a moment, while the archimandrite fixed him with his full interest. "I've been thinking about it myself. You see, this delegation from the town has made trouble. It didn't get what it wanted and there are some silly rumours about." He lowered his voice. "Now Mr Oldenburg is to give a talk at the town hall on Thursday about copper-mining in the Levant. It's a long-standing engagement. The lectures are free and anyone may attend. Perhaps he could add some words about the Company's plans in Kalepia—just a few hard facts and assurances, pointing out the advantages in terms of employment and so on. Something to baulk rumours."

The archimandrite was sipping his fourth glass of brandy. His body felt comfortingly immovable. All he had to do was to concentrate on the motions of his hand, bringing the glass to his lips as steadily as he could, and not spilling the brandy in his beard. "But those lectures—" he managed to say, "they are never well attended, are they? Just a sprinkling, mostly retired people ... I seem to remember...."

"That's true," Lerides said, "but it would be easy to spread the news that Mr Oldenburg will be making some statements on Company plans. That will bring the people in. The hall can hold three hundred."

All other voices had dimmed into a single murmur for the archimandrite. Even his own sounded like somebody else's. "That sounds a good idea," he said. "Yes, that should bring them in...."

"It would be useful if we could say that in the event of sale the Church would dedicate another shrine," Lerides went on. "I imagine that is so?"

Lerides' face seemed a long way away to the archimandrite, little more than a milky oval under its crinkled hair, while Ekaterina had dimmed to nothing but her eyes, pleasantly vivid and green. "A new shrine, certainly ... the Church would not neglect to honour the saint ... you may say so ..."—his own eyes were watering—"the new site, yes, if that will quiet the people ... I quite respect your judgment, Mr Lerides."

Leave it to him, the archimandrite thought, he seemed to know what he was doing. Mr Oldenburg had better say what he pleased. Nobody would quite believe him anyway ... people didn't respect companies and institutions here, it wasn't Germany ... but it would calm things down ... surely. To the archimandrite it seemed as if all his troubles were gliding away from him. Within the amber of his brandy glass he could nearly see them, passing in a gilded procession of saints and consciences, like pagan gods abandoning a city. The glow inside him had cleaned them away. He had himself become this glow. That was what it must be like to sit in a halo, he thought. And there was the holy procession deserting him, while he criticized it a little. Sages and law-givers, those who found decisions easy, with their one eye each. Oh yes, that was good. These country people. They might not be such a bad lot....

Ekaterina touched her husband's arm and whispered: "Don't go on at him, Michael."

Lerides looked away from the archimandrite, who was in any case not seeing him, and turned so fully to his wife, throwing one arm over the back of the chair, as to exclude anybody from their conversation. He was angry. "I'm trying to repair your damage." The effort to quieten his voice filled it with breath. "It's been our business to persuade him that a new shrine will get rid of superstition, and you have to say precisely the opposite."

Ekaterina faintly blushed. "It's true," she said. "The opposite is true."

"That's not the point." He sighed sharply, frustrated by the way he sounded. "The Company's going through a difficult phase, and we'd all be grateful if our women were behind us. Muller's wife does nothing but moan about illness—says he's getting silicosis when he's fit as a bull. And Claudia only helps as far as her duties go. And now you. Why did you have to tell the archimandrite that? All this about truth." He took a cigarette and struck a match fiercely. "What about loyalty?"

"Oh Michael." She stared round the table, as if she would talk to somebody else. "You can't make me loyal to whatever happens to be around me. I'm not a tribe."

He asked acidly: "Do I just happen to be around you?"

She laid her hand gently on his shoulder. He immediately held it. She smiled at him, but she was feeling something like despair. She whispered: "Let's not start this now. I was only trying to help the archimandrite. He doesn't know what to do; his conscience keeps ..."

"Conscience! Are you being serious?" Lerides dropped her hand. "He's a man of expediency."

"So you don't think he has a conscience?" She half turned to glance at the old man. The water was dribbling from his eyes, so that he appeared to be weeping, and she felt an impulse to touch him, as if she might soothe his torture away. "Why is he drinking like that? Don't you remember what he was like when he first came to Kalepia? He was quite a robust old man. Now look at him. You'd think he had cancer."

"So I suppose you're feeling sorry for him."

"Yes I am!" she answered hotly. "It's only men who find pity degrading. Yes I do feel sorry for him! Think what he has to contend with. Not only all the practical considerations, but with dogma and traditions. He's probably tangled up in the Great Councils and the Church fathers." Why was there such contempt for tenderness, she wondered? "And on top of it all he thinks there must be some perfect answer. I suppose the Church implies that: if he fails to find an answer, it must be his fault. It can't be God's, can it?"

Lerides was softened by her defiance.

"Anyway," she went on more quietly, "the archimandrite knew perfectly well that superstitions follow the saints about. He didn't need me to tell him. He respects frankness"—she smiled faintly—"because he's not very good at it himself."

Lerides seemed mollified. He said half affectionately, half in irritation: "You're too clever."

"If I was clever I'd conceal my views. That's what clever wives do."

Lerides finished his glass of brandy. It always hurt his pride if she felt differently from him about anything. She linked her hand over his arm, yet looked away from him. Her face and her hand might have belonged to different people.

Lerides poured himself another glass and started, morosely, to drink it. On her other side the archimandrite was propped up comfortably by the arms of his chair. His cheeks looked as if they had been rouged.

Ekaterina felt rebellious about the whole issue of the new mine. She had watched other towns in the Republic grow rich through mining, and the process had dispirited her. She preferred the settled patterns of an agricultural people, their kindly slowness, their health, their candour. But nobody around her felt as she did, and she had learnt to stay silent until angered beyond endurance. Then she would bare her teeth at the Company's concept of progress, and spit out such heartfelt criticisms that people would say: "Ekaterina's got no sense of reality."

As for the archimandrite, she could not really like him. Self-importance always alienated her; and he seemed to fall into that wide category of men who strained to be strong, yet who were both better and more lovable when they were weak. But now he looked so peaceful, with his eyes almost closed and his face nestled into its beard, that she could nearly like him.

Beyond him, Julian Alastos was still talking with Sofroniou. The schoolmaster was listening strenuously, white wisps of hair sprouting comically from his head. He kept picking up his brandy-glass to find it empty, but when pressed to drink more would answer "No, no. One is quite enough, quite enough."

Alastos, with his dogged questioning, his restless desire to work everything out, was growing intense. He had forgotten to drink anything at all. The schoolmaster would lecture him in a plaintive, conciliatory way; then Alastos would say "Yes, yes, I think you are right there, I see that, but what about—?" And Sofroniou's face would pucker again while he tried to phrase a reply to something which was upsetting his ex-pupil's ideas. Sofroniou recognized this agitation from the man's youth. He was like a child trying to reshape the senseless data around it into something fair, something absolute. It was desperately exacting, thought Sofroniou, and he attributed it to a religious upbringing—moral sensitivity at war with rational evidence.

Certain things seemed to nag at the man like ulcers. There was this child which had died of typhus, for instance. When he spoke of it you suddenly noticed the aggression in his face. The child's death had committed an outrage against him. You might think that an embryo Socrates or Shakespeare had been crushed out. Well, Sofroniou thought, perhaps it had, but it was not likely. Children died every day. But the fact did no violence to any order of justice in the world, because there was no such order. Alastos admitted so; his reason agreed. Yet still this metaphysical turmoil went on, this fury to cure it all, as if the earth might be made to glisten if only some light were played on it. Yes, that was what was most peculiar. When all the evidence pointed one way, he nodded agreement then walked off in the other. Sofroniou sighed. If you saw a child dying of typhus, it was dying because its mother did not wash the lice out of its clothes. Its birth was pointless, its death sordid. There was nothing more to say.

Alastos, Sofroniou thought, was like a priest without a god. He was troubled, for example, that human character could be changed by chemicals or that a bad upbringing could pervert what he called a child's "natural right" to develop. What, Sofroniou had asked, was this natural right? What did it mean? There was no such thing as a natural right. And Alastos had clenched his teeth in frustration, and been unable to explain. The schoolmaster shook his head and lifted his brandy-glass again, forgetting its emptiness. All the same, he felt an affection for the man; he had not been in the usual run of students. Rather him, thought Sofroniou, than the ex-pupil sitting on his other side, returned from an insurance company in the Capital for a few weeks to flash himself among his friends. The old man always found that insufferable, and wished such people had remained tilling their orchards.

The archimandrite was now fast asleep. One of his hands dangled down, and the occasional silences revealed his gentle, regular wheezing. Ekaterina and Alastos were talking quietly across him. "I wonder what sort of a noise the archimandrite would make if you tapped him," Ekaterina whispered. "I believe he'd sound like a drum."

"Don't you dare tap him."

"I wasn't going to." She glanced at the archimandrite mischievously. "He looks so peaceful, I think he's dreaming of wines. Or is he asleep at all? I believe he's listening." She said in a tiny voice: "Archimandrite?"

Alastos was smiling at her fun. Perhaps she had not changed so much after all. She used to deflate him terribly. But now these humorous moments were rarer than he remembered. He found himself saying: "When you're making mischief you seem exactly the same." He used to pretend that she had inside her a monkey called Horrid, which needed exercise. It was one of an affectionate vocabulary which he had mostly forgotten. But he remembered this one, and said: "I hope Horrid has been taking regular walks."

But the moment he had said this it sounded, for some reason, sad. It seemed to be trying to reach a hand across the years, which could not be done. Ekaterina too felt a faint hurt. For both of them it had created an unwanted intimacy. "Oh, Horrid," she said, "he has his days." She was growing used to Julian now; she no longer distinguished between the past and the present man. They had grown together. "When you're puzzling something out you seem the same too," she said. "I was watching you with Sofroniou. I could tell exactly what you were up to." She could not help looking amused. "But you must have slackened off while you've been away. I've been waiting all this time for the world to be reordered, and it hasn't happened. 'What on earth's Julian doing?' I kept saying."

He laughed too loudly, then looked down less happily at his

hands, as if they had indeed failed. "You know, Ekaterina," he suddenly wanted to talk seriously with her, "it's depressing to look back on, that's true. You wonder what the hell you've been doing. After a year in Utah I thought: 'I must consider what I should be trying to achieve.' And then another year went by and before I knew it—five of them! Time goes like the devil if you keep doing the same thing, then you look back and can't tell one year from the next." His shoulders were tucked in, as if with self-reproach. "In fact by the fifth year I was so disgusted that I took the first job in England which offered. Just to move."

She was looking at him attentively; for some reason she badly wanted him happy. As she watched him, he was struck again by the strangeness in her good looks. The green-flecked eyes, stroking backwards, held a hint both of softness and emotional violence. She said: "But your work was only part of your life."

He wrinkled his nose. "Was it? Yes, I suppose it was." But work had been almost his whole life in Utah, all that he could much remember. There were women, of course, but he did not care to tell Ekaterina about them. In any case, he could barely recall a face, except Matty's. He had liked Matty just enough to deceive himself over her. She had worn a dreadful peaked cap all one summer, and he'd said it was great. There was a thing called a Go-Go Show, he could remember that. Everybody danced and shouted Wheeee! And she had said: Isn't it great? and he'd said: Great. And really it was awful and all he wanted to do was to go home to bed (with her) or just sit and read a book. The fact was that women were difficult to get in that town, and Matty had a lissom little body. Looking back, it was all rather pointless and you couldn't be proud of it. At least now that Ekaterina was staring at him in that slightly puzzled way, he began to wonder all over again how the years had slipped. There had simply seemed nowhere else to go, nothing which was more worth a man's doing; and the pay had been high and the miners a good lot.

And yes, there were the vacations. He told her about those, they seemed to give some purpose to it. He had even gone east and spent a week in West Virginia. "You should have seen the trees in the fall, Ekaterina, whole mountains on fire! I got a horse and trekked to a bluff of rocks where you could see the valleys spreading into the Carolinas—you'd have liked that." That had been something. There was a moment saved from the wilderness!

Ekaterina watched him with this gravity which was not precisely new to her. He wanted to tell her that she made a fine-looking woman, but he thought that this would beg a compliment in return, and she would be unable to give it.

As for her, she felt anxious, as if she was responsible for whatever might have happened to him. She wondered why he had not mentioned any woman; it seemed that either there had been somebody important or nobody at all.

He had been pulling at a bunch of grapes on his plate, and peeling them in a fastidious way which looked ridiculous in so big a man. Now for some reason he remembered the ballet. He thought he would tell her about that. At least it was an evening which he could distinguish, although he was quite unmusical. "But there was this ballerina," he said. "She was different from the others. She looked like a beautiful antelope. And she danced heroically—that's the word for it—as if she was not among the rest but thinking something all of her own. That was magnificent, I thought, that was the way to dance. Or was I biased?" He stopped suddenly, but he had gone too far with this story now. He pretended to take some grape pips out of his mouth.

Ekaterina repeated: "Biased?"

"Yes." How should he say it? He did not want her to imagine that he had thought about her more than he had. He felt a fool. "Well, you will laugh at me, but she looked like you. At least from the gallery. I thought: I didn't know Ekaterina could dance." He grinned sheepishly. "Of course I knew it wasn't you, and afterwards she came out of the stage-door and ..."—he turned back to his grapes, and added harshly: "she had enormous orange lips painted over her real ones...."

He noticed how odd his own voice sounded. Ekaterina was not saying anything. But he had never forgotten the effect of those lips, painted on an almost-familiar face. He said: "That was my first year in Utah—I was twenty-two, and what an idiot! I drank a bit too." He looked at his full brandy-glass; he never wanted to drink now. "But here's a curious thing: all the time I was working on that pit mine I told myself that I was gaining important experience, although I did not really believe it. But now—" he lowered his warm, too-powerful voice and glanced at the archimandrite, who still slept—"now, with this new mine, it looks like coming true."Can you imagine anything better for a man than to apply his experience to something he believes in? If it wasn't for my father, I'd be the happiest person in Kalepia ..."

He rolled some grapes about in his mouth. All the time he had been telling her this, he was thinking that she would now owe him some confidence in return. Perhaps that was why he had talked so much. But when he said, "Now what about you?" in his blunt way, she answered:

"Me? Well, I have a little girl now." Then she stopped. She did not know what to tell him. There seemed nothing to add. Sometimes she was fired with a mute rebellion: the mines, her husband, her whole life. She became aware of things moving—strong but half formed under her calm—things she had never articulated, and could not now. So she went on quickly to ask: "And what about your future?"

He turned round to her, shovelling away his plate. "My future's here. With the new mine." If he could have seen himself, he would have been mortified, because his arms had spread over the table and his hair, which he had damped down before coming, had sprung up again. But he could not see himself, and in his enthusiasm he had forgotten his anxiety about how uncouth he must appear to her. "I don't have to explain it," he said. "You'll understand. Of course it's the people's lives here. I suppose being abroad ruins your peace—when you come back and see this poverty, and hear this endless talk of money, money ... how-much-is-this? and what-did-you-pay-for-that? You'd think the whole world was composed of nothing but small change." He was growing excited. "It's not that education makes people happier. What the devil can do that? The important thing is that it develops you, it makes you more aware. Doesn't it? It gives you a choice. It's almost as if people have no choice here. They're born into prison."

Ekaterina said: "You speak as if you want people to develop in a special way."

The archimandrite moaned. His head flopped forward and pulled back. Then he burped, closed his eyes and was quiet again.

Alastos said: "To develop in a special way? No, not really. You make me sound like a missionary."

"And what's wrong with missionaries?" she asked. She wanted to tease him; she longed for him to laugh, to be as she remembered. It was like breathing another air.

"You're baiting me, Ekaterina. I remember this trick. Missionaries suffocate ..."

"And you?" Her face kept its mettlesome look.

"I wouldn't suffocate anything. I'd like people to evolve." He made a great scooping gesture with his arms. "To discover themselves!"

"And what if you disliked what they discovered?"

"Yes, I know. I've thought about that." He looked like a schoolboy who had anticipated some difficulty in a carefully-laid plan. "But by education I didn't mean knowledge or morality. You can stuff a man's head with those but he'll stay a fool. I meant imagination. It's the root of intelligent sympathy, isn't it? Clever men and even moral men may destroy each other's civilizations. But not imaginative men."

He sat back in his chair and gazed at her with an expression of earnest triumph, as if to say "Don't you see? That is what civilization is." He so much wanted her to see. Surely she understood, this intelligent woman?

But she was looking into her wine-glass, turning it in her fingers so that the lights in it twinkled. He wondered if he had offended her, she was so silent. He almost regretted his outburst. He had forgotten how to speak at dinner-parties, or perhaps he had never known. Looking at her turning and turning the glass with its lights, it seemed extraordinary to him that those fingers had once touched him, that he and she had actually been in love.

At last she said: "You may be right." But she was sure that he was wrong. Men learnt other things before imagination.

He toyed with his grape-stalk. Sofroniou was talking to the other young man, the insurance broker. Alastos had found nothing to say to that man. Men like that irritated him. The Republic was full of them. Sofroniou's wife was chattering to Lerides, who stared at her in a saturnine way, barely replying.

Alastos leaned towards Ekaterina again and asked: "Do you still think I'm a missionary?" He had been worried by that, but whether at the idea, or because it was she who had thought it, he did not know.

"Dear Julian, you mustn't be hurt by me." She was ashamed at worrying him; she'd only wanted to make him laugh; in fact she could only bear to talk of the new mine by creating laughter round it. "I tease because I've nothing to answer. You used to say I was intelligent, but I'm not in the least. I thought you'd have discovered it now that ... now. No, of course you're not a missionary!" Yet she found herself adding a little tensely: "But you must admit to two things in common. One is the certainty that you're right. And the other is your faith in people's potential."

He frowned, at himself rather than her. "Don't you have faith in people's potential?"

She said: "I'm afraid of it."

"So you'd have people kept primitive?"

"Oh," she answered, suddenly laughing, "that wasn't a government programme. That was just a fact."

Alastos burst into laughter. "What a nuisance I am! Sofroniou tells me I would find cosmic significance in a chick-pea!" He ran his hands through his hair, and asked her with his heavy humour: "But how can I change? My father told me that when he was a boy there was a widow who used to go round Kalepia selling a powder made from terebinth berries. Nobody ever bought it, but they said that two pinches in a glass of *ouzo* and you were under the table, laughing! Perhaps it would have cured me. But that widow must be dead by now. . . ." He looked at the exhausted face of the archimandrite. "The thing is, I'm not accustomed to believing in what I do. It's gone to my head. . . ."

"You organize the power excavator?" she asked, and added: "One day I'll come up and investigate this mine, since the next one will rule our lives."

"Yes, come, do come." He liked that idea. He could already imagine her walking along the rim of the excavating bench. That was what you missed in those arenas of rock; there was never anything feminine, not even a plant. "I'll expect you now," he said. "Come in the lunch hour. And next time I won't antagonize you with generalizations. That's a promise."

"You'll be tongue-tied," she laughed. "How will you speak?"

"I'll listen. You'll speak. You haven't said a word about yourself. Ten years is a long time. And I think you've learnt more than me."

She kept her tone bantering. "We find new mistakes."

"Then we'll talk of the future!"

This time she shook her head and said almost fiercely: "Of your newly-educated town? No."

"Why not?"

She leaned towards him, her hair sliding over her shoulders. She said: "Look opposite you."

Alastos looked. Opposite him Sofroniou's ex-pupil was turned towards the schoolmaster. Alastos realized that he epitomized the Republic's newly-educated élite. His outspread elbows seemed to corner the old man in his chair. His hands gestured near Sofroniou's face, touched the table with a scrape of gold-plated cufflinks, then lifted again, their fingers splayed out for the counting of figures. "The premium's only fifty-two drachma a week," he was saying. "This would cover not just the fabric of your house, but all fittings. That's against fire, theft ..."

"But as I say," Sofroniou's voice had dwindled to a mew, "I'm fairly well satisfied with my present policy. Yes, I know it's only a small firm...."

The man put up his splayed fingers again. "But I don't consider the sum sufficiently covers your library, if your valuation is accurate. Now we will cover you against everything but war or what is termed an act of God, that is to say earthquake ..."

Sofroniou managed a wisp of smile. "So you cannot insure me against God?"

"... and a premium of seventy-five drachma would carry added advantages...."

Alastos turned back frowning to Ekaterina. She was not smiling. At the other end of the table Mrs Sofroniou was making a move to stand up and usher her guests into another room, but she could not attract anybody's attention. Even Lerides, sitting next to her, was working out something of his own, tightening and slackening his jaw and narrowing his eyes; while the archimandrite had awoken—but only a little. Deep in their nest of beard his lips were moving, saying prayers.

Chapter Twelve

An acrid smoke filled the hall above the heads of the people, rising from cigarettes which were tapped away on to the floor and stubbed out against the backs of chairs. Two beams of sunlight hung solid and golden in the haze, like ingots. The people's voices were hushed, except for the harsh chatter of the fisherwomen at the back of the hall. In the first row of seats, beneath the platform, sat several of the Company's executives, while seated behind them were throngs of sallow miners. But the whole of the centre of the room was occupied by a black mass of sombrely-dressed men, fidgeting and muttering. Many of the classes and professions had grouped themselves together, and although they were dressed much alike it was obvious at which place the tradesmen and small officials merged with the dockers, and the dockers with the fishermen. But at the back of the hall were a few rather comical rows, varied as a line of saints on an iconostasis in which class and sex were helplessly jumbled; and at the last moment the imbecile God-Asleep ran stooping in and squatted by the feet of the policeman at the door.

Matheopoulos sat in the middle of some twenty workers from his flour-mill: a severe, spreading figure who now and again lifted his watch from his breast pocket; he would flick open the little silver cover and touch the timepiece to his ear to make sure that it still ticked. In the centre of the mass, Kallis waited with Philippou, the fisherman. The thin, sleek man was dressed unobtrusively. The fat genial one sat in shirtsleeves and a pair of oil-stained trousers, which he tried to conceal by balancing a straw hat over his knees.

The place started to overflow. Some thirty men were left at the back, leaning against the wall whose chalk rubbed off on their suits. Alastos could only find a chair at the side of the room. From there he could see along the row of mining personnel and could talk to Caroline without raising his voice. Claudia sat on one side of her, Howard on the other. Claudia looked too pale, he thought, and was smoking hard. Beyond her were the young Armenian and Muller, the Mine Superintendent, with Lerides, Ekaterina and two Americans—the Chief Engineer and the Mine Safety Officer. Lerides kept turning round to look over the faces of the audience. Ekaterina was biting her lip. Only the German, Muller, looked unperturbed, and sprawled with his legs apart and his hands on his hips, thumbs rammed into the pockets of his overalls. On the other side of the hall Sofroniou, squashed between two weathered farmers, wore such a look of squeamishness that Alastos had to hide his smile.

While one of the town councillors introduced Oldenburg at unnecessary length, Alastos looked round to see if the archimandrite was there. But he only glimpsed a chubby deacon who had perhaps been sent to report on the meeting.

Oldenburg's lecture was delivered in a terse monotone. He only had recourse to notes when he was reading statistics. Raised on the platform, he struck a powerful figure, well dressed and groomed for him, and never hesitating in what he said. Of course it was all slightly ridiculous. Somewhere in the dense blackness of those three hundred were the twenty or so people who had come to listen to a lecture on copper-mining in the Levant, but the rest were simply waiting for the General Manager to finish as he promised with the 'brief survey of the Company's future'. Yet the bulk of his speech was delivered without concession to the audience. The few allusions which he made to Kalepia were buried in their context. He talked precisely as if the people's total interest was in the exploitation of low-grade ore-bodies or in how the top-slice system had given way to the block-caving system.

The tension slackened. After five minutes the men began to look down at the floor or pull on the creases of their trousers; after ten minutes heads were held in hands, cigarettes lit surreptitiously and whispered conversations began. By the end of three quarters of an hour, during which the ingots of sunlight moved up the walls and melted against the ceiling, these conversations had risen to a respectful purr. Even the mining personnel looked bored, and Lerides was cleaning his nails, one with another. Only Caroline remained gazing intently at her father, leaning forward on her folded arms.

After reading out another group of statistics, Oldenburg tucked his notes into his pocket. The purring instantly died. He talked a little about the future of mining in Cyprus, but everybody knew that he must be nearing the end. Alastos desperately hoped that he would speak with tact and that when it came to questions he would not crush individual complaints with his usual monosyllables. Alastos was afraid above all that the Company might turn into some grim-faced philanthropist, whom people used but did not like. It must show sympathy at the outset. And although Alastos now knew Oldenburg's manner well, he could not believe that the General Manager would not soften a little at this important moment.

Everyone's face was again turned in the direction of the platform. Oldenburg moved quite smoothly from the Company's past year to the possibility of the new mine, so smoothly, in fact, as to make it seem entirely official and just. This was not a device, but lay naturally in his manner, and when he went on to say that the Company would hope to employ a minimum of a hundred new men in its first year, the figure sounded as solid and verifiable as a company record. He then gave the categories of semi-skilled labour in which these men would work, remarking perfunctorily that he hoped the workmen would all be recruited in Kalepia. This figure for new employment, he added, was more than double the number of young men who generally emigrated each year, and must represent a boom in a town of less than six thousand. Then he gave examples of salaries, which were a little lower than Alastos had hoped, but higher than those of workers in any other field, and he said that there should be an added need for mechanics and lorry-drivers after two years. He finished by remarking that the dues which would be paid to the municipality for various rights—he mentioned port installations—would be heavy enough noticeably to raise the quality of life in the town; and that the Company had offered the See of Nikitari, at a modest price, a suitable site for a new shrine.

Nobody in the hall stirred while he spoke, and there was no interruption. The people seemed impressed but not enthusiastic. They did not look as if they disbelieved Oldenburg; but at the same time they did not seem to connect this spate of figures with themselves. Perhaps they would have to see before they understood. This ocean of faces was not stupid. Many of them, in their intense concentration, struck Alastos as sensitive and sharp. Their eyes glittered like blackberries. But their vision, he knew, was drastically limited. For a space they saw keenly; beyond, they saw nothing at all.

He felt relieved by Oldenburg's speech. The General Manager had given public promises, and they sounded generous. He had obviously worked over his figures with Lerides, and had decided on all the solid assurances which could be offered. When the good of the Company coincided with that of the people, all went well. It remained to see if it could show understanding on the personal problems, on indemnity and environment. Oldenburg ended with no change of tone: "That concludes the lecture and I will answer any questions now."

He ended so abruptly that a second's silence followed. The row of Company executives had brightened. Claudia's cheeks showed a touch of colour, and Lerides sent Muller a curt nod of approval, although they hated one another.

It was the Mine Geologist who broke the silence: "This training you intend giving for semi-skilled labour, Mr Oldenburg—will the trainees be paid?"

Alastos felt an immediate disgust, the question was so obviously manipulated. And when Oldenburg answered "They'll be on full pay," a number of simple folk at the back started clapping and cheering.

"And what about sickness benefit?" asked Lerides. He was looking at Oldenburg in perfect seriousness.

Alastos grasped his knees in anger. As far as the bulk of the hall was concerned, these were disembodied Greek voices whose demands were being handsomely answered. The audience had been given fifteen minutes question-time, which was being whittled away in tricks. He glanced down the rank of executives. They were all looking at Oldenburg with satisfaction, except for the women. Claudia and Ekaterina gazed into their laps, while Caroline appeared puzzled. It was a revolting device. Alastos suspected that Lerides was responsible, because Oldenburg, when he answered "Sick men remain on full pay provided the circumstances are reasonable", did so in a voice of faint surprise, as if to say "You know that, don't you? You pay them." Now the cheering was louder, and several women at the back were murmuring "Yes, Oh, yes", "Very good", "Blessed Virgin."

But this time, before the clapping had died, somebody from the centre of the hall asked: "How long is the average life of an open-cast mine, Mr Oldenburg?" Because the man was hidden and his voice unnaturally raised, Alastos did not at once realize who he was; but the phrasing of the question was familiar.

"It's hard to be exact," Oldenburg answered, "but I'd expect nine years of this one." Whatever one felt about the General Manager, he was not evasive.

"So after nine years," the voice continued, "the men you have trained will be left without employment or qualifications for any other work?"

The people in front of this speaker had turned round to look at him, and Kallis was visible sitting back very coolly in his seat, his head tilted up. He was creating unnecessary difficulties, Alastos thought. No pit miner expected to work on the same location all his life.

Oldenburg stumped across the platform to obtain a better view of his interrogator. "After nine years," he said briskly, "the Company would negotiate another site. We're not going out of business. There are several promising sites in this area, though none as rich as the present one. But that is far in the future."

It had to be admitted that Oldenburg was impressive in his way. Alastos was reminded of those brightly-lit cabinets at the Capital fair. You pressed a button against whatever question you wanted answered, and out it came on a slip of paper: exact, almost official. The trouble had been, Alastos remembered, that all sorts of questions were not printed on the cabinet at all. It was no good kicking or banging it or enticing it with a ten drachma piece. It simply did not contain the machinery for that sort of answer.

Now Kallis said: "So you can guarantee to keep up a steady level of employment, Mr Oldenburg? Why then have fifty open-cast workers been laid off the present mine during the last fourteen months?"

"Because while that mine was expiring, our negotiations with the Church for a new site were complicated by Kalepia's loss of episcopal status," said Oldenburg. "That is why we weren't able to hold on to the men. The situation was unusual. It will not recur."

The faces of that intent, dark mass in the hall centre were neither pleased nor disappointed, but they looked at the General Manager with respect. On their fringe the deacon sat mildly, cradling his headgear. Only three minutes' question-time had expired.

But Matheopoulos was agitated. His fingers were running up and down his waistcoat buttons as if he was playing an accordion. "You mean ..." he said suddenly, but his thin, melodious voice gave out. He cleared his throat. "You mean that in nine years all this will be finished, and we will be left with a disfigured town?"

That was precisely the sort of question which Oldenburg was unable to accept on its own terms. He stood foursquare, his arms stiff at his sides. Some of the women still murmured "Oh, yes," "Oh, fine," at the back, and God-Asleep was audibly mumbling "... says Mr Oldenburg says Mr Kallis says ..."

Oldenburg answered: "Nothing will be finished, Mr Matheopoulos. The men will continue to be employed. And the conveyor installation at the port will go on serving mines over the whole district. The appearance of an expired mine is not an economic factor."

Matheopoulos took off his glasses as if he no longer wanted to see Oldenburg, since Oldenburg refused to perceive him. He said something which even those close to him did not hear; it was meant only for himself.

A faint commotion had been taking place at the back of the hall during this exchange. Two or three stout peasant women were pushing forward a bow-legged man whose head was sheathed in flattened white hair as if normally compressed by a hood. Every time he tried to step back the women behind pushed him forward, and at last, as Matheopoulos finished, he remained standing where he was and said: "What will happen to the olive trees, Mr Oldibur?" His voice was so small that the question had to be relayed up through the audience.

"The olive trees." Oldenburg peered at the back of the room. He liked to see his questioners, but the man was invisible. "It's up to the Church to indemnify the needy," he said.

The man had not understood. "Where?" he asked. "Where in ... indem ... ?"

Oldenburg grunted: "Can you speak up?"

Caroline gave Alastos a look of mock despair. She and her brother were for once in agreement. Howard was shaking his head and adjusting his glasses as if this stupidity was beyond belief.

The peasant women whispered and nudged the man. They were all but speaking through him. At last he said: "We went to the residence and asked ... this morning ... asked the bishop." He evidently thought Drosinis a bishop. "The bishop said the Company would in ... in ..."

"Indemnify," said somebody else.

"I can't help that," Oldenburg answered. "We've made ourselves plain."

Alastos felt a hot dryness coming into his mouth. Somebody had to do it. All the same, he was surprised when his own voice said: "But if the Company and the Church both expect each other to compensate the poor, who is going to do it?"

Somebody should do something, he thought; it seemed a natural thing to point that out. So he was astonished to see the whole row of executives turn and look at him with hostility. Lerides, Muller, the two Americans, the Mine Geologist, the senior foreman—every one of their faces seemed to be saying "Shut up!" He stared at them for a second in amazement, then glowered back. They turned away. The only face which remained staring was that of Howard, which wrinkled its nose inquisitively. Caroline was blushing at her lap and biting in her whole lower lip as if she might burst into tears.

Alastos continued to gaze at them, but quite newly. He had no idea that things had gone this far. He wanted to touch Caroline's shoulder or whisper something to her, but she was too far away. He planted his elbows on his knees and bent his head into his hands. Why hadn't he noticed it before? They were afraid.

"This lies outside our field," Oldenburg said. "I'm here to answer questions on copper-mining."

Immediately Kallis called out: "I have a particular question. How large an area will the new works cover?"

"That's impossible to say." Oldenburg drew his lips against his teeth.

"But they will be as extensive as the old mine?"

"More so."

"Ah." That quick, smooth "Ah" escaped Kallis like a warning. Nothing could have sounded less like a light being switched on, but it was precisely of this that it reminded Alastos. "I've been making some calculations myself, Mr Oldenburg—very careful ones," the silky tone continued, "and if the new pit works are even the same size as the old"—he stood up to make sure that he was heard all over the hall, while the quietness of his voice in the silence created its own tension—"every house within five hundred metres of the summit of the Mountain will have to be demolished."

This remark had the most extraordinary effect. For a moment—it was almost possible to see the lifted faces—everybody in the hall mentally gazed up from his home to the summit of the Mountain. With its white hump of shrine and scattering of dwarf oaks, it was like a physical presence in the room. For a full ten seconds it hypnotized them all. How far was it from each of them? Was it five hundred metres? Could it be so much? Was it four hundred and fifty? On a clear day . . . Six hundred?

Then, one by one, the alarm touched the people. It ran and jumped up like an underground weed all over the audience and in every profession. Instantly the germ of respect which had been growing in the people's minds was smashed, and they reverted to the distrust which generations of misrule had made natural to them. In every row men stood up and shouted: "Tell us everything! Give us the truth!"

"Forty families will be moved! That's the truth!" shouted Kallis.

Yet in spite of their alarm, these faces looked as though they had found their own nature. The strained deference had gone. It was as if they had only been awaiting this discovery, as if it had never been a question of whether or not they were being betrayed, but a question of how. And now, shouting and demanding, the black mass was relieving itself of a huge frustration, seeming to say "What fools we were! Of course! We ought to have known! Nobody gives anything!"

It was this acceptance of the selfish and unscrupulous as natural which blurred the edge of their indignation, and which made Alastos feel as if all his entrails were slipping down inside him with despair. It was as if within their enmity the people also laughed a little, were a little triumphant. They had discovered the fakir's trick. For a moment he had almost convinced them. But now the game was up.

Even Marangos had momentarily sunk his jealousy of Kallis. Slouched immobile in a crowd of gesticulating dockers, he smirked slightly and nodded his massive head, muttering "So that was the hitch."

After sufficient disappointment, Alastos thought, five or six generations of rotted hopes, a whole people could be turned like that. Suspiciousness leaked from parent to child like a hereditary disease, until in a village, a city, an entire nation, there remained no single person who trusted or expected any more. That was what four hundred years of Ottoman rule had done to the Republic.

Oldenburg remained expressionless, waiting for the hubbub to diminish. The voices now agitated for particulars. Several were crying "Give us the names of the householders! Give us names!" Alastos thought that what Kallis had said about the mine's extent was roughly true. But forty families? Could that be right? He had himself wondered about the houses scattered in the folds of the middle slopes, but they had not seemed so many. Now they had suddenly grown formidable. Forty houses meant two hundred people.

The miners and staff had mostly turned round during the clamour, and in the fading light their faces looked more strained. Matheopoulos was rubbing his forehead with both hands, but as the noise died a little he called up: "That must include the homes of the goatherds. They are not even represented here." But Oldenburg could not hear him.

Alastos felt bewildered. He averted his stare to Caroline and Claudia, sitting together. Caroline's face remained turned to her father, impatiently waiting for him to refute. Claudia was gazing at nothing; she appeared not to belong in the hall at all. In the superficial similarity between mother and daughter, one might have been the other twenty years before or hence.

Oldenburg had stood stolidly all this while, occasionally looking down at the silent miners. But as the noise stopped he barked out: "These are not the Company's figures! We have no finished reports whatever! And anybody who has to move will be rehoused at the same standard as he was housed before—or better. This will be our first priority."

A number of voices, more subdued, asked "Where? Rehoused where?"

"It's too early to decide."

Kallis asked "On Company land?"

Oldenburg again walked to the edge of the platform so that he could get a clear view of the man, and addressed him directly: "Mr Kallis, you are spreading unnecessary alarm. I have given my answer on rehousing. As to the numbers, it's impossible even for the Company to know at this point, let alone you. The engineering of an open-cast mine is not as elementary as you seem to think—there can be many approaches to a single site. Please speak within your knowledge."

Kallis, who had remained cool until now, flushed. "My knowledge, you say! My knowledge is enough for yours not to blind me!" His voice rose to falsetto. "Unnecessary alarm you call it!

When you plan to pollute our sea, demolish our houses, desecrate our saint and turn our town into a living pit! Unnecessary alarm!"

A few of the dockers cheered, but the rest of the crowd seemed to think that Kallis had overreached himself. He was starting to spoil his own argument simply by his manner. A tactitian in debate would have tried to pique him further, but Oldenburg simply shrugged his shoulders and returned to the centre of the platform. Kallis, alone in his rage, saw that he was in danger of losing the people's confidence, and recovered himself. "If rehousing is your first priority," he said in a voice dark with control—the change in it was too sudden—"you and the municipality must surely have some idea of where you intend to build. You'll not only have forty families from the Mountain, but thirty from the port."

"Those are your figures, Mr Kallis, not mine."

"They are the minimum figures," replied Kallis confidently, "the bare minimum."

"Cunt," exclaimed a coarse voice. Marangos did not move a limb or even bother to look at Kallis. "Pure goat's cunt," he said.

Kallis continued as if no one had spoken. "Even if the loading installation were to run into the port from the side of the Mountain, it would remove thirty houses, coming out, say, through the Angira Restaurant."

A man jumped to his feet and bawled: "Through my restaurant! Who's sending anything through my restaurant?"

Oldenburg jerked his shoulders in exasperation, and looked up at the hall clock whose minute hand moved on with an obedient click. Question-time was half over. He said: "If nobody has any more questions..."

"My question still stands!" Kallis shouted. "Where will you rehouse all these people? You must have plans, if you care at all. We have a right to know!"

"True! True!" cried many voices.

Howard, with a judicial look, exclaimed "True!" His voice died among the rest like a woodwind among brass, but Caroline turned on him. Her fingers tensed, as if they might tear him.

"Howard!" She bared her teeth. *"Shut up."*

"It is true," he said.

Kallis called up again: "Where will you rehouse?"

The room fell silent; the mass stilled itself for an answer. The summit of the Mountain of St Vichinos still haunted them all.

Many of them, Alastos sensed, had continued mentally to pace those five hundred metres to the crest, and probably dozens of people in the audience, including everyone living round the port, felt unsure of their future. During this instant's quiet the drivel of God-Asleep was distinctly audible: "Forty-three for seven then eh? Those are my figures and yours then. How's that? That's a minimum. Can't quarrel with that then eh?..."

Oldenburg ran his tongue round inside his cheeks. His square body and shining head looked less like a man and more than ever like a piece of machinery. Until now his answers had come pat and expressionless; but he hesitated a moment before saying: "Land can't be wasted. The Company will probably make part of the present open-cast site available when the mine expires."

Lerides sank his head in his hands.

Six or seven voices rose together and an ominous hum of conversation spread behind them. "So you'll house us in your waste!" "You've bribed the municipality!" "You can't do it!"

Oldenburg barked back: "The municipality has power of compulsory purchase if it considers the circumstances beneficial to the town as a..."

"No, Frank, no!" Lerides was furiously shaking his head. He looked as if he was about to get to his feet.

But a tremendous hubbub had arisen from one part of the hall. Some thirty fishermen had got to their feet and were voicing a single, deep-mouthed complaint. They did not want to be rehoused away from the sea. They stood with their woollen caps in their hands, shouting their rights as they understood them. Their frayed waistcoats were unbuttoned over their shirts. Most of them were middle-aged or old. Between the high boots and baggy trousers hitched in at the knee, their legs showed wan and spindly. One man, in particular, with bright blue eyes, caught Alastos' attention. The lines of his face bit deep, and a snow-white moustache plunged over his mouth. He must have come expecting to defend his saint, not himself, for he had tied a reproduction of St Vichinos round his neck. "Leave us the sea!" he bellowed. "We're seamen! Leave us alone!"

Alastos noticed the fisherman from the delegation too, in the same brown coat, and the man who had rowed him into harbour two months ago. The complaint of these people had a sober ring, less impassioned but more sturdy than that of the tradesmen. It neither threatened nor pleaded. But it expected justice. And now the women had joined in, holding their scarves modestly to their mouths but shrieking from behind them.

Some bank employees near Alastos were passing cigarettes between each other and enjoying the spectacle. The postmaster and the district inspector of schools were sitting with them. They shrugged their shoulders.

"The fellows can't even speak coherently," said a banker.

"Look at the one with the sun-hat. Oh mother!"

"The sea belongs to them, does it?"

These other men, Alastos thought, looked well cared for. Their glossy hair crinkled at their ears and necks. They were the type of men about whom you first noticed the immaculate cuffs and manicured hands. He glared at them. The prejudice of his own hard profession stiffened him. Everything about them riled him. Why did they have to hold their cigarettes like that—disdainfully, since they drew on them with such delectation? How they savoured! And they seemed entirely self-confident, which could not be true. Yet these were the favourite children of the Republic. Go into any government office, any bank, and there you would find two or three of them, seated at their desks with cups of coffee and bags of small sweets which they inspected like cats in their little nurtured hands, before deigning to gobble. All very well for them to laugh at the burnished fishermen! A dying business, of course, fishing. You could discount it.

The seamen were still shouting hoarsely. Alastos wondered what such fishing felt like. Quiet work, he supposed, but laborious and paid next to nothing. Sometimes you followed the shoals all night. Red mullet was the main catch: a slim, delicious fish, but never big. In winter you banded together in the larger boats, because the storms could be sudden. Mending nets, caulking timbers. It was not a business which left much room for dishonesty or laziness. Which was more than you could say for civil servants. Then one day, out of the blue, you hear that you might be moved two kilometres away and housed under slag heaps. A Greek, his father used to say, should never lose sight of the sea. It was the spine of his people.

The men were still calling out, sporadically, leaving Oldenburg gaps in which to answer them; but the General Manager stood like a schoolmaster who feels that his presence is sufficient to require silence.

Someone tapped Alastos' shoulder. He looked up and saw Sofroniou rather pale, his hair dishevelled.

"It's growing a little rough over there," he said. "Could I share your seat?"

Alastos moved over. "Not as rough as I'd be if I was them," he said heavily. "Especially at that age. Half of them must be over sixty."

"Oh I'm quite in agreement with you." The schoolmaster shot him a look. "Quite in agreement. A fisherman should not be taken from the shore. It would make for all sorts of inconveniences ... all sorts."

The district inspector of schools, a friend of Sofroniou, leant over from among the bank officials and said: "Getting jumbled with the fishermen? They might have slit your gills for you!"—then added his favourite disparagement: "No education, that's the trouble—none at all!"

"All the same," Sofroniou said tentatively, "it's wrong to move them."

"They'll get used to it," the inspector said.

Alastos writhed. He asked rudely: "Since when have you been walking two kilometres to the office every day?" He thrust his hands into his pockets.

The inspector glanced at him up and down, then withdrew his conversation to the bank officials.

Sofroniou looked peevish and edged further on to the seat. "You should not have said that."

"Why not?" asked Alastos. He jerked his thumb at the bankers. "Look at that lot—I'd like to see them on a rough sea!"

"There's nothing wrong with a little self-respect," said Sofroniou.

"Self-respect!" Alastos was growing thoroughly angry. "How dare they have self-respect! Laughing at fishermen! Just try housing them in somebody else's industrial shit."

Sofroniou made a hushing noise. "Listen," he said quietly. His glasses had slid on to the tip of his nose; he pushed them back. "When men like these have bettered themselves in a single generation, they naturally..."

"Bettered themselves? What's better about them?"

"Their education is better," said Sofroniou, "and only the other evening you upheld the value of that to me ... only the other evening."

Alastos was silent. He rasped his hands over his cheeks and ran them through his hair. His body felt sticky. He thrust his shoulders angrily against the wall. The fishermen were still on their feet. It seemed to him as if the old delegate in the patched suit had been duplicated thirty times in them. They looked grizzled and foolishly innocent. And they continued to shout, asking was there nowhere else for them?—not demanding higher wages or threatening to strike as workers did at the Capital, but asserting the meanest fact: that fishermen live by the sea. They threw all statistics to the winds. And he felt a terrible urge to jump to his feet and start shouting with them.

But the tumult was dying down. The fat fisherman sitting next to Kallis called out: "Mr Oldenburg, is it true that copper occurs in the human liver?"

"Yes," said Oldenburg, frowning. "That is correct."

He asked: "Then wouldn't it be simpler for you to chop out our livers and use those?" He gleefully clapped his hands at his own joke and banged Kallis on the back. But nobody laughed. The people seemed to flinch. The macabre fantasy remained in their imaginations. It epitomized what they felt.

"Question irrelevant," said Oldenburg.

But the whole meeting was relapsing into turmoil. Men sprouted from all parts of the audience and shouted their anxiety or defiance. The questions were mainly about the shrine now and a trill of *"Panaghia!"* and *"Christos!"* ran back and forth among the women, while the older men crossed themselves. Oldenburg refused to answer most of these half-articulate demands, and stared at the clock as if to bully it into motion. There was a minute left. Anyone less self-demanding would have quitted the platform long before. But the official span was fifteen minutes and he would give fifteen minutes.

In the middle of a lull, it was Kallis who stood up to ask: "And where will the site for the new shrine be?"

Oldenburg's face tightened. Alastos searched for a strain of triumph in Kallis, but there was none at all. His eyes had that unhealthy, perspiring look and his lower lip was drawn down bitterly from his teeth. He was shaking. He leaned his hands forward on the back of the chair in front. It seemed to support him. For a moment Alastos thought that Oldenburg might evade the question, since again a second elapsed before he answered. Then the General Manager said: "We have offered the See a position above the present open-cast site."

"Oh Lord," whispered Sofroniou. "That in the waste too?"

A peculiar, muffled sound escaped the crowd, like a tired groan. It was as if some diluvian creature was dying after a long torment. The people had suddenly assumed one identity. The officials and bankers had been absorbed or pressed away at its flanks. And now, unmistakably, the creature was shaking its head, groaning. It was saying "This is the finish." For a few seconds it seemed to accept in despair this last act of ungraciousness. Then, slowly, the notes of its great voice grew harder and louder. The mass began to stir. It was swelling itself upright, flexing its sinews, roaring. The noise was terrible.

Alastos felt Sofroniou's bony grip on his arm. "This won't do. This won't do at all. We can't reach the door."

But whatever else the creature threatened, there was scarcely a hint of physical violence about it. Why this was so, Alastos could not say. It was not that the monster was harmless, not at all; more as if it had only just awoken, and now stretched itself, feeling its power. The men stood in the ranks where they had sat, moving their arms in short, cutting strokes to the rhythm of their voices. Slogans exploded and died amongst them, but the only ones discernible were a taunting cry from the dockers: "Think again, think again!" and a deeper, more consistent baying which rose from the end of the hall: "Ayios Vichinos! Ayios Vichinos! Ayios Vichinos!"

Matheopoulos pressed himself to within a few feet of the platform and called up as loudly as his voice permitted: "Mr Oldenburg, this is too high-handed! You see what is happening! I beg you to reconsider!" The town councillor, who had climbed on to the stand to read his thanks to the lecturer from a slip of paper, tried to perform this duty in a ludicrous effort to quieten the people. But even Alastos, who was standing nearby, only heard "I'm sure . . . most interesting. . . ." The paper quivered between the man's fingers. Oldenburg descended without a word.

Looking round from his superior height, Alastos saw that the policeman had discreetly vanished from the door. He also glimpsed Kallis. Now that everybody else was angry, Kallis looked slightly green; his lips were parted against his tongue. He was continually staring round him, but it was difficult to tell if he was exhausted, or bewildered by the sheer volume of noise; or whether in his heart he was not alarmed at the monster which he had set free.

The miners had also stood up, and now that Oldenburg was amongst them they turned away from the platform and found themselves facing the crowd. The staff looked haggard, except for Muller whose face had reddened with exasperation. "Bloody fools!" he ranted. "What do they want to do? Go back into caves?" He shouted at those nearest him: "Pull yourselves together! Wake up!" But his Greek, bawled in a coarse Bavarian accent, went uncomprehended. So he folded his arms over his chest and simply shouted at them: "Boo! Boo!" Some ten or fifteen of the miners started to boo also, tentatively at first, then more loudly, and this lowing sound penetrated the whole hall.

Caroline stepped over to Alastos, her teeth clenched. "Doesn't it make you sick?" She glared at the crowd. "They're just afraid their silly little pilgrimage profits will go. I suppose they sell a few things. Boo! Boo!" She jabbed him in the ribs. "Come on! You've got a big voice. Boo!"

He laid a hand on her shoulder. "Stop it! You'll only make things worse. Stop it."

She stared at him. She looked defiant. He thought that her anger was going to be deflected to him, but she said nothing. He scrutinized the rest of the mining people. Howard's hands were fidgeting about his face, incessantly readjusting his spectacles. Ekaterina stood with her back to the platform, looking not afraid but miserable. Claudia and Adourian were next to her. That was the only sight which brought a smile to Alastos. The Armenian's right arm rested along the platform behind her back, curved in a protecting gesture which did not actually touch her and which she did not notice. She stood perfectly composed, bored almost, waiting for it all to end.

But Lerides had turned white. He had probably anticipated the crowd's mood earlier than anybody. Now he was obviously afraid that this passive creature would start to reach forward. Even a casual pawing would sweep them all away. He was pushing grimly among the booing miners, jolting and snapping at them to be silent.

But possibly the only important person in the hall at that moment was the man through whose eyes the archimandrite would see. The deacon, jostled on either side, had laced his hands meekly round his headgear to prevent it being knocked away. But underneath it he had been concealing a bag of tomatoes and several of these were now rolling about under his feet. Every time he bent to collect one, another was jogged out onto the floor. So while the crowd roared its anguish, the deacon was for much of the time bent double, scooping about among the stamping boots.

As for Alastos, he stood mesmerized by the crowd, one hand on Caroline's shoulder left over absent-mindedly from a gesture which had not been to protect, but to restrain. The noise of the people had lessened. Some were even starting to leave. But now he could hear more clearly, in his own head, a sharper sound which promised its own misery. He wiped his hand across his forehead. Inside his skull a pressure was building. Everything was confused. All the delicate structure of his belief was shifting. It made him sick. He thought: "Just as everything was so good." But the pressure went on. It throbbed and hardened. He drew his fingers in slow exasperation back and forth over his scalp. His hair had gone lank and sweaty. Wait, he thought. Tomorrow. Leave it until tomorrow. Now he was tired, he was not seeing things in perspective. He must pause. Then he must rethink. He would rethink it all.

Where the road from the town went down to the mines, crossing the river on a stone bridge, there grew an eccentric mulberry tree. Every winter the local farmers said that it would not last another year; but every spring, for three hundred years, it had thrust out leaves as huge as trays. Now its branches sprawled along the ground on struts, and in summer it looked like a badly perforated umbrella.

Alastos and Caroline approached this tree on the way back to her home, she walking in a brisk, determined way, he lumbering disconsolately beside her. The conversations in other streets were growing indistinct, and although it was still light Kalepia had reverted to its usual lonely appearance of a late evening. During the past week Caroline and he had several times sat in childish fun under the mulberry tree, concealed inside its tent of leaves, listening to the evening noises, kissing. To pass it without stopping now seemed an insult to one another, and they both halted uncertainly, he dragging his feet and she half turned away.

She said vehemently: "Did you ever see anything like that? It was just a rabble! Shouting about their rights. Don't they ever want to give up anything?"

Alastos began: "It's all very well for..." Then he stopped and grimaced. He could not think coherently. A hundred different ideas and sympathies were galloping in disorder round his head. Caroline, by her averted shoulders, might have been asking him to touch her; but he could not. He felt fixed to the ground; all his weight had plunged down into his legs. He looked at the back of her head, the separate strands of yellow and brown. They appeared beyond his touch.

"Nobody here gives a damn for anything but themselves," she said. "Can't they give a single thing? Nothing?" She turned at him, flushing. "They ought to be made to! They ought to be made to sacrifice to the town!"

Alastos looked at her uncertainly. "They are the town," he said. He was so tired that he thought his eyes were going to close then and there. "Those people—those are what we're talking about. That's Kalepia." If he had been alone, he felt, he might have gone to sleep under the mulberry tree. "And they feel they're being sacrificed to the Company." That at least was obvious, he thought. He held his neck with both hands and gazed up where two bats fluttered like blown ash.

Caroline was not listening to him. "And you didn't help, did you, going on and on about the olives?" Her tone was resentful but not really bitter. She had only just remembered. When she looked up at him, the hurt was concentrated in two little furrows between her eyes.

"I didn't go on and on. I asked one question."

"Well, they went on and on," she said, "and you added to it."

He stared down at his feet. There was no point in arguing. He kicked the ground gently with one boot. The earth was noiseless with the rust of decayed leaves. He thought they had better walk on, but Caroline did not move. She was standing closer to him, yet she appeared still to be a long way away, as if he was looking at her through the wrong end of binoculars. She continued to talk and he to gaze. Her indignation was only strengthened by the challenge of his silence. All the weight of his back and shoulders was demanding to be laid down. But instead he kept up this slothful stare. She, who was always rejuvenating him, now made him feel old, far older than he had ever thought to be. It was like a distance down which he watched her.

The householders, she was saying, couldn't they be broad-minded? He mumbled something which dissatisfied her. But hadn't he said the same, she demanded, the evening after the delegation? Something had to be sacrificed. You never got anything free.

He said with his dogged humour: "But the price of this is soaring!"

She frowned and took him seriously. "Not compared with what people will be getting back." Her head turned from side to side in fury. "Nobody talked about the benefits. Did you notice that? Nobody once said 'That's good, Mr Oldenburg' or 'I'll be glad of that opportunity'. Oh no! Nothing like that. Just difficulties. Just 'We want everything!'" She clenched her fist again. Her voice was faintly tearful. "And those ridiculous men in waistcoats shouting about the sea! They don't deserve better standards!"

It must be the evening which was grey, he thought. It couldn't all be in his mind. The evening grey and pink. "Kalepia, famous for sunsets," said the tourist brochures. And now this grey-pink evening was washing everything together. Houses, sea, valley-side. And here was this girl, for whom he felt affection, talking to him with all the conviction in her, and he was scarcely able to listen. She jerked in front of him like a marionette, a pretty marionette whose vitality was inexplicable. He touched the side of her cheek as he had often done, but the gesture was almost inquisitive, as if to say: Ah yes, I see, it rises over the bone there, dips in here....

It reminded him of a dream which had recurred to him as a boy. In this dream he and another person were walking towards one another from a great distance; but always he woke up or the scene changed before they had met. Sometimes this happened almost at once and the person never became fuller than a silhouette. At other times they had come to within a few paces of one another and he had thought he knew the person and had held out his hand.

So this was where he and Caroline stopped short of one another; and it was not their decision, even if they thought it was. They simply could not go on. Would parting hurt her? Not much, he thought; that buoyancy, that self-assurance, were genuine. Again the tiredness enveloped him, the heaviness all round his chest. It was an effort to breathe. The evening so hot and close. Perhaps he had been wrong to look at her at all. He must have used her to relieve the pain of his father in him, but he was too tired to discuss that with himself, and Caroline was not the sort of girl who gave the impression of being used. He went on kicking the soft ground with his heel.

No, he felt certain; she would not be much upset. That was a relief, and a slight humiliation. As for him, it was depressing. Not sad; just depressing. Perhaps, he thought, he was past feeling that proper grief any more.

He looked up. How pretty she still was, with her brown skin and brown eyes! Even the gold in her hair looked confident. She was smiling at him. Happiness, certainty. To turn away from her seemed to be to say "These things are not so." She was still talking and he still pretending to listen, but he only heard notes and tones, which seemed sufficient, with now and again a "should" or an "oughtn't" or "Daddy"; and once or twice "you said yourself. . . ." People were always using that against him; he seemed to have said everything at one time or another. A fool could never shut up. All the same, these two people, unable to approach one another closer, had nothing to do with the mining controversy. That had only pointed out the distance between them.

For a little while she had been accusing him. "And only six weeks ago you were thumping the balustrade and saying you cared, that you'd always care."

He couldn't let that pass. He pulled himself upright. "I do care. It's just . . . not going to be as easy as all that. We've got to think more carefully. It's not so simple. . . ."

"Oh Julian, it's just as simple, if only they'd let it be. It will be anyway. They can't stop it." She looked at him in disappointment. He found himself examining the tilt of her nose and chin. They gave her a look of brittle affirmation. "It's a matter of whether you believe in the mine enough. If you believe, then you'll be able to enforce it." She crossed her hands to her shoulders as if she was cold. "But if you don't," she added, "then I suppose you give up."

Alastos could not tell whether this "you" was personal or general, but he thought that it was for him. She was giving him a last chance to be positive. Then she walked on over the bridge. So, he thought miserably, that's that. She had finally lost her freshness. The street lamps seemed to cast down pools of dimness instead of light. If you had to separate, he thought, this must be the most painless way. The break was disguised under their opinions about something else. Both of them recognized what it meant, but there was no need to say. He was not sure whether he liked that way of parting, but this, he supposed, was because of his urge to have everything definite, everything known. As if that was possible.

He watched her out of the corner of his eye, walking beside him. She looked depressed too, but firm. She went with a rather girlish stride. When they reached the house she apologized that she could not ask him in, her parents would be tired. Before she climbed the steps to the door he said: "Sorry." But precisely what this clipped word regretted was not certain. It had simply squeezed itself out, and remained suspended unacceptably between them.

Chapter Thirteen

The flour-mill ran to the hum of grain flying up and down transparent pipes, and to the throb of grinders. The whole plant seemed to function of its own accord on the flight of compressed air. Even the floor was spotless. The upper level, where two sieves shook together, was occupied by the brushing and cleaning units. Over the years, before the modernization of the mill, numberless backs had been crippled while hoisting the flour sacks on to the lorries which took them to Nikitari. But now the old millstones, with their steel rims still in place, lay disintegrating on the side of the road, and the lorries reversed under an overhead chute which sent the sacks thumping into their crates.

Matheopoulos had a small office on the upper storey. Through its glass door his figure could be seen on most days answering correspondence by hand on plain sheets of paper. Before midday he would emerge, tucking his gold-rimmed spectacles into an inside pocket and putting on a horn-rimmed pair, and would walk among his machines, paying them the same scrupulous attention as he gave to the men. But for the last week, since the night of Oldenburg's lecture, he had been preoccupied. His mill had become an unofficial headquarters for resistance to the new mining project and all through the middle of the day, in spite of the heat, people arrived, complaining.

Marangos rested his weight against a flour porter's trolley, slumping over the handles. He watched Kallis with a look of loutish indifference, but in fact he was thinking: "He's in his element now all right. He'll be running for mayor next." Kallis sat on a sack of flour, dangling his feet and keeping his back upright against another sack. That was a suitable perch for the little fellow, Marangos thought—a poor man's throne; he could sit puffed up half the day while the people came to him, and he would answer "We're doing this—" or "We mean to stop that—" and "Would you affix your name to this petition?" Smooth as a girl, flickering his pen in his hands. He made a man want to pulverize him. What would happen, Marangos wondered, if he slammed Kallis with a right hook to the jawbone? His eyes followed the trajectory which the body would take, over two piles of unstitched sacks, somersault against the floor, land up by the grain-washing unit.

Kallis was irritated by Marangos' leaning his great sweaty body on the trolley and watching him with that unblinking stare. But this was the only disharmony in the place. Several fishermen sat among the mill workers, eating lunch. Matheopoulos was checking the refuse from the cleaning and brushing machines, matted clumps of dirt and husk which he kneaded thoughtfully between thumb and forefinger.

Kallis ate a plate of cold *dolmades* which had been sent him by the owner of the Angira Restaurant. This proprietor, a fat young man who overcharged for his wines, seemed to think that Kallis knew precisely what the Company intended, as if he sat in on board meetings. But it was not for such as him that Kallis meant to stir a muscle or utter a word. Such people were a miniature bourgeoisie who sucked at the poor without anybody noticing. The restaurateurs, the owners of the larger shops and little businesses, they were the smaller pigs in the muck-house. Now they were alarmed because their pools of profit might be earthed in. All week they had been dribbling round the port and the flour-mill: warehouse proprietors, garage owners and the like. It was well to use them, but not consider them.

Of course they all wanted to know where the conveyor-belt loading installation would be, whose premises it would affect. His answers never precisely contradicted themselves, but somehow he had channelled this ghostly installation through half the town. A week ago barely a soul had even heard of such a thing. Now it haunted them all. There was nowhere it might not go and nothing it could not demolish.

During the past week Kallis had collected the signatures of all the householders along the dock and on the middle slopes of the St Vichinos Mountain, and they had been handed in at the municipality. He knew perfectly well that the municipality would do nothing, but the gesture had bound these people together. They were starting to speak for themselves. When nothing was done, they would feel personally slighted.

The whirr of Matheopoulos' machines was soft and conciliatory. Matheopoulos was the only successful person whom Kallis tolerated. But no one yet realized—let alone this old man—that nothing would be achieved without violence. That was how things had always been in the Republic. And in most other places, for that matter. Kallis wiped his palms on the sacking. If you wanted something, you had to grow strong enough to take it. As for these company businessmen, they would worm along on promises for as long as you let them. They'd flatter and placate, as they were trained to do, until only one answer remained: to put a fist in their face. Not because the poor could not speak in any other way, but because nobody listened to them any other way. So Kallis, with his delicate face and hands, anticipated violence.

He looked down from his height at the mill workers, sucking and gnawing their lunches. Philippou, who knew him better than anybody, was sitting with his back to one of the grinders, chewing olives, and called up: "Eh! Where will you send this loading installation next? How about weaving it round Nikitari? We could do with some support from there." He picked some olive stones out of his mouth and dropped them on the grinder belt, which snatched them away. "Or could it threaten the Capital?"

Kallis allowed him a smile. "We'll get all the support we need from here. You'll see." His eyes had narrowed. The narrower they grew, the harder he was thinking. Sometimes thinking closed them altogether and it looked as if he was asleep. "Everything's starting to move," he said. "The priest has set himself up in almost open opposition to the archimandrite."

"Oh Virgin!" cried Philippou. "So now we have two gods! What a purgatory!" He threw up his gaze to the roof, then suddenly bent forward earnestly: "Which will you take, now? The archimandrite? No offers? Fine old fellow, the archimandrite—all sniffle and shuffle. If a man asks a loaf of him, he gives him a reason. As for the other—" he crossed himself, "Christ preserve us! Look at the beard of him, clotted with last year's fodder. A ram from the herd of prejudice!" The mill workers burst into good-natured laughter.

Marangos remained propped against the trolley, but flicked his eyes towards Philippou. The fisherman was cradling his well-fed stomach in his hands and this, for some reason, irritated Marangos.

"The priest'll be the one for you," he grated. "No brain, just bladder."

Philippou abused Marangos, mimicking the priest's groaning voice, and the millers laughed again, rocking themselves with their arms clasped round their knees. Marangos' face did not change, but his hands, which hung loosely, clenched. Philippou noticed this and stopped talking.

"The priest'll suit us well," said Kallis. "He's not like the rest of them."

They were a solid crowd, these flour-mill workers, he thought, glancing round them: cheerful, straightforward. But this cheerfulness was also a drawback. They took everything too easily. The whole mill, in fact, ran as smoothly as a strong heart. The answer of these men, and most others, to any imposition from authority, was invariably "It can't be helped", "That's life". It scarcely occurred to them that life could be altered. They accepted treatment from the municipality which they would never accept from their next-door neighbours. They had no developed sense of rights. Instead they retained a self-perpetuating fatalism—acceptance of bad employers, bad government, a bad world. They would lie down before they were hit.

But now! They were beginning to stir. It was exhilarating to see. Most of them had at least a relative whose home was threatened. Continually they were asking would this house go or that house be spared? They were growing angry. The only way of safeguarding themselves, he had said, was to find their voice. Why did the municipality have power of compulsory purchase over their property, but not over that of the Church? Because the Church was holy? No, but because it was strong. Now it was up to them to grow strong. Find support. Multiply themselves.

He had made his calculations minutely from the large-scale military map of the Kalepia area which hung in the customs office. Then he had walked round the site itself. He had also accurately calculated the effect which this revelation would have on the lecture audience. He knew these people. The only reaction which he had not anticipated had been that of Oldenburg. To admit that the Company planned to resurrect the shrine on a slag heap! What was he thinking of? Was he a man or a ledger?

Kallis passed his hand across his face at the memory. The crowd round him had seemed to buckle for a second, as if everybody had cramp. Then this tidal wave. Listening to it, hearing its thunder released by a question which he had not even expected Oldenburg to answer, he had felt afraid. Not with the fear of what he had done, but of what he would now require of himself.

Unnoticeably, over years, he had been approaching that stage in failure when the past hangs too heavy, when a man evades thinking of his own waste and the passage of time, and when lack of opportunity becomes necessary to feed his self-pity; he attracts it, needs it.

And now, suddenly, he was pleading success of himself. The forces inside him were countermarching. They were trying to trample down his sour self-isolation. He did not want to reflect on their progress, in case he lost heart. He must take hold, keep active. Nothing must stagnate.

He watched Matheopoulos examining the grain-washing unit. The foam bubbled from under its casing. The old man was turning over in his hands the waste of tiny wet stones, and dropping them back in the refuse bag.

There was something else which Kallis had been considering. He wanted to know how far the people were prepared to commit themselves. He tried to introduce an idea.

"Do you suppose, Mr Matheopoulos, that there is any chance of the archimandrite refusing to sell?"

"I don't think so." Matheopoulos held up one of the tiny stones to the light. "The tall priest is the only conscience among our clergy."

"So we must hope the Company withdraws its offer."

Matheopoulos did not bother to look up. "How could that happen?"

"If it felt threatened."

Marangos had gone. The mill workers were listening. The old man did not answer, but went away and checked over the panel of machine switches. Kallis enjoyed the curiosity of the others. They affected lack of interest. They all had ideas of their own now. But they wanted to know his. At last one of the porters demanded: "How can we threaten them? Haven't we threatened already?"

"Only in theory," said Kallis, "not in practice." He liked dropping these enigmas among them. It was an easy trick, but it had its effect. They all wanted to know. They looked up at him, their hands tucked into their flour-covered overalls. "Talking doesn't mean anything to those people." He slid off the sack and dusted the back of his trousers. The dry, pleasant smell of the flour was inside his nostrils. "A token—that's what we owe them. A warning that we're serious."

Philippou piped up: "Let's kidnap Mrs Oldenburg!"

One of the fishermen asked Kallis woodenly: "Do you really mean that? Are you going to kidnap somebody?"

Kallis squatted between the two most intelligent millers, two brothers with simian faces. He glanced over the others, and waited until Matheopoulos, who had reached his office, had closed its glass door behind him. The men's curiosity made them all look alike. Their dark eyes had woken. The question was whether they were prepared to participate, or whether they merely wanted to be in on the secret.

"Here's the crux," Kallis said quietly. He knew how this quiet voice could hold attention. "If we're to dissuade the Company we must act at once." None of the others said anything. They agreed. They were waiting. "Now there's only one way to dissuade such people; that's to threaten their pockets. And a mine is one of the easiest things to sabotage." His fingers started tapping on his knees as though he was spelling out a code, if they could only decipher it. "I don't mean anything dangerous. Just a token, something to show them how vulnerable they are. A stick of gelignite would do it, exploded in a haulage incline—enough to bring down a strut or two. That would say 'Watch out.'"

He had walked into unexplored territory, alone. The legal penalty for sabotage was death. For a moment he forgot the others and noticed his own reaction. Was he afraid of what he had proposed? No. Only the faintest airiness about his heart, as if he were marking a new altitude. Exhilaration, not fear. Because people still made their own justice here. The laws of the state were younger than theirs, and further away. And these men were trustworthy. They would close about him like a fist. Everybody would suspect, but nobody could prove. The whole town would sympathize. It was this warm, imagined mass about him which encouraged and justified the idea. It was a passive mass, certainly, but sabotage was exactly the action to waken it.

The men had burst into animation. They found their anger again. Not one of them disagreed. As far as they were concerned, the whole world was on their side. Kalepia was the only world they knew, and they had seen it, hadn't they, at Oldenburg's lecture, waving its three hundred arms against the Company? The Company deserved it, the Company had asked for it. What were the struts of a haulage incline compared to seventy dislodged families? Were they going to let themselves be driven from their homes by foreigners?

"What about six lots of gelignite?"

"Ten!"

"Blow up the ventilation plant!"

"Who'll get the gelignite?"

"I know where to get that," said Kallis. He knew a man in Chakistra.

"And I know a miner who'll lay it," said one of the simian men. "He'll be glad to. Works on the seven-thirty shift this month. He'd stick it up Oldenburg's arse."

Kallis concentrated his stare on the man. "Is he a relative of yours?"

"No, but you can trust him."

The door of the office rattled open. Matheopoulos was folding his reading spectacles into his pocket, and fumbling for his other pair. "I'd like to see this man of yours," said Kallis, getting to his feet.

Matheopoulos dawdled above the stairs, watching the men return to work. He was preoccupied. Four years ago he had imported a beautiful wheat from the United States, but the operation had proved too expensive; he was always wondering whether to try this again. He had liked that fine, pale flour. That was real quality. Most of his product now was a buff-coloured substance used for semolina, useful enough, but not good in itself.

Kallis was standing alone with his hands behind his back, his head bent and his eyes half closed. Matheopoulos asked him: "Do you remember that flour we sold four years ago? The baked loaves had a light but firm texture. A very white bread."

Kallis scrutinized the old man. It was a curious fact, he thought, that however well you knew a person, if you scrutinized him for a while he became a stranger. "No," said Kallis, "I don't remember." Matheopoulos had never known what it was to be poor. You could tell. Those born well-off were always a little blurred. Oh yes, Matheopoulos was a very white bread. Even the deferential way he treated his workmen grew from not quite understanding them, from a tinge of romanticism even, which a man could only give to a class not his own.

Kallis said to him: "The temper of the town is so high I believe there'll be bloodshed if the Company doesn't retract."

Matheopoulos lowered his head and stared at him. His jowls overlapped his collar. He did not answer. Kallis went on: "We ought to impress on the Company that there will be violence if they buy."

"They wouldn't listen."

"Not to words, no." Kallis kept his gaze on the old man's face. "But suppose there was an explosion in the present mine—a small one, say in a rail passage? It would create a little inconvenience, no more, but it would be obvious what it meant. It would also be obvious that it could be multiplied by a hundred or detonated under expensive equipment. It could even make the business unworkable."

Matheopoulos sank his head in refusal. His pale-veined eyelids slid down like hoods. "No," he said wearily, "no, that wouldn't do."

"It would prevent bloodshed later," Kallis said. He was not sure how strongly he believed this, but that did not worry him. He was not used to delving into the roots of his own behaviour (the roots did not matter; the point was to use yourself to best effect). "If we don't show our teeth, they'll think we don't have any."

Matheopoulos' head was quivering slightly. "Anything," he said, "anything is better than that."

Why, Kallis wondered? Why was anything better than that? He did not understand this attitude. So a whole town should sit idle, should it, while a foreign company shifted its people about like counters? All because nobody was prepared to say, with a stick of gelignite, "Beware! Your money can't trample out the world!"

Kallis said: "If we don't do something, the householders on the Mountain will band together and resist. I'm sure of it. And so will the people at the port. If the municipality wants to evict, it will have to call in soldiers, and the last time a municipality did that, seven people were killed." He stared hard at Matheopoulos. "If that happened here, would you still say that anything was better than an explosion in an empty mine-shaft?"

The old man's hands were blotched light brown; they fingered the silver watch-chain across his stomach, back and forth. He did not know what to make of this pale, intense man. He felt that something was wrong somewhere, but he could not discover the words to express it. He pulled out a handkerchief and dabbed it against either nostril. "We must find some other way," he said, "within the law."

Law! When that word was mentioned Kallis felt something burning along his cheekbones. It made his whole face pucker. These words of authority—"law", "the municipality", "the Company", "the government"—what were they? They were just men, conglomerates of men protected by names. He had known about "law" from his youth, and it still sent this acid along his cheeks. The tragedy was that these names hypnotized people. Tell a peasant that Mr Alpha and Mr Beta were coming to take away his house and he'd be at his door with his rifle shouting "Let them try!" But deliver a stamped paper headed "Urban Council of Kalepia" and he'd shake his wooden head and throw in his hand. Yet even in the Republic people confused law with justice. What sort of man was it who said "It's law" and so accepted it? An infant!

Matheopoulos noticed the sweated expression on the other man's face, and frowned. Kallis was remembering a time twenty-five years ago, when the law had arrived at his mother's door. He could remember the official to this day, in minute detail. He had merely been some lap-dog of the local justiciary, but to his mother and to himself he had embodied the law. They could do nothing about him, because he had a little brass badge pinned on his lapel and a bit of paper in his hand. He had stood insolently on their doorstep, and delivered this form to his mother: the one which said that since the defendant had pleaded guilty she was fined the maximum sum of — drachmas under section Christ-knew-what of an act invented by the civil authorities for extorting money from people who took in lodgers. His mother he knew, everybody knew, could not pay. A week later the bored official had come back with an order that if she did not pay within five days she would go to prison. She had to sell their house within five days. For months afterwards the thirteen-year-old boy had dreamt, literally dreamt, that he was tearing the face of that official to the bone. But later he had realized that behind that bored face were other faces, and others behind those. They folded one upon another like shadows into the horizon of "the law". You could go on tearing, but you would never reach your tormentor.

That was why Kallis spat "Law!" in a way which made old Matheopoulos jump. "There's no law to protect these people! They must make their own. And that means violence. It's all they have left."

That was the lesson. Prove yourself hard and you cut your swathe. Now, if they were to fight, it would not be they, but the

Company which was to blame, which would have brought this upon itself. The Town would not have murdered; the Company would have committed suicide.

Matheopoulos straightened his jacket and stood against one of the grinders, staring absently in, watching the crushed husks whirling, whisked away. He answered uneasily: "We are too ... too weak to try violence, even if it were right."

"We're only weak if we refuse violence," Kallis said hotly. "How did the Syrians throw out the French? Or the Cypriots the British? By finding their own spirit, that was how. By realizing that the law of others need not apply to them. That the rules had been made by the rulers." His words were coming in bursts, as if he was breathing too close an air. "And you don't have to look so far away either. Only last year the Nikitari dockers got what they wanted by beating up a few policemen and town councillors."

What was the reason for his looking like that, Matheopoulos wondered, as if he were sweating out a fever? Perhaps the man was not well. But his mind was working all right, that was sure. He seemed to have all sorts of arguments for everything. Matheopoulos could not keep up with them. The Syrians, the British. The old man was a little hazy on history. He could not find any reason for rejecting these arguments. They sounded forceful. All the same to him, to the whole of him, they were wrong. Matheopoulos closed the lid of the grinder. "To make your own law for violence..." His forehead crinkled. "You have to be very sure."

Kallis felt exasperated. He was wasting his own time. The old man was all right in his way—he dealt well with people—but he had no backbone. "It's the same pattern over and over again," Kallis said, "the owners against the owned. Two kinds of people. And until that ends, there'll be battle."

Matheopoulos was examining a rotary belt. He mumbled something about "plenty of kinds of people" and continued running his fingers over the frayed fibre to feel its extent. He was never happy about giving these machines inferior grain. Not that it harmed them, just that they seemed to be made for something better (after all, you could grist semolina flour in a donkey-mill).

Kallis had quietened. He was leaning on the trolley as Marangos had done, watching Matheopoulos bent beside the grinder. "After my father died," he said, "my mother used to take in lodgers to pay for my sister and me at high school. We were reduced to a single room, almost to begging. If you've always been poor, you may not recognize what poverty is. But if you grow poor, then you know all right." He stooped to see what Matheopoulos was doing to the grinder belt. The old man looked as if he was massaging a body. "So I know the difference," Kallis said. "It's in every bone of me."

Matheopoulos straightened himself. "You have that advantage over me," he said. He did not want to hear about Kallis' private life. He thought the man ought to go and lie down. He was not standing steadily, but resting on that trolley as if he expected to be wheeled off.

Kallis did not know himself why he was speaking to Matheopoulos like this. Could the old man understand what it was like? Not physical misery, but degradation. That was what he remembered. Not his torn clothes, but the way people looked at them. The things which humiliated, which were ridiculous. One day, he said, he had found his mother sticking cardboard inside her shoes because the soles were worn away, and later he saw her skip over the tarmac road because it scorched through to her feet. Could Matheopoulos understand what that meant to the boy in whose imagination his mother had always walked like an empress?

Matheopoulos nodded sympathetically. All the same, he thought, what was the point of all this looking back? He found that his eyes averted themselves from Kallis. Scratch a bitter man, he thought, and you find a sentimentalist.

Kallis was staring behind him at the switch-panel, green and red lights. He understood Matheopoulos' silence enough not to go on talking. But he thought that the old man was genteel. He had an urge to shock and disgust him with other parts of his childhood, but he did not. He went on watching the lights and listening to the throb of wheat and husk running through their tubes all round the room, as if through the arteries of a body. His mother had taken in two Lebanese prostitutes as lodgers. They had been reduced to that. The spare men of the town had run in and out like wolves, shouting and arguing most nights. (That was how they had been detected keeping lodgers without a licence.) And once these women, half drunk, had caught the boy, and one of them had teased him with her body. Fascinated and revolted by those sagging pendulums of flesh, huger than anything he had imagined, he had lain helpless while the creature had pressed his penis between her reddened thighs. What would Matheopoulos think of that, who had not played with nasty boys in his street? By then Kallis' mother, who five years before would have lacerated those women until they were wrecked for their profession, had become anaemic; that's life, she'd said, he'd better learn. But he had learnt that it was not so much life, as poverty. Poverty was not malnutrition or tattered clothes. But what happened inside you. That.

"There's only sympathy between equals." He was flicking the patches of flour from his sleeves. "It only comes from standing in the same line of fire. And in the case of this mine, nine-tenths of Kalepia share the same threat." That was the fortress: numbers. He sensed the town like a warm nest around him.

Matheopoulos was walking among the sacks, jotting down the numbers on a note-pad: so many for semolina, so much for second-quality, so much for macaroni.... Every time his mind considered violence, he turned it away.

But Kallis was not looking at him any more. He had shut himself off from the endless shaking of the sieves and humming of grinders, and from Matheopoulos with them. He was gazing at a window as if he could see through it, although it was filmed with flour (even the dust was clean here). Distinctly he could hear the tap of his ageing mother's feet on the tarmac, and was watching their ludicrous skip as he walked behind her, feeling as if the whole heart of him was coiling up and burying itself away.

Chapter Fourteen

There was no escape from the dazzling rock. The heat was so fierce that a bare hand or arm which brushed against the excavator received a searing rash, and to reach the driving seat the shovel-operator had to lever himself in with the delicacy of a cat to avoid burning his forearms on the metalwork. Once inside, and with all windows open, this man still sweated in a glass and steel oven, and when he took off his helmet to relieve the crushed wetness of his head, it was Alastos who was supposed to bawl at him: "Obey the regulations! Put your helmet back on!" Supervising the excavating bench from outside was little better. Alastos felt he was walking along the rim of a blast furnace. Today, on top of this, his sunglasses had fallen out of his pocket and been run over by a dump truck; and somebody from the night underground shift had borrowed his overalls from the change-room, and the sleeves had been burnt through by acetylene flame.

He had gone the previous morning to complain about conditions to Oldenburg and had virtually demanded altered hours for the men. One of the truck drivers had vomited half the night from heat-stroke. Oldenburg demanded: was he wearing his helmet? Yes, Alastos answered, and that had probably been part of the cause. Heat-stroke was a matter of body-temperature, not sun-rays; he remembered that from Utah. Alastos had grown nearly offensive by this time. His temper had been at surface level for a good ten days. It was time the men inside vehicles were relieved of wearing helmets in July, he said. The shovel operator was half asphyxiated even without his.

The result of this was that a three-hour break was permitted at midday instead of a two-hour one, and the evening period was lengthened. Towards five o'clock a thin breeze blew up from the sea, perceptible more from a lightening of the air than from any movement. Alastos knew that the heat must be failing because his eyes were no longer forced into slits, and the sweat was dry on him. The haze had washed off the surrounding hills. By six o'clock the sun had turned pleasant and the sea's horizon showed clear. The men worked with great precision.

Alastos had grown more exacting—the tougher the conditions, the stronger the discipline had to be—but to the men it only seemed as if he was augmenting their discomfort. During the past ten days they had been asking "What devil's jumped in him? Aren't things hell enough?" During the noon heat his mind, like his eyes, operated through chinks, which let through only the necessary thoughts, and these in isolation. His actions were automatic and if he remembered some disquiet in him, he would curse the heat, as though that had caused it. The men needed closer watching too. Yesterday the operator had released the bucket flap too soon, and it was only because his load had been fragmented that the truck had escaped damage. Then the maintenance depot had notified that the import of large-diameter cables had been delayed. If he broke one of the present ones, he would have to revert to the old-fashioned ropes for two weeks. That meant that he could not take his eyes from the excavator. All the same, he recognized that he was not himself. He had kept his humour in worse conditions than this. Twice already, seeing the shovel-operator crowding the rock a little, he had bellowed at the man: "Where's your co-ordination, blast you? D'you want to snap the whole damned arm? Drop it!" And when the operator's glazed eyes had scarcely seen him, Alastos had bitten back his anger and added: "It's this devil-sent heat. Take it easy, just take it easy."

Now, with the sun waning and his eyes able to endure looking at the rock, he wondered if he had not been sounding like Muller or Oldenburg. He had always detested supervisors who burdened their men with their own frustration. But he himself was probably doing the same. For one thing his father's condition was visibly worsening; the old man's flesh pressed so dry and discoloured against its bones, that you would think he contained no bead of moisture in him; yet every morning his pillow was soaked and he was coughing up more blood.

But the noon sun purged even these thoughts away. As for

Caroline, she remained little more than a greyness in his mind. He simply missed her gaiety and was depressed by his failure to feel more. When at night or in early morning he felt any personal loss, it was not this affair that he remembered; instead, he found himself thinking of his parting from Ekaterina years ago. But during the day the sun evaporated everything except what he was doing: spacing the blast holes four metres apart; checking the delay ignition; watching the iron grab and its squealing cables. It was all this which seemed to have changed.

It faced him in the evening coolness. He had put it unresolved from his mind for days: that the business had become senseless to him. His brain, when he allowed it to work, was in chaos. Sometimes it seemed as if the machines were condemned to trundle round this white inferno simply for their own misery. It had become a hell.

Since the day of the lecture he felt that his reason had given up. His mind was not only crowded by the same questions, but was plagued by imaginings which teased it with the force of arguments. Whenever he tried to subject the matter to rational scrutiny, a crowd of figures almost physically jumped up in front of him and shouted "What about us?" The fishermen, in particular, had the power to overturn logic. Half a dozen of them recalled themselves to his mind with pinpoint clarity. He remembered everything from their fretted waistcoats to their robust, injured expressions. It was all very well for him to talk of sacrifice, but these were the victims. No wonder they waved their sweaty caps! You could go on juggling forever with the gains and losses which would accrue from the sale; but these men were being relegated to the waste dumps. You could not compensate one group of people by giving to another. Such equations only kept their force if you considered the question as a whole, which was like treating a crowd as if it did not consist of persons.

Alastos turned abruptly from the machines, reached the access ramp and climbed to an upper bench. His thoughts came clearer when he walked; but he went in a businesslike way, striding past the blast-holes whose dust lay mounded above them like ant-hills.

Theories flourished by forgetting human nature. It had sounded fine to talk of sacrificing the present to the future. But the present had suddenly cried out, and the benefits of the future appeared less certain. It was still a matter of degree. But the degree vacillated whenever he looked at it.

He was walking faster. He was almost marching, swinging his long arms. There was a question, too, of the Company's right to impose its will. The town was solid against the Company. It had got to its feet to say so. That dark mass of indignation! It had its own ideas. It seemed to demolish the right of anyone to interfere with it.

He stared down through the aperture of the hill at the mining offices. Beyond these showed the squat miners' houses, with their television aerials and car awnings. Their newness no longer seemed an asset. They looked soulless and transient. But he told himself that his alienation from the Company must also be transient. He could not go on like this. Perhaps he would never feel again as he had done two months before, striding along this great serrated bowl of a mine, and speculating on the opposite valley. That exhilaration had been a luxury. But wouldn't he return, with reservations, to his old conviction? It was not as if he had ever thought that his values were those of the Company. Only a fool would think that the Company was interested in anything but itself.

But he continued to pace along the vast arena as if one by one he could trample out the knots in the question and restore it to simplicity. He lowered his head until the rim of the helmet deflected the sun from him; and he thought. He thought hard—as if by sheer mental effort he could erect himself a structure by which to justify the eviction of seventy families. But at last he only felt tired with himself. He had set himself to restore a town which did not want to be restored, at the hands of a Company which had no interest in restoring it. He had got what he deserved.

Eventually he sat down exhausted on the edge of the rock and gingerly lifted off his helmet. He took a comb from the pocket of his overalls and pulled it through the crush of his hair. He was thinking of himself now. He was working with men and machines for a purpose which had never been theirs, and was no longer his. It was deeply humiliating and made a man want to give up and start doing something solid and simple. Perhaps he could buy a citrus orchard or go into the timber trade. But he had no money.

What, he wondered, did other people find worth doing? But other people were never explicable. All the same, where were the ones, like him, who had not devoted themselves? Or were those the ones you saw in the bars of the Capital, lolling over glasses of pale brandy? The ones who were sick in the gutters.

He got to his feet. He knew perfectly well, in fact, that such men were everywhere, in every profession. They were not so much the slaves of their occupations, he thought, as poor in themselves. In the West they became absorbed half-heartedly in business. In the Republic they sat on the pavements. And now he was one of them—he might just as well be one (we always despise what we are). Like them he would sit and wait. Coffee, a little argument, sleep. Fondling strings of amber beads. (The men of Kalepia had a special way with theirs, manoeuvring them in a circlet beneath the thumb.) Yes, he thought bitterly, that would suit him.

He rubbed a handkerchief over the back of his neck, beneath the collar, then wiped the stone-dust from his face. He walked back towards the excavator. His feet made a hollow crunching. He shovelled his hands deep inside his overalls. He thought: to hell with it, I must try to give myself time. In Utah he had gone for months without thinking at all, without worrying in the least as to whether what he did was worth a dime. But then he had told himself: "this is not permanent, this is gaining experience". And that had saved him. But how long would he go on pretending that his life was a preparation for something? From childhood he had kept this premise that he was moving towards some triumphant completion. Yet no such completion existed. He could not even envisage one. It was a mad figment, but something for which he did practical things; in London he had even taken a course in hydrometallurgy in the interests of this chimera. No doubt, he thought bitterly, his whole life would be spent only gaining experience.

The dust around the site hung as thick as ever. The machine's caterpillar feet were lolloping back and forth, and an empty dump truck was driving up the access ramp and turned along the bench. Beyond the dust cloud he thought it must be one of the office clerks walking towards him, but the figure looked too small. He passed the excavator and shouted instructions at the truck driver. Then he saw Ekaterina. She had stopped ten yards off with her hands behind her back, watching the machine. He thought how disgusting they must all appear to her. Still, that was the job. He wiped his hands on his overalls. Her presence made the business less depressing. It seemed that if she could stand there on those slender legs watching so respectfully there must be some purpose to it after all. The truck drivers grinned out of their windows and the operator began to show off, swinging the shovel arm with an unnecessary flourish.

Alastos took off his helmet and held it in one hand, smoothing back the hair from his ears. He went towards her. "So you came."

Her white blouse emphasized the blackness of her hair. She was flinching from the noise. He always forgot the noise; after the first day or two you became used to it. He thought she shivered slightly, the sort of shiver which used years ago to make him put an arm round her. They walked farther away. She wanted to know how the blasting was done, why the pit was engineered as it was, how the machines operated.

"And is that," she asked light-heartedly, "the machine which is going to dig us into our future?"

A harsh look crossed his face. "There'd be four of them for the new mine," he said. The future! It was his own fault if her teasing stung him.

They walked away from the site. The air was almost cool and the lightest wind brushed the dust over the mine's rim and into the sky. The ground had cracked underfoot, threatening to fall on to the bench below. There was nobody else near, but the siren from the underground mine was sounding on the north side. The sea looked very calm and the coast was visible for thirty kilometres on either hand.

Ekaterina was relaxed. Her green eyes were half closed against the glare—he noticed their tilted lashes—and she walked springily. Now that they were away from the mine she could make her voice heard. She stared at the horseshoe of ground at the bottom of the pit. In one corner shone a pool blue with copper sulphate. "Where do they plan to rehouse these people?" she asked.

"Not down there anyway," he laughed. "A well-engineered pit like this one will fold in after a few years." He shortened his stride to hers. "It's to the south. We'll go up the ramp." He felt more at ease with her outdoors, where his movements were in scale to the mine and to the land which faced them from its summit. They stopped there. She gave a sigh of pleasure, and gazed at the view without saying anything. He remembered these silences as a sign of emotion. He watched her out of the corner of his eye. She had changed less than he had thought. She was only a little sparer. Her waist looked so slender that he felt certain he could still have joined his thumb and fingers round it. But he had something more uncomfortable on his mind. He was waiting for her to pick out the mutilated piece of land where the Company planned to rehouse. Had she noticed it yet? No, she was enjoying the view with her eyes still half closed. That was her single sign of age: the little amused lines in the far corners of her eyes.

Suddenly her expression lit up with anger. He followed her gaze. The Company's plot of land stretched below a ridge of andesitic lava which had been tipped back from the mine. Nothing grew on it. To the east the site was overhung by a black iron waste. On the far side lay eroded limestone foothills and the south was dominated by a long chute on struts, which carried the ore from the primary crusher to a lorry-track. As Alastos looked at this suffocated little valley, he felt a deadness in himself. In fact he could not bear to look at it at all. He fumbled with the padding in his helmet and stared at his feet. Even his feet looked embarrassed. They were turned in. He could envisage the place easily, crammed with duplicates of the miners' houses. In winter the rains would trickle down from four sides; in summer it would be airless. He was afraid of what Ekaterina was going to say; she was still staring with that look of desolation. He was remembering things which he had said at Sofroniou's dinner, but he had given up trying to think of any excuse. He was blushing, but chiefly in rage, and hoped that his dark suntan concealed it. He had cast the Company in the role of saviour, and it had answered by this decision to shift seventy families into its own excrement. He fixed his gaze on the Asproyia mountains far away, which showed clear and blue as if cut from glass.

Ekaterina's hands clenched at her waist. "I wouldn't house my cat in that place!" She still was not looking at him; she had a horror that his face might show no outrage, no grief. If he approves, she felt, he's finished as a human being.

Julian heard himself begin feebly: "I suppose the Company doesn't feel it can afford . . ."

"Feel!" she cried. Her gaze on him was like that of a primitive statue, slanted and violent. "The Company's given up feeling anything! It only calculates. Don't make lies for them, Julian. If they corrupt you they'll corrupt anybody!" She turned to look at the land again. She felt tears of misery behind her eyes. She wanted to plead with him, but she could not manufacture his decision. "What about that chute? They'll surely remove that?"

Julian's mouth felt thick. They'd never demolish the chute; it wouldn't be an "economic factor". Oldenburg wouldn't spare a man to cut down a line of corpses.

Suddenly Ekaterina turned her back on the place. She did not know whether her tears were for the townspeople or Julian.

"They must find another place," he said.

She answered more calmly: "What place? How can you compensate people for their homes? Country people, sea people."

There was no answer. Julian swung his helmet angrily back and forth. "I'd better get back to my work."

"All right."

"Why do you say 'All right' like that?"

"I don't know how I said it."

He stared away from her.

She said: "You don't sound happy."

"Happy?" Something long pent up in him exploded. "How the hell should I be happy? D'you think I'm some company pundit? Shuffle one lot of people here, another lot there!" He grabbed her arm and forcibly turned her round again. "Just look at it—slag on three sides, barbed wire beyond! D'you think my eyes are different from yours? I see it too! And a chute which'll rust there for another half century!"

She said softly: "You're hurting my arm."

His hands fell to his sides. The weight of his self-exasperation was almost more than he could bear. "Oh, Kat." He half raised one hand again as if he would touch her, but noticed a mark above her elbow where his fingers had been. "I'm sorry. I don't know what I was thinking of."

He stared at her so much as if he had really harmed her, that she said quickly: "Don't be absurd, Julian, don't look like that. I'm not made of china."

"I don't seem to understand what I'm doing any more."

She said: "I know."

Yes, he thought, she always did. It used to madden him sometimes.

He felt emptied. With a self-conscious tenderness he held her forearm for a second on his fingers. "I'd better get back to the men," he said. He told himself: you'd better. That was what he was best at. Digging and blasting. A man's hands, his whole body, grew insensitive with this work.

They descended the ramp and watched the mine from a distance. The work went on smoothly. A good shovel-operator grew to know his foreman's mind. It was only in the heat that anything might happen. Opposite, on the Mountain of St Vichinos, the goats had awoken out of the shade and were trailing along their tracks. He shadowed his eyes and examined the hillside. He no longer knew what to say to her.

But she was quiet now, and had even started to regret her outburst. She hated to hurt him. Standing beside him, gazing at the hill, she asked: "It's about forty homes, isn't it?"

"Yes, I think so." The houses ran in a seam along the middle slopes. He could count them.

"They line the pilgrims' path to the shrine," she said.

"Is that it?" He noticed now. They traced a curve. "Yes, I see. I didn't remember that. I used to follow the pilgrimage as a child, when old Fantousis was alive. I confused him with God."

Her laughter was mellow, fond. "The next pilgrimage may be the last."

He shrugged his shoulders. "I don't regret that."

"It's not your shrine." But she mustn't argue again, she thought.

"It's propping up an idiotic myth. That child died of typhus because its mother took it to the saint instead of to the hospital. Did you know that?" He looked harsh again. "It had been diseased for eleven days, before the doctors heard. Eleven days with typhus! You're a nurse. You know what that means." He was glad to have stated something he knew. His beliefs seemed to be eroding all around him.

But Ekaterina, he remembered, had never seen the need to change things. Old ideas and ways seemed to please her. If people believed in impossible saints or legends, she regarded them only with quizzical interest. In fact she had no respect for education. But in argument, he thought, she had a clever way of escaping the consequences of her illogic.

"The poor people here don't go to doctors in any case," she said. "The fees are too high." She shot him a half mocking look. "Leave them their shrine."

"I know you," he said, but quite softly. She'd give up a sea of truth for a trickle of happiness.

They started to walk again. He wanted to ask how she and Lerides managed to differ so widely, and yet continue to exist happily. But then perhaps they were not happy. She gave him no idea. She always spoke of Lerides matter-of-factly; she did not surround him with any special tone. He asked: "Doesn't your attitude to the mines make for ... doesn't...?"

"Doesn't what?"

"Does your husband mind you feeling as you do?"

"Yes," she said. She looked away from him. She felt vaguely alarmed.

He began again: "Doesn't that make for rather a lot of..." Again he could not possibly go on, although he still fumbled for the word. "No, I'm sorry, I've no business to ask."

Ekaterina still did not look at him. "Yes, it does," she said, "rather a lot." Her voice was sad enough to make him feel ashamed. So he knew the answer but not, precisely, the question. What would it make for rather a lot of? Irritability? Coldness even? He was struck by her sudden silence and feeling; he wanted to show her some affection, but did not know how. He remembered how quickly she could pass from humour to an almost frightening intensity, and now clearly she did not want to carry on this conversation.

They had reached the edge of the excavation bench and could glimpse the sea. It was still and very blue. Off the northern headland, the stern of the drowned cargo boat glistened in the waves. A few cars were moving along the coast road to Nikitari. Inland he could see the lower course of the river, and above it the slopes of St Vichinos where the new mine would be. Now, in the faint sea-wind, the whole valley-side trembled with the movement of its trees: myrtle, olive, eucalyptus. Their green and silver branches were shimmering, as if some god were breathing down from the hills.

"How fine they are!"

He shifted uneasily. "I know, I know. It's hard." His voice rasped. "But still, it's no good." He kept his eyes on the excavator at the far side of the pit. "You can't get sentimental about trees when there are people to be considered."

"But the mine isn't people." She touched his arm in a way he remembered, very lightly, with her fingertips. "In fact people don't want the mine." She spoke gently, to prevent their arguing again, running her fingers through her hair and tilting back her head to feel the breeze. Julian turned his back on the valley. They walked along the pit towards the machines. It was very pleasant in the evening, circling the emptiness with her. The odd thing was, he thought, that they behaved so much as they had always done. How else he expected either of them to behave he did not know. All the same, he thought, it gave you a slightly peculiar feeling.

She did not believe in the future as he did, and he thought he understood what she meant now. But she was wrong, she must be wrong. If you stopped believing in the good of people's development, you stopped believing in everything. He began to tell her so, but went cautiously: "I'll tell you something funny, Ekaterina. There was a group of bank officials at the lecture—they were sitting right in front of me. They might have been planted there for my instruction!" He knew where this chatter was leading him, but he was in no hurry to arrive. "Now these bankers were sneering at the fishermen. The inspector of schools was there too, saying how uneducated everybody was. It made you want to retch." He was laughing and shaking his head. "Anyway, there they all were, just like a parable, the newly educated élite! And after listening to them for a while, and watching their cuff-links sparkle and smelling their hair lotion I—yes even me!—I began to get the idea that there was something wrong with my own expectations." He was grinning to himself, as if the scene no longer affected him. "But Sofroniou called those men a first generation"—he looked closely at her—"and perhaps they were. And I suppose there'll be other generations very like them, and others, on and on—but slowly, Ekaterina, won't they be getting better? If a person doesn't believe in this, isn't that the end of everything?" Suddenly he seemed to be pleading with her. All he wanted was for her to say "Yes, I grant you that at least—things will get better." His hands were cupped in front of him, as if they were holding something solid. "That's a minimum belief, isn't it," he continued, "that we'll be capable of treating each other better as the generations go on?"

He stared into her eyes, and she smiled back at him—a smile which was warm and upset, which wanted to agree. "Oh Julian," she began—that was her affectionate tone, the one which said: you haven't changed. It depressed him, because he did not even respect the Julian of two weeks ago, let alone the one of past years. "If you place three educated men you know beside three uneducated ones, do you find them kinder or more honest?"

"But you always had trust in the future."

"Did I?" she answered. "I don't remember...."

"Yes you did, always! Why have you changed?"

She said: "Perhaps when you're married you want to preserve things, not develop them. It's not a reason, it's an instinct." Then despite herself, her voice filled with urgency. "These fishermen for instance. If you deprive people for the sake of a future which you think you foresee, there may be no end. The next generation will do the same. They will see another future, and another lot of people will suffer for that, and all the time people are suffering for this vision of a future which never arrives." Alastos had the impression that she was talking as much about herself as of abstract generations. "I don't mean we shouldn't change things. It's just that this fever seems so ... unnecessary." She opened the palm of one hand as if she was releasing a moth. "No, I'm sorry, I can't see why."

Alastos was scowling with frustration. He insisted: "But supposing you're wrong? Supposing the sacrifice is worth it after all?"

"By that time," she mocked, "people will be able to climb to heaven on the pyre!"

He could sense her becoming mischievous. He said forcefully, to forestall her: "The fact is that educated people understand more than uneducated ones. That speaks for itself."

But her face had its monkey's look. It seemed unavoidable that Horrid would be exercised. "What a world you'd create! No love, no hate. Just education and understanding. We'd die of dullness."

He scowled and laughed together, did not answer her. But as they walked on he began to take her seriously and to wonder, in his cumbersome, analytical way, if love and understanding often excluded one another. The only person with whom he had fallen in love was Ekaterina, and it was true—he had not understood her. Even after the bitter and degrading arguments with which they had parted, there had followed weeks of remembering her almost as two girls—the one he had loved and the one he had just discovered. Who had played the trick? Why had he loved a mirage? No, he had never understood her. When they were together, love had been like a perfect body. You didn't hurt it by delving into its intestines. What did they matter? It was a shining, living being. There was nothing pertinent you could discover about it.

Until it died.

He exclaimed gruffly: "Loving and not understanding!"

She looked up.

He said: "The fact is I don't have too much respect for those feelings any more." He glanced at her quickly. Was he hurting her? He could only see her profile. It looked calm. But he had a foolish idea that the other side might be sad.

He began again: "I was lucky to have loved you"—the words went fluidly, easily between them; her profile remained steady, it did not turn—"I wouldn't give back an hour of it. But I didn't really know you. I might just as well have loved a monster for all I understood. It's not a thing to base your life on, that feeling, do you think?" Now it was all tumbling out, this conviction; he could not stop it. It had been formed out of their unhappiness, but she was not to know that. It all seemed far enough away for him to speak it dispassionately. "Isn't it mainly sex which deludes us? Just when we need to see clearly?"

Ekaterina stopped dead and turned to him. For a moment he had no idea what to expect of her. Was she angry?

No, she was smiling. But in her warmth there also showed—and he was perfectly sure of this—almost a desolation, the sort of look which somebody might fix on a back which had been turned away and was vanishing down a street. He looked away from her, but did not move. Then she put her hand on his arm in her light gesture and said: "Were you so much hurt then?"

Soundlessly, deep inside him, without Alastos having been prepared in the least, something collapsed. He faltered in front of her. His whole body appeared to be dangling from some invisible wire. "Was I . . . ?" His hands began to trace a gesture, then gave up.

Ekaterina's forehead ruffled into small lines. She came to his rescue. "A woman, at any rate, doesn't think love a deception," she said. "More likely she feels transformed into whatever the man believes her to be."

Alastos pulled himself upright. He wondered if that was right. Transformed. Did women feel transformed? He touched the rim of the helmet, as though he were greeting her. Then he tilted back his head as if to say "So love is all right for women!"

Yet Ekaterina was still staring at him and he avoiding her gaze, as if no longer sure of himself.

Chapter Fifteen

Alastos walked through the town on the way to the mines, thinking of nothing now, keeping his hands in his pockets and allowing his feet their slow, rolling lope. It was not yet seven-thirty. Women were washing their doorsteps, and the fan was already whirring in the barber's shop; an old man sat inside, leaning back in the luxury of the raised leather chair, while the barber, looking intent and grave, pinched up his client's nose as he scraped beneath it. Alastos noticed the windows of the older houses as he passed them; they showed balconies of thin metal, like filigree; and in the gardens the hibiscus had poured into flower.

The harbour was quiet. The sea flopped on its wharf. Some goats stood in the back of a lorry, poking their beards through its railing, so that Alastos stopped to tug gently at them.

"You from the mines then?" the driver asked. He seemed to know.

Alastos said yes. He used a different tone when he answered that question now. It sounded apologetic. But the man was cheerful. He took goats between here and anywhere you liked. He gave his prices. Alastos said he did not have any goats.

"But if you should have any, remember. . . ."

Alastos walked on along the wharf. The bell of the church announced another saint's day with a high, soft Beng-beng-beng. Some schoolchildren in squashed sunhats were being led on an early outing. Two of the girls were talking at once to the schoolmistress, who was trying to be impartial, then they all stopped to gape over a wall at a man snoring under a mulberry tree.

Alastos took the path beside the river bed to the mining offices, slurring his feet through the grass. He felt restful and vacant. In front of him, wobbling along the path, its rider half concealed by a pile of cucumbers and vetch tied with string, a bicycle teetered on flat tyres. It seemed to balance only by luck. Its rider was half asleep. Alastos watched this miracle go past him, then, where some arbutus bushes overgrew the path, saw the front wheel make a right angle with the rear and the whole apparatus pitch into the bushes.

There was silence. A thin voice said: "Oh, the Devil." The man picked himself up and pulled a thorn out of his hair. "Must've had a terrible night."

Alastos gathered up the cucumbers for him. "You need new tyres."

The man looked at them quizzically, then remounted the machine and leaned his weight first on the back, then on the front. "They'll do," he said. He picked out one of the long local radishes from among the vetch. "Here," he said. "Take this."

Alastos stuck it behind his ear, watching the man bicycle on round a corner. The offices were close now. He crossed the dry stream and walked through the barbed wire entrance past the repair depot. He strolled into the change-room and began to undress. His body looked humorous, he thought. His hands were so sunburnt that he appeared to be wearing gloves. He buttoned up his overalls to his neck. As the heat increased, he would undo these top buttons one by one to dry his sweat. But it was best to start with them assembled; that left you a way of relieving the heat. Then he searched for his helmet. Other miners were always taking his, although the cat-lamp socket had been knocked off; but it was the only one which fitted him. He attached it to his belt at the back.

The offices sounded quiet. The only noise was that of a Land Rover coming from the underground works. It was being driven so hard that he thought it must pass by. Then he heard the driver's fast, heavy stride. The next moment Muller was trampling through the staff offices. Only Muller walked like that. There must be some emergency. The Mine Superintendant usually went down with the morning shift at seven-thirty. It was past eight-thirty now. Alastos went to the back of the building to look under the car-awnings. Two of the staff had already arrived: Lerides and the mine geologist. He went back to the entrance in time to see Muller burst back through the door and glare round him. The sweat was pouring off his face and he was caked in dirt.

"Why the hell's nobody here?" he bellowed at Alastos. "Where's the G.M.?"

"He must be at the mill plant in Nikitari," Alastos said, "it's the last Thursday of the month."

"What about the Safety Officer?"

Alastos looked at his watch. "Not for another hour." Muller must know that, he thought, he's lost his head.

"Then is nobody here but that puling geologist?"

"Lerides' car is here."

Muller spat. "Bloody lot of use...." He grimaced. "Lerides...." He thought hard for a second, baring his teeth, then grunted: "Better than damn-all!" and charged back into the building.

A moment later he reappeared. Lerides came behind him in shirtsleeves, looking disconcerted. He was running his hands over his hair as if he was being asked to meet some important personage at short notice. "It's your responsibility," he was saying. "If they won't listen to you I can't see why they'll listen to me."

"Try, man, try!" shouted Muller, and added something in German. "The whole bloody shift wants to surface! You pay them. Tell 'em you'll starve 'em if they don't go back!"

Lerides seemed undecided. He was turning the gold ring back and forth round his finger. He looked too pale and fleshy, Alastos thought; he did not look well. Muller refused to wait for his deliberation and bawled at him: "You're the Company blasted Secretary! You could fire the lot!"

For a second Lerides looked as if he was going to shout too. But the German thrust his fiery face still closer, and Lerides took a pace back and said sharply: "I have no experience of this. I'm an accountant, not a miner. If you want to show one of the staff down there, then take the mine geologist. He's one of yours."

"Take him?" Muller drew breath noisily. "He doesn't even speak Greek."

"Then you'll have to wait for the rest to come."

Muller exploded. "You bloody people! You're all the same! A line of corpses sitting at desks!" He wrenched off his helmet, lifted it high over his head and dashed it on the ground. He looked like a vast, frustrated schoolboy, his chest black and sweltering where his overalls ripped open, and his hair matted over his skull like a second helmet. "The men are rioting down there and you stand on your arse and quibble!" He strode to the Land Rover, leaving his helmet behind him, pulled the door open and stopped. For a moment there was no sound but the gentle rocking back and forth of the helmet on the ground. Then he said over his shoulder: "I'll go back alone if you haven't the guts."

Lerides' eyes squinted as if Muller had flicked a piece of dirt at them. He shifted his weight and planted his hands on his hips. The Mine Superintendent had marched back to pick up his helmet. "All right," Lerides said, "but this isn't my job. It's yours."

Muller answered: "It's got beyond all that." He turned to Alastos, looking him up and down. "You're the foreman of the open-cast, aren't you? You come too."

They crushed into the front of the Land Rover—all three big men—while Muller drove as though urging a horse. They circled the waste from the open-cast mine, bounced over the single-track railway and followed it for five hundred metres. Alastos knew that he had been chosen for his size, which made him uncomfortable. Muller and Lerides did not speak to one another. The German was concentrating on the track. Lerides leaned back in the seat with his lips compressed, and slowly rolled up his sleeves. Evidently he thought his appearance too refined. His arms matched the heaviness of his throat. They were ample and pale. He kept running a finger beneath his moustache. After a while he glanced at Alastos, looked harder and said: "What've you got behind your ear, man?"

Alastos' hand fumbled up and felt something long and cool. The radish fell into his lap. It seemed to arrive from another world.

The hum of the ventilation plant had turned to a bellow, and soon its great silver cylinder appeared beyond the compressor house. The old mine-shaft was sealed up now, and a railway tunnel sloped into the hill. The train was waiting for them at the adit. The driver was turning its wheel restlessly round and back with one hand, and eased it forward as soon as they had crammed in. It collected itself in spasms—its trucks were heaped with tie-beams—then moved into the dark, where its lights lit only an interminable corridor of rock. Muller was the only one with an acetylene lamp, which he set on the floor between his feet. All three men had to bend forward from the hips, trying to avoid their faces being crushed against one another. Alastos' head was pressed down beside Muller, whose sweat had dried in dirty runnels down to his neck. The rims of their helmets clashed together with every jolt. Meanwhile the train trekked forward on its own patch of light, and the lurching of the trucks was underscored by a continual creaking, like a ship's timbers complaining in a heavy swell.

Alastos asked Muller: "What's the trouble then?" Muller, he knew, could deal with trivial accidents unflickering. This must be more serious. It meant at least that one of the caves had burst or the blasting had miscarried.

Muller shoved out his lower lip. He said in a rough, quiet voice: "One of the men climbed into the haulage incline to check a runner—against safety regulations of course—and found a stick of gelignite poking out behind the props. It never got detonated, but it was waiting to be. Instead of telling me, the bastard sent up a yell and the whole mine had heard in two minutes. They wanted to surface."

"Who'd have done it?"

"Who?" he grated. "Anybody." He wedged the lamp tighter between his feet. "The whole fucking town wants to do it."

Lerides was looking sullen. The light illumined only the puffier curves of his face, ignoring his eyes and firmer stroke of jaw. His hands pressed against his knees. He was obviously reluctant to ask Muller anything, but he said: "I thought the mining families kept away from the town people. Half of them came from Nikitari."

"But half didn't," said Muller, "and you can bribe anybody."

They stopped talking. Alastos could see neither of their faces. Muller's was concealed by its helmet, while Lerides had pushed out his feet and battened the base of his spine against the train wall. Alastos' back was starting to ache. He eased it by leaning sideways, and watched the tunnel passing. There was now no day at all, only the glow which they took with them. On either side the rock was a dead, grey colour, and fitted itself tightly round them, as if they were travelling down the innards of a worm. Alastos wanted to ask more questions, but he could barely make his voice heard above the stage groans and screams of the trucks. Now wooden props had appeared, bolstering the passage against meteoritic clay, and stretched like columns thickly in front.

Muller told the driver: "If you see any men walking this way along the track, don't stop. They haven't had permission to come up. Make 'em get to the wall."

Alastos grimaced at the wall. Lerides looked up. "You mean they'll be walking back to surface?"

"Could be."

"How did you leave them, then?"

Muller gave a low, raking "Huhuhuh". This noise set Alastos' nerves jangling. "It's a paradise in there. Some of 'em tried to hit me with rocks while the rest shouted encouragement. The foremen were too scared to move."

Alastos still could not see Lerides' face, but he felt that most of the blood had seeped out of his own. It would have seemed all right if some ordinary superintendent had retreated up the mine. But when a man like Muller surfaced, it sent your stomach into your boots. And what was Lerides going to say to the men? He was obviously trying to work something out. His fingers were tapping his knees.

They were half way there when Lerides' head tilted up, his lips bitten in. He said: "It'll be dangerous to give direct threats. I'll have to judge their mood."

"Mood!" Muller grunted, almost laughed. "They want to stick their rock-drills into your guts, that's their mood. For the first few minutes they were scared yellow—went flitting about like house-elves on a bloody mine-field. But now—uhuhuhuh—you'll see."

Alastos slid his back down the train wall, easing his shoulder-blades, and sat on the floor with his knees bunched at his chin. He surreptitiously touched his fingers together to see if they trembled, but the mine-car shuddered so violently that he could not tell. To him there seemed to be two kinds of miner, and he could not associate them. One kind filed home from the shower-rooms after the seven-thirty shift looking refreshed and cheerful, and played with children in the gardens of the square houses. The other kind lived in this secret Hell, toiling in the dungeons of the earth. He knew that these two groups were one, but his imagination could not link them. And now it was this second group, the damned, which was marching along the track towards them, perhaps, or was scattered through the different levels in bellicose clusters, with picks and staves. He remembered their white arms and stooped backs.

He glanced at the others, at Lerides' fingers which now tapped ceaselessly, and at Muller's bulging shoulders. He caught Lerides looking at him in precisely the same way, sizing up his strength. It was always other men's strength which seemed most reliable. He was bigger and younger than both these men, but he placed more faith in either than in himself. That must be because of fear. In any case, if things came to that, the sallow muckers could pull them piecemeal like a flock of baboons tearing a leopard.

He took a grip on himself. His imagination was running away with him. The most they could suffer was a few bruises. If the miners wanted to surface, they could do nothing to stop them.

Lerides had given up thinking. He caught Alastos' eye and they smiled uncomfortably at one another. It was tough on the man,

Alastos thought—perfectly true, this was not his business. What could he do, except threaten to withhold the men's pay? And that was not the way in which Lerides liked to argue. He relied on his charm and on an apparent reasonableness. Besides, nobody but Muller would openly threaten sixty angry miners.

And Lerides' face had changed. This showed in no one feature, but came from a tautening of facial muscles which numbed its whole expression. It was the kind of face you would hesitate to address. It might not hear you.

"Why don't you sit?" Alastos said. "You'll kill your back."

Lerides looked at the floor, and sat. He smiled again, the twitching smile which affected only his mouth. Alastos noticed his own hands. Yes, they were trembling. Lerides said tightly: "How's the open-cast going?"

He was obviously not interested in the open-cast. He wanted to hear a voice.

"Another six weeks left." Alastos shouted to be heard above the train, but shouted too loud, so that his voice clanged on their silence. "It's blazing hot there!"

"Ekaterina said."

"Yes." He tried to adjust his voice, but it either seemed to shout or whisper. "And she came in the evening. It was almost cool then."

Seated on the floor in the glow of the acetylene lamp, with Muller's feet between them but his head far above, they created a momentary pool of intimacy.

"She was fascinated by it," Lerides said.

Alastos felt his own smile as tense as the other man's. The jarring and shuddering round them appeared to be increasing. "She was always inquisitive about everything." They must both be afraid, he thought. Why else were they sharing Ekaterina between them? He said more quietly—Lerides leant forward: "She's a fine person, Ekaterina. Always made me feel a bit of a bear, I must say." That was not true when he thought about it, but it seemed to be what he ought to have felt.

Lerides gave a wider smile which might normally have been a laugh. "Women do," he said.

Alastos noticed his pitted neck and jowls. It was a curious thing, he thought, how some women did not seem to care about men's physical appearance. Muller was married to a delicate Austrian from Styria; it was impossible to imagine her loving Muller. As for Lerides, one could understand some women, but Ekaterina.... Did Lerides, he wondered, murmur endearments, or did he just use her? He could not imagine Lerides precisely growing sentimental. He would simply become more charming. And what did they do in the evenings? Did they read or talk or play with the child? And did she have trouble giving birth to this child? Why hadn't they had another? It was surprising how little he knew of her now. Sad and indecent that a person could mean so much at one time, so little at another.

Muller's boots suddenly shuffled. Was Muller nervous too? Alastos rested his head on his arms but kept his eyes open. The boots were still again. Their rubber lining was half peeled away, and they smelt of limonite. A minute later they moved against the mine-car door. Alastos and Lerides got to their feet. Lerides tucked in his shirt. Alastos settled his helmet more firmly on his head and chafed his hands. He looked outside, but the passing rock-face kept its putrescent greyness and the fresh water and compressed air pipes ran along it unchanged. Muller stamped his feet as if in irritation. Suddenly the driver turned a pale face to them and said: "There they are."

The train's light cast a blob for only thirty metres ahead. But out of the darkness beyond, choking the divided tunnel and overlapping the rails, the lamps were flickering in a dense river of sparks. As the train moved closer they resolved into a glint of helmeted heads above a flowing seam of bodies. These heads turned and craned forward, flashing their cat-lamps, and other men were holding up acetylene flames which lit up the whiteness of their shoulders and arms. Alastos saw that it was only their lights which turned and moved. The men themselves were banked solid and motionless, waiting for them. Their murmur could not be heard above the grinding of the wheels. Muller said: "The bastards have gone quiet."

They reached the first men. The train eased past faces whose eyeballs showed white under their helmets but whose expressions were invisible. They were playing their lights over the cabin. The engine halted. Opposite the footrail stood a fat mucker who raised a lamp high over his head and shone it down at them. For a moment all they could see was this lamp and the obese, glistening armpit. Then Muller pushed himself out and they were standing with their backs to the train. The battery of lamps dazzled and confused them. They were pinned against the steering-car. For a while they could see nothing but the spears of light. The voices did not address them, but muttered among themselves.

Then Muller said in his harsh Greek: "I see you've got yer senses back. You've lost an hour and a half's work already."

The answer came sullenly from in front of him: "Where are the rail trucks? We're coming up." Nobody else said a word. He must have spoken for them all.

"The rail trucks are at surface!" Muller shouted. His voice rang and resounded along the tunnel. "And you'll come up at end of shift!"

So many voices sounded in a rising temper that it was impossible to distinguish them. Lerides pressed himself up beside Muller and shouted: "Listen! Listen!" The first word sounded wavering and throaty. He held up both hands like an orator. "If you come up now, when do you intend to return?"

Confusion answered. One man shouted "Tomorrow!", another "After there's been an inspection!" and somebody else bawled "When we say!"

Lerides waited for quiet. "I want to tell you two things!" His voice was firm now. "The first is this: that it's against the company's policy to pay miners who abandon work without permission. We never did it for the open-cast workers, and we can't do it for you...." Before the roar of their answer could drown him he shouted "And the second thing is this!" The anger waited. Their breathing was heavy all around the three men. "And the second thing is this!" he repeated. "You're perfectly right to demand an inspection when there may be more explosives concealed here. But the mine staff are too few to carry out a search which would properly safeguard you. Now I want to make a simple proposition, which would enable you to retain both full pay and a full measure of safety." He paused for a second while these words matured behind the soiled faces. The trouble was that it was hard to see these faces beyond the barrage of light. They shifted. Every movement of their heads sent out new rays and coruscations from the cat-lamps. "Nobody knows these mines better than you do," Lerides said, almost quietly now, "and I don't imagine you would feel anybody else qualified to inspect them. So I simply want to propose this to you: that under Mr Muller's direction you carry out the search yourselves in the Company's time. That would satisfy us all."

This was greeted by a merciful silence. Four or five of the men in front of him turned their backs on Lerides and consulted in whispers. They seemed to be spokesmen. One voice, which held an emphatic, angry note of its own, cut through the muffle of the rest. When they turned back to Lerides, this voice rasped out: "We want danger money for that."

"Danger money!" Muller strode forward at the man and bumped him with his chest. "Just because you may find a stick of unignited explosive! Do you get danger money for handling your Ammo-Nitrate then? By God! You'd ask danger money for baby-sitting!"

Immediately the voices rose and multiplied. "Danger money!" Some of the muckers were holding up their fists and several of those in the front row hitched their lamps into their belts so that their arms dangled free. Their dirty-vested torsoes, few of which would have been formidable alone, were pressing from all sides. The whole multitude moved fractionally forward.

But Muller yelled at them: "A miner's pay takes danger into account! You bastards get danger money automatically!"

Lerides tried to shout above him "I'll discuss it with the General Manager," but the roar had grown terrible. "I'll discuss . . ." Now the men behind were pushing those in front. Their eyes were indecipherable, deep under the rims of their helmets, but their mouths showed flashing arcs of teeth. Alastos and Lerides both found their backs flat against the cold metal of the train. Muller stood a pace in front of them, his fists bunched at his shoulders. The agitation of lamps had a mesmerizing effect. It throbbed on their eyeballs. Now less than the length of an arm separated them from the mass. The train-driver, crouched in the cabin, whined: "Get in, get in quick."

Alastos had watched what was happening as helplessly as if he witnessed the unrolling of a nightmare. It was as though some part of him stood aside, observing his own body with the backs of its hands cold against the train under the lights. Muller and Lerides were the actors, he the spectator. It was not his place to speak. But now they were all reduced to the same. They were going to be beaten up. The noise was horrible; it resounded and redoubled in the vaulted dark. The men were being carried forward on the swell of their own fury. The faces opposite him were so close that he felt their breath. It was these which jerked him to life. Their rage looked personal. Their eyes were fixed on him, and the fibres of their shoulders gleamed in stringy lines.

He remembered what a pit superintendent in Utah had done when threatened by miners who had found one of their number run over by a truck. And suddenly he lunged forward over the two men nearest him and pointing at a shifty-looking mucker in overalls bawled at the top of his big voice: "You! You! You're the one!"

In the shouting only the miners nearest to him heard this, but they turned round to look at the man, creating a pocket of silence and bewilderment. Lerides, realizing what was happening, shouted "Yes! That's the man!", plunged forward and managed to grab the mucker's shoulders over the heads of those in front. By now the confusion had spread into the core of the crowd. Alastos and Lerides continued to bellow at the mucker, who shrank away in astonishment. They went on and on until their lungs screamed, and at last the doubt and silence spread and the yelling dwindled to the rim of the crowd.

Lerides and Alastos were left in the centre of a mob whose voices were no longer united. The din faded. It was not even necessary to shout. Alastos wanted quickly to exculpate the man, and asked: "You're the winder-operator on Level Seventy-six aren't you?"

"No." The man was almost whimpering. "No ... no it's not me. Giorgios ... where's Giorgios?"

Several voices shouted "Giorgios!"

A squat man pressed forward. "Are you the winder-operator on Level Seventy-six?" Alastos demanded.

The man glowered. "So what?"

"We want to question you. You're the one in charge of the incline where the gelignite was found. Well?"

The operator frowned thickly. "I went down with the winder supervisor. We've been together all shift. We've seen nothing."

"Who was there when you arrived?"

He said: "Spyros."

"Spyros!"

This time a thin, stooped man raised his hand. He was almost elderly, and his voice sounded husky with years of stone dust and pyrite. "Me? Huh! I couldn't climb that incline."

The mass was quiet now. The lights twinkled like fireflies. But Alastos' fear was releasing itself in a burst of half-angry exhilaration. "Who's responsible then?" he boomed. He glowered round them and shouldered himself into another group. "Somebody' been endangering the lives of all of you! Haven't you any idea who it is? Come on!"

The men remained stolidly standing, or muttered to one another. Alastos glared into their eyes. Most of these eyes looked back dumbly or in defiance. Some evaded him. But he was getting carried away with himself. This mob which had threatened to squash them! It was built of nothing! He was striding about it like a king! He jolted them with his shoulders and thundered: "Can't you say anything? There's a criminal among you! Who's got gelignite on him?" He felt like adding, as Sofroniou used to do in the classroom: "You stay here until one of you owns up!" but instead he seized on the most burly man he could see and banged him on the chest with the back of his hand. "You! Can't you answer?" The man did not reply. Alastos' exuberance carried him on. He was positively enjoying himself. He shouted and knocked them with his body. He was acting against everything he considered reasonable. A dictator was marching in him. He trod over the men's boots if they were in his way and bellowed: "Damn you! You're all implicated if none of you'll help!"

He had not noticed that for the last minute his words had planted spikes of resentment in his wake. The men were gritting their teeth and swearing under their breath. The shouting leapt up again in the first sharp, angry detonations. The men pressed closer and wedged him in so that he had to ram his chest sideways between them to reach the train. "Nobody's implicated!" they yelled. "Somebody from the night shift could've done it!" "Anybody!"

All this time Muller had been glaring from man to man as Alastos confronted one after another. He did not know what was going on. It was Lerides who quickly held up his arms and shouted: "Nobody's being blamed! The Company blames nobody!" He pushed himself forward confidently. He could be heard clearly. "Listen! I will talk to the General Manager about danger money when he returns tomorrow! I cannot authorize it myself! But I promise I will talk to him!" He took the situation in hand. He stood with his back squarely to Alastos and Muller, as if to stop any more of their attacks. His voice was conciliatory and, Alastos thought, oily; but he spoke with precisely the balance of reason and emotion which the men required. Their voices died away, and slowly Lerides cooled his own; it took on a soothing texture. He started to flatter them with "As experienced miners you will I'm sure know..." and "I'm only an accountant myself, but I imagine..." He slid in a shaft or two of humour, and although nobody laughed, the whole crowd had visibly softened. All its tenseness seemed to be sliding away through its dangled fingers and heavy feet. No spokesman opposed him. He began to gesticulate. His gestures all implied fairness, and after a minute or two his thick, pale hands appeared to be kneading the multitude in their fingers. They left it slack and gutted. He made the Company seem almost generous in not firing them all for this piece of sabotage, but ended by implying that it was the aberration of a single man and that the Company's faith in its personnel was unshaken. The front row of miners looked positively bored by now and several had taken off their helmets and were scratching the dust out of their hair, or running their hands over their necks. Lerides answered a few surly questions in a way which bestowed dignity upon their questioners, and finally recalled the miners to responsibility. Their safety, he said, was in the interests of the Company; Mr Muller would now organize them in a thorough examination of the mine which would be undertaken, since they insisted upon this, at full pay during their working hours.

The miners forgot that they had never even mentioned this, and after a few minutes of murmuring in disorganized knots, which Muller interrupted, they drifted away down the branch tunnel, swinging their lamps and dragging their feet and wondering why they felt so jaded.

Clanging back in the train, Alastos and Lerides alone, the same twilight and jarred, shuddered bodies, the same shrieking of wheels—they both slumped with their heads on their knees. Alastos' limpness—he was sure that if he tried to stand up his muscles would not obey him—must be the final arc of this alien and repulsive cycle in him. He had been inhabited by foreigners and nightmares of himself. They had risen in him like the devils in church frescoes which leap from the mouths of penitents. And now this unstringing of his body. He felt slack as a doll. He could barely keep himself from falling sideways. Yet his heart pounded....

Pricked out of the blackness before them, a minute semi-circle of light announced that they were emerging. How good it would be to surface and recognize himself! The rail which joined them to the semi-circle shone silver and strong. It pulled them up, an umbilical cord into the day. They moved through sunlight. They stood up. His foot on the step-rail was firm. The ground was firm. He walked with Lerides to the Land Rover. Lerides looked exhausted. The back of his shirt was opaque with sweat. When they reached the mining offices he offered Alastos some coffee, so they sat in Oldenburg's office and closed the door against disturbance, but had nothing to say.

Alastos only asked him: "How much danger money will they get?"

Lerides made a disdainful "Puh!" He gave a last flicker of his hands. "They won't get a thing. By tomorrow everything will have cooled down."

Alastos enjoyed the trickling warmth of the coffee. It spread its relaxation deep into the trunk of him, along his shoulders and limbs. It eased him back in the chair and closed his eyes. After Lerides had gone he found in his pocket the bicyclist's radish, and chewed it. So the men would get no danger money. He should have realized that. He supposed that cheating was natural to Lerides.

When he stood up, his back ached. He stretched himself, bracing his knuckles on the table, and noticed the map by Oldenburg's blotter. Its heading read: "St Vichinos Mountain Area. Preliminary Geological Report. Lythrangomi Mining Co." He looked harder. He took in the swirling contours of the mountain and the coloured bulges for pyrite chalked over them, with a cross-section alongside showing estimated depths of ore. There was nothing especially surprising about the report. He had seen these maps before, and every time he had been stimulated to picture how the great theatres would be engineered—their ramps, their chutes, their tips. But those had always been excavated out of a landscape as barren as the one they would create; whereas here small dots and squares of ink denoted houses. He counted those which would have to go. Forty. Exactly. The pale docker must have worked it out carefully.

The map told Alastos little new; but from it, for the first time, he could envisage precisely how great an extent would be ravaged—the ore scooped from the very edges of the town, its waste tipped out above the suburbs. Now he could imagine Kalepia as if it lay upon that map, under his knuckles, suffocated. He pressed his thumb and forefinger against his eyes. They still hurt. Why did it take a map to tell him what he had already known? Or was he growing sentimental about landscape? Landscape, he reminded himself, did nothing for these people. They never noticed it. It didn't tickle their nostalgia or turn them into poets. The farmers tilled it for a hard living—it was pitted with limestone—and the rest were glad to escape it.

The sunlight was brilliant when he walked out again. He was already an hour late for his work, but his legs refused to stride.

Chapter Sixteen

Tonight Ekaterina had to go on nursing rounds to two incurable patients, and she could feel their hopelessness weighing on her. Perhaps the evening would revive her, she thought, it had been a stifling day. She took down her black case from its shelf in the passage and ran her fingers over its contents, unscrewing the pots to check if they were full. Then she walked into the kitchen to collect the anti-histamine cream—she had put it in the refrigerator because the heat melted it—and up to the bathroom to unlock the medicine cupboard. As she reached up to it, she saw her own face in the mirror—a face surprised in the moment of living. It looked almost ghostly to her. She examined it closer. Its eyes seemed tired. When she pulled down the skin at their corners, the mesh of tiny lines vanished. When she released it, they reassembled. These traceries, she thought, were like the start of tracks. You could tell where they would lead and how they would deepen if they continued to be used. Two of them intruded on her cheeks from the inner corners of her eyes, and threatened to dribble down. In ten years time, perhaps, they would give her a look of amusement.

She climbed on to a stool to examine the top shelf of the cupboard. The syringes and fresh needles were there, and the sleeping-pills kept away from the child. She took these downstairs with some phials of penicillin. It was still only six o'clock and the babysitter had not arrived.

So she took a book, picked off her shoes and sat in the deepest chair. It was a poetry book which she had not opened for years, but at the age of seventeen or eighteen she had pencilled stars against lines and pieces she liked. She discovered these and began to follow them. The thick, confident stars surprised her now. "... As the moon through golden clouds, so her shoulders faintly shone...." She had enjoyed that. But she had read without comment "The Sacred Road" of Sikelianos, and Maria Polydoure's "I sing, only because you loved me in years gone by."

But at seventeen nobody had yet loved her. Her mother had been strict with her, and at school she had been shy (and rather skinny). She had discovered far more about death. As an auxiliary nurse in the hospital she had laid out bodies for six months. But love, no—not until a gangling young man stopped her at the hospital entrance, holding a nurse's cap which he had found on the pavement and which he thought might be hers. Plenty of youths had tried to flirt with her before, but they had all been so confident of their charm that they had made her afraid. And now she was confronted by this heavy, awkward man, who did not look like a Greek at all. He coughed continually to excuse the hand which kept coming up to his face, while she glanced at the cap—it was disgusting—and said "No, certainly not." But he looked so crestfallen that she took it from him. She found herself saying "Well ... I don't know ...", then compromised by suggesting it might belong to a friend of hers.

"Perhaps," he said, "you will give it to her," but he uttered the words so strangely, as if this would be a wonderful and difficult service on her part, that she had looked quite hard at him to see if he was not teasing her. But his face was even solemn, the eyes set well apart under a wide forehead. It had, she decided, a pleasant expression.

"Thank you, I'll take it to her," she said.

She was already late for duty but he still stood there. "Well then ..." he said, "goodbye, Maria ... Despina?..."

So he wanted to know her name. There would be no harm in that.

"Gardner, Ekaterina Gardner," she said.

He looked at her astonished, clenching his hands to his chest as if some gift had suddenly been floated into them. "But that's an English name!"

"Yes," she said abruptly. "My father's English."

She had almost turned on her heel when he said: "But I'm half English too!"

Well, really, that was too much. He would pretend he was a surgeon next. She looked sharply at him—his face had the effrontery to remain serious—and said: "What is your name then?"

"Julian Alastos," he answered. "But my mother's name was Emerson. She came from Hampshire."

Ekaterina, tucked in her chair, was smiling at this memory. It had been her turn to look embarrassed then. Her father had entertained Andreas and Helen Alastos several times before they had separated. And now here was the son, beaming at her and still clasping his hands against his chest while she, in confusion, was agreeing to let him walk home with her after work that evening. The pleasant thing was that her disbelief had gone unnoticed. It had not occurred to him that anybody would mistrust him.

She stopped reading. The more she thought about it—and she supposed it natural to think about it now that Julian had returned—the stranger appeared the people they had been. How little they had known! And such years ago! But she remembered his exact words (which were now so ordinary). "You see, Ekaterina, I'm too young to marry." They had made her feel she was no longer precisely alive. He was twenty-one, he had said, he wanted to make his way in the world. She must wait for him. And she had answered through her angry tears that age had nothing to do with it. If you loved somebody, you wanted to be with him—at once, for ever. (She had been a terrible prig.) Why shouldn't a young man's love be the same as a young woman's? And where it differed, she had refused to call it love. How could it be? It was she who felt love. Under her ribs, in her throat, all through her. She knew! How could he say he loved? He might think he did. But that was not love. "Love". She had held the word above him like a dagger, in its absurd simplicity.

Alastos could have answered that the simplest affection tries to understand and be patient. But instead he had been thrown into turmoil. Even she, in her self-righteous misery, had felt alarmed for this diseased, clumsy creature trying to unravel what was wrong with its affection. But they could not help one another. Because her conception of love had also been his—something direct and complete—and now that his nature was transgressing it, he could not say, as other people said, "Well, that is my nature!" He suddenly believed himself an aberration, a monster, and he could only try to restore harmony by a titanic affort of analysis which pulled the affair to shreds and left it there. That was why, when at the mines he had denied the importance of love, she had felt as if her own narrowness had destroyed a part of him, years ago. That denial still pained her. It was unbearable that a girl's ignorance should have stunted a man's heart. She could plead blindness, it was true—most crimes were deeds of blindness. But the damage remained. And you could never quite restore. Never.

Alexia, her child, was touching her knee and holding up a drawing: two dark green circles for sheep, a yellow scribble of a goat. The girl was staring into her face as if she had been holding these up for approval for a long time, and had been met with silence. Ekaterina kissed her, and consciously put the past from her mind. Alexia looked like Michael, unless the childish fullness of face was deceptive. She had the lighter brown of his eyes, and was bigger than girls of her age. There was a danger of her being pampered, because she was probably all the children they would have. Ekaterina had suffered three miscarriages since. The birth of Alexia had damaged her.

Ekaterina's fingers slipped out between the pages of the book. It hit the floor without her picking it up. She did not want to read any more, but she knew that she ought to do something or she would go on thinking in this saddened way. She got up and rearranged the ornaments on the mantelpiece, wondering why she always arranged ornaments so that they faced inwards. Today they would face outwards: the two lean dogs in bone china, the bronze Artemis which her father had bought, the beakers of Damascus silver. She wound up the clock. Then she took Alexia upstairs and undressed her, while the child struggled to avoid going to bed.

Ekaterina wished above all that she could have given her husband a son. Her own father had never had a son, and had not minded; he had been devoted to his daughters. But a Greek must have a son. In those first years, she would listen to the feel of her body in pregnancy and grow convinced that it nurtured a boy. She willed it. At first Michael told her that it did not matter. But more recently, when he was drunk, he would talk about it as if his own life and continuity were being snuffed out in her. And although he never accused her, she felt accused.

But her third miscarriage was different from the other two. Before it happened, everything was good. Michael was gentle and had given up drinking in the house. And because it was no longer any use pretending indifference, he said that he was sure the child would be a son. It was true, he seemed to have convinced himself. He always looked jubilant during these days, and walked as if flourishing himself. Yet she felt quite alone, as if the unborn child had nothing to do with him. It was only hers. She did not want anybody to know; and when it became obvious, she refused to talk about it. Before, she had been proud of her distended belly—let the whole world admire! But this time she hated to hear people talk of her faintly thickened waist, fussing her, tacitly debating its chances. They threatened it. People told her afterwards that she had become rude and silent. She was always glowering about her. She was not understood, and she did not care. Other people inhabited other spheres, while she lived only in the chalice of her own body, the body which was no longer simply hers, waiting for it to overflow. Nor did she mind any longer about the sex of this frail commotion inside her. She simply wanted to go on bearing it, to ease it triumphantly into the light, to hear its scream of liberation from the dangers of her own darkness.

Then, quietly, for no clear reason, it died.

It slipped out of her in a bloody mass. After much pain.

This completion of her, this thing which was she herself—a scarlet lump. She wanted to take it in her hands, to kiss it. She did not understand.

The doctors carried it away.

After that she had thought of returning to the hospital as a full-time nurse on the maternity staff. Nothing, not even caring for Alexia, had then seemed more important than preventing this from happening to other women. But Michael had objected, and he had probably been right. Besides, this did not seem to happen to other women here. They were fertile as cats. There were children everywhere.

But not hers.

She thought, for the thousandth time, as she put Alexia to bed: this child must not be spoilt.

"No, you can't have an apple."

Michael was more lenient than she. He adored the girl. He gave her the whole-hearted devotion which he no longer spent on Ekaterina. All the same, her failure to bear more children had not deeply affected their feelings for one another; rather it had pointed out changes which were already there, changes which had subtly taken place. Their kind of building did not fall all of a heap. It was chipped away. Or it rotted. The sudden, definite things might be remedied. But the unacknowledged ones, which divided people with the silence of curtains dropping year after year, at last formed a wall which you did not dare point out and which it was useless to discuss. You came to recognize features unnoticed before: pettiness, shallowness, small insincerities. He and she must always have been hopelessly different. Why had she thought otherwise? Only because, for a while, they had been drunk on one another.

Perhaps Julian was right that love was "not a thing to base your life on". But everything in her rebelled against that. For years she had worked hard to hold her relationship with Michael, and had flung herself into helping him in his business (although the mines slightly nauseated her). But after a while she could find nothing to discuss any longer. She could not keep up any interest. Where she differed from him, she found that she was damaging his dignity. In the end it was usually wiser to be silent.

Sometimes she wondered what they had talked about in their first years. They had filled each other's company with words! But it was mainly his flattering smile and his attentive manner which she remembered. That was rather humiliating. Yet she hated to believe that they had not been closer than this. Both of them had been different, fuller. Hadn't they? They had elicited more from one another. Then somewhere, unnoticed, they had lost the secret.

She thought that it was mainly her own fault. She had gone on regarding life in a childish way, as a spreading out of herself, farther and higher, limitless. But now everything inside her seemed to have stopped. Each day, each minute was a compromise. And she was filled with a violent, hopeless longing to get away—to burst into some other system, to touch on something real, something responsive.

She thought that she had never been fair to Michael. She had expected too much. His limitations (and hers too) could not have changed. It was no good demanding things which people did not have.

The peculiarity was that his love—and he did still love her in his way—elicited a condescension of her own: a spasmodic but perfectly genuine affection which seemed to be saying: "I don't understand why you still love me; but thank you, thank you for failing to realize how far apart we are—that means we can carry on." This softening of gratitude, almost of compassion, overlay her disillusion, concealing it a little from both of them. She was too emotional to feel indifferent. They had rows. He hated her to think differently from him. It insulted him. And so from time to time a furious dispute arose, he trying to make her see his way, she standing out.

But now, she thought, they were beginning to learn a little. They had barely discussed the new mining project. Argument on this would be especially damaging, since his future must be invested there, and in any case the quarrel would be certain to end as many of theirs did: he calling her impractical, she calling him inhuman. He would then start to drink. She dreaded this. There was a strong local whisky and a cheap brandy. She would ask forgiveness almost at once. She could never sustain anger. So sometimes she would dissuade him, saying that she was sorry without precisely saying she was wrong. But generally she would fail and would go up to the bedroom, if it was evening, and try to sleep early, and he would come in much later too stupefied to want her.

She turned out Alexia's light. The child was already asleep. It was seven o'clock. Michael would not be back for another hour; on most evenings he worked late now. She softly closed Alexia's door, thinking that there were many things of which she ought to be glad. She walked briskly into the bedroom and slipped into the white dress which gave her a semblance of privilege on her nursing rounds. Then she went downstairs, took up the case and walked out into the evening.

It was cool. The breeze touched the pines in the municipal garden, and stirred the pennants on the arch which said "Welcome to Kalepia." Some of the gardens were pretty in their ramshackle way, and the hibiscus were in flower, with a few cannas. If it were not for the thought of her two patients, she would have been positively happy.

But treating incurable patients made her feel guilty. Even when the relatives knew that nothing could be done, they would greet her with a stirring of hope. And she was more vulnerable to the sight of death now. She looked back on her hospital experience with astonishment. The first time the matron had said "Nurse, prepare the laying-out trolley", she had felt these little wings beating inside her. But she had already grown used to the nearly-dead. So she had washed the corpse of an eighty-five-year-old man—the first time she had ever seen a man's naked body—had cleaned his nails, brushed his hair and replaced his ring on his finger. Then she had conducted his relatives to see him with a feeling almost of pride. Because now his hands were twined in his beads among flowers. And they said how peaceful he looked, just as if asleep. But in fact he had died in agony. They were not to know that she had closed his eyes or that the matron had shown her how to pad the caved-in cheeks with lint and to twist cotton strips up the nostrils; or that she had shut his teeth and his flared lips over the deception until, yes, he looked peaceful as a waxwork.

Ekaterina was much weaker now. She was not sure if she could have touched a dead body. Perhaps this was why she found her hands trembling while she gave Andreas Alastos a cool wash. His flesh had shrunk against his frame to show every bone. She was fond of him, he had been a friend of her own father. But he could not have much longer to go, she thought. He was barely even sweating. His pulse was high. His temperature touched 104°, and he no longer had control of his bowels. She dabbed the sponge over his ribs gently, because they looked as if they would break. The skin was turning yellow. And all the time she had to joke with him—his mind remained clear—and to talk about trivia to Julian who sat with his hands spread lightly at his sides, as if he would suddenly get up.

And then came the gratitude, as if she had done something solid for the old man. That was the worst of all. Zena gave her a lemon drink and sat her down in the drawing-room. But after a moment Ekaterina looked at her watch and said that she must go, although she was not expected with her second patient for twenty minutes. Julian was smiling at her as if she was some kind of healing angel. She could not bear these unearned thanks. She had been stronger at eighteen, she thought.

He followed her on to the verandah and stopped her above the steps.

"You don't have to go yet." He said it like a fact, not a question.

"Not quite yet."

"And where are you going? Do you have another patient?"

"Yes. One other." She put down her case.

"And what does he have?"

"It's a woman. She has cancer."

He seemed shy with her now, as if he did not know her well. The respect he showed must be for her married status, she thought. But this status had leant her only a superficial poise. And it was precisely with Julian that she felt it least. He brought out the girl in her. It made her wonder whether she had really changed at all. It was faintly disturbing (because the girl was happier and more vulnerable). It gave a slightly irresponsible feeling.

But she was conscious of not looking irresponsible at all in her white dress, with the clinical case at her feet. It was just a feeling.

"You must let me know if you think Zena needs anything," she said. "She doesn't look strong."

"You mean drugs?"

"Yes. Something mild."

"She wouldn't accept them. We'll manage without."

Ekaterina had expected that. Drugs could choke off love as well as pain. Later it could seem as if a person had not loved so much, that he had cheated the dead. All the same, Julian looked so exhausted that she wished he had accepted an anodyne.

He said: "Zena's stronger than she seems. And for me it's easier. By the end of a day at the mine you feel played out. You heard about the gelignite, I suppose?"

"Michael told me. Muller antagonized them."

"Yes, I was there."

She knit her brows. It was just like Michael not to mention that, as if he had done everything alone. "You went down with him and Muller?"

"Yes." He did not seem to want to talk about it. He was pouting slightly. His face wore that puzzled look: the child trying to work out something. "I happened to see the geologist's map of the new mining area too," he said. "I must say..."

But whatever it was he must say, he only gave a slight shrug. In fact his whole body, propped against the balustrade, suggested surrender. Remembering his certainty and enthusiasm of a few months before, she was touched with sadness. Now, perversely, she found herself wishing he could recover confidence in the new mine. But she knew he never would. His feelings wavered so frailly that she only had to question something for him to frown and narrow his eyes and perhaps throw it into the balance against his own wishes. This conscientiousness appealed to her. Most people, she noticed, created the beliefs they needed. But not him.

Even now, she suspected that he was invoking her, as if she was his conscience, expecting her to say "I'm sure that map showed that the town outskirts would be ruined." But she felt that she could not talk about it any more. It was all very well for her to object; she did not have to work for the Company. And it was ridiculous how she was always disagreeing with him; because she had more respect for his opinions than for those of anyone else.

He was inexorably turning against the mines, and she was not surprised. It was natural for him to be on the side of the town, of the deprived. He often used the word "stunted". He hated anything stunted. His most typical gesture was an ungainly evocation of something bursting into flower. He used it continually when expressing an idea, and while he had been away it was like this that she had envisaged him, standing with his feet slightly apart and his hands bent upwards in a delving and lifting movement which involved his whole upper body.

"Have you seen that map?"

"No," she said, "but Michael has. He explained to me."

He nodded. "But to actually see it is different. Before, I'd envisaged a town with a mine attached to it. But this'll be a mine with a town attached. It'll absorb us all."

She was wishing more and more that he had kept his illusions. She simply said "Yes." After all, she would ride on the back of this dragon, but he, she was sure, would not.

He seemed to have been thinking the same because he said without any resentment (he never resented, he simply grew angry): "But your husband should do splendidly from it. It'll be good for you and the child."

"Educating one girl won't be a problem."

She did not mind him realizing that there would be no more children. He pursed his lips. She knew he wanted to say something sympathetic, but could not. He had never been any good at these short, tactful expressions; Michael would have found the right words at once. But Julian put his rough hand on her shoulder and said almost belligerently: "That's a shame! That's wrong. You always loved children. Look at all the children here not properly cared for! And you can't ... That's heartless, Ekaterina. I hope you've had proper attention. I hope..." Then he stopped and looked at her as if he might have upset her.

She could tell that he wanted to understand her marriage too—he hovered round the subject—but she had never confided that to anyone. Perhaps this was why she so often felt constricted. To tell somebody, just one person, would be like vomiting after a long nausea. And since she would not tell anybody she knew, she thought that one day she was going to pour it all into the lap of a stranger, some housewife, perhaps, travelling on the train between the Capital and Nikitari. That would be a little like confessing to a star or a tree. Not a betrayal, just a harmless bleeding.

But if she divulged it to Julian he would start at once to build up some extraordinary solution, as if a huge mental exertion could solve everything. All the same, he was the one whom she most nearly wanted to tell.

"There are women who have no children at all," she said. She wondered why she immediately had to be cheerful when somebody sounded sorry for her; but her brisk voice continued: "It's futile to worry. In fact anxiety can be harmful to conception—or so we were told in psychotherapy lectures."

"Then is psychotherapy quite respectable now?"

"Good heavens yes!"

"In fact if you believe you will recover from an illness, you increase your chances?"

"Yes, in some diseases."

For a long moment Julian was silent, thinking, then he started to laugh soundlessly to himself, she had no idea what about. He said: "So you mean the cult of healing round that wretched saint may be doing good all the while?" He went on laughing then stretched his arms above his head, half exasperated and half relieved, as if he had given everything up and was laughing at the world. "Oh Ekaterina! I don't know!" He turned and looked out from the verandah. "Even though that saint was invented in early Christian times?"

"Oh yes," she said. "People can be cheated back into health. But I expect you'd object to that. You'd stay ill."

He was still shaking his head. "Ekaterina, sometimes I get a feeling ... as if I'm only real with you. Explain that."

"I can't explain that." But once or twice she had felt the same with him—this sensation of sliding back, of girlish regeneration. As if some stratum in her was being disturbed. She thought that this must be because her life had run through itself so suddenly. The important steps had come too close together: love, disillusion, marriage, childbirth—she could hardly have caught up with herself! And that was how old people said existence was. Gone in a flicker. When she had first loved she had felt as if years and years awaited her—the child's feeling of endless life.

Julian was scratching his forehead and chuckling. "I think I'll become a goatherd! If I graze them will you milk them?"

She began to laugh. "My English half may, but my Greek half will charge you for it. That's solid service for an intelligent price."

This joking about their different halves—she'd forgotten all about that. She could not help smiling back at him. It was odd, she thought, but she felt no bitterness: perhaps because of her impression that he had suffered as much as she. (These debts of suffering!) Or perhaps it was because she recognized now that he had, in fact, loved her, and she had not been just to him. It had even occurred to her to tell him so, but the idea hurt her intensely.

Julian had stopped laughing. His hands, which had been dangling over the balustrade, now held each other so that their veins stood out. The vigour and lightness had left his voice. He asked: "Tell me frankly, Ekaterina, have I changed?" He seemed to have steeled himself against her reply. He looked strained and depressed. She wondered what on earth he was expecting her to say. Of course he had changed. But she was almost pained to tell him so, because she had loved him as he had been. She realized that she wouldn't have cared if he had matured or not. To her it was more important that he should not have lost any part of himself that she had cherished. Yet now, to a woman, the youth's gaucheness had become something more protective. That was what she would have expected.

So she told him precisely that.

It was true. He had become a man. That was why this feeling of sliding back must be spurious; he was not the same any more than she was.

Was she? She did not ask him. He was relaxed now. But it unsettled her that they kept the same manner together. Sometimes she felt pangs of apprehension with him, just as if she was a girl again. It was almost as though they were carrying on in the same way, without physical contact. He even looked at her in the same way.

But she could not imagine what new manner they might develop. When she stood up and said she had to go, it even seemed strange, momentarily, that they did not start kissing. Julian returned to looking over the verandah and stood attending to the glow of a cigarette as he inhaled, watching it flare close to his lips then die again. Her shoes rapped loudly down the steps. She crossed on to the road. The house of the cancer patient was almost at the street's end. She felt neat and contained walking along the pavement in her white dress. She listened to her shoes tapping. She had a silly desire to skip. But she did nothing of the sort. She continued walking in her responsible way with the slim case in her hand.

Chapter Seventeen

The archimandrite was sitting in his armchair and gazing at the beam of light which floated countless particles of dust into the room. Extraordinary, he thought, how every moment he must be inhaling that dust and breathing it out again—God knew how many specks!—and yet he remained healthy and went on living.

All the same, these August afternoons were insufferable. In the Capital it had always been possible to escape into the mountains—but here! There was not a developed resort within a hundred kilometres, only a café or two near fresh-water springs which would be dried up by now. He mopped his forehead with his handkerchief. All day he was mopping and dabbing. No sooner had he cleared the sweat from his forehead than he would feel it trickling at his neck. Then his scalp would itch and he would stoop over a basin and pour water over his head, before combing out his hair and twisting it back into a knot behind.

He was sure that if only the heat had allowed him, he could have reached a decision of his own on the St Vichinos Mountain instead of letting circumstances decide. All he had needed was a single bracing day in a Northern climate—somewhere like Sweden—and he would have sat in the cold with a few sheets of paper and developed a vigorous thesis. That must be why they got things done in those parts: simply a matter of temperature. Whereas here the moment he began wrestling with the problem his head started to ache as if a manacle were tightening round his temples, until very soon the matter hazed itself over and he ended up by sitting in his chair, just like this, staring at the sunlight.

He had reached the end of his resources. He had scooped everything out of himself and it might as well have been nothing. And he had suffered a good deal in the process. The only feeling left to him was a subdued bitterness that he had tried to do right yet had been answered by silence. He felt deserted—but precisely by whom he did not know.

Even now that he had decided, it did not feel like his decision. It was not he, but everybody else, who had assumed he would sell. Oh yes, everyone had known how he would decide, except him! He dabbed the water from his eyes. Of course people were the same everywhere. It had not occurred to them that anybody could turn down a profitable deal. All right then! They had decided for him! He would not disappoint them. Even if he refused to sell, they would not say it was an act of conscience. No, they always had to level a man to themselves. They'd simply say he was frightened (which was true). And in any case—he mopped his neck again—he was already incurring the same hostility as if he had sold. When his decision was known, the reaction would not be a howl of outrage, but simply "We knew that" or even "Naturally—the man's not a fool—they must have offered a good price." That was the sum of these people: money.

He stood up and stroked out the folds in his gown. It was almost six o'clock and still hot. He placed his *kamelauikon* carefully on his head and arranged the cross over his chest. Only a few minutes separated him from his resolve—the few minutes which it took to walk from his residence to the Oldenburgs' house. He had promised to be there by six. He crossed the garden and started up the street. He thought that when walking he took smaller steps these days, and more delicate. Until now he had not thought of himself as a man whose powers were declining. But then for years his powers had not been put to the test. He had grown flaccid without noticing.

He folded his hands into his sleeves and promised himself: everything will be better after the act. Already the Company was bearing the brunt of disapproval, whereas his own struggle had gone unnoticed—in fact scarcely anybody believed he had been struggling at all. And it would be up to the Company as to how it dealt with the town. He could not be held responsible for that. The Company was equipped for decisions. It could go into consultation with itself. But he was alone.

He avoided the main street, and went among a network of houses and small shops. As for the future, he was afraid that Company decisions were no better than personal ones. On the contrary, an organization could lose its conscience quicker than an individual. Because within it your actions were never quite your own. That was how armies worked.

More of the shop windows showed notices or reproductions of the saint now. They were pasted up from inside so that they could not be blown away or torn down. The handwritten slogans almost all said the same—these people, he thought, could not even write differently—"Ayios Vichinos pray for us", "God will be the Judge" or simply "Ayios Vichinos". The shopkeepers themselves, loitering in their doorways, never looked at him as he went by; they stared straight in front of them or turned back inside. The carpenter, planing a chair-leg in his open workhouse, did not look up (but then he never did). This, the archimandrite thought, must be what a Turk felt like as he walked here, or a negro or a Jew in other societies. Such a man could never know how people behaved normally. There was no way of telling whether the scowl on a face was natural to it or was intended for you. Already he had forgotten how these people had looked before the issue of the mine arose, and he had a sudden ridiculous urge to sit in one of the dingy restaurants and wait and watch—as if, when it believed him gone, the whole street would burst into smiling life.

Then, coming round a corner, he saw a notice in a grocer's window, very large. It spelt out the single word: "Judas". His step faltered. What should he do? He walked on. How dare they! They did not know his mind! And they had not seen his suffering! So. That proved it. They deserved nothing. Nothing.

He was striding now, striding like a young man. A woman leaned over a balcony in front of him and emptied a bowl of potato peelings into the gutter. Insult or coincidence, what did it matter? These people did not deserve a saint or a Church or a single priest. No. Not a cabbage! The police chief greeted him in passing. That was something. Responsible men, the police. They knew that things weren't always simple.

By the time he had reached the Oldenburgs' house his heart was beating hard and he decided to stop for breath before he pressed the bell button. He felt faint. But here at least were civilized people, who knew how to treat a person properly. They did not rush into assumptions or set themselves up as judge of things in which they were not qualified. No, they showed a proper respect. He straightened his collar. It was always the little people, the narrow people, who knew everything—the ones who kept petty stores. Oh yes, they were pocket sages, all of them! Nothing they couldn't tell you! "Judas" indeed! Had they been through theological seminary? Did they have a bean's-worth of learning on the saints, or anything else? Had any of them so much as heard of the Seventh Council of Nicaea? And they called him "Judas"! He set back stray wisps of hair over his ears and tried to compose himself. An odd thing, he thought, but the more intelligent people were, the more likely to be diffident. Look at old Sofroniou, for instance, hedging his comments with "perhaps" and "possibly" and "on the whole". Sofroniou had never told him how to do his job, any more than he would have told the schoolmaster how to teach. No, it was only a grocer who would presume to tell an archimandrite how to behave! He lifted off his headgear and smoothed his hands over his scalp. The ignorant should be silent. Let the whole world be silent until it understood!

Claudia Oldenburg opened the door. She had seen the archimandrite climbing the steps, and had waited, wondering whether the bell had broken. Even after she had sat him down in an armchair with a drink, he did not regain his colour. Oldenburg was in his study and had asked to be told as soon as the bell went; but the bell had not gone, so she let the archimandrite sit for a minute, while he caught his breath. She could not tell what kind of decision he had reached. He merely looked worn out, so that even his agitation—he had been mumbling to himself fiercely as she opened the door—had now subsided.

"It's hot out there," he said. "Too hot for an old man." He set down his whisky and relapsed tenderly among the cushions, easing back his shoulders after the rest of his body was still. That was the first time he could remember calling himself an old man, and Mrs Oldenburg had not contradicted him. Ah well.

Claudia offered him a cigarette which he took in shaking fingers. She lit it for him. Whatever decision he had reached, she thought, he did not look pleased by it. She went back to the drink cabinet and poured, very slowly, some whisky for Frank, while the wheezing behind her grew measured and soft. As for her, she would be glad to have the thing resolved—if Frank did not buy this site, he would only find another. This one or that one, did it matter? If it was this one, the townspeople would fuss about the changes for a while, then settle down to make more money, or whatever it was they wanted. As for the Company, a few more expensive cars would jam the streets of Los Angeles. But that was all.

"I'll fetch my husband," she said. Frank had been almost excited for the past hour. He reminded her of a boy, or of himself as he was when they were first married. This sudden showing of emotion and uncertainty pleased her; but she could not become excited herself. If the deal was concluded, she and Frank might become very rich. But that wouldn't change them. And it would not help their children. Caroline was the only one who might be affected by money, and not for the good. Howard simply needed independence. In general she did not see what the rage for money was all about. If Frank should ask her whether there was anything she wanted, what could she say? All the things she wanted were already lost.

No, she would answer. Nothing.

So he would conclude that he had done all he could for her. Although she might, of course, say that she would like to ask a piano-tuner down from the Capital. ("Now be sensible, Claudia.")

She opened the study door and he was up in a moment and into the drawing-room, extending his hand to the archimandrite and smiling. Yes, he was smiling! It altered his whole face. His smiles, Claudia thought, were like words of praise from the most exacting critic. They warmed her. She was smiling too.

But the archimandrite was not. "I'm afraid I'm late," he said. "This weather..." He laid his drink carefully on a side-table. As he did so, he noticed how his hand shook. It was like another person's hand, bloodless, the sort of hand which he saw when conducting funerals, laid on the breast of the corpse in open coffins. He looked away from it. "Have you seen these notices in the shops? I find some of them intolerable."

"The people here are like that," Oldenburg said. "If one shouts they all shout. They're not worth your worry."

"No," replied the archimandrite. He noticed the bitterness in the word. What was he saying? These people were his responsibility, his sheep. Of course they were his worry! He, like the saint, was a part of their way to God. He too was a mediator. "I dare say they have their reasons," he said. With closed eyes he sipped at his glass of whisky and tried to collect himself. But really, he thought, there was nothing to collect. He must resemble those dead molluscs which were washed up near the port. Their innards, little by little, had been scoured out by the sea, and even their shells thinned through constant friction. Soon they would disintegrate. Of course to other people he only looked tired. But there were various sorts of tiredness. He wanted to say "I require more time to think about this sale; I will give you my decision next week." But it would be no use. He had no decision in him. "Yes, these are a difficult people," he said vaguely, "not like in the Capital."

How far he had come from loving them! Now it was a struggle not to hate them. He must always be reminding himself: "These are your responsibility. These are poorer than you." That was the easiest way—to keep telling himself that they were, in a sense, inferior. That way he could forgive them. He felt the water gathering again in his eyes. A man could not love people in general. If he loved them all, he was a fool or a child. It was all very well for monks to talk about the human brotherhood. They were not much exposed to these brothers, with their loud voices and foul-smelling bodies, to be cheated and insulted by them. ("Judas" indeed!) Life was easy enough if you refused to live it.

He took up his drink again; the glass was cool in the palm of his hand. The Oldenburgs were expecting him to speak, she very reserved (how well these foreign women kept their looks!), he impatient, tapping the arms of his chair. The archimandrite looked slowly from one to the other, running his tongue round his lips, but eventually he said more for his own benefit than theirs—he was thinking aloud: "The people are against this deal—except the municipal councillors, and since they don't speak for the people, they're deprived of moral authority."

Oldenburg said curtly, harshly: "But still it's these men the town has voted to trust. The people are going against their cooler judgment because of a few rabble-rousers. That trust must hold until the councillors' term of office expires."

The archimandrite lowered his gaze. This argument reminded him of certain theological tracts. "The fact remains," he said, "that the majority don't want it."

Oldenburg was gripping the chair hard. "But the decision of the majority is invariably simple-minded," he rapped out.

The archimandrite sighed silently to himself. "So you may disregard it?"

Oldenburg's lips had tightened. Poor fellow, the archimandrite thought, he imagines that I'm not going to sell. Whereas the fact was that you could never know what was good for people. The people themselves didn't know. As far as he was concerned, he found it easier to think about the Church. It was the Church which had nurtured him. The Church was his family. Now that no other clear answer came to him, now that he was this scoured-out shell washed up from feeling and reason, he could act only on the judgments of others—and everybody assumed that the sale would benefit the Church. He, like the people, could not turn down a profitable deal for his family. That made it possible for him to sell. Nothing else. Just that. A kind of tribal feeling. Even his desire for advancement, he thought, was now merely a nugget inside him. Nothing much any more. One day he might wake up to find that even that had gone. After all, who was a bishop? Was a bishop, after death, more privileged than an archimandrite? It was only in frescoes that bishops stood around the throne of God. What really happened, nobody knew.

Oldenburg was saying: "But these people may change their minds tomorrow—or somebody else may change them. They can't reason for themselves. I've been working here seventeen years now, and I can tell you the only motive here is money. As soon as they come to see that the mine is profitable to them, they'll support it."

"I dare say," answered the archimandrite. The people were not stupid, just ignorant. "Our race has been adapting for centuries. We can squeeze wine out of a boot." Yes, these shopkeepers would soon accommodate to whatever filled their pockets. They wouldn't suffer—not for the world! It was the poor who would get the worst of it—and that reminded him. "The only question left concerns the olive trees. There are not many on the Mountain, but several families would suffer without them. I think that the Company should make a gesture here, if only to set aside a small piece of land for replanting."

At those words "the only question left" the strain in Oldenburg's face changed to a vigorous pleasure. So the sale would go through. But Oldenburg would make no concessions. His price had been agreed among the shareholders. No more, no less. This was not a bazaar. "We have insufficient land to spare as it is, archimandrite. I've pledged to the municipality that we'll reaccommodate all the householders who are evicted. And our expenses only begin with this purchase. We have to buy machinery, pay dues for rights at the port, house our new staff and so on. No, I'm sorry. The olive trees cannot be our responsibility. We're a business, not a charity."

A few months ago the archimandrite would have fought this; he could have flattered, bluffed, threatened and opened up new avenues of approach. But now his mind went dead. In any case, who were these poor? He had never seen any. Everyone had some sort of business.

He toyed with the arms of the chair. The Company had offered a good price. His lawyers had compared it with cessions of land for both copper and chrome mining in other parts of the Republic, and they had been satisfied. He said slowly: "If that is so, it is so. I dare say the bishop will make an allowance." He had no idea if this was likely. "But one more thing, Mr Oldenburg. The shrine is to be demolished at the Company's expense, and we must have warning at least a month beforehand. The icons, you understand. . . ."

"Certainly."

There had been no special reason for demanding this. Perhaps he was seeking a token concession before he surrendered (he felt it as a surrender); or perhaps he was simply postponing the moment. But one thing was certain: he did not in the least care who demolished the shrine. He felt nothing for it beyond faint nausea.

Yesterday morning, while the air was still cool, he had climbed the path to the Mountain's crest. It was as if he were giving the saint a last chance. What he expected from the visit, he had no idea. Instead he was laying himself open to ideas outside him. For months he had been talking and arguing. Now, in exhaustion, he would not talk, but listen.

Beneath him, down the middle slopes, the trees had dropped away. Along the path only a few holm-oaks clustered, and an army of burnt-out plants—thistles and asphodel—stood bolt upright and transparent in the brightness. Three-quarters of the way up, the archimandrite had sat down on a stone, his heart thudding. It was undignified, but there was nobody to see. By the time he had reached the summit the air was no longer cool, and the sun flamed over the upper valley. The shrine showed a dazzling whitewashed dome. It rose from the rocks with a numinous starkness. Beside it stood a holy tree, decked with the rags of those who were diseased and had asked for healing. Behind him the whole valley plunged to the sea. He replaced his *kamelauikon* and crossed himself. The shrine rested in front of him. The mountaintops were drawn about it like glass, blue and grey. The waves shone far off. Listen, he told himself, listen. There was no wind. Utter silence. The brilliance of the light! It did not flow. It was golden, still. It held the whole land in suspension. Listen. Not a cicada, not a bird. But some other presence. This presence also not moving, waiting. Almost the stillness of midday, the Pan-hour. Yes. He felt it. Something was holding its breath.

Should he go forward? Yes, go forward. Cutting through the silence, the light, he pressed his hand against the wooden door. A pale pine-wood, hard and old to the touch. Push. Something would speak (why hadn't he done this before?). Do not think. Listen. Pushing harder now, to enter the sanctuary, the bleached wood gently gave way at his touch.

Then plop! And plop! He jumped back, shuddering. Black, loathsome, they trailed along the floor and up the walls: beetles. Hundreds of them. Ugh! He whipped off his kamelauikon and dashed his hand over it. They were creeping under the lintel too. He had always detested them. The place smelt of bats' urine. In the steaming air he was shaken by cold. His shoulders convulsed. He slammed the door. That proved it. Nobody ever went there.

"The Church agrees to sell," he said—Oldenburg had been waiting many seconds for him to speak—"We'll get our lawyers to meet as soon as we can."

"Excellent! Delighted!" Oldenburg was on his feet and vigorously shaking the old man's hand. "Marvellous! I'm sure you've acted in the way most advantageous to the Church. It is a great opportunity. Excellent!"

He was beaming, he was literally beaming. His blue eyes were almost genial. Claudia was reminded of other times, years ago, other things. She felt suffused with warmth. She leant over and laced her fingers into Frank's, and he smiled back at her and actually placed his other hand over hers, and they were smiling at one another. She wanted to laugh. Could this begin a new life for them, new characters? Could the play be changed? Frank was still beaming. Scrap those characters! Let's have these ones! Could it happen? Could you, after all, retrieve? His hands (at least one of them now) were still linked to hers. She went on smiling at him.

Well, thought the archimandrite, that was something. At least somebody was happy.

"Have another drink!" Oldenburg said. "Drink to it!"

The archimandrite looked at his glass. "No," he said. "This will do."

Oldenburg began: "Now just one or two points for the lawyers..."

"No, no," interrupted the archimandrite. He was almost pleading. "Leave all the details till later. Let the lawyers deal with them.

We can correspond and so on, and sort out the rest ... and ... everything...." His voice tailed away. His face seemed not to look straight out, but to be hanging down. Only the small, red rims under his eyes gave them life.

"As you like, archimandrite," Oldenburg said. He still smiled, a tight, set smile. "But you must remember that the Company is grateful to you. As Mr Lerides mentioned before, we feel in your debt for this trouble. We certainly wish to make a gift."

The archimandrite stood up and stroked his hands over his gown. He repeated "Gift?" in an expressionless tone. He touched a finger to his beard. "I don't want a gift, Mr Oldenburg. Thank you." He listened to these words of his without surprise. Of course he could always change his mind on this point before contracts were exchanged. But he did not particularly see why he should. The gift would not be worth the trouble. Why invite another factor with which to do battle? Why complicate everything? That gift would only arouse something inside him, something with which he had not had to contend before. Not a spark, just a dull, unhappy resistance.

A man wanted peace, not money.

Oldenburg's jaw was working back and forth as he opened the front door for him. "You're sure about that? I understood from Mr Lerides that you would accept."

The archimandrite wished this man would not look at him as though he was a fool. It made him feel as if he was. He drew himself as upright as he could, and although Oldenburg would not recognize the words of St Chrysostom, answered: "'Within conscience, there are no flatterers, no wealth to corrupt the judge.'"

Which was true, no doubt. Even if the judge was incapable of judgment. Even if he had been corrupted years ago.

Chapter Eighteen

The branches of the trees interlocked too closely to let in the moonlight. They overhung the path in many layers, which from beneath appeared solid as a ceiling. Only their white trunks showed up paler than the leaves, where the bark had fallen from them in rotting heaps. Since his adolescence this path had reminded Alastos of Ekaterina, and it saddened him to walk on it with her again—she married, he alone—accompanying her home after she had nursed his father. But the olive-pickers sometimes slept by it on warm nights, so that it was considered "not safe", and unpleasant things—although nobody could be specific—were said to have happened here.

Several times already they had almost stopped, he dragging his feet, she trimming her pace to his slowness, as though they meant to dispel the situation's tenseness. It was absurd, Julian thought, to be walking through these trees where they had spent their love, and to pretend that they had forgotten.

The night was very still. They talked impersonally, and even discussed the shrine. Ekaterina no longer disputed with him. If he put out an argument, she retired before it, but usually he would answer himself much as she would have done, and once he even looked at her in open exasperation and said "Ekaterina, you're always changing my mind!" But she had scarcely said anything.

And all the time, underneath, he was thinking of something quite different, and so was she (he was sure). The path was blatantly the same, and the trees.

He said: "Kalepia seemed half dead when I came. But now I feel it almost pleasant again, like I remembered it. I don't get so infuriated any more."

"Oh you," Ekaterina laughed, "you'll always be a bit infuriated." Nevertheless, she thought, he looked more at ease.

"Well, they do make you angry," he said.

"Who are *they*?"

"The men on the streets, sitting, sleeping. . . ." But he was scarcely attending to his own words. The night had turned the path into a long, velvet corridor.

Ekaterina was feeling a lightness in her legs, walking so easily over the powdery ground. The trees were thinning out. She glimpsed the moon-filled sky through their branches. Julian talked on disjointedly about the new mine, even admitted his disgust. But his face and voice showed no sign of misery. He was smiling. She watched this smile develop and remain, and a deep relief came over her. She would have liked to take his arm (but not here, not among the trees) and tell him how thankful she was. Not because his feelings were right or wrong, but because they were resolving. She said at last, as lightly as she could: "So you don't favour the new mine at all?"

He said almost vaguely: "No."

He was looking at her white dress which showed up like an hourglass, tiny at the waist. His feet were wayward, they wanted to stop, but above them his chest and shoulders, for weeks so heavy, felt no weight at all. It's wrong, he thought, that we should be walking here like this. Other people talk about their past relationships, even laugh about them. Why do we have to go in this silence?

They had reached a place which they both remembered. The blackness of the overhanging trees was intermittent, and beyond them were other trees which stood in moonlight. The ground was covered in its pallor, like a frost. They were both walking noiselessly, almost, it seemed, on tiptoe. Neither of them spoke. The path curled greyly ahead. They had almost reached its end. He could remember that. This was the last clearing, here, among the rough, quiet trunks of the myrtle trees. These stood taller than myrtles usually grow. Their branches drooped untidily, and were filled with purplish berries.

Julian's walking petered out. He began: "I've been meaning to ask you something." He wiped his hand coarsely over his mouth, for no purpose. He felt clumsy again, standing in front of her, and she, for some reason, not looking at him. "Don't you feel sour with me?"

While she had stared at the ground she might have been feeling anything. Now she looked up quickly and said "No."

He answered with relief: "It seemed wrong to be walking here and pretending and . . ."

"Yes I know." Suddenly she put down the nurse's case. "And I know why you asked that." She was standing with her back to the trunk of one of the myrtle trees. I must say it now, she thought. She owed it to him. "I want to apologize to you," she began. "It's ten years too late, but I want to, all the same. I was very hard on you. Looking back, I can tell you loved me. I can remember certain scenes distinctly. But I was too narrow to believe you. I thought love could only be like mine. I'm not going to ask you to forgive me because I know you'd say there was nothing to forgive. But I think there is. When you said the other day that you didn't believe in love, it was like something you'd suffered. That was my doing. Wasn't it? Or am I being conceited?"

He breathed "No . . . I mean, not your fault. . . ."

She looked so wan and sad, he could not collect himself. This sickly moonlight was drugging him. He had no idea what to say to her. She went on in the same tense voice: "Do you remember what you said those years ago? You simply said that a man needed to feel himself worthy of a woman. You wanted me to wait for you. You were just twenty-one. And I answered—I remember this distinctly—that my love should make you feel worthy. I demanded to know why it didn't. And you couldn't answer. And I couldn't forgive you." Her hands were still pressed behind her against the tree trunk. "But I could answer now, and so could you. That it's only a woman who feels transfigured by love in that way—it alters her being. But that doesn't happen to a man. He has to feel worthy in himself. Which seems more respectable when you come to think of it. But I didn't allow you that. No, when I was twenty I knew everything." He was astonished at her; she was bitter with herself, not with him. He had never seen her like this. She was perfectly controlled, but her grief—and that was the only word for it—was spoken in terse phrases emitted under a hard pressure of feeling. "That's why I'm not sour with you," she said. "I have no business to be. You may not recognize any of this, because you no longer believe in love. But there was a time when you did—which I remember—and it was a good feeling, a generous feeling, killed off by a self-opinionated girl. Please don't say anything—" She raised the palm of one hand and kept it there to silence him. But the gesture, he thought, looked more like a blessing from some pale statue under the tree. "Don't talk about logic. Don't say the real fact is that love is irrational and so on. I'm just a woman and the truth to me is what I feel."

His face was puckered by deep, furious lines of disagreement. But he could not get himself to say anything. She seemed to have mesmerized him. This frozen light—he hated it now—made her look gaunt. And if she appeared like that, he must look ghastly. Now Ekaterina had lost her tightness of voice and said dully: "I dare say it's true that love is nonsense. After all, its wreckage is everywhere. You're probably right."

He shook himself as if he was shaking off somebody's grip. "Don't say that."

"But you said it."

"Yes, but I don't want you to say it." How childish he sounded. "You always believed so passionately."

"So did you."

He suddenly felt an irrational panic about her. She seemed broken, and he felt her sliding beyond his control. All at once she was not at all the person he had known. She was adult and lonely. He fumbled for words to correct her. She was talking nonsense—all this about killing parts of people as if they were hydras. He did not feel anything dead in him.

He said in an almost imploring tone: "I haven't the slightest bitterness, Ekaterina. Do I look bitter? If you'd killed anything in me I'd know it."

For God's sake believe me, he thought. What had happened to this adorable woman? He had been used to curing her moods before, but this was a new person with a contained, mature sorrow. Something in him was profoundly alarmed. "Listen, Ekaterina," he said; he was positively comforting her now. "People often say those things when they're not in love. I expect it's just the same with me. I didn't experience that again. But if I do, I'll suddenly feel quite differently—I'm bound to, aren't I?"

Her face did not change. It wore that expression which was older than him. "But the fact is you haven't loved again."

He held her shoulders tightly; they were small and soft (he remembered). He bent towards her and almost whispered, as if to a child; "Look, if you'd killed that in me, I'd hate you, wouldn't I?" He waited. "Wouldn't I?"

A faint lightness appeared in her voice when she agreed. It was like a chink opening.

Then he added triumphantly: "Do I seem to hate you?"

"No."

"There you are!" He released her, as if he was giving her freedom.

She stared back, puzzled, wondering why she had not considered this herself. She could not yet quite believe him.

But she must, he thought. He would make her. "Really I don't see why I said all that about love being delusion! I wasn't deluded in the slightest. You're just as fine as I thought you—every bit! But don't frown like that." It was true, he thought. His love had been well placed. He gazed into the green eyes, trying to convince her. They stared back at him. They were filled with confusion.

It crossed his mind that in a way she was right—his opinion on love had grown from bitterness with her, years ago. But now that opinion was like a suit of armour with no one inside. You could knock it over at a touch. Why he suddenly regarded so lightly a conviction which had been born in such pain, he could not tell. All he knew was that this leftover theory troubled him not a bit—no more than a conclusion on some remote academic subject.

"You forgive me everything, Ekaterina, so you ought to forgive yourself. I criticized your affection too, didn't I? I accused you of being half in love with your own feelings. A woman's subjectivity—" He laughed boisterously. "I had plenty to say about that! I seem to remember treating you like some sort of alloy, as though I could melt you down into component parts and pour half of you away!"

She was laughing reluctantly. It sounded funny now. And he looked comical as he was talking about it—and his face, she thought, was full of affection. Yes, she could remember these arguments well, but they had not damaged her because she had ignored them. The more she thought of herself then, the less she liked the person she discerned.

She felt warmed by his forgiveness. It spread all through her. She became filled with a kind of love for him. He reminded her of those dancing bears which could still be seen in central Turkey. They were too gentle for the wilds, but civilization constricted them and could make them ridiculous. In fact they were a little unsuited to anywhere.

It seemed so easy to talk intimately—they might have been standing in a drawing-room instead of this circle of moonlit trees—

that she asked him straight: "Why didn't you love anyone else?"

He pouted slightly. The peculiarity, he thought, was that people did love, not that they didn't. "I spent most of those years in a mining town in Utah," he said off-handedly. "It was difficult to meet the sort of woman you might like. The miners had a bad reputation. And the young people mostly worked in the cities, just like here. The small towns were for the old." He knew that he was not being quite frank. There had been girls, after all, but he remembered them as little different from one another. In his eyes their fault had simply been (if he was honest) that they were unable to replace Ekaterina. They were only charades. He was sure of that now. In his memory they had resolved into a composite girl. On a good many mornings he had woken up to see this girl's head on the pillow beside him, and her curled-in shoulders. Her clothes would be scattered over the furniture among his, her bra hung on a chair-back. And he would glance at this closed-off creature without the slightest desire to touch or speak to her. The fact was that he had never slept with Ekaterina (if you had such a relationship with a girl in Kalepia, that was the end of her) and it was frustrating to have had such physical contact with other women, yet barely to have touched the one he loved. On these white, tired mornings he would ask himself why he bothered with it. It was not only subtly disappointing, but this way it was a little sordid.

He said: "I dare say a man's lucky if he loves more than once or twice. Perhaps a woman is."

"Yes." But she did not want him to speak coldly about love again. She only wanted to take away his forgiveness still warm in her. She picked up her case and said as if to match his own sang-froid: "The past always seems better. People deceive themselves." She took a few paces along the path.

But Julian did not move. Was she talking like that about their own past, he wondered? He refused to follow her. He remembered their love perfectly well, even if she didn't. It was one thing to say that this happiness could not be repeated, but quite another to pretend you hadn't had it. That was a double poverty.

She was standing a short distance away. She did not look the same to him. It was hard to tell how strained she was, or how much came from this detestable light. But he had the feeling that their past was being corroded. He thought: if you stop believing that the good things were good, everything goes to hell. You wouldn't believe in a future either, let alone a present. And this was not like Ekaterina at all.

She took the few steps back to him. He looked so outraged standing there that she felt ashamed of herself for having upset him with this lie. And of course it was a lie. Of course they had been happy. "I'm talking nonsense." She thought that if he did not understand, she had better tell him. The painful words came fluently: "It's simply easier for me to try to forget." Then she started to walk.

He followed the white shape, the hourglass. The moonlight caught the calves of her legs, darker than the dress. "Easier for me to try to forget." So his return had upset her. He could feel where the words were, in a nest in the core of him, just between his ribs.

Chapter Nineteen

Now that Andreas Alastos was dying, only a few strands of his life held significance for him, and it was to these that his mind returned when it looked back to justify his existence or to assure himself that he had existed at all. His three decades in the copper mines were forgotten, one year like another, and instead his memory rediscovered the time when he had crewed cargo boats with Yugoslav and Arab sailors, and had joined a freighter travelling through the Panama Canal between the West Indies and the South Pacific.

His head on the pillow was so shrivelled that the bones almost broke through its skin. His body looked stiff and narrow under the single sheet, and lay formally with its feet together. The life in it seemed no farther from death than the pulling of the sheet over the head. Yet all morning and into the afternoon his memories returned, vivid, as if demanding a last breath before their rich world crumbled with the frame which could no longer contain it.

Zena sat as she had done for months, her hands plunged in her lap and her head inclined to him. She scarcely spoke, only listened like somebody who has suffered for so long that nothing more can be inflicted. Occasionally she reached to the basin of cold water on the bedside table, took a flannel and passed it over his forehead, but now his body did not have the energy to sweat; and it was still only five o'clock in the afternoon, three hours before the peak of his fever.

"I wish you could have seen that," he whispered. "They say you shouldn't sleep under a Polynesian temple ... the spirits ... But there I was and opened my eyes in the night to see it gliding over the water. They'd lit a flame to attract the fish, and a man standing absolutely still at the prow.... The fire glittered on the tip of his spear ... its flame made an orange path over the water." He gazed at the ceiling but whether he saw it, or Samoa, or nothing, she did not know. "Papeete was disgusting ... there were these sea-turtles they caught, lying still alive in the mud outside the houses ... sticking out their tongues...." He gave a soundless cough. "But Moorea island comes vertically out of the sea. You should go to Moorea." She nodded, although he could not see her and although she had no more chance of going to Moorea than he did. So she just imagined it, rising straight out of the sea.

"We put in at the Fiji Islands for supplies. The Indians had set up businesses there ... and grown more wealthy than the natives ... who were friendly fellows with bushy hair. But they got bitter. The Indians were showing them things they didn't have so ... they got bitter...."

Although his whisper was almost effortless, she wanted to say "Stop, you're tiring yourself." But there was no point. Was he to lie without expending himself on action or thought or speech, and simply wait?

"So did the natives attack?"

He closed his eyes and eventually answered: "I don't think so. I don't know. We sailed off. But I expect they ... accommodated." He puffed through pouted lips: a cough which scarcely moved his chest. Zena held the basin under his mouth in the hope that this might give him strength to cough properly; but he could not. He whispered: "Extraordinary how ... you never think about your lungs ... until ... but after that you never forget them ... Now in the Marquesas..."

Zena remained without speaking, which was what he seemed to want. Everything inside her was dulled. She was never angry now, never upset, never anything. She thought that she would not again feel anything sharp. The instruments inside her were irreparably blunted. She was sitting at her husband's deathbed and she could not weep, only look down at his unrecognizable face and wish that even this cask of a man would remain. Even this half-life. Anything so she could know "He is alive! He still breathes! He is still with me!"

But she was so tired that after he had stopped talking and appeared to sleep, she dozed off with her head on her breast. She did not hear Julian and the doctor climbing the verandah steps. The doctor was elderly, and stopped half-way up, wheezing. He had been trying to keep pace with Julian all the way from his house.

"I know there's nothing you can do," Julian straddled the stairway behind him. "That's not the point. My step-mother's completely run down. She'll have a breakdown. It doesn't matter what you do. Just go in and take his temperature and mumble something—anything to make them both feel he hasn't been abandoned."

The doctor was still catching his breath. He asked: "Why is it you think he's reached the end?"

"He feels it himself. He can't cough up anything. His flush has come earlier too. And he's talking a lot. Is it true that people get this spate of energy before death?"

"Yes, that's true." He mounted the steps; on the verandah Alastos stopped him again. The doctor had been trained outside the Republic, and that commanded respect.

"Tell me. Why should he get this disease in a climate like ours?"

"We get it among older people, especially men."

"Why? Why? Bad conditions, bad diet? But my father hasn't had either."

The doctor sighed and looked away from Alastos. "To tell you the truth," he said, "I think mining has something to do with it. I don't mean to alarm you, mind. But along with the usual cases—silicosis and the rest—we get these instances of tuberculosis. It's the men at the rock-face who suffer. The lungs get infected by stone-dust. And then—did he ever work in a smelting mill?"

"Yes. Two years."

"That wouldn't help either."

Julian did not follow the doctor into the bedroom, but could hear Zena's voice intermittently, welcoming and hopeless. He stood in the centre of the sitting-room. The sun sprawled his shadow over the floor. He strode across to the drink cabinet, stared, slammed it shut without taking anything out, and lit a cigarette. All the objects in the room looked pointless and lost. He sat down and gazed through the verandah door at the blue rectangle of sky.

So the mines had killed his father. If his father had stayed on the sea he might have lived to a fine old age. You could not be sure, of course, but that's what it looked like. His father had pawned his life. From time to time he had hoped to retrieve it and to spend it some other way; he used to talk of jobs in shipping offices, even of investing in a small business. But it had never quite been possible.

He must pay for his children's education while stone-dust got in his lungs. Not that he would have seen it that way. But that was the fact.

Julian clasped his arms in front of his stomach. He felt as if he had cramp in the belly. He was bending forward with his eyes narrowed. He wished he could weep. All over the Republic, all over the eastern Mediterranean, people made such sacrifices for their children, and their children repaid them nothing. If the parents had been to high school they would somehow lift their sons into university; if they had been to university they would get their children to a better one. Before a man left the world, he would raise his stem higher.

Julian fervently wished that his father had not done this. There was nothing a son could give to justify its cost. His father should have lived the life he wanted to lead. Nobody should surrender himself for an unforeseeable future. That was why the new mine was not worth the cost either. The future would not be what anybody expected. It never was. It would turn round and spit.

He drew numbly on the cigarette. It was always the present which suffered. People did not allow it to exist. Every second of life, he thought, was taken up in preparing for the next second, or the next hour or the next year. If a man opened the door of his car, he did so in order to climb in; and when he was in, he must go somewhere; and when he was somewhere he must do something.... And none of these actions was complete in itself. They were merely preparations. All living, in fact, seemed to be a long trail of anticipation, which burnt itself out in the dark.

For Alastos, with his passion for absolutes, this was deeply disquieting. It seemed that only death was not a preparation. A man's attitudes had to change then. He had noticed that in his father. Suddenly there was very little which the old man found worth doing. He simply wanted to think—he would lie for hours staring at the ceiling—and speak with his family and perhaps read a few books: not the clever, urbane books, but the other ones at which a man in better health might sneer. When you were dying you didn't sneer at anything.

Julian stared at the rectangle of sky: deep, solid blue. The other day his father had been wondering how he had once filled weeks of ordinary life, yet had scarcely thought a thought in peace or said to somebody he loved "I love you." The dying man felt that he should have tried to achieve less and to have listened more. Instead of indulging this rage for activity, he had said, he should have made himself more sensitive, like a perfect glass. Then perhaps he would have grown to understand something. After all, what could a man do if there was nothing in him?

The doctor came out of the bedroom. He looked grey and rather querulous. "I think you're right," he said. "If you like, I'll call a priest."

Priest? Julian frowned. Yes, he supposed they should do that. "He doesn't care for the archimandrite."

"In such cases the priest's character is of no importance," the doctor wheedled. "He's no more than a delegate. He..."

"Damn these delegates!" Julian interrupted. "Is there a decent churchman here? I've never seen one."

The doctor stared back at him fretfully, wondering whether it was worth explaining, then moved to the verandah door. "I'll find somebody."

Julian strode after him. "Thank you, doctor. I'm sorry." He spoke at the doctor's bowed back as it descended the steps. "Of course I'll trust your judgment." But he added: "Just let's have a good man."

The doctor did not look round.

Julian turned to Zena, who was standing behind him. He put an arm round her and kissed her. "You should get some sleep. I'll stay with father now."

He pushed open the door and entered the room. The sunlight lay in slabs over the floor. Everything was as usual: the semi-circle of chairs, the bookshelves, the ottoman stacked with old editions of *The Republican*, the side-table with its litter of medicine bottles. Only the bed looked larger—a great white wasteland around his father's head. The fever had painted the old man's cheeks with two bright crescents. The rest of the face showed as white as the pillow, but it was a different sort of whiteness, almost translucent.

Julian sat beside him. As so often, but now more intensely, he felt how rude were his own size and health—these sunburnt hands on his knees, this whole powerfully-working body which beat and pulsated without any sound or effort that he knew. He had sometimes had the urge, almost unbearably to move his hands over his father's chest and spread them round his ribs, as if he could electrocute the aged body into health and pour his own strength down through his fingers. But now his father's frame was so hollowed that he scarcely dared to touch it. He even tried to control his own breathing in case it should deprive his father's lungs.

"Zena tells me..." Andreas began, then stopped and with frightful slowness turned his head to his son. Julian noticed that the glitter in his eyes did not touch the heart of them; their pupils looked blind. "Zena tells me that the archimandrite has sold."

"Yes, he has."

His father closed his eyes. "I don't understand."

"What don't you understand?"

The silence was so long that he thought his father had not heard or had fallen asleep. When the old man spoke again, he kept his eyes closed, but his voice came fluent and oddly high. "It's as if the earth was turning over underneath us." Unable to sigh, he paused before saying: "When I was a child the church was filled, every Sunday, young and old. Nobody questioned that here was wisdom ... everything.... My brother, your uncle—did I tell you?—used to carry the standard of the Cherubim at the Entrance of the Gifts, and when the priest elevated the Gifts, there was a moment ... the choir singing for the Holy Spirit to come upon them ... there was a moment ... you could feel it ... when something was changed, something happened." He opened his eyes. "It does not seem to happen any more now. A faith needs people. And now people will do anything...." Julian lowered his eyes, though his father could not see him. "And now they've sold the Mountain. Even five years ago I wouldn't have believed that. But today it's perfectly credible, almost ..." his voice died "... natural."

"The Church may withdraw the sale if the people make enough trouble." Julian did not know what his father was hoping.

Andreas' eyes settled their gaze on him. "You can't withdraw the times." Yes, they looked different from normal eyes. As if death began from a man's core and spread outwards. "I don't understand. I don't understand what God is planning...."

Julian did not want to listen to this bewilderment. He tried to remember how his father had looked years ago. Because soon, he told himself, this shrivelled head and voice, this last memory, must take its place among earlier, better memories. It was not the total man. It was only the end. His father's lips were rubbing together again. Pulled back from his teeth, they had to move to find one another, before he spoke. Julian bent to catch his words, but they refused to come. In a moment of panic he could not properly remember what his father used to look like. He saw only this whispering skull. There was nothing else to love.

The old man said at last: "The sale of the Mountain will be good for the Company ... for you." His features and voice were as expressionless as one another. Julian could not decipher what he was feeling. Should he tell him that he meant to quit the mines? Would he be glad? He leant forward and spoke near his father's ear: "Do you think the Company should have done that?"

"The Church should not have sold."

He asked with a trace of desperation: "But should I work on the site?"

He felt that whatever his father answered, he would accept as the truth, at least for this moment. But Andreas only said: "Should I know?"

Julian's hands clenched in frustration. His father had always been so positive. He had always given directives. And now this querulous whisper.... Did he really feel nothing strong himself?

But the mines seemed far away to his father, that was obvious. Everything seemed far away, except God. This unimaginable God was occupying his mind. As for Julian, he had long ago exhausted everything important to say. He was left with repetitions: love, reassurance, gratitude. Nothing else was worth repeating. So he said these things again, whispering too. Sometimes he was not sure whether his father heard. The old man's speech had grown less coherent as his heat rose. The fever was spreading over his cheeks.

And suddenly he was sweating. The beads were collecting along the line of his hair. They were too small to roll or coalesce. They stood out tiny and hard. Julian began to sweat too in his tension, and the muscles of his stomach were aching. He dabbed the flannel over his father's forehead, but scarcely dared press hard enough to remove the perspiration. With horror he sensed in that old body the frail and delicate clockwork purring to a stop. Life seemed to continue only in his fragment of a voice, which he forced to go on whispering. Julian held himself utterly still. He knew that half of what his father said did not even make sense, but he gathered the words to remember them, and nodded at the gleaming, near-dead eyes, saying "Yes, father ... yes ... I see ... of course ... yes." In the intervals he spoke softly, briefly—the only message important enough, "I love you", as if his father must take this talisman with him into the grave; as if it could make up for years of idle talk, poor letter-writing, impersonal discussion, silence.

It was growing dark outside. For a time, when Andreas gave up talking, Julian did not turn on the lights or draw the curtains in case the whispering started again. On the wall a red bulb weakly lit his father's icon. After a long stillness, he stood up quickly and switched on the bedside lamp. The moment he had sat down, his father began to speak. Now the clownish flush burnt on his skin. He said simply: "St Andreas."

Julian held the icon close to his face. He might have been sickened that his father should need this piece of wood and pigment now, at the moment when he deserved truth. There was so little time. But instead he wished him only peace. Peace through a lie—it did not matter. Besides, Julian did not know any more what was a lie.

For several minutes his father moved his lips in prayer. Then he said "Closer." Julian touched the icon to his mouth, and he kissed it. When he spoke again, his words were distinct, but hurried. "Don't look like that, Julian ... there's no need." How was he looking? He had forgotten that he looked like anything. He brushed a hand over his face. "Over the years ... I've come to see myself as less and less important. As a child I was everything ... later, by stages ... less.... I believe that's how we're reconciled to death."

He might have tried to cough. There was simply a pause. No sound or movement at all. His eyes, bright with their fever, suddenly shut. His voice stopped dead.

Julian remained frozen, bent double, his ear close to the mouth. Between its lips the teeth shone white and strong. Julian's throat contracted and trembled. His father could not be dead. The face was turned to him, its eyes shut. But no, not dead. He placed the glass of his wrist-watch under his father's nostrils, held it tenderly, like an offering. His hand was shaking so much as he withdrew it that at first he could not see the glass clearly. Then, sure enough, he saw that it was faintly misted over. His father still breathed. He had fallen into coma or sleep. He might not speak again. But he was alive.

Julian folded his arms hard against his chest, as if to keep himself together. He refused to think of this as the end. He did not know what else it could be, but it was not the end. If he thought hard enough about it, he would see. Death was not that closed chamber. If you stared long enough you would discern a door. Nothing was for ever.

The room was in darkness. Through the utter silence of the house he heard the siren calling for the night shift. It must be eight-thirty.

The miners would be assembled at the adit. Beyond the verandah window, on the other side of the valley, the lights of the surface installations still shone. Julian went across and drew the curtain.

He remained sitting and staring for what seemed a long time. After nine o'clock he heard footsteps on the verandah stair, slow, two at a time. He had forgotten the priest. A tall, dark man had arrived alone with a censer, a flask of oil and his vestments over his arm.

Julian said: "There may not be much time." He was glad not to recognize the man. He did not want one of those mundane clerics from the archimandrite's residence. This priest had a swarthy, aquiline face. He did not offer any oiled consolation. He looked precisely right.

"If you wait for me in the room," he said, "I will join you in a moment." He was preparing to put on his petrahili, praying. He looked up and said: "The incense is not obligatory. Do you want it?"

Julian said yes. Perhaps his father, in his sleep, would smell it.

The priest entered. He stood outlandishly tall in his glistening vestments. He seemed to fill the room. Some imperfection of the palate gave his voice an odd resonance; each note he sang momentarily throbbed in the air after he had released it, and he chanted as if the dialogue between God and himself was part of an ageless relationship. Julian was exhausted; but nothing seemed to be required of him, not even a response. This man was priest and choir and congregation. He did not appear to belong to the world. He was creating God in the room.

The incense filled the air with a blue light. Julian closed his eyes. The priest's intonation was thickening with the incense—not one note only, but the ghosts of all the others—they seemed not quite to die. In Julian's ears they hung diffused, like a remote booming of gongs.

Perhaps it was as well, he thought, that he could not concentrate on the words, because he would not agree with them. Paradise, damnation. He rubbed his eyes. As a boy he had been brought up on this childish hereafter. But he was not a boy any more. He could remember the very moment, at thirteen years old, when he had ceased to believe. He had been playing in an ancient necropolis on the headland south of Kalepia, and had looked up and seen an epitaph carved above one of the tomb doors. He had expected to see some pious formula of hope inscribed there. But instead he had read the two words: "Even Thou". Then the boy had stood on tiptoe to have a better look. Surely he had read that wrong? But no. It was perfectly clear: the knowledge of his ancestors. Undeluded, final.

Beyond the blue air the priest still shimmered in a cloud of song and perfume. There was pressure round Julian's temples. He thought the incense must be drugging him; his eyes were watering and his heart was beating against his ribs as if it wanted to be let out. All around him some mass was pressing in. It was closing off all knowledge and certainty. It was isolating him. It seemed to be saying: Nothing explains anything. Nothing apparent is true.

The flame was fading from his father's cheeks. Julian shook his head; he must keep awake. He tried to imagine some universal spirit with which his father might be merging. But where was the comfort in a universal spirit? His father was passing away under his eyes. That was what died: a unique face, a mind's temper. Nothing would resurrect them. The individual would never come again. Never.

His eyes were not watering, but weeping. The drops were on his sleeve.

The priest had finished anointing his father on forehead, cheeks, chin, hands. A drop of oil had trickled from Andreas' forehead down his nose and into the corner of his mouth. And although the priest had ended the ceremony, and had blessed him, he now seemed almost to be addressing him personally. He was praying near the old man's face: "Whoso dwelleth under the defence of the Most High, shall abide under the shadow of the Almighty...."

The prayer finished, and the priest turned on his heel, gathering the oil-flask and thurible. His movements were all rapid and certain. He did not look at Andreas again. He had no reverence for dying men. There was no such thing as dying. He changed his robes in the passage without speaking, and accepted payment.

Julian said warmly: "I'm glad the doctor sent you. My father is very exacting. He doesn't approve of all clergy."

Instead of a dogma, the man boomed back: "Priests are just men. The Church is filled with rotten ones." He looped the censer over his arm. "Your father is well spoken of."

The sound of the priest's voice in the passage woke up Zena, but she did not leave her room until he had gone. She was not religious. When she saw the oil on her husband's cheek she took the flannel and wiped it away. Andreas was a man of God whatever anybody prayed or sang, she said; he did not need his face dirtying. She was still so tired that towards midnight she fell asleep in the chair at his bedside, and Julian could only keep awake by getting up from time to time and pacing the room. He no longer resented the Church. He was distantly grateful to it.

Zena moaned in her sleep. On the icon, St Andreas traced a ritual blessing with his fingers. Julian felt grateful to the icon too. His old anger at the saints was remote and absurd to him. He had treated them as living beings instead of as an effort to people the darkness. Now they seemed almost friendly.

He curled an arm round Zena's shoulder to prevent her from falling forward. An hour later he fell asleep himself but woke up remorsefully almost at once, wondering whether his father had spoken and he had not heard. But Andreas' face had not changed—he looked neither peaceful nor in pain. His appearance was dictated purely by the thrust and pull of bones and wizened flesh. The fever had left him and would not rise again, for at midnight he had quietly died.

Julian's head fell on to his chest. For a while he kept his eyes open, then they closed while he told himself: I must not sleep.

Then he slept.

PART 2

Chapter One

In late September news reached Kalepia of an aborted *coup* at the Capital. It was difficult to be sure how such news percolated, because the official channels were silent. But within a few hours the whispering in the cafés had become a fierce drone, and the next busload of passengers from Nikitari brought more details. A general was named. A loyal tank regiment had hurried down the main road between the Capital and the second town of the Republic, Chakistra, where the garrison disobeyed its commanders and surrendered. Security police had been carrying out interrogations in Nikitari. It was at these times that the people of Kalepia became grateful that the town contained no barracks. Even the shopkeepers, who were jealous of the money which soldiers spent in other towns, would mumble: "It's not worth it. After all, you lose more from pilfering in the bad times than you'd ever get back. Better to have peace. . . ." And some of the older men would recall other times and towns and say "Remember Nikitari in '33", or "Remember Margo in '57", and the rest would nod agreement, although memories about these events were confused and exaggerated, and many of the men in fact remembered nothing at all.

For two or three days everyone listened to the radio news bulletins, but nothing was broached. There were no forthcoming trials, no 'deluders of our faithful army' and no 'agents of foreign aggression'. The newspapers ran headlines about the success of the government reafforestation scheme, the new areas forbidden to goat-grazing and the grant of an oil-prospecting licence to a well-known international consortium. The people were used to not being sure of what was going on. The Republic was only a republic in name (but names were important here). The real news came by word of mouth, and even then it was often vague and contradictory, so that public figures were always blurred by fantasy. In any case guessing at events was a game of no importance. The people were impervious to changes of government, because no change had ever made any difference that they knew.

By October this insurrection had almost been forgotten. The town was busy with its own revolt. In the shop windows the notices were multiplying. When the Company moved in two brand new bulldozers which could only be intended for the clearing of the St Vichinos Mountain, word went round that the rumours had been true and that the archimandrite had sold his saint for a fistful of silver. Nobody was surprised. People had been saying that he had sold as early as July, long before the town had been awake to the dangers.

The division between the Old Town on one side of the river, and the Company's New Town on the other, was now more marked. Their communities mingled less than before. The miners could not afford to jeopardize their jobs and their homes by sympathizing; they accused the townsmen of being backward and jealous. The townsmen taunted the miners for supporting foreigners who were destroying their homes and religion. There were several fights in the cafés.

For a month after his father's death Alastos took no interest in the dispute. He carried out his work automatically, and late into the night he read aloud to Zena to pass the time. He knew that his ideas of what the new mine might accomplish had been folly; and it was a relief to relinquish them. The Company was losing its head. Everything seemed to have changed proportion. Here was a whole town which wanted to be left alone, yet a handful of profiteers was bent on converting it into an industrial Gehenna.

The time came when he could scarcely bear to shout instructions at his men any longer, or blast another cubic metre of rock. It was time to tell Oldenburg that he was quitting. In the gentler warmth of one October day he looked down at the mining offices and realized that he literally hated them.

From the crest of the open pit he could envisage how Kalepia would look once the new mine had been excavated. The town would be ringed by giant steps mounting five hundred feet. Not a soft thing would rest the eye. All day and all night the machines would roar along its flanks. The blasting would become so regular that people would forget what quiet could be. The waste would pour over the ends of the valley.

Then, suddenly, in about ten years' time, the ore would be exhausted. The dust haze would lift, and they would look up to find themselves encircled by a wilderness where nothing grew and nothing moved. The people would start to leave, because the Company was certain to find other deposits—he had seen the signs all over the hills—and the men would have to follow them, tied by their training to the creature, copper. Then fresh villages would be built for them, and for all anybody knew they might spend their lives in a new underground mine, their lungs heavy with silicosis, until the Company buried them in those fenced-off graveyards between the slag.

"Reverse another two metres, damn you!" The dump truck driver seemed half asleep.

He looked back to Kalepia again. Even in ten years' time, after the new mine had been abandoned, that would not be the end for the disfigured town. Because soon the whole valleyside would begin to crumble, as a well-excavated site must. The rock walls, heaved outward by the push of the mountain, would split vertically at first, then fall on the benches beneath them, until the stairway lost its shape and rolled down in boulders the size of houses to settle in the green, sulphurous pools. He had seen just such an expired mine in Montana. Eventually a slurr of rubble, silicate and iron-stained waste would surround Kalepia.

He laid off the men ten minutes early and made for Oldenburg's office. Another week would see his job here almost done, so his resignation would cause nobody inconvenience. With every step he took the weight of the mine was sliding from his shoulders. He would slough it like a dead skin. He was singing robustly to himself, swinging his helmet in his hand. The Company's plans and decisions would no longer be his responsibility.

He would start a new life.

Of course in its way it was humiliating; today he would be destroying his old hopes. But now he felt more at ease with the town, more at ease with himself. The need for change no longer stared him in the face. Nothing was so certain, nothing so obvious, any more.

Oldenburg was sitting as usual in shirtsleeves with his tie strung loose round his neck and the sweat showing at his armpits. The

Armenian assistant looked up at Alastos and tentatively smiled. Oldenburg said "Yes?"

"The job on the open-cast will be finished next week, Mr Oldenburg. I've come to hand in my resignation." It had been surprisingly easy to say. The words had simply rolled out, natural and untroubled.

Oldenburg frowned slightly. "But you realize we were employing you on a permanent basis?"

"Yes."

The General Manager frowned harder and started knocking his knuckles on the top of the desk. "You've had several talks with our Chief Engineer, haven't you? He's in favour of taking you on as his assistant for the new project. What d'you say to that?"

Alastos merely said "I'm sorry."

Oldenburg was thinking hard. Alastos looked at him mildly, smiling. The General Manager seemed to think that the decision still lay with himself; he looked grumpy and bellicose. After rapping the table, he finally seemed to make up his mind and snapped: "All right, Alastos, this is completely against my principles. But I'll raise your salary to thirty-two hundred drachma as from next week. But in future remember: rises are given by the Company, not extorted from it." He nodded sharply once, in dismissal of both the man and the subject.

Alastos continued to gaze at him in his detached, friendly way, thinking with wonder: "so he can't believe that anybody should want to leave the Company; he imagines I'm bluffing." He stared down at the man's bald head, wondering what went on inside, then let his glance chase round the enormous filing-cabinet of a room.

"Well?"

"I can't accept," said Alastos. For some reason he was feeling almost benign, almost sorry for Oldenburg.

"You've been offered another job?"

Alastos half shrugged. "Mr Sofroniou has offered me a post teaching English and history at the primary school."

"That can't be well paid."

"No," he said vaguely, "not very."

Alastos was surprised to see a shadow of hurt in the other man's face. Oldenburg in any case appeared different, tireder. At some stage in the General Manager's life, Alastos thought, there had been smothered a man he might have liked. "You're not afraid of repercussions from the town, are you? Because I can tell you for sure: there won't be any, either now or in the long term. Once we've woken this place up, it'll like it."

Alastos did not want to argue. He simply wanted to go. "No," he said dully. "I'm not afraid."

Oldenburg was nonplussed. The man did not look afraid either, standing there with his great arms dangling and his shoulders stooped forward. He had always seemed a sensible, balanced fellow, Oldenburg thought. All the same, half of him was Greek and you could never tell what that was after. He was probably raking up some business on the side. If he did not want the job, there were plenty of out-of-work engineers in the Capital who would crawl for it.

"What is it then?" Oldenburg demanded. "Why are you quitting?"

Alastos thought that he had better say it. It wouldn't impress Oldenburg in the least, but it wouldn't harm him either. And he didn't owe the Manager any politeness. "I disagree with Company policy over the new mine."

Oldenburg's stare hardened on him. "Disagree? Disagree? What d'you think we're trying to do then?"

"Whatever you're trying to do, the town doesn't want it."

Oldenburg rammed his elbows forward on the desk. "Look here, Alastos, get one thing straight. We've bought this land from the Church. The town has nothing to do with it. The municipality has granted certain rights to us, that's all. If the Church was concerned for the welfare of the town, it should not have sold."

"No," said Alastos, "it should not have sold." That was what his father had said.

"You can argue that with the archimandrite. It was his decision."

Alastos was starting to get irritated. "But priests in this country are no better than anointed businessmen. Didn't you know that?"

"I know nothing about the Church," said Oldenburg roughly. His face had its look of controlled temper. "We dealt with the archimandrite as the legal representative of the land's owners. That's all. The land is now ours. We hold a government mining licence for it."

What was the point of arguing? Better to talk to a tree or a bulldozer. Alastos relaxed and let his hands fall to his sides. "Anyway, Mr Oldenburg, I've made up my mind." He hoped Oldenburg would not go on staring at him like that, because while the General Manager could keep up this unchanging gaze indefinitely, Alastos could not. His face would be certain to grow more stubborn until it became insolent.

But Oldenburg seemed suddenly to realize that he was wasting his time—the Company's time—and grunted: "When do you want to leave?"

"The job will be finished by the end of next week."

"All right then. Next week." Oldenburg bent his head to his work without another word. Alastos was left staring for a moment at this glossy pate bent beneath the production charts with their confident ascent of grey and red lines. It looked less like a head than a piece of furniture.

Then he turned on his heel and was out in the open air. Free.

Chapter Two

Alastos sat at a café table on the quay, looking up to the houses which ascended almost on top of one another along the valleyside. The fig trees were turning brown in their gardens, but the hibiscus and geraniums were in flower and cyclamen were growing in the clefts of the stones along the wharf. He was smiling at nothing in particular, but felt as if he was greeting the town. The dark pink roofs looked tender and clean. It was almost noon, but the October light was young and enhancing. It glittered over the sea and picked out each pine on the headland beyond the breakwater.

A smell of charcoal passed him every time the owner of the restaurant went by with *lounza*. A plate of roast squid and a glass of dry red wine cost only eight drachma, and for this a man could sit half the day and watch the tankers crossing the horizon on the way to Nikitari. Occasionally some girls walked arm in arm along the wharf, flirting with their eyes, or one of the old barges slouched into port for the crane to pick up its rag-bag cargo and dump it on the jetty. All this reminded Alastos of his childhood, and the memories, faintly sad, yet set him at ease. He felt he might fall asleep here for months, sniffing his wine like any retired sailor, and listening to the waves. He wanted to be immured in his surroundings instead of being at war with them in his old, pig-headed way. He was feeling tired. The sea was very blue. There was nothing to do for two weeks, until he took up his appointment at the school. He ordered another glass of wine and took out a book from his pocket, but did not open it. Here in the Republic, with the weather so warm, most activity cost too much effort to be worth it. The most important thing, as his father had said, was to still yourself, like a perfect glass, almost as though—if you were quiet enough—everything would clarify in you.

A glass, holding the light.

The dockers had finished their morning's work, leaving one of the barges half emptied, and a gang of them sat down at the next door table, tugging off their gauntlets and slapping the dust from their trousers. Two of the flour mill workers came over to Alastos and wanted to buy him wine—they had heard of his resignation from the Company. This had been happening all morning. Everybody seemed to have heard of him and to have a different, exaggerated account of his leavetaking. He had told Oldenburg to go to the devil; he had knocked the Manager over; he had refused to complete his work; he had smashed up his power-excavator, and so on. Alastos had momentarily become a popular hero.

As soon as the dockers noticed him they pulled their table up to his, shook his hand over and over and ordered bottles of wine.

"Good man!"

"God bless you!"

"That's a fellow for you!"

In no time they were clashing glasses, joking, drinking to the failure of the foreigners, clashing glasses again and bursting into renewed roars of laughter. Immediately he warmed to this circle of bronzed men, with their black eyes and gnarled, working hands. What a good lot they were after all! They had the right ideas! The wine splashed and gurgled. Alastos held up his glass. It glowed like a ruby. He drank to them all, twice, three times. The glasses clashed again. They drank to him. Everything looked mellow and good-humoured to Alastos, even the lean wharf cats. Then plates of mullet arrived. The dockers held them by the tail and gobbled them backbone and all. They forced a plate on Alastos. "Eat! There may be nothing tomorrow!" He found that he was still hungry. The crisp, rosy skin was delicious. He ordered bream for them all, but the mill workers paid for it behind his back. The bream too were sweet and succulent, fresh that day. And the bread still warm. And the wine, how had he ever thought it acid? It was sweet as a bird! He wished them everything good—these genial, generous faces. They ordered humous. Everyone plunged his fragment of bread into the bowl. The humous dribbled down their chins and sat on their moustaches. They began to joke vulgarly.

"Panos has a yellow beard!"

"Humous has made a man of him!"

"Look at Nicos! Yellow whiskers and black hair! What's the colour between your legs then, Nicos? Green?"

"Ask Despina."

"Old goat. . . ."

"Here's to Julian!"

"To Panos! Spyros! Nicos!"

"Here's to the green hair between. . . ."

"May the devil swallow the Company!"

"May God spit it out!"

By now everybody's arms were linked round his neighbour's shoulders. The tall docker Panos rose, let out a long, boiling hiss and clicked his fingers. But he had drunk too much to dance, and slumped down again. "Holy Virgin!—drunk at this hour!"

"Marangos'll sack you."

Panos burped. "I don't give a puke for Marangos."

The wine was slumping them all together. They looked as if none of them could sit upright if his neighbour should move. Julian's hands were dangled round the shoulders of the two flour mill workers. The drink was spreading all through his body, dazzling the sea in his eyes. A week ago he had been supervising an excavator tugging cupreous rocks out of the hill. Why? What for? Who seriously wanted them?

"Here's Cat's-Bottom!" shouted somebody. "Come here my only!"

The wharf prostitute lumbered over. She smacked a kiss at one of the dockers; but her expression was bitter and heavy.

"Sit and drink!"

"Not with you crowd."

"Going to Philippou, then? By God, the fellow can't catch fish but he can land a whale!"

But she was out of earshot, teetering fatly down the quayside on high-heeled shoes.

"Who can sing?" shouted Alastos. He was quite drunk. "How about this? Does anyone remember this?" He threw back his head and chanted strongly:

". . . a young Armenian girl, the daughter of a witch.
She casts a spell upon the stars and sky. . . ."

Two of the dockers roared at once:

"The little birds enchanted cannot fly.
The rivers are bewitched and flow no more. . . ."

The others joined in with wine-sodden voices, banging the bottles on the table at each pause in the chant and slopping the dregs into their glasses which they tipped to their mouths whenever they forgot the words. A voice behind them chimed in reedily:

"*She captures me, who never can return. . . .*"

The imbecile fisherman was grinning and swaying at them backwards and forwards from the waist, as if he bowed slightly to each one. All the lines of his face ran together at his mouth, giving him a look of secret amusement.

"God-Asleep! Who'd ever capture you, you mistake? What news?"

It was a habit of people to ask God-Asleep the news. He always seemed to know something. "News is Mr Alastos he say say Goddam to Mr Oldenburg he say Pooh! So go Mr Alastos. . . ." He suddenly caught sight of Julian and lifted his frayed cap. "May you go to the good, Mr Julian!"

"Sit down!" Alastos demanded. "Drink!" Two men prised open a space between them and forcibly crammed the frail fisherman into it, so that he found himself sitting on their knees. They banged down a glass in front of him and grabbed the bottles, tipping and shaking each one as if something must come out. But the glass in front of the old man remained empty.

"Never mind. He won't know. Drink, God-Asleep!"

"Nothing there," he answered squinting. "Nothing for a bargain, eh? Forty for seven, then?"

"Here!" Panos yelled. "Bring a bottle for God's-Nod!"

The bottle came. The old man seized it by the neck and poured a jet down his throat. The dockers roared and urged him on. He did it again and started to giggle and urinate in his trousers. The wine coursed down his shirt like blood.

"What'll your wife do with those trousers? She'll kill you!" Everybody except God-Asleep knew that he had no wife. She was his pet idea. He talked about her more than men ever talked about their real wives.

"Trouble's trouble," he babbled. "Got a length of soap. She's a proud washer. . . ." Three quarters of the wine had vanished into his throat. The rest flowed down from his neck among the grey hairs of his chest, tickling his stomach.

"Dance then, God's-Nod, show us your dance!"

The old man cleaned his face by rubbing it all over with his shirtsleeves, like a cat. Then he placed his hands on the shoulders of the men on either side and tried to rise. They stood up, supporting him, and in a moment they were moving in disunion along the quayside. Borne between Panos and Alastos clear of the ground, God-Asleep kicked his feet in a ghostly *syrtos.* Alastos, watching the mosaic of pebbles along which they stumbled, could no longer tell one from another. They blurred and flew together like the grain in old Matheopoulos' grinders.

Then Marangos was ordering his men back to work. Panos dropped God-Asleep, who folded up like a marionette, and the mill workers collected him and laid him in the shade. The sight of Marangos, and the sound of his gravelly voice, had sobered everyone, and although the dockers winked at Alastos and clapped his shoulder, they looked sheepish as they collected their gauntlets scattered over the table.

Alastos was left alone with the empty plates and bottles stacked around him. A puddle of urine and wine shone under God-Asleep's chair. The imbecile was curled like a foetus on the dried nets, with his mouth open. Alastos tried to pay the restaurateur, but the others had already paid for him, just as if he was a foreign guest, which he supposed he was. He yawned and sank his head on his hands. The sea sounded from the headland. Here on the quay it made no noise except where it slopped among the ribs of old boats rotting among the rocks. But out there it rose and fell with a regular, sighing hush. The only other noises were those of glasses clinking on a far table, and the crane cables whining as they plucked scrap iron off the barge.

Then Boom!

He smiled at the familiar sound. Toe blast hole drill (six and a quarter inch). Delay ignition. How good to be removed from the thing, to hear it merely as a cough on the horizon! His face remained sunk on his fists. The reverberation died. But the tinkle of glasses went on, with the far-off sound of the waves like a blurred but continuous clash of cymbals.

What were they blasting? There was nothing left worth scooping out. But he did not even bother to look up, although if the excavator was working on an upper tier, it would have been possible to see it. Oldenburg could never keep men or machines idle. He must have decided to scrape off a little more in the hope of exploiting a lower-grade ore body. It would not be worth it; it would merely create work.

Dressed in jeans and a tight black shirt which emphasized the thinness of his body, Howard Oldenburg was wandering along the wharf with his hands in his pockets. The sun caught the discs of his spectacles which he adjusted whenever he stopped to stare at anything. He was always wrinkling his nose. Alastos expected him to go by without speaking, but instead Howard came straight up to the table and sat himself down.

"Did you really give my father the sack?" He eased his buttocks into the seat and pulled himself as close against the table as he could. "I don't blame you."

Alastos scowled slightly. No Greek ever spoke of his family that way. But Howard was enjoying it, adjusting his spectacles with one finger pressed to the rims, condemning his father.

"I sacked myself from the Company, not from him."

"But he *is* the Company. He administers it, plans it, he even owns twenty per cent of the shares. The other shareholders don't know a mine from a drug-store. My father likes it that way. He couldn't stand interference." Howard was anxious that Alastos should understand. "Basically, you see, he's a megalomaniac. He dreams of being God."

Alastos was picking his teeth. "Basically" and "fundamentally" seemed to be Howard's favourite words. Alastos did not see why he should be defending Oldenburg, but he did not want to agree with Howard. "Your father's got a difficult job."

Howard's thin fingers flicked this aside. "Whatever his job, it's his nature to dominate." He was enjoying the chance to speak like this of his father. It gave him a feeling of relief, almost of victory. "But the danger is this: he's not just an isolated phenomenon. Not at all. You might say he's the ideal modern businessman." He pointed a finger didactically, and said in the tone of voice which was not his own: "You see, the whole thing goes back to the aggressive factor.... We all know what happens even to a primitive society in war. Democratic elders are replaced by dictators. Which proves that aggressive authority grows with friction and competition. Are you with me? Now there is nothing more subject to competition than a commercial company. Therefore a company must, by nature, be aggressive. Its ethics are those of war. Unless it's bad at its job, of course, and at least you can't say that of my father." He added, compressing his lips: "Most of modern society is moving towards this aggressive ideal. This is what I repudiate."

Alastos scratched his neck. It was strange, he thought, how one man, perhaps a fool, could say "God is One", and you were fascinated; while another could divulge a whole argument and you found that you had been listening to the sea instead.

"You can't expect people here to share ideas like that," he said roughly. "While your people were dabbling in theories, these ones were trying to keep alive under the Turks. The humanities to them mean school Plato and Aristotle, and that's where they stop. That's why art and philosophy are a dead letter here. People don't want ideas, they want something to put in their stomachs. It'll be generations before they get an idea." He hunched his shoulders aggressively. "Generations!"

Howard had been agitated while Alastos was speaking. He was bursting with something to say. "Generations? But don't you see that by then it will be too late? Without proper reasoning people will fall a prey to anything. They'll be sucked into the same patterns of business and aggression."

"Greeks are all businessmen anyway," Alastos grumbled. "I don't like it either, I grant you. No, I don't. But that's the fact. And what the hell's 'proper reasoning' got to do with it?"

"Everything." Howard wanted to explain. He wrinkled his nose again. "Now look. Forget about the town and the Company for a moment. If a man reasons clearly and questions scrupulously all the time"—he pointed a finger—"*all the time*—what will come of it?"

"He wouldn't be a man at all," said Alastos rudely, "and he wouldn't have a friend in the world."

Howard did not see why he should go on talking to this man. Barely one of these people deserved civilized conversation. But he decided to ignore the interruption. "The fact is," he went on, "that the questioning man won't delude himself. For instance if my father only thought honestly, he'd give up calling his career a duty to industry—copper's on the way out anyway—and accept that it's a drive to power."

Alastos scowled. Nothing looked less rational than Howard, he thought, with that eager but strained expression whenever he spoke about his father.

"But questioning is a habit," Howard went on, "that's the point; and he's never developed it. He's just invented for himself the virtue of serving industry." Howard shook his head as if it was almost too pathetic for his comprehension. "Sometimes I think the whole corruption of society comes from sentimental moralizing and so-called virtue. Nietzsche said that virtue was our greatest misunderstanding. And he was right. Most accepted virtues fall to pieces under reasoned examination."

Alastos yawned. He did not need Howard or Nietzsche to tell him this. And in any case, what was the use? Even if the whole town knew its motives, it would go on behaving in precisely the same way. A pig was a pig, however it reasoned.

Howard had splayed out his hands and raised his voice: "Now you're a Greek. It was the Greeks who first stood against the superstition of religion. Can't you accept your own heritage? It was the Greeks who invented reason."

Alastos was growing thoroughly irritated. Any fool respected reason, but this man reminded him of his days at university—the busy intellect talking significance, pretending that life was a thing of logic. That too was a kind of inhumanity. It bred contempt. And that, no doubt, was why the man's mouth looked as it did, too thin and self-nurturing. Alastos muttered: "Nobody's rational. It's good to attempt, but why be insulted by the lack of it?"

Howard's eyes appeared to withdraw further behind their spectacles. He said peevishly: "Few people have the stamina for pure reason. It's easier to accept the current myths. Take the people here for instance. They can't even think themselves clear of folklore. These people . . ."

Suddenly Alastos shouted: "I'm one of 'these people'!" Several heads turned from the other occupied table. "You and your pure reason! There's no such thing! There never will be until there's a pure man! It's a lot of rot. As for the people here, just you try being sat on by a Turk for four hundred years and see how much reason you'd have." He had no time to consider that he was defending the people whom he had himself attacked a month or two ago. They had suddenly become his people, and no pimpled graduate was going to wipe them off the slate with cant. They were as good as this man was, more generous, more robust and, by the look of him, happier. Alastos was too worked up to stop himself now. He was marshalling his arguments, rushing ahead. "Don't you tell me I don't question things! I've spent half my life questioning, and I'm still a fool. As for reasons, I make them up for whatever I want to do in the first place." He pointed rudely at Howard. "And so do you, even if you don't know it. There's something for you to question!" He banged both his bear-like hands on the table. "A reason wouldn't take me anywhere. I need a compulsion. Sympathy, hate, sex, anything. That's how I am. That's what makes life. And anybody who says it isn't true is a muck-worm."

"Bravo! Bravo!" shouted a voice behind. It was the fisherman Philippou, standing with his hands on his paunch. Kallis was with him.

Howard shook his head and stood up. He tugged his shirt down where it had crinkled round his chest. He looked at Alastos with a mixture of condemnation and awe. That was the trouble with all these people, he thought, they wouldn't face up to things. They would never admit to being wrong. They always knew everything. This man at least had resigned from the Company, but his reasons were typical of muddled thinking. Of course if people refused to be guided by logic, they were prey to every sort of fear and sentimentality. He glanced at Philippou. Yes, you only had to look at their silly, grinning faces. Logic was what was missing in the whole country. Nobody could plan a town without building its factories upriver so that the water arrived polluted; and the streets were sure to run in fifty different directions. Even on his deathbed a man would split his land into different parts, depending on how many sons he had, so that most of the farmers owned tiny plots scattered miles from one another. Look up in the hills at any time of day, and you would be certain to see these absurd people riding their donkeys to some puny orchard the other side of the valley. They must spend more time riding than they did farming.

As Howard turned to go, the fat fisherman fingered the cloth of his shirt. "How much did you pay for that?" he asked.

"Two hundred drachma."

"You were cheated."

Howard stepped back. He did not see why this dirty-looking fellow should finger his clothes. Then the fisherman asked: "Wearing a black shirt—are you a Fascist?"

"No!"

Philippou laughed, still clasping his calloused hands over his belly. "I thought your father might have trained you. Ha-ha!"

Howard's lower lip was quivering uncontrollably. He considered that he had suffered enough from these people for one day. "I don't have anything to do with my father! I don't agree with anything he says or does or thinks! Nothing!" He stared at the man, hoping that this had penetrated, but he saw only a face whose eyes, like very small and mean chestnuts, seemed to be saying that the world was empty of anything but jokes.

"He's teasing," Alastos said. But Howard had walked away. He had moved a few paces nervously along the quay, and now turned and vanished among the houses.

It was Kallis who sat down by Alastos and asked: "Did you hear what plans the Company has for the port?"

Kallis looked less pinched and sallow. Alastos felt well disposed to him. He was the sort of man the town needed. It was odd, he thought, how a person's appearance seemed to change with one's conception of him. Here was this man, whom he had disliked before, with a face which now looked eased and sympathetic. The sleekness of his movements was no longer repellent, but reassuring. And what if he did feel bitter? He had good cause.

"No," Alastos answered, "I never heard plans. I was just a foreman. But a loading installation..." he looked round him at the cramped wharfside shops "...could demolish half these."

Kallis seemed eager to know exactly why Alastos had left the Company, how much new machinery it would have to buy in, and how many new men. Were there any other miners who might defect, he asked? No, Alastos answered, none. Where would the road to the mine be engineered? When might the Company attempt to demolish the shrine? Would they do anything before spring? He questioned on and on. He wanted detailed answers. He did not so much amass information as slot it into gaps already in his mind. He had imagined and anticipated a great deal. It was technical information which he lacked, and he absorbed this quickly before asking more complicated questions. Then he would return to some point which seemed to have been contradicted, and would argue it through until he was satisfied.

Alastos, whose brain worked in a more unwieldly, ruminative way, was impressed. He started to ask Kallis questions about how the people were organizing resistance. Had they approached anybody for help? Had they written to the Holy Synod or any government ministry? But Kallis' answers made him feel naïve. Where had he been all this time? The Republic was not the United States. A letter wouldn't be worth the five minutes spent on it. Nothing here was managed in ministries or offices—*nothing*. Decisions were taken in the sitting-rooms of businessmen and senior civil servants. It was a matter of passing money, how much and to whom. And the people of Kalepia, even if they had known whom to bribe, had nothing.

Kallis and he walked among the houses along the quayside. These fishermen's homes had not been thrown up from poor concrete like the modern ones, but had been raised with care in hewn stone, and plastered over—the work of many months, even years. Here and there the plaster had fallen and the well-dressed limestone showed palely through; or if the wall had been exposed for a long time, it was weathered to the same gold-brown as the plaster. Inside, the rooms were austere, and cold during winter. The fishermen were in from the night's catch, and lay on their big wooden beds under quilts; but as soon as their wives told them who was there, they came padding barefoot over the flagstones, ushered the two men in and gave them coffee. They did not speak much. Kallis gave the impression that Alastos' resignation was only the start of a widening crack in the Company. Alastos felt discomfited by this. But he supposed that lies were needed to support the men's morale.

The fishermen looked steadier than the small tradesmen, and were without self-pity. If life went wrong for them, they were not used to blaming it on anybody but themselves. So now they did not whine, but sat in their striped pyjamas with their blackened hands curled round the coffee cups and their woollen fishing caps, which they wore even in sleep, askew on their heads. A few of them said that they wished they were younger, and it was true that fishing was dying out in Kalepia—their sons did not follow them—and most of them looked grizzled and old and dark as monkeys.

Kallis knew them all personally. He and his mother, when they first came to Kalepia, had lived in a house similar to these. He could not go into them now without remembering his youth. Many small things reminded him: the curves worn in the threshold stones; iron hooks hanging out of the walls; the dried smell of roof timber and rush panniers heaped in corners. But he knew that these things, which had meant poverty to him, were the only wealth which the fishermen possessed: solid houses. The sea was on their doorstep. That made life tolerable. A man could stroll out when he pleased and mend his nets and floats, or go indoors out of the noon sun and sleep.

"You see what I mean?" he said fiercely, after they had left the last house. "Their only real possessions are their boats and their homes, and the Company means to separate them from both. Men of sixty, seventy! But it won't happen. Provided the town remains united, it won't happen." They were walking up the main street now. It was still only three o'clock and the men were dozing on their chairs in the shade. The street was dusty and colourless. But Alastos felt no irritation at the men any more. He knew many of them, and they were no longer a bored mass to him, but were sharply differentiated. Some he wanted to avoid; others he would have liked to sit with. Now he passed among them easily, greeting some, forgetting others. As for any desire to change them, he had quite forgotten it.

Kallis received attention. On all sides people asked him to sit with them; but he scarcely ever did. He walked in a dapper, self-conscious way. "The crisis will come with the first man the Company tries to evict," he said. "All the petty clerks and civil servants, of course, will evaporate. They won't take sides, and it doesn't matter. Those who don't care don't count. But ask any of the working men what they feel, and you'll get the same answer. Just ask one!" He insisted almost proudly: "Point to any one!"

Alastos pointed to a nut-seller at the corner of the street. The man looked too decrepit to care about anything. "Here!" Kallis called. "Antis! Where will you be when they try to take our town from us?"

The man shuffled across to them. "We'll fight for St Vichinos," he said, "and St Vichinos will fight for us." He thumped his stick on the ground. "Did I tell you my son has another child? They live too high on the Mountain. Would the foreigners try to evict a family with seven children? It's not possible. We'll fight...."

"You see," Kallis said, walking on, "you won't find a dissenting voice, not among the poor. And this is a town of the poor. They cling together like a bee-swarm." Kallis wondered how far Alastos would go in the use of force, or if he would condone it at all. He did not feel that he quite understood the man, and this made him uneasy. Alastos came from an unfamiliar class and he was only half Greek. Kallis could play on most men as confidently as on a lute. Touch a certain string and you knew what would resound. But there was something cumbrous and inflexible about Alastos. He had not the quicksilver attunement of most men. That must be the English in him. The whole world might decide one thing, but these stubborn people could always cling to another. Perhaps it was that which made him wary of Alastos, and slightly respectful. But he would try him out. "In the end there may be nothing left to us but force—force of numbers and arms. I don't mean anything heavy—just a few shotguns and a rifle or two, enough to make the people's resistance mean something. After all, if they have nothing, what can they do? Nobody'll take them seriously."

Alastos was frowning. His arms had suddenly stopped swinging with his walk. "And what if the municipality calls in the army?"

Kallis answered quietly: "That means the government will have to take notice. Then anything might happen. The Company might change its mind, or the municipality might. Or the Church could try to rescind. Provided the town stands firm, something else will give way."

Alastos was still frowning. But it sounded rational. He said "Yes." If you stood firm, something else gave way. The Church, the Company, the municipality—none of these had their homes at stake; their lives were not being distorted. It was up to them to change. Whatever happened, the town must not submit; and that meant—yes—it must be armed. If it bared sharp enough teeth, it would not have to bite. The more he thought about it, the more inevitable it seemed. In a country like this, unarmed resistance meant surrender.

Kallis was scrutinizing him. "Do you mean that 'Yes'?"

"Certainly!" Alastos answered. He was striding out. People were not dummies to be knocked about. People had rights, natural rights. If they surrendered them they invited bad law and an empty future. His stride was almost angry now, but pleasurably so. He rejoiced in this certainty. How had he not seen it before? He, who talked about developing people's minds! These people were doing precisely as he had always wanted them to do: they were thinking for themselves.

If people did not defend what they knew to be true, it was the end of everything.

Chapter Three

Without warning of his mood Oldenburg looked up from lunch and asked Howard: "When are you going to get a proper job?"

Claudia dropped her knife with a clatter on her plate. She had been dreading this moment.

Howard said: "I don't know." The room was filling with tension. Caroline went on eating with her eyes down. Howard steeled himself; for the past three months he had been giving English tutorials to young men who were more certain of their aims than he. All he knew was that he did not want to go into business. He refused to become a travesty of his father. He had thought of teaching or publishing, but neither seemed right.

"I don't know why you don't try social work," said Caroline.

Howard shook his head. "I'm not going to start a job just for the sake of working."

Oldenburg stiffened. This languor infuriated him. He felt responsible for Howard, as if one of his own limbs was dangling out of control. "You think you're going to sit on your arse and wait for a vocation? When I was your age I'd already been working three years as an apprentice."

Howard said softly: "I'm not you."

Claudia went cold. She knew this confrontation was inevitable, but she said quickly, and rather loud for her: "Jobs in the Republic are difficult, Frank." It was true. In the whole country the only good jobs given to foreigners were those in American mining corporations and the Italian-owned paper mills.

"I'm not talking about the Republic," Oldenburg said.

"Everyone knows a history degree's useless here." His gaze moved between Howard and Claudia. "I'm talking about home. Why don't you go back to the States?" If Howard went, Oldenburg did not know if he would miss his son. What mattered was to stop this aimlessness and lethargy.

Howard said: "I don't like the States."

"Why the hell d'you suddenly decide that?"

"I didn't suddenly..."

Oldenburg reached his point with sarcastic force. "It's not the States you dislike"—his jaw shot forward—"it's work."

The didactic tone, very muted, appeared in Howard's voice. "That's true. I don't see the point of work for its own sake. It depends what the work's for." Sometimes he felt as if he occupied a different world from his father; as if they were shouting at one another over an impossible distance.

Oldenburg said: "Any sensible work contributes to society."

Howard was starting to flush. "I don't want to contribute to society. Society's lost its balance." His eyes fidgeted behind their glasses. "I'd rather work in a backwater—like here."

Oldenburg laid down his knife and fork. "This won't be a backwater much longer." He was staring at Howard, who felt his gaze on the side of his head. "If you work here," his father went on, "you work for the mines—unless you want to be a dock-hand or a beggar. You can earn seventeen hundred drachma in the clerical department."

Howard felt the air high up under his chest. Fear of his father turned him more truculent than he wanted, yet his voice came small: "I don't want to work for the mines." Now he was ashamed at how weak he sounded.

Oldenburg's eyes were hard on him. "Why not?"

Claudia said quickly: "We've had all this out before."

Oldenburg might not have heard her. He repeated: "Why not?"

Howard saw his mother's strained face. He was going to go too far, he knew. He was afraid of his own anger. "Because I don't like what you're doing to this town," he said. His voice shook. "They all hate us. The mines aren't a god, they're just an industry."

Oldenburg's head trembled slightly, but his eyes remained fixed on his son. They exerted a gleaming pressure. His voice was rock-hard: "I didn't send you to college to criticize things you don't know. Or to mess about giving tutorials in your own language. That's all you've done in the last three months—apart from flirting with that niece of the archimandrite's." He leant a fraction closer. "So pull yourself together. Find yourself a job and a decent girl."

Howard stared back at him, his mouth sagging. For the past minute he had been holding a piece of potato foolishly suspended on a fork. Now he put it down. Claudia watched him in dismay, he looked so abject. His lips were quivering; it seemed he could not even speak. She thought: a man like Frank suffocates the son he wants to have. She felt that Howard was going to weep. She wanted to take his hand, but that would be the worst thing.

Howard had put the potato down on the polished table. The movement seemed to take a long time. He was shaking, yes, but from indignation. How could he stand against his father while he ate his father's food? That was why he was so weak—he was always in his father's debt. He nudged away the plate with the back of his hand, pushed it halfway across the table. Then he got to his feet and said quite softly: "How dare you speak about Helen like that!"

In the second's silence Caroline breathed: "Christ."

Howard felt isolated and strange above their three upturned faces. His chair jarred noisily behind his legs. The old mixture of fear and anger shook his voice. "You don't tell me who I'll love! And you don't tell me where I'll work or live or anything else! I'm not a child. I'm twenty-one." His glasses slipped from his nose and he took them away, although he was short-sighted. Now his father's face was no more than a pink balloon beneath him. He said: "I don't want to go, but you've made me." The words had an edge of tears, which annoyed him; he turned to the pink balloon and repeated hoarsely: "You've made me." He sensed that his father's fury had reached its limit, still trapped in his eyes; he could go no further. Howard felt as if he had passed through an atmospheric force and escaped into the void on the far side. He brushed aside his chair and went through the door, then began to climb the stairs, two at a time, to his room.

"Howard!"

He shouted back: "I'm sorry, mother. I've had enough. It's not my fault—is it my fault?" Is it my fault, he wondered instantly? But it scarcely mattered. He and his father, he knew, were not arguing about his job or about society or about Helen. The issue went unfathomably deep. And he could not stay now even if he wanted. "Talk to father, not me. If he can't change . . ."

He listened, heard a faint choking, then the dining-room door close again. He stopped himself thinking and went upstairs to pack.

Oldenburg listened to his son's footsteps on the stairs. He expected them to return, but they did not. Then Claudia appeared in the doorway. She was white-faced. "He's gone." Her distress offended him, made him angry. He wanted to say "He'll be back," but he was not sure of this. They looked at one another in silence.

Chapter Four

Ekaterina's cancer patient died one October afternoon, and Julian, sitting on his verandah in the dusk, noticed her white nurse's uniform as she walked home along the road. He called out to her and she climbed the steps to sit down with him. In the semi-darkness the oval of her face and the white curves of her dress gave her a simplified, abstract look.

He asked: "Did the patient have much pain?"

"Yes. Carcinoma of the stomach." But she did not want to talk about it. Tonight she wanted to talk about nothing serious, simply to sit in the shadows with him and know the luxury of being herself. Herself was not such a poor thing, she thought, that she could ignore it for ever.

He gave her a cigarette. She unbuttoned her nurse's coat and laid it over the verandah railing. "I'm not supposed to smoke in this." He poured her a glass of wine and she touched it against his. "Here's to your new job as a teacher. I hope the children obey you." She liked the idea of his teaching.

Beyond the trees the street-lights were filtered green. A nightjar cried from the eucalyptus wood. They sat without speaking, as if eased into the darkness, the tips of their cigarettes brightening and dying alternately. They had always been able to sit like this in quiet, he remembered, and the silence was like a proof of their unchangedness. Once it would have been disturbing. But now he felt a glow of possession, as if he and Ekaterina had never been parted. There had risen up in him an extraordinary recognition of her—it was like seeing anew—and it filled him with longing. He felt vibrant and sure as he had not done for years. And now that she was sitting beside him—the black tumult of hair he remembered, her vivid face—the idea grew in him: I love her.

The night moved with a faint wind, rustling down the inland valleys. He did not dare ask her indoors in case she said she had to leave. They finished their wine while one by one the lights appeared in the mining offices on the far side of the valley. He said at last: "They must be working late."

"They often do now. The planning staff's been working a ten-hour day." She was glad to feel so distant from them tonight. She thought of the mine as a monstrous child, growing, consuming, demanding all the time. But they—she and Julian—were far away from it. They were free.

Julian asked: "And your husband?" He was still unable to call the man Michael.

"He's been working twelve hours at a stretch, even more."

Julian longed to know about Lerides and her, but was afraid of discovering that she still loved him. Sitting beside her now, it was impossible for him to believe that anyone was closer to Ekaterina than he. After longing to see her for weeks, he now did not know what to say or do; he was simply consumed by this elation, which he was sure must be burning in his face.

He heard himself say: "What does your husband feel about the new mine, then?"

She said mockingly: "You and your feelings! You've got enough for everybody! Michael's a businessman."

"Yes, I suppose." The fellow would trade in slaves or missiles as readily as in copper. "At least he likes his work."

She said with definitive deadness: "He is his work."

Julian grimaced. This was the Ekaterina he did not know: mature, contained. In the shadow she had only to stare down and her face became invisible, but he ached to put his hand under her chin and force it up, to see how she looked. And now he heard his voice go on quietly, very easily, to say: "Are you happy with him?"

She pulled hard on the cigarette. He waited in limbo. Then she said· "Perhaps I'm not naturally a happy person."

He said indignantly: "You are—yes, you are!" She certainly was, he thought. But then he had no right to be indignant—he had been the first to injure her. "You were always happy."

She touched his arm in a gesture almost of consolation. "Perhaps with you."

"Not only with me." He hoped it was untrue, but added: "You'd have been happy with most people."

She laughed. "You make me sound an idiot."

It was very strange, she thought. For years the sadness of her marriage had been growing so tense in her that she felt it must one day explode; but instead her confession had come as a natural release, like changing into more casual clothes. She imagined that Julian was right and that she used to be what is called happy. Why else did her present life fill her with rebellion, so that she wanted to scream? Why else should she yearn so for another landscape of desires and emotions? But she could not go back; her youth seemed so far away that it might have belonged to somebody else. Only sometimes, as when Julian said "You are—yes, you are!", she felt uneasy, as if his presence had recreated her girlhood, which of course it could not do. It must simply be that his directness made him seem more real than other men. He used to caress like that too, with a mixture of animalism and reverance. She wished now that they had slept together.

He stared at her. "I'm sorry. I'm making you sad."

"No you're not," she said defiantly. "Don't start me pitying myself."

She pretended to examine her nails. But Julian did not want to comfort her—she seemed too intelligent for his comfort. He wanted physically to touch her. The back of her neck showed white; he could see where the hair made a soft nest above it. He felt a tightening round his jaw. He sensed that he was pushing towards some barrier. He could even hear his heartbeats. He said: "How can you go on?"

Now he was gazing at the hand at her side. He longed to hold it. But if he did, he had no idea whether or not it would withdraw.

She said: "Go on? By not thinking ahead, I suppose. Women are good at that." That was the trouble, she thought. Every day was bearable. But if you added up the years, you'd cry out: "Where is my life?"

He said: "Don't you still imagine things?" But he was looking at her hand, how beautiful it was, and sensuous with its delicate knuckles and fingers.

"Everybody imagines things."

He told himself: take her hand. It was no good waiting for her to take his. He said: "Do you remember how you used to imagine something, and I could tell you what it was?"

"It didn't work."

"Certainly it did! Don't you remember?" He smiled into her eyes: grey irises with long green flecks. "You have a pessimistic memory." Then, without thinking, he took the hand. The feel of her fingers—they closed around his a little—almost stopped him speaking. Ekaterina. . . ."

She looked up at him, startled. She could tell that her face had gone white. And her insides had turned to water. She said: "You don't feel that for me any more."

"Yes."

"What?"

"Yes."

She lowered her head. "You sentimental fool!" But suddenly, without her knowing why, she was weeping.

Julian was taken aback. He did not know what these tears meant, but he overcame his surprise and took her other wrist, as if his fingers were pouring warmth into her. "I'm sorry," he said. "I'm sorry, Kat. I didn't want to upset you."

But he was not feeling sorry in the slightest. He was holding her almost fiercely. And he felt no nostalgia either. This was not the past which was writhing through him—neither this blinding adoration nor violent sexual arousal. Over and over in his mind the words were repeating themselves: I love her.

"Why do you still feel that for me?" She shook back her hair, as if trying to wake herself up, then slapped the tears angrily from her cheeks. "You don't believe in that any more."

He was too happy to feel foolish. "Who on earth knows why?" Yet even now he was glad she had called it "that" and not "love". The word "love" could mean so many things.

She tried to steady herself. "I don't understand." She left her hands tight in his; staring into his face, she did not know what she felt for him. But she had again that sensation of shedding her oldness; it was as if he had exhumed a corpse of herself, and it was living; as if her maturity was no longer important. Yet she said in a voice feeling its way: "You know we can't go back."

"I'm damned if I want to go back," he said. He felt in command of himself, in command of her. "I loved you like a priest then. No, Ekaterina. Nobody's trying to go back. You have to be sceptical about love if you want to keep it." It was he who had used the word love. There seemed no other.

She said half to herself: "You're not the same."

"No." He did not want to be the same either; he did not want to go back; youth was too unsure. "Did you think I was?"

"I've tried not to think." As his hands closed on hers again she felt breathless. It was mad to be returning like this, as if into adolescence, yet faced by an older man than she remembered, perhaps by the man she had once accused him of not being. She felt a little as if she was swimming, attempting to touch on something solid. It was warm and beautiful, but it was not solid. She moved her hands in his. "I'm a married woman. I have a child."

"Yes, I know."

"But you are free."

"Not with you. I don't even want to be free."

"You haven't been married," she said. She was in confusion. She kept saying to herself "You have a husband and a child, husband and child." And these words stifled her.

Now he saw only the whiteness of her bent neck again. Something about it distressed him. He knew he should be treading discreetly, cleverly, but he did not know how to begin. Ekaterina—at least the ivory slope of neck in the dark—looked resigned. He wanted to hold her, but her legs were crossed in front of her, between them. He had never noticed such difficulties in holding a woman before, but even her shoulders looked enclosed and unassailable. He thought angrily: Lerides must be a bastard to have lost such a woman's love.

He said: "Marriages can't all be prisons."

"I didn't mean to sound cynical."

He felt he would suffocate if they went on talking like this. He heard his own clumsiness as he demanded: "Won't you ever leave him?"

In their silence an owl called hoarsely. Ekaterina hesitated. He could not see her face properly, and he suddenly did not want her to reply, because she would have to answer discreetly, or lie. His hands found her waist and turned her towards him. Her flush was perfectly visible in the night, high along her cheeks and in her eyes. She looked astonishingly beautiful. It was strange to him, in that moment, that she could feel anything for him at all. But when he pulled her against him she accepted his embrace with a look of someone drowning. Her fingernails bit into his shoulder. He wanted to be gentle but there seemed no time. His lips closed with hers. They fitted naturally (he remembered) and the whole softness and suppleness of her small body entered into the angles of his. He crushed her harder as if to remember her. He covered her face and neck in kisses, on and on. A terrible urgency was taking hold of him. And she was answering it with her own. She loved the roughness and strength of him, her own helplessness. She wanted him to hurt her. He fumbled with the buttons of her blouse, with her bra, until one breast escaped into his hand. It was high and delicate, like a bud, the nipple a tiny roughness under his fingers. He pressed it against him, her mouth clung to his kiss. And in this fierceness there was a feeling of comfort, for their bodies had slipped together in remembrance, and he even recognized the dazed way in which she spoke his name. If his conscience was moving at all, its noise was smothered. He was simply returning home.

It was Ekaterina who at last put her finger against his lips, and withdrew hers. She looked dreaming, lost. He let his hand drift over her neck and hair. He said: "Trust me."

"Of course I trust you." She was listening to her own depths, not knowing how to interpret what she heard. "It's myself I don't trust."

Julian held her shoulders as if steadying her—it was like touching silk—and kissed the corners of her mouth. Her look of intoxication was draining away. With sinking heart he felt that the real Ekaterina was older in loving now, had lost that early wholeness. As soon as she withdrew from his arms this sadder woman began to reappear. The girl's clarity was lost. She pulled herself upright and said breathlessly: "Oh Julian. I don't know why you still feel as you do. All the same, thank you."

Julian said vehemently: "It's not a gift. I can't help it."

Her face was filled with emotion; but it was the kind of emotion, he thought, which a woman can afford when she is once again in command of herself.

In the room beside them Zena suddenly coughed and stirred. Ekaterina gave a start and glanced at her watch. The next moment she was standing in front of him, buttoning her blouse and saying she must go. He watched her in a fervent frustration as she descended the steps and disappeared along the street.

Chapter Five

There were banners looped across the streets of Kalepia now, proclaiming the rights of the people to their town, and invoking the saint. The walls were smeared with threatening or obscene slogans, and a huge mural appeared overnight on one side of the town hall, showing the Lythrangomi Mining Company in the guise of Uncle Sam copulating with Mother Church. The police were unable entirely to scrub this away.

The river bed which separated the mining settlement from the Old Town flowed with autumn rain and carved out a gleaming no-man's-land between the two. Miners were rarely seen in the main town, and only came in groups of ten or more. They could not even find anyone with whom to argue. People watched them in open hostility; the shopkeepers turned their backs and the brothel "artistes" were warned not to accommodate them.

For five weeks the tall priest had preached against the sale of the saint's shrine. His hollow, passionless delivery lent his words a half oracular magic, and every Sunday his small church was choked with people. A mile away, in the vaulted emptiness of the cathedral, the liturgy sounded frail and empty to the archimandrite, as if God Himself had abandoned them.

The docks had become the heart of Kalepia. People came simply to sit or to walk up and down. They were waiting. Old Sofroniou, who for years had liked to sip coffee on the wharfside, wondered what the town would do after its troubles had subsided, and thought: it will have to create new ones. In particular he wondered about Kallis: surely nothing would content the little man now.

Kallis and Philippou stood on the quay among boxes filled with ice and with the night's fishing catch. Three mornings a week a dour contractor weighed the mullet and bream on an iron rod, paid the men in soiled twenty-drachma notes and took the catch by van to Nikitari, selling what he could in villages along the way. The autumn had brought good shoals but poor prices. The men were all but inured to this. If mullet fetched a hundred and fifty drachma an ochs, squid was sure to be down to fifteen drachma. Few of the fishermen of Kalepia could even afford the nylon nets which were appearing on neighbouring coasts.

The tall priest was walking among the piled boxes, buying cuttlefish, which were cheap. He held one in each hand. Philippou sniggered and nudged Kallis. "Did you ever see such a fellow? He looks like God cradling the souls of the blessed. Look at their eyes—dead as bricks, the eyes of the blessed!"

Kallis watched the priest attentively as he approached. The lank figure stopped in front of him. The priest did not even bother to brush away the flies which crawled on his own lips. Kallis smiled at him uneasily. "Good morning, father."

The priest said: "You have some news?"

"No. The Company's been quiet all week."

The priest took time to digest this, while Philippou said in a voice of theatrical disgust: "Did you hear, father, that the children of Satan are living behind the wharf?"

The priest's eyes narrowed. He only said "How?" as if it was perfectly possible.

"Oldenburg's son." Philippou came close to him, fingering the whiskers of the two cuttlefish. "Living above a restaurant, father, and giving tutorials in the American language. And at two hundred drachma an hour. Doesn't that shake a poor man's blood? It's as if he caught a shoal of grey mullet every hour.... May the Lord puke on him!"

Kallis was glaring at Philippou, who refused to meet his eye. Instead the fisherman began to stroke the front of the priest's soutane with his oily fingers. "And he is living with Helen Drosinis, the archimandrite's niece."

The priest stood darkly above him. He seemed as still and numinous as a totem pole. "Dog breeds dog," he said; but whether he referred to Oldenburg or the archimandrite was not clear.

Kallis was still glaring at Philippou, but the fisherman continued to take no notice, and instead gazed into the priest's face with a look of mock respect. "Won't you exorcize the couple, father? Won't you fumigate them with the censer?"

The priest seemed neither humoured nor insulted. He merely stared at Philippou with a hard expressionlessness, still holding the two cuttlefish which added their dead gaze to his.

Philippou looked sad. He picked one of the cuttlefish from the priest's hands, examined the long, pink body, then held its face level with the priest's. "Look, father. The eye of the cuttlefish. There's the world for you! The outer rim's like mother-of-pearl, but look at the core!" The core was filmed and dead. "You see?" Philippou became convulsed with his own ingenuity. What a sermon! Even God shrivelled into the pupil of a cuttlefish! The rim was a beauty, but the heart—yes, the heart was dead.

Kallis pulled the fisherman away and the priest walked on as if nobody had spoken. "Don't fool with him," Kallis said angrily. But Philippou went on laughing. If he could have laid hands on a dog-fish he would have shown the priest that too. There was a match for the man. Because the eye of the dog-fish held a sinister, green translucence, endlessly nothing. Look into the eye of the dog-fish and you could see forever, forever.

Kallis said: "Never make fools of people."

"I wanted to find out if the priest was alive." Philippou picked a squid out of one of the boxes. "There's no way of telling."

"It doesn't matter what he is." Kallis glanced at him in frustration. "He's on our side. Haven't you heard how the people talk of him? They say he preaches like St Chrysostom."

"Preaches—oh yes. He's a regular holy man. A dash of madness is necessary." Philippou's shoulders shook with soundless laughter again. "After he's dead they'll discover that his body exudes holy liquids—*ouzo*, I dare say—and some other priest will make a fortune selling the glue of him."

Kallis stared hard and seriously at Philippou, until the fisherman looked a little ashamed. "Antis, you are my best friend." He took his arm. "But I warn you. For God's sake don't alienate the priest. And don't antagonize Marangos. That's all I ask of you."

"And what about Howard Oldenburg?"

"What about him?"

"Can I strip him? Foment him and bottle him? He's coming towards us now. He's looking at you."

Kallis leaned against one of the crates of fish with affected indolence and said stonily: "You leave him to me."

Howard had been looking specifically for Kallis. Even among the miners the sleek, sallow man was recognized as the focus of rebellion. Howard did not care to be involved with his cause personally, but he wanted his own attitude known: that he was not a part of his father. These townspeople disgusted him; but fools, he thought, could sometimes embrace a rational cause, and it seemed to him that they had sensed the worthlessness in the Company's promise of well-being—that well-being which could only lead (as Niedermeyer had said) to spiritual slavery.

Howard had found a room over the Seven Brothers Restaurant behind the port. Surrounded by his books and posters he had continued giving tutorials, had arranged for various periodicals to be sent him from America, and had settled down to studying for a future which still eluded him. He had seen Helen only once before she joined him. Sitting in the restaurant below his room, he had made his feelings clear. He was not in love with her. That kind of passion, he said, was an insult to a woman, who merely became a focus for her lover's fantasy. Under the white strip-lights his face looked more gaunt and pared than ever. Falling in love, he explained, was simply a neurosis which had become socially acceptable. In a healthy sexual climate it would not exist. He had never felt it, and he had no intention of inducing it. If she wanted to live with him they could enjoy one another physically, but emotional demands were out of the question. On the other side of the restaurant window the idiot God-Asleep, his face squashed against the glass, stared in and mimicked him like a monkey.

Helen said she understood. She knew all about the new concept of partnership from university. She chain-smoked while he talked. God-Asleep went on mouthing at them beyond the glass; his saliva dribbled down the pane. So they finished the discussion upstairs, sitting on Howard's bed. He spoke to her quietly, but precisely. People's lives were ruined by sentimentality, he said. He hated sloppy thinking. She must not be sloppy. He unbuttoned the top of her dress and slid it down over her swarthy shoulders. And they must accept each other's independence. Two people could not become one. But they ought to make a fuller two. Did she understand? Yes, she said, clasping his arms, she understood. Now his hands were sliding over her back and her heavy breasts. He began to kiss her. Half an hour later she had given him her virginity, and they lay asleep in the dampness of her blood while the street lights were extinguished outside and the restaurant below became silent.

A long time afterwards Howard awoke in darkness. Helen's face lay against his shoulder, curtained in her hair. He turned on the light and she woke up and washed herself at his basin, quickly and self-consciously. Then she wedged a pad of cotton wool between her thighs, and got dressed. Tonight she was expected home; but tomorrow, they agreed, she would remain. He came down to the door with her. He reminded her of what they had said: their relationship would not be a return to childhood but an act of maturity. People were separate; they had no right to one another.

She let herself into the street. It was empty as she walked back. She was dismayed to find tears on her cheeks.

Howard knew very little of the Company's plans, and if he had known more he might not have told them to Kallis. He sought the man out only to make his own stance clear. After Philippou had gone, he found Kallis leaning against the fish-crates. Howard respected the quickness of the man's mind, but he did not like its quality.

"Ah," said Kallis. "It's Mr Oldenburg's son."

"Howard," he said stiffly.

"I hear you're living by the wharf." Kallis tapped at his cigarette as if he was standing in a drawing-room. He looked far too dapper to be a crane-driver. He had female wrists and hands.

"I've got a room above the Seven Brothers Restaurant. It's small, but cheap."

Kallis thought: the man's playing at poverty. The real poor hide their condition; poverty is weakness. He said: "A change from your family."

"I'm not returning to my family."

Kallis faintly lifted his eyebrows. "Your father?" He appeared interested, but not too much so.

Clouds of flies were settling on the fish in the boxes all round them. A smell already stale filled the air, a stench of flaking scales and offal. Howard was aware that several other men were listening to them. He tucked his hands slowly into his pockets. "My father disgusts me."

Kallis smiled laconically and took a step towards Howard, but did not shake his hand. "You're with us, then?"

"I'm with anybody who stands against old-fashioned ideas of progress," he said. "That's why I'm against the mine. Industry dehumanizes men. Its workers are just highly-paid slaves, and as for its directors . . . they're power-mad." He raised his voice. "And my father's one of them." Why shouldn't he say these things, he thought? Loyalty was nonsense unless it served a good master. A knot of men had gathered about them—dockers, mill-workers and fishermen. They smelt of oil and the sea, and they peered curiously at Howard, who felt embarrassed and rather elated. He said still louder: "Industry is creating a whole society whose ethic is aggression."

Kallis thought that sounded much like any society, but he smiled at Howard. "Our people think the same," he said, although he imagined that not one would think anything so metaphysical and unnecessary. The rest of the crowd was simply riveted by the sight of the General Manager's son repudiating the Company. They did not understand much of what he was saying—their English was poor and the fellow did not seem to know many simple words—but his gist was clear.

"There's something else I should tell you," Howard went on. He was starting to enjoy himself. The faces around him were attentive and almost friendly; and Kallis was more civil than he had thought. Howard waited for their silence before saying in a voice thinner and rather high with tension: "Today the Company is starting to lay a stake and wire fence round the Mountain. Did you know that?"

Kallis turned noticeably paler. The crowd around them—it numbered some forty people now—shifted and stared up, and sure enough, like flies on the wall of the Mountain, groups of men were strung out at some invisible task, while the roofs of their trucks gleamed among rocks.

For a second there was no sound among the people but a vague susurration of voices, as if each was confirming the sight with his neighbour, then they started to shout oaths and threats. Every instant the crowd swelled. A few picked up knives or boating-hooks. All around him Howard could feel their decision ripening, until the will to march on the Mountain had grown like a hard tumour in the core of them. He felt a little afraid. Kallis was asking him harshly: "How long do they expect to take?"

He shook his head. "Three, four days. I don't know."

Kallis grabbed Philippou and shouted into his ear: "Get me something to stand on. I'm going to speak to the crowd."

The people had overturned one of the crates, and its fish were slithering and squelching underfoot. Philippou grunted in a voice terse for him: "You're sending these men against the miners?"

Kallis jerked back his head. "You think I'm mad? They haven't a rifle between them. Get me the empty crate. Anything."

The crowd was growing all the time. It overlapped into adjoining streets, and the balconies and windows above the wharf were crammed with women. The men below packed shoulder to shoulder, and their shouting might even have been heard from the Mountain. Yet it was the grim, disciplined anger of people whose feelings were tempered by responsibility. Already they looked more like an army than a mob. They were steadied by the knowledge of their own size and power.

But while Philippou and Kallis were trying to set up the crate, the priest, standing a head taller than most of the people, flung out his arms and began to speak. His huge, ceremonial voice silenced the gathering. "Not yet! Wait for God to support us! Wait until the foreigners defy the pilgrimage!"

Howard understood little of the priest's Greek, but its lurid magniloquence made him afraid that this horde was being induced to riot. He prised himself towards the houses on the edge of the quay. He had a sense that at any moment the whole mass might start to move, with himself imprisoned in it. The crowd was unbearably dense and glutinous. He could not breathe properly. From time to time the priest's words reached him like a far, dislocated thunder. The crowd shifted and murmured. The man seemed to be telling them to wait until the St Vichinos pilgrimage. Would the Company dare stand against them then, he was asking, swollen with greater numbers and the strength of tradition?

Somebody shouted: "But that's not for four months!"

The voice boomed back: "God is eternal!"

By the time Howard reached the houses he felt bruised and rank with other people's sweat. The priest was still speaking. The crowd had grown so silent that you could hear the grain whirring in the pipes of the nearby flour mill. Now and again the priest lifted his arms in strong, deliberate gestures, like a great black bird threatening to fly.

The day of the pilgrimage, he cried, would be the day of reckoning. Then the fence would be peeled like a scab off the holy Mountain. If the Company tried to stop the people's ascent, would not the saint himself leap down to aid them? The people roared in answer. Dazed by his words, they half believed him. Yes, the saint would come down. Standing on the hushed wharf, under that translucent sky, anything could happen. The priest's voice shook the walls. The shrine of St Vichinos, he said, was a lodestar chosen by God. Beside it the mine, the Company, America itself was no more than a blink in the eye of Eternity.

Kallis heard all this with satisfaction, and watched the priest end his speech as abruptly as he had begun it, without a blessing. The day of St Vichinos, Kallis knew, would give them numbers and authority. The pilgrimage must take place as it always had, ascending from the seashore to the shrine, and if the Company did not want to see its fences torn down it would have to man them. This prepared a flashpoint which the people could approach with confidence.

He watched the crowds trickling from the wharfside, wending up the streets, returning to work. The priest went with them, grasping his cuttlefish in a bag. Already, high up, a group of men had appeared on the mountainside and were watching the miners staking their fence.

Marangos straddled up to Kallis and said: "That's settled it." He scrutinized Kallis with contempt. He was hoping to detect some resentment of the priest's speech, the priest's assumption of leadership. But Kallis only smiled back, letting his cigarette smoke drift between them. He felt no resentment of the priest. You could not be jealous of God.

He merely said: "It's as well the Company's made the first move," and waited until Marangos went away. By now the core of dockers and mill workers was gathered round him: men he trusted. He glanced round at them, sardonically amused. "Guess who drew our attention to today's manoeuvre? Howard Oldenburg, the General Manager's son."

The dockers stared at him. "He's come over to us? The G.M.'s son?"

Kallis laughed without pleasure. "He's one of those intellectuals they breed in the West. They come over here and teach us about principles, but they can't tell reality from dream."

"All the same," said a mill worker, "he's joined us. And so's the foreman, Alastos. The Company must be cracking."

"Don't deceive yourself. When the time comes that Oldenburg youth will still be talking cabbages. After all, what's he got to lose?" Kallis kicked away a squashed pickerel; it left its pink gut behind. "You can't count on anybody except the ones who've been wronged." He scrutinized their faces, watching for an opinion. He was growing used to his strange authority. He was both less euphoric and less afraid, and the men had altered with him. Their old anger was replaced by something grimmer and more patient. It was a mood unnatural to his countrymen: the mood of long battles. He was glad of it.

"We'll be ready by the saint's day." He lowered his voice although the quay was empty now; this quieting of the voice, a way of emphasis. "The money for the weapons is collected. They're coming by road from Chakistra. It's arranged. Just twenty repeating rifles. Placed in the right hands, those'll be sufficient." He turned his foot in the gut of the pickerel. "I repeat: we don't mean to fire a shot. Our determination should be enough."

"And whose are 'the right hands'?" asked one of the simian millers. "Marangos'?"

Nobody laughed. Philippou lifted his eyes to heaven and muttered something. "Yours are the right hands," Kallis said.

At the far end of the wharf the crane was moving again. It swung its neck twice above the water, then dropped the grappling-hook on to the quayside with a crash and a shriek of cables. Marangos was sitting in its cabin alone, waiting for the men to work, and singing sarcastically.

"He'll hear about the rifles sooner or later," Kallis said. "So we'll take pains to tell him—a little."

He had no more intention of telling the truth to Marangos than he would have told it to Oldenburg. Secrecy was more important than the most cunning plan. Now, almost of its own accord, the pattern of the future was beginning to flower. In four months everything would be over. Those four months gave a focus and a limit to their energies. That was what they needed. Almost calmly now he could contemplate the possibilities of the day: the tearing down of the fences; the mediation of the Church, perhaps; the renegotiation of the Mountain; the will and solidarity of the town. He could even imagine the collapse of all diplomacy; bloodshed; death; perhaps his own. But he refused to envisage defeat.

Chapter Six

For more than twenty years now Sofroniou had run the largest primary school in Kalepia, and despite constant upheavals in the Department of Education—in recent years there had been seven changes of government, four of them bloody—his regime had been an uneventful one and his children, by the standards of the Republic, promised well. The girls, in their green and white uniforms, were as docile and cunning as hares; the boys generally showed an extrovert confidence, were vain and mercurial, and successfully passed their exams into the *gymnasien*.

But his pupils came from a complexity of backgrounds. Since the school bordered on the Lythrangomi property, most of the miners sent their young there, and because of Sofroniou's reputation the children of officials and bureaucrats came too. The curriculum was based on the German system: dense, rigid and entirely unsuited to the Levant. The Department of Education (the least coveted Ministry in the government) enforced it with patriarchal sternness, so the students, year after year, gobbled outdated information and regurgitated it in monthly exams. They were, on the whole, happy.

But on the very day that Alastos began to teach, Sofroniou ushered him into his empty classroom, sat down in the bay of the window and said in a querulous voice: "I must warn you that things here are not as I'd wish. In the past few months the atmosphere has changed, and it's getting worse." He seemed tired, Alastos thought, and even thinner; his neck looked as if it should rattle in its collar. "I'd always hoped to keep politics out of school." He kept sniffing and sighing. "Yes, I'd always hoped that. But children are sensitive, like white mice, like barometers. Yes, if you want to discover the state of a family or a community, observe its children."

Alastos was depressed by this snivelling. He hoped Sofroniou was not losing heart.

"It was nothing specific at first, just an unease." Sofroniou pulled out a giant pocket handkerchief. "But then came a falling-off in concentration, and it's been growing worse. The children are arguing about the mines openly. Several of the girls have gone sick. We've had fights too." He dabbed the handkerchief to his forehead. "I feel hot. Do you feel hot? It can't be more than twenty-two degrees." Children's feet hammered on the stairs, then went quiet. "I'll be glad to finish with all this." He looked up at his ex-pupil. "I don't like to think where it will end."

Alastos said calmly, hoping to encourage him: "It'll end with the Company's retreating. Nothing else would be just, or even possible."

"Just," Sofroniou echoed. His smile was sour. "You've been away from the Republic too long." He stared over the classroom. The sun threw their shadows grotesquely long across its floor. "There'll be people killed before this is over." He remembered children he had taught who were now men: dockers, miners, shopkeepers. Their adult foolishness amazed him. He looked at Alastos. "And where do you stand in all this?"

Alastos could remember praising development and modernization to Sofroniou, and he now felt deeply embarrassed. He said curtly: "I'm with the town. People were happy enough before all this started. Let them stay as they are."

"Stay as we are?" Sofroniou faintly smiled. "We're still barbarians! Am I co-opting a schoolmaster who doesn't believe in education?"

Alastos laughed. He had examined himself too often to keep much vanity. "Of course I believe in it. . . ." He gazed out of the window at the bright spine of river. "But I'm more sceptical. After all, Oldenburg and Lerides were fully educated—and look at them."

"Lerides. . . ." Sofroniou stroked back his wisps of hair. "I think there's something to be said for Lerides. . . ."

Alastos snapped: "I can't think of anything." The very mention of the man riled him. Lerides: the name suggested an expensive scent. He realized that he would take a positive joy in crumbling Lerides in his hands.

Sofroniou noticed and was puzzled. Alastos wasn't a natural hater. The old man's gaze became shrewd and a little predatory, as when he would prise a confession of idleness or cribbing out of a pupil. "But I think Lerides may be our best chance of peace. He understands the town, he's more sophisticated. . . ."

"Oh yes!" Alastos almost spat. "He'd sophisticate the devil." A bastard like that wouldn't create peace for anyone, he thought, unless it served his interests. "When the miners rioted in August he promised them danger money—but no sooner was he safe on the surface again than he rescinded it. I feel sorry for these executives' women—Claudia Oldenburg, Ekaterina Lerides (he spoke the name softly), Gretchen Muller. They're married to ghosts."

Sofroniou frowned. "Have you had an argument with Lerides?"

"I?" Alastos said in surprise. "No!"

"But you think Kallis a better man?"

Alastos nodded. "He's more real, he's more human, whatever you say. He loves, hates, has ideals."

"*Po-po-po.* Do you still imagine we think of those here?" Sofroniou took off his glasses and wiped the lenses on his lapels. His eyes, without these spectacles, showed exhausted and small; it was a different face, Julian thought, less kindly, almost mean. Momentarily he found it odd that Sofroniou had allowed him to see it. "Ideals!" the old man said. "Down here we don't have room for such things. We mature early and disillusion early. We're older than you in the North. As for Mr Kallis, I don't know him—no, I don't. Although sometimes I see him in one of the dockside restaurants." He replaced the glasses tenderly; his eyes resumed their kindly size. "Do you know how that man eats his lunch? He always sits at a table facing the wall."

"Well?"

"Well, that is how he feels when he only has himself for company. He faces the wall."

Alastos shrugged. He did not much care what kind of man Kallis was. Kallis had stood up for people who were threatened. Such leaders were often hurt men; but they did good work. He said: "All these people ask for is to be left alone." He rested his forehead against the glass of the window and stared along the valley. He thought: old Matheopoulos was right. It was something to be proud of—a valley of fine trees, and olives for the poor. He was thinking of Ekaterina too, of everything real and natural, everything she loved: old rhythms of life, animals, orchards. "Why shouldn't they keep their saint and their Mountain?"

Sofroniou sighed. "You're not a Christian any more than I am."

"But they are."

Some girl pupils, arrived early for school, were whispering behind the door; but the classroom remained empty except for themselves and for a feeling, old and distinctive as the chalk-dust in the air, of generations long since adult, who had sat in the vacant desks, learning and forgetting the same things. "Irregular Verbs," said the blackboard. "*Nuire*, to injure. *Falloir*, to be necessary. *Poindre*, to dawn."

Sofroniou said: "You seemed to speak personally."

Julian answered very distinctly: "My father's death hasn't turned me Christian, if that's what you were thinking." A man could not create God because he needed Him.

Sofroniou said apologetically: "No, I didn't imagine that."

Alastos was staring beyond the old man's shoulder into the room. He found it hard to think about his father with any sense of reality. The more one had loved the dead, the farther away they seemed. He was even glad when sadness, as now, caught him sharply and unaware. He fixed his eyes on the blackboard to stop them watering. *Être*, to be. *Croire*, to believe. *Suffire*, to suffice. He said: "Why can't we be content with what we've got here? The sea, the sun. People in my mother's country travel hundreds of miles to find them."

Sofroniou bobbed backwards and forwards impatiently. "And people in our country will travel hundreds of miles for what you have in America and Britain."

"The frustrated ones can always leave," Alastos said intolerantly. Those ones, he thought, were always the least likeable, returning home to sport crude clothes and spreading jowls. How good it always was from where they came! A fellow could get anything he wanted—the right car, the right job, the right girl. Well then, Alastos thought, let them go. There were new businesses all over the country now. The mines at Ambos had turned the place into a cess-pit, and Chakistra had grown full of heavy industry and social pretension. He said: "But the people here have different ideas. And they're going to fight for them."

"No. No." Sofroniou was starting to become concerned. He could see that Alastos was going to enmesh himself in this trouble. "Don't you remember our country at all?" His voice grew high and plaintive. "It would be a great mistake if you were to ... to ...

Yes, a great mistake. Don't get involved. People here use issues as a cloak for what they want. Sometimes they wrap it round them so hard that they even come to feel it. But in the end you find them selfish, ordinarily selfish." He thrust his finger at Alastos' face. "And even you, trying to put everything right ... It's just an intellectual vanity. You can't do it. Leave it alone." The finger returned to his lap. "I've never known the people like this before. Brutes. They're becoming brutes."

Alastos said firmly: "They have a right to defend themselves."

The old man rubbed the corners of his eyes. "I don't trust 'defence'." He felt worn, yet it was not even eight o'clock, he thought, the day had not begun. He could not tell if Alastos was blind to the approaching danger, or whether he understood it and was not afraid. He said palely: "I for one will not be here when it happens. My wife is frail. I want to take her away." He began to shift and bob again. "All the reasonable, moderate people seem to have gone, although where and why I hardly know. Kallias and Perikentis are dead. But they were old. And the Grikos family left for the Capital. Do you remember these people from your childhood? They were your father's friends."

"I don't remember," Alastos said. He was not listening; he was watching the children creep into the room, and they, in turn, examined him insolently. Sofroniou suddenly noticed them too and got to his feet.

"You must find your classroom. Epsilon Beta. You'll remember what I told you, won't you, about these children? Although I can't see there is anything one can do ... I can't see there is."

Alastos made his way towards the classroom down a passage filled with children rummaging in their satchels and exchanging items of picnic lunch. It was a measure of the poor teaching standards in the Republic, he thought, and of even poorer salaries, that he was employed here at all. He had never confronted a class in his life. He was sufficient in English and history for twelve-year-old children, but the standard government text books were thirty years old.

He was faced by a class of forty, ranked in desks five deep. This ocean of faces seemed to wear an expression of veiled ridicule. They were watchful of any faltering, and restless. But for the moment his imposing size and his unfamiliarity commanded them. He found the class list and called through their names. Six of the desks were empty. Where, he asked, were Chloe Kostis, Io Polemis, Alexander

Philes, Polixenia Sathas, Maria Elytis, Penelope Mylonas?

At the mention of these absent names the faintest ripple of anxiety travelled along the class, as if some plague had carried them off and might still be lurking among the rest.

"They're sick, sir," said a boy in the front row.

"What's wrong with them?"

Nobody seemed to know. Their stomachs were not good. They were exhausted. They were simply not well.

That day Alastos and the class did not grow used to one another. His teaching, his occasional jokes, his effort to develop their enthusiasms only aroused a grudging servitude which was not at all what he had expected. He realized that until now he had rarely noticed children. Were all the young of Kalepia like this? And how long had they been so? The boys looked sullen; and the girls, although staring at him through the lustrous and faintly sorrowful Greek eyes, were evidently paying no attention. He was glad when they started to giggle at the back of the class, and when Vassos, a stout farmer's boy, ventured a question about the Battle of Salamis and asked if history was really true.

The government text-book was of such grinding dullness that after twenty minutes Alastos put it away and read from Herodotus. All children like a story, he thought, so all children ought to like history. " 'After dark, in the midsummer season, there blew up a terrible rainstorm which lasted all night and was accompanied by thunder from the direction of Pelium. Corpses and wreckage, drifting up to Aphetae, washed against the bows of the ships which lay there. . . .' " From time to time he glanced up and thought that the strangely combined tension and boredom was starting to ease. He also noticed the face of a boy—a dark youth—so heavily bruised that his left eye was shut and his mouth swollen purple. Alastos wondered how he had come by such a hurt. " '. . . The sound of the storm threw the Persian troops into panic, and indeed they had suffered greatly. . . .' "

He closed the book. His own concentration was lacking. He asked the boy: "How did you get that bruise?"

The youth continued to look at him without a word; his mouth seemed to be leering. Alastos thought he might not have heard.

"You," he repeated. "I said how did you get that bruise?"

Somebody muttered: "Stelios gave it him."

Then, growing from the back of the room in splinters of argument, and spreading quickly forward, there arose so terrible a crescendo of noise that he thought the whole school must be struck dumb and listening. A dozen boys sprang to their feet and began shouting at one another, while a plump, puffy youth sat sneering at the back and yelled: "What if I did bash him? He asked for it."

Alastos could not make himself heard above the din, and strode among the desks pushing the youths back in their seats. At one moment a frail, fair girl—he thought she had Circassian blood—clung on to his wrist and piped: "He's the priest's son. That's why they did it."

"What priest?"

"*The* priest," she said.

Now the pupils did not dare stand up, but they were twisted in their desks and bawling almost in miner's language. Alastos bellowed for silence until little by little the shouting stopped and only the sound of his angry feet could be heard trampling in the quiet. The Circassian girl was crying.

Alastos said with controlled fury: "I'll not have outside squabbles repeated in this class. Do you hear?" It was as if to say: "your parents are behaving like children; you must behave like adults." And looking at their flushed faces he could already see the adult in them. Their expressions were more guarded and knowing than those of children in happier countries. The boys already showed a dark down on their upper lips, and the girls were heavy-breasted. Perhaps Sofroniou had been right when he said that they matured too early.

The surly Stelios called up: "Whose side are you on, sir?"

"He's on our side!" shouted Vassos at once. "That's why you left the mines isn't it, sir? My father said."

The shouting began again, and in the desk immediately in front of Alastos one of the miner's daughters, a brown sinewy girl whose smock was torn at the neck, turned round and spat in Vassos' face. Again Alastos found himself marching between their desks and roaring for quiet. He plucked out the worst offenders, the fat Stelios, the loutish Vassos and the dark miner's daughter, and stood them in front of him. Then he began to lecture the class. He told them, through gritted teeth, that the mining corporation meant well; it wished to improve the town. His own voice sounded strange to him, its hypocrisy distorting it. He said that the miners must understand the town too; it was natural for people to be apprehensive of their future. His sentences dropped like stones into the silence. The faces which looked back at him were filled only with their own fever. Their expression did not change, and nor did the remote tone of his own dishonest voice. "The Company is of value to everyone ... The townspeople understandably think..." He could scarcely bear to continue. He felt his words crawling like flies about the room, to be flicked away. He thought: this class seems to have gone on forever. "The shrine is sacred..."

"Is it sacred?" the miner's daughter asked suddenly. "My brother says there isn't a God anyway." She shook her tight curls. "Is there a God?"

"Yes, there is a God." He glared at the girl. "People often think that what they can't understand doesn't exist." Who was he answering? His voice was creaking, terribly old.

"But how...?"

"Shut up!" He wanted nobody to speak again for a long time. He was choked by the role he was being forced to act: lying to children. But what should he say? That the Company was a rapacious monster? That the town should fight to the death to preserve its own heart? That God, if He existed, might be a jester, a sadist? With the three pupils still standing in front of him, he went back to his chair and opened the history book again. He felt as if he had nothing important to teach these children. They were already taught, already old. He and they, sitting in this classroom, were merely conspiring in a silly game. Yet the silence was absolute. His hands trembled slightly. The pages rasped as he turned them. Far away, on the flank of the valley, they heard a shepherd crying to his flock.

" 'The news of the Persians' advance caused panic at Delphi, and the terrified people consulted the God as to whether they should bury the holy treasures or escape with them to another land. But the God answered that they were not to be disturbed, because he was well able to stand guard over his own possessions...' "

Chapter Seven

Nobody could say that the Company was not trying its hardest. For the second time that year, in early November, the Oldenburgs gave a party to which was invited almost everyone of standing in the town. It was one of those autumn evenings, quite frequent on the western coasts of the Republic, when the air had kept the day's warmth, and guests came as lightly dressed as in May, the women feeling the night's softness on their bare arms and saying to one another "Perhaps there'll be no winter this year." As before, the servant boy met visitors at the foot of the steps and led them along verandahs where datura plants now dangled cream-coloured bells. In the drawing-room the white tuxedos, the gliding waiters, the air of settled but faintly exotic privilege, gave the feel of a function in some old-world colony.

Outside, intoxicated by the sounds in the house, the imbecile beggar was squatting in the dust of the pavement, and called to each arrival: "Good morning! Good morning!" although the sun had already set.

It was hard to tell exactly what had changed, but the old undercurrent of ease and success had gone. Many of the guests stood in awkward cliques, talking softly together, whispering almost, noticing who had accepted and who not. The conversation never settled, but blew about the big room animating groups whose jollity then became noticeable. Claudia Oldenburg had the strange feeling that although more people had come than before, the room was emptier.

Oldenburg, who had organized the occasion, hated it as he

always hated parties. He stumped impatiently among the senior guests, looking for something practical to effect. The Greek fluidity and politesse exasperated him. He received the impression that none of these people—not even the mayor, the judge or the police chief—mattered any longer. They were at the perimeter of a battle-ground in which the threatened townspeople and the baulked Company stood alone. Momentarily he wondered whether the police chief—a stringy man with drooping moustaches—would ever turn his carabiniers against fellow-townsmen; then the thought left his mind.

Caroline linked her arm in his. "It's going all right," she said. He grunted and patted her bottom. It was not going all right. There were more than a hundred people in the room—civil servants, councillors, businessmen—but the noise of their talking was often only a susurrus, as if each was listening to somebody else's conversation. It was less a party than a gesture of concord, of gratitude almost, to those in responsibility who tacitly stood with the Company. But nobody was enjoying it.

Claudia Oldenburg, pausing to talk with Ekaterina, murmured: "Rather sticky."

Ekaterina was sad that Claudia should have to play hostess to such an occasion: a business necessity but a social fraud. "You've done all you can. In fact you've done beautifully." She put her arm round Claudia's waist.

"I'd like a vacation," Claudia said. "Frank and I used to make trips on the Canadian lakes. You could sail for miles and not see a soul."

Ekaterina thought Claudia needed to rest. Beneath her eyes the carefully applied makeup hid grey half-moons. "Why don't you go away for a while?"

Claudia shrugged woodenly. Ekaterina held her wine-glass to Claudia's lips, smiling mischief: "I'm going to make you drunk. Yes, you have a holiday. Take Caroline. Why not go to Rhodes or Turkey?"

"Too cold at this time."

Ekaterina said: "But go somewhere."

Claudia suddenly looked down, took the glass and held it against her cheek, steadying herself. She was near to tears. Ekaterina stood close to her so that her face would be hidden from the guests, and laid her hand gently on her forearm. Claudia said in a hurried voice: "I keep thinking ... I keep thinking he'll come back. I mean

Howard. If he does, I want to be here." She fastened her stare on Ekaterina. "Could anything happen to him? The people must all know who he is. They're growing violent."

"That may send him back to you."

"Yes." Claudia trusted her friend's judgment. Ekaterina must understand the town more intimately than any foreigner could. Claudia often forgot that Ekaterina was half Greek. Her gaze took in the black hair and the paradoxical green eyes, as if these were a talisman for knowing the secrets of these incomprehensible people. All the same, she did not want to talk about Howard any more, and turned to look at the guests. Frank was still pushing himself from one to the next, while Lerides, leaning against a sideboard full of drinks, had begun an argument with Muller. The party was picking up a little, she thought. The men were beginning to show off in front of their uninteresting women—these men so sure of themselves, she did not like them.

She said suddenly: "Sometimes I see no point in going on with it."

Ekaterina did not look at her. In that "it", she felt, was comprised not only Claudia's marriage, but her own. She was reminded, suddenly and painfully, of the insignificance of themselves: women who had given their lives to men, wrecked on the swell of their emotions, falling in love. And this, of course, was the pattern of women in the Republic: their duties were passive and physical. Generations, centuries of these women had passed with little more self-awareness than ancestral orchards, proud in their fruitfulness, neglected if sterile. Now she watched these other women, who for all their drabness seemed sufficient, and envied them their calm. She thought of her own dissatisfaction as a part of her Englishness, inherited from her father. But like Julian she supposed herself in tune with neither world.

She said: "One must have somewhere to go."

They stood without speaking, in a detached intimacy. Ekaterina kept her eyes on the guests. She noticed Julian's head above the crowd, on the far side of the room. He was looking for her. Something made her want to turn away and dissolve among the others. But instead she stood a little back from Claudia, so that her profile showed clear. This act of submission slightly appalled her. She tried to concentrate on Claudia, and, searching for something which was both sincere and happy, she said: "Howard needs you all."

Claudia said: "We'll see," and gave Ekaterina her glass of wine. "I must talk to the poor archimandrite."

Nobody mentioned the archimandrite now without prefixing "the poor", he looked so ill; and the moment they were speaking together Claudia was conscious of their mutual concern: Howard and Helen. She was afraid that the archimandrite might be angry with her for not controlling her son. But he was not. He was too concerned about what she must think of his failure to control his niece. And because each could feel personally the other's suffering, they came near to sympathy, so that the archimandrite sighed without thinking: "I don't understand it. The young."

When Claudia looked at him, she saw a very old man. "Things change," she said with brittle cheerfulness. "That's all. They're just ourselves under other conditions."

The archimandrite tilted back his head in disagreement. His lips looked bloodless in the coarse cloud of his beard. "I think we are the last generation that knows God."

"No." Claudia's gaze wandered to the cross on the archimandrite's chest. "The children become as the parents deserve."

The archimandrite smoothed his hands over his soutane; it was not as clean as it might have been, but nothing seemed to embarrass him any more. "How can anyone know what he deserves?" He sipped at the wine; it was acid and dry. "You'd have to know a great deal to know that."

Alastos was shouldering through the crowd in the direction of Ekaterina. He had purposely arrived late and had noticed at once how muted the party was. He knew that he had only been invited out of courtesy to Sofroniou's establishment, and he despised himself for accepting at all. He had come only to see Ekaterina. Without looking to left or right, he pushed towards her. He was not going to endure the coldness of the mining personnel by staying even to pick up a drink. But half way across the room he encountered Jon Adourian; they were both moving in the same direction, to where Claudia and Ekaterina were talking. "Oh, Mr Alastos," the Armenian said, "what a lot's happened since we last spoke."

"Not as much as *will* happen," Alastos said sombrely.

"No, I dare say not. Just think of it—the whole town standing against the Company! And Howard Oldenburg has joined them. I think that is very wrong of him."

Julian said impatiently: "It's his decision." He was more than ever conscious that he too stood against the Company. He wanted to leave at once. But he had not seen Ekaterina for two weeks. He said: "I have to speak to Mrs Lerides."

"They're over there."

For a moment the two men looked at the women together. Claudia, with her starker hairstyle, her ice-blue eyes and handsome facial bones, stood in sharper focus; Ekaterina subtler—a Greek face, kindled and intelligent. Alastos glanced at Adourian and thought how absurd, how degrading other people's love could appear. Momentarily it was unaccountable to him how they could watch these women and not love the same one. But then desire—an old country song went—was as various as beauty, and there were men in Troy who had no eyes for Helen.

He felt sorry for Adourian. Ordinary relationships found their true level; but this kind of love could only ferment in secrecy; it must be like breathing your own stale air. He could not have tolerated it. If Ekaterina refuses me, he thought, I'll return to England.

But now the women were no longer together, and the archimandrite had gone. Claudia Oldenburg was concealed behind the broad back of Lerides and his voice, its words coarse and slurred, could be heard above the noise in a blubbering aggression: "Why shouldn't we call in the army? If the bastards won't move we'll have them bombed out!" He lifted his empty brandy-glass into the air.

Claudia said with irony: "That would be too much fuss," and edged away.

But Lerides was very drunk. He turned on Ekaterina, teetering in front of her like a bull on its last legs. The sweat shone in wide seams along his jowls and his eyes were filled with heavy-lidded contempt. "Fuss! Christalmighty! Anything's too much trouble when it comes to the Company's affairs, isn't it? Claudia won't lift a finger unless ... Bloody Hell. She's no enthusiasm, no ideas, nothing...."

Ekaterina said: "You must talk to somebody else. I'm helping look after the guests."

But Lerides grabbed her shoulder in one hand and held her against the wall. "Now listen. We run a business, not a fucking nature reserve." He fingered her necklace. "Otherwise you couldn't even afford a brooch out of a goddam Christmas cracker. You'd..."

Ekaterina said urgently: "No more arguments, Michael. Please,

please." The people around them were blatantly staring and in the rest of the room the crowd had thinned, so that Lerides' voice could be heard through half the place.

He looked revolting, Alastos thought, with his hair crumpled and his neck leaking sweat. "God rot you! You sit in judgment like a bloody angel. . . ." One of his pale, broad hands was hovering near her face; in a moment it would touch her. Then, Alastos thought, I'm going to hit him. Where the flaps of his tuxedo parted, Lerides' stomach seeped over his trousers. Alastos prepared his fist for this spot. He did not want to hurt the man, but to remove him, like cleaning the air.

But Ekaterina, staring once into her husband's face, flinched visibly as if recognizing the extent of his drunkenness. When she turned away he tried to follow her, shouting uncontrollably, but she went quickly through the door, leaving him isolated between whispering groups. Alastos glared at him; he felt cheated. Lerides muttered: "Bitches. Bloody bitches."

Alastos hesitated, then followed Ekaterina. The verandah was empty. A single light shone among the datura trees, whose huge trumpets hung luminous. He ran down the steps and looked to either side along the road. There was no sign of her. But something moved among the myrtles in the garden, and he saw the beggar squatted, defecating in the shadows with his knees at his chin.

He asked: "Did a woman come out here?"

"É, a woman came."

"Which way did she go?"

The old man got to his feet, pulling up his trousers, and waved along the road. "É and fast . . . and fast." He started to hobble. But Alastos strode too quickly for him, reached the crest of the road and looking down saw nobody. She must have followed the track through the trees; he walked softly where the path went like a grey stream under the starlight. On the far side of the valley the lights of the mining company were still shining, and seemed to hang in the branches of the eucalyptus trees. He thought that Ekaterina would be a little way ahead of him. She must certainly be on the track; there was no other place.

He broke into a gentle lope, feeling the ease of his own limbs over the earth. She must be close now. He felt weirdly exhilarated, as if she was running from him. The air was warm as an August evening. He stumbled on a pair of olive-pickers asleep, and stopped for a second to stare at them in amazement, remembering his childhood when these strange people had made him afraid. They lay—the man and the woman—like bundles of clothes among the maquis, snoring at the sky with bloated faces. He moved on again through trees so close-knit that his shoulders scraped their branches.

Beyond a clearing the way narrowed. She was walking fast where the eucalyptus gathered thick on either side. The darkness of her cape merged with the trees, but her legs showed white. She stopped when he called. He said: "Why on earth didn't you go by the road?"

She looked at him with the kind of face which has composed itself a moment before. "I didn't want him to follow me." She was breathless. "When he's like this I'm only an incitement to him. I'll drive back and collect him in an hour."

He came close to her until her head nearly touched his chest. He said: "I don't understand how you can go on."

She did not understand either. Except that Michael and the child were all she had.

He repeated vehemently: "Can you go on? Do you know how?"

She did not know what to answer. When he domineered like that she no longer felt herself. And suddenly he was undoing the clasp of her cape. It fell on to the path and she stood with her fingers at her throat. Her arms and shoulders looked unearthly white. She was seized by trembling, by the fear that this feeling of youth and wholeness was a lie. Surely she was too old for that, too damaged? There were parts of herself which could no longer be given. She whispered "No, Julian." But she wanted him to take her.

And now he kissed her hard, as if stating a fact. His hands covered her back. He could feel its suppleness under the dress. Then he said: "Is there anything left between you and him, that I would destroy? Is there?" If there is, he thought, I'll destroy it.

But her composure had deserted her. Instead of answering him, she kept sighing through her teeth. She was thinking: whatever he might have destroyed is already dead. But she could not bring herself to say so. Julian saw that the decision must be his, embraced her and lifted her in his arms like a toy. In the trees' darkness where he carried her he could barely see her expression, only the smooth swelling of her shoulders and the paleness of her throat. As he let her down his fingers found the zip at the back of her neck.

Not before, in a whole summer of adolescent loving, had he dared to touch her body as he did now. It was as if all other bodies which he had held—brown bodies, coarse bodies, sleeping bodies—

had been fantasies, and he felt only the extraordinariness of this flow of flesh and bone which was hers and which filled him with a blinding agitation.

Ekaterina had not meant to be modest with him. It seemed to her that she had known this would happen, had dreamt and longed for it so that now she was hypnotized. She heard the remote rustle of her dress falling to the ground, and automatically covered herself with her arms. Then his touch electrified her. He could not be tender. His hands covered her with a rough amazement, bringing the dimmest regions of her body to life, parts which she had forgotten, but which now burnt until she wanted to cry out. He was kissing her throat, her breasts, her stomach. He seemed almost angry with her, although she knew he was not, and it was this threat, this dark threat of him which made her afraid yet caused her to gasp and writhe until she heard a voice, desperate and scarcely her own, crying: "Please, please, please."

But suddenly Julian had straightened, his body taut. She stared at him in bewilderment. He was listening. But she could only hear silence, a dense, night quiet. Not a car, not a bird, not even the sound of the sea. Only their twin breathing, heavy and secret. But he continued to listen, and now she could hear it too: a reverberation, as of some creature thumping feebly, persistently on the dry earth. Yet no sooner were they still than it grew faint, died.

He whispered: "Only olive-pickers."

Their eyes had grown used to the trees' darkness. A few stars showed directly above. In the sudden quiet they stared at each other. He realized that he was fully clothed, while Ekaterina stood almost naked. So he began to undress and she, in tacit collaboration, her hands no longer trembling, began to undress him too, equalling her guilt to his. She did this with a deliberation which made its meaning unmistakable.

He slid the brassière from her shoulders. Her breasts quivered into his hands. For a moment she looked embarrassed again, then let her arms drop to her sides and gazed at him as if asking: "Am I all right? Are you pleased with me?"

He lifted and lowered her on to the fallen softness of eucalyptus bark. Momentarily, as he looked down at her in the faint starlight, she seemed wild and oddly lost, with her hair shining loose and her arms extended to him. But the next moment he was above her, hot and abrasive, like an animal, aware of his weight, pressing her apart. His touch in her was sudden. She wanted to cry. Then she began to moan at his depth with little sobs of half-pain, tears in the angles of her eyes, until he made out her suffocated smile in the darkness, her approaching ecstasy, and they were struggling and crying into stillness.

For in spite of tenderness it was almost as if the thing had been a battle, something which they had committed against one another to hush themselves and to reach this moment, this perfect suspension of time, when her arms curled round his back and they were wrapped together, feeling their union in the moment of its being lost.

He slid to her side, looking up through one eye at the stars, which seemed alive and benevolent. The earth breathed obscurely round them both. Its half-surrendered heat embalmed them. He felt the beauty of her grow meaningless under his hands, felt dazed and remote. He stretched his arm across her breast and kissed her.

Ekaterina smiled. She did not want to think. Her hand remained sticky and limp in Julian's; but she let him lie sleepily beside her, and was filled with a deep, triumphant gratitude. For these moments—they might have been seconds or hours, she could not tell—were for her a victory over time and age, moments salvaged for ever from the wreck of her commonplace personal tragedy. So she lay startled and wondering at herself, listening to the leaves falling with dry, metallic clicks among the branches: the year already dying.

Chapter Eight

The police post of Kalepia was a group of blockhouses surrounded by barbed wire and enclosing a courtyard. Behind them spread a vegetable garden where the prisoners were put to work, and usually the same men were to be seen digging or sowing there: the culprits of drunken brawls. Whenever a policeman was noticed working in the garden the townspeople would say: "Watch out. They're short of gardeners." And sure enough, during the next few weeks, the police would make energetic attempts to secure new prisoners. On overcast nights a truck-load of men would set out, grumbling and half asleep, to ambush one of the boats bringing contraband to the small bays north of the town. Such were the laws of the Republic that while a whole range of "crimes against the State" was punishable by death, these men, smugglers of Lebanese hashish, were rarely condemned to more than six months' imprisonment.

Marangos did not want to be seen visiting the police post, either by prisoners or by the local people, so he arrived at noon when the town was so still that grey-jacketed crows leered and cawed from the rooftops. The sentry seated at the barbed wire gate was doodling in the dust with the butt of his sten gun, and only looked up, grunted, spat and settled into torpor again. Even the lumbering of Marangos' feet over the forecourt did not disturb the place. He passed the patrol trucks and the radio pylon, then ducked through the entrance and into the main yard. Under its verandah six or seven carabiniers were lounging in half-sunlight, tilted back in their chairs with their rifles against the wall and their feet over the railing.

Marangos ignored their jokes. Years ago he had spent nine months in prison for knifing a man in the arm. He made for the chief's office. He remembered it by its brown shutters and door. A radio was blaring inside. Nothing ever changed here. The sergeant was sitting in the anteroom, playing backgammon with one of the corporals for a soiled fifty-drachma note. Marangos loathed the sergeant. He was fat, with shifty eyes, and he enjoyed imbuing the simplest transactions—stamping an identity card or renewing parole—with difficulty and delay, until he had reduced his subject to pleading.

He looked up from the backgammon board, took in Marangos with his close, suspicious eyes, and continued throwing the dice. The corporal was losing.

Marangos said: "I've come to see the chief."

"So?" The sergeant hid his surprise, but stopped playing and shifted his holster to the back of his hip. "What about?"

Marangos pretended to be chewing gum, while in fact his mouth was empty. He chewed for several seconds in the sergeant's face, fixing him with disinterested eyes. Finally he stopped and said: "Secret."

The sergeant threw the dice again. "I'll pass your secret on to the chief."

But Marangos remained in front of him, chewing laconically, and powerful as a tree-trunk, his grizzled head sunk without neck into the slope of his shoulders. He spat on the floor. "Buggered if you will."

The sergeant's eyes narrowed threateningly. "We've plenty of empty cells, Marangos." He stubbed out his cigarette an inch from where Marangos' hand rested on the table; the hand did not move. "Get out of here."

Marangos smiled. With the knowledge that he had, he could afford to ignore this man. He stepped over the sergeant's chair with a look of saturnine contempt and rapped on the door which said "Chief of Police, Kalepia district".

"God break you!" the sergeant hissed.

But Marangos took off his cap, entered, and closed the door behind him. The chief sat at his desk under a picture of the president, in which the glass hung broken. He was of middle age, a sour but not a ruthless face, softened by drooping moustaches. He was of a different class from Marangos and the sergeant—Marangos preferred that—and he was said to be almost honest. But he did not understand why Marangos was here; he thought the man had been arrested and said brusquely: "What? You back?" He scuffed his papers. "Where are the charges?"

"There aren't any." Marangos stopped his abstract chewing. "I've information for you."

The chief looked at him coldly; he did not offer him a chair. But Marangos took one, scraping it close to the desk and away from the door where the sergeant would be listening. The chief said: "Well?"

Marangos cleared his throat and let out in a quiet, gravelly voice: "We're on the verge of a war. Kallis is getting in arms."

The chief's face, which had seemed blurred before, suddenly gained definition. Above the greying fall of moustache his eyes turned to needles, very small and hard. "Arms from where?"

"From Chakistra."

The chief picked up a pen. "Who's supplying them?"

"I don't know. Kallis keeps us in the dark. But there's twenty rifles and some explosive. They're coming by road, I can't discover when. They'll probably be hidden somewhere along the coast the same night."

"You don't know where."

"No. But I'll find out."

The chief looked at him hard, working his jaw with a dry, regular rhythm. He could see no reason why Marangos should be lying, and there might be many reasons for the truth. He asked: "What do you want for this?"

"Nothing."

The chief frowned slightly. He got up and slammed the window against the wind, which was blowing dust over the room. Then he slid open the lower drawer of a cabinet, took out a bottle of whisky with two glasses and set it on the table. Whisky was a state monopoly, hugely expensive.

"Want a drink?"

Marangos gathered the phlegm in his mouth and swallowed it. "Christ, yes."

The chief poured the liquid neat. It stood thick in the glass, like stale blood. He proposed the toast of the country. "To the people."

"To the people."

Neither showed his irony. Marangos sighed and ran his tongue over his lips. The chief lit a cigarette and remained sunk in thought. He knew that it would be mad to apprehend arms in the town, where almost the whole people supported Kallis. Safer and simpler to capture the boat while it was landing them at their hiding-place. He raised his glass to Marangos. "There are criminal elements in every town. I'm sorry about Mr Kallis. I'd thought him more sensible."

Marangos grated: "Kallis? He's got the sense of a shit-beetle. This thing's gone to his head." He tipped back his glass, gulped. The whisky warmed him. He hissed through his teeth with the pleasure of it, then grinned and sneered: "Little bastard'll run for president of the Republic next. After that he'll vote himself God."

The chief squinted at Marangos, drawing quietly on his cigarette. "When you know the hiding-place for the arms, you will inform me."

"I'll send a note. Place, time, date. I won't be seen coming here again." He stared levelly into the chief's eyes. "And I'll send a note to Oldenburg."

The chief understood that he was not trusted. And it was true that some police might have preferred to leave the matter alone. But it was not his intention to tolerate any arms in the town except his own, and Oldenburg, certainly, would ensure that action was taken. The chief was surprised at the depth of Marangos' vindictiveness.

He demanded: "Is Howard Oldenburg still living by the port?"

Marangos grunted. "He's just a kid."

The chief picked among his files. He ran his finger down lists of names. Marangos could see them whenever the chief held the thin paper near the light, but he could not read well. The chief said: "And Julian Alastos?"

"Yes," Marangos answered. "He's with them. He's not quite trusted, but he's with them." He licked his tongue round the inside of the whisky glass.

The chief scribbled something against the name.

He looked up at Marangos with the faintest sign of satisfaction, his expression relaxed. It was possible, just possible, that this whole affair might die still-born. If its ringleaders were caught smuggling arms they would be guilty of a crime against the State. Nothing could save them then.

Chapter Nine

For a month the winter rains had fallen densely on the littoral. At the Lythrangomi mines the open-cast pit, already unsafe, was cracking and unsettling in its upper tiers, so that the last of the power excavators had been called off work, and the last litre of copper sulphates drained away. The new bulldozers were busy levelling the valley where the housing estate would stand, and the householders of the Mountain had been told to quit by April.

But these expulsion notices were met by a unanimous silence. The Mountain itself was silent. A giant circle of stakes and wire now demarcated the Company's privilege. It sliced across the wood along the stream, climbed the western slopes above the town's rim, then sunk again to a long semi-circle; it embraced a whole region which seven centuries of tradition had pronounced *theobadiston*, "trodden by God", and on the summit nobody had yet dared to touch the whitewashed shrine. The householders came and went through barbed wire gates which were picketed by helmeted muckers swinging batons. No glance or word passed between them. The factions were like races which had never learnt each other's tongue.

And now the winter mud was trickling off the Mountain. Every year the rains eroded its crest with wadis which the spring flowers covered and the summer stripped again. Oldenburg spent hours each week with his Chief Engineer and the Mine Geologist, pacing the site and laying down coloured stakes and markers.

In the mining offices the Armenian, left alone with little to do, passed the time gazing out of the window through his deep, melancholy eyes, drifting into day-dreams of Claudia Oldenburg. So obsessive were these fantasies that when she appeared at the office one day, looking for her husband who was still at the new site, Adourian stared at her stupidly, unsure if his imagination had not created her. She was standing by Oldenburg's desk, casually dressed in a cotton blouse and a pair of slacks, while Lerides, who was signing Oldenburg's letters, answered her questions. Adourian was hypnotized simply by the quality of her voice—that clipped, formal softness. He could not both listen to its timbre and digest its words.

"Half an hour," said Lerides, "I'd give him half an hour and he'll be back."

She was saying: "All right, I'll wait around."

Adourian sensed the enmity between them: she very cold, polite, decisive; Lerides conscious of his drunkenness at the party, and hearing his own suavity ring false, ill at ease. Adourian was breathing harder. He wanted to watch some part of her, and found that by twisting a little in his chair and shielding his eyes with his hand, he could see a triangle of space beside the corner of Oldenburg's desk. Into this triangle appeared one of Claudia's feet.

"I hope Frank wasn't caught in the rain up there." The soft-hard texture of her voice!

"They had the Land Rover. . . ."

The foot wore a leather shoe. Between its rim and the bottom of the slacks, isolated as if for his gaze, was a delicately boned ankle. Its skin was crossed by a trickle of pale blue veins so frail and light that they might have been pencilled there.

"All this commuting between one mine and another. . . ." She moved. The triangle fell desolate. "I'll be glad when it's all settled."

"So shall we all." Lerides was walking to the door.

"Don't mind me. I'll wait here."

Adourian heard the door close, Lerides' footsteps fading outside. He remained hunched at his desk. The silence was so complete that for a moment he was unsure if she was in the room or not. In a second of panic he nearly swivelled round to see. But he knew she must be there, she had not left. Was she sitting or standing? She might even be reading, but he could hear no pages turn. She must be simply standing there. And perhaps, he began to colour, perhaps she was looking at him. The stillness was growing unbearable. Outside, near the newly deserted mine, some orioles were singing.

Suddenly her hand appeared on his shoulder. "What are you working at, Jon?" Her voice was friendly.

"Me?" He looked up and for a second bathed in the luxury of

her pale blue eyes. "Oh me, I'm working at..." What was he working at? He had no idea. For a terrified instant he thought he would not be able to look away from her face. The paper in front of him was blank. "I'm just ... planning out something."

"Oh."

Her hand was still on his shoulder: strong, slender fingers. He stared at it.

She said: "I see you've noticed my ring. I bought it from your father yesterday."

It was a tiny, gold-mounted aventurine. It was certainly beautiful. He pretended to examine the stone, and to his own amazement he took her hand. He felt the firmness of her palm, the pearly nails.

She asked anxiously: "Do you like the stone?"

"Very much."

The hand withdrew. He watched it hanging at her side, as if it might return. He said proudly: "They say my father is the best jeweller in Kalepia."

"I imagine he is."

He thought she was observing him, but he could not meet her eyes. He had never felt closer to confessing. He took up his pen, but was at once afraid she would go away. So he put it down again. "My ancestors have all been jewellers."

How could he look back at her, this statued goddess with her carved face and smiling lips?

All the same, he knew that worshipping was not enough. Half a year ago he had told himself that if only he could see her once a month, while working on the flotation figures—then he would be happy. But ever since, he had longed to take her hand. Several times already he had held it (twice while pretending to guide her across a road where no traffic was passing). And now this too was not enough. He wanted to kiss her lips. He told himself that if he could do this once, just once ... But already he knew that this also would not quiet him.

She was saying: "Do you share in this enthusiasm for the new mine?"

Adourian thought for a moment. All opinions and morals were drained out of him by her presence. They were simply to be arranged as she would best approve. All the same, as he answered her, he believed that the opinion was his. "Oh no, the new mine rather worries me. I feel it would have been nicer to choose somewhere else. The Company's doing very well as it is...."

"You tell Frank so!" She sat down on the chair near him.

He watched her mouth as she talked, and wondered how he would ever come to kiss it. He wanted also to know why she looked so sad, so detached. He felt childishly sure that he could expel all her sorrow simply by kissing her lips. Nothing painful could survive that.

He began: "I'm sorry your husband's not back."

She said: "I have you to talk to."

He flashed a look at her—hot, suspicious—but she was not a mocker. He thought she looked very tender; her cheeks had coloured. "Thank you," he said.

A light rain was falling outside. Claudia looked up at the ceiling. She was aware, of course, of the young man's infatuation, but could not altogether dismiss it as schoolboy idolatry. Instead she felt softened. Strange to be looked at like that again after so many years. But the feeling was not unpleasurable. Just a little disquieting. After all, he was not a boy. His figure, she imagined, would still look young in middle age, and so could the well-cut face whose delicacy a woman might envy. Yet there was an estrangement, somewhere, between the submissive nature and the lithe body. No, she certainly could not think of him as a boy.

Above all she felt this odd gratitude. It was ridiculous, she thought, for a middle-aged woman to be feeling so, but even now—without makeup and her hair untended—she could sense his gaze, his adoration, ranging over her body.

Surprised that her feeling was so definite, she was reminded of a time several years before, the first summer that she and Frank had not slept together. An occurrence slight but bodeful, the start of a watershed. They were on vacation in Sicily, sprawled on one of the beaches under Taormina, the day blazing. She sat in her bikini, Frank with his back to her, reading. And the scene was completed by three young men lounging nearby, who began to stare and whistle. She turned away from them. Then she thought: why? Why should they not enjoy looking at her? Why should her body be left to die? That was how she felt of it: as dying. If these bored Sicilians found her beautiful, let them gaze. So she twisted a little towards them, her body still firm and very brown. Their stare intensified. She shook her gold-streaked hair and lay with her eyes closed, facing them, and once or twice arched back her shoulders so that the fullness of her breasts almost spilt from her bikini. And the young men continued to gaze, murmuring, and eased their buttocks restlessly on and off the railings, and grinned.

Adourian was saying: "I think men feel differently from women about business. Mr Lerides should understand that. It's no good people getting angry at one another."

"Business doesn't represent anything to a woman," she said.

Adourian smiled. "That must be the difference." He dared to add, although unsure how much this meant to her unhappinness: "That must make living hard. I mean very hard to be married."

This time, he noticed, she did not look at him. He thought himself in love even with her sadness, even with the grey shadows under her eyes. "Well yes," she said. "Perhaps you would understand that."

He was watching her profile, she knew. A year ago she would have felt surprise at this, because she had grown to think of herself as unattractive. She discovered her face too hard, too masculine. Her figure was still firm, but again, hard; no, she was not beautiful. There was no longer any fullness, any bloom.

Yet for a moment, sitting in his line of vision, all this had ceased to be true.

She looked at her watch. It was half past four. She stood up and went to the window. The rain had stopped, leaving its pools along the concrete sill. There was still no sign of Frank. She felt rather ashamed of herself, and continued to stare out of the window at heaps of slag fading in sunlight. Beyond them the Asproyia mountains rose bald and colourless, cutting off communication. Looking at this scenery made her feel dead.

Adourian was pretending to work again; but the pen in his hand stood bolt upright and motionless. She felt sorry for him. Then a thought—sudden, irresponsible, shocking—rose in her, rose like a fish in the grey calm of her mind, flashed, fell with the tiny lisp of something parting, something out of reach. She nearly laughed aloud—a self-contemptuous laugh which she suppressed—then opened the door, looked back and said to him: "Tell Frank I couldn't wait."

Chapter Ten

He had seen the trees, with the man and the woman. Grey, in starlight. The trees spread their sails to the sky, a thousand million leaves dangling like Turks' scimitars, cascades of silver. And the woman like the trees, beautiful.

The beggar God-Asleep, walking on the path through the eucalyptus, had heard people murmuring. But it was the trees he remembered most, white, like men's limbs stuck in the ground. And the couple too were trees, standing under the silver cascades, under the stars. Except they spoke and moved a little.

His eyes were very keen. Yet at first it was hard to be sure. Things changed. If you could, it was best to touch. You touched a bottle, you stroked, and its shine was on your fingers. But when you went away it became . . . eventually a flash of light on the other side of the street. So you ran back and stroked it so that it was a bottle again.

So he went forward slowly. He wanted to touch. It was the woman facing him, although her eyes were shut and she almost naked. He made no noise going forward. Her face was joined to the man's. It was some ceremony. But he could not touch because she was a woman. And he recognized her. And he only knew one man so tall. But they were jerking about together, like you saw the crane drop bales of wool on the freighters. They were quivering like that.

He went away, softly.

He ran on the path, stopped, listened. It was too dark to see, but somebody far away, one of the trees, whispered: "Only olive-pickers."

Chapter Eleven

Ekaterina saw little of her husband these days. He rarely arrived home before nine o'clock, ate his supper poring over plans and figures, and sometimes worked in his study until midnight.

Yet she imagined that he must have noticed her nervousness. She thought she looked thinner, as if sucked inwards—her hands were never still—and when one evening she heard his car on the drive as early as six o'clock, hissing through a thin rain, she began to shiver as if something must have gone wrong. But he came in unhurried, and walked down the passage to the kitchen, while she remained sitting on the drawing-room floor, and composed herself. While clearing out drawers she had found letters from her father written ten years earlier, and had started to read them. They seemed to come from a century ago, and at first they saddened her. They used phrases like "the excitement of being young" and "all the world in front of you". She wanted to do something violent, but instead she stayed kneeling on the floor reading them, and wondering why her father, whom she had loved, had given her to expect so much. Eventually she folded the letters back in their envelopes, knowing that she would not read them again.

"You're back early," she said.

Michael smiled perfunctorily. "It's the rain. Makes a noise like hail on the office roofs. It's impossible to work there."

Looking up at him, she noticed how the creases had deepened about his eyes. She felt as if she had put them there, and resented him for this.

"But we made progress today," he said.

She answered feebly: "Did you?" The whole mining project

frightened her now. Its smug single-mindedness seemed to have found its way into Michael's face, even into his voice's inflexion. But she thought she should be glad that he had come home early—perhaps it had been done for her—so she talked about Alexia, and how the child had been missing him.

He came behind the sofa where she was kneeling, and saw her father's letters in her lap. "Clearing out?" But he was jealous of her father; he knew she would not throw away the letters.

"Tidying up," she said. She wondered if her smile looked false too. She detested herself this evening, hugging her own sourness. She hoped for something from him which would ignite her laughter or sympathy, but instead she heard herself say, too brightly: "Are the plans developing well, then?"

"Still a long way to go," he answered.

She let out a barely audible "Oh", and the silence was thick with their disagreement. Now her disgust was confused by guilt. In Julian her opposition to the Company was defined, solid. It was a total betrayal.

She could not think of Julian calmly. If she had loved him with her old certainty, she would have felt (she was sure) a simplicity and completeness instead of this nervous confusion. When they were together she abandoned herself fiercely to him, obliterating all thought and conscience; but as soon as they had parted this ecstasy leaked out of her, like a drug thinning in her veins, and the question which she had thought exorcized returned coldly and left her lost. What was she to do?

She thought of the child and she thought of Michael. She had a terror of hurting people. For a long time she had realized that if she were ever to leave Michael it would break him, and she recoiled from meeting the blubbering child inside that self-sufficient man with whom she had fallen in love.

Above all she thought of her return to Julian and what it meant. She loved his warmth and vigour, his sexuality, his honesty; but his innocence distressed her. She grew close to him only through that trick of time, that sliding back into girlhood, becoming vulnerable again, and shared his youth. But she knew that his artlessness was his and not hers. Her own was spurious, just a feeling with which he endowed her. She bitterly wanted it, just as she bitterly longed to be young again. He was naïve, and she loved the feeling in that word. But she—no sooner had she left him—felt irretrievably old, separate. People had even called her mature, although she did not feel this thing, and they assumed that her natural place was precisely here, with Michael.

Yet it was only away from Julian that these thoughts upset her. While she was with him, she became as he believed her. It was a little like dreaming. And like dreaming, it faded.

Michael sat on the sofa with a newspaper. She sat beside him in case his coming home early had anything to do with her. But her indifference was like a stiffness all through her.

"Have you seen the newspapers?" he said. "A lorry-driver ran over a crowd of twenty-two people in a suburb of Chakistra. On purpose."

"Was he mad?"

"No. The police found him sitting on the side of the road, having a smoke. He'd simply felt like it, he said. That's all. He'd run back over them until they were all dead."

Ekaterina got up and switched on the table lamps. They did not seem to brighten the room. Twenty-two people.... Michael was wearing his reading-glasses which turned his eyes oddly watery. He started to read the football results aloud. She said suddenly, without knowing why: "Shall we have supper out? Alexia's already asleep and Mrs Avakian will come and babysit. Why don't we?"

Michael laughed. "I hope you're joking. Nobody from here goes into the Old Town after dark now. You know that."

"But there's a little restaurant near the river, quite close. Nothing can happen."

"Can't it?" He was keeping something from her; he looked rather pleased. "No. Let's eat here."

"All right. Let's eat here."

It was only very late, while she was combing out her hair before sleep and he sitting on the bed in his pyjamas, smoking, that he told her about the town arming itself. Within a week, he said, as soon as the popular leaders could be caught handling illegal weapons, they would be arrested and the heart of the town's cause plucked out.

Ekaterina was surprised that he had not known of the arms before. Julian had told her weeks ago. She went on combing out her black cascade of hair, keeping her face averted. She did not want Michael to say any more, anything she might betray. She realized how completely he trusted her. For a while she watched his profile in the mirror: the puffed cheeks and straight, shallow nose scored by lines. Then, tiredly, she stood up and folded her arms on his shoulder. She was beginning to feel afraid. He squeezed out his cigarette and ran his hand through her coils of hair. She said: "Take care."

She felt a little afraid for all of them now. She did not understand this man's world, which had to fight, and change, and persecute itself.

Michael was pleased by this softening on his shoulder, and immediately began to pay her attention, but his courtship had become a game to her, in which his expertise was faintly revolting. She knew he needed her love for his self-esteem, needed it desperately. She bore with him. She no longer wished that he would show her his heart. It would only humiliate both of them.

Half an hour later, lying beside her in the dark with a cigarette at his lips, he asked: "What were you doing today?"

She heard the words through her half-sleep; her eyes opened and stared at the wall. She tried to remember. "I took Alexia to the park. I did some cleaning." How trivial it sounded. "Oh, and I read."

Michael fidgeted. Mosquitoes were whining in some recess of the room. He could not enter into this world of his wife's reading.

She asked: "Is there any news of Howard?"

"No. Nobody's seen him. Even Frank seems a bit tense, and Claudia's looking ghastly." He blew smoke into the darkness. He felt almost sorry for Oldenburg; Howard's behaviour was making him look a fool.

Ekaterina said softly: "Poor Claudia."

Michael grunted. He thought: women like that deserve what they get; if she had supported her husband more, and made a self-respecting home, this could not have happened. He did not understand these Northern wives, with their complicated longings and independent ideas. Such women never quite belonged to a man. That was the puzzling part of Ekaterina too. He sometimes glimpsed sides to her which he did not know at all.

She said: "I can't see what's going to happen. Frank's made it impossible for Howard to go back."

"He only wants Howard to do well," Michael answered.

"Howard doesn't believe in Frank's idea of doing well."

Michael frowned. "You mean Howard doesn't want to go into mining?"

"Not that." He thought her words carried a faint despair at his incomprehension. "I mean he simply doesn't want to make money."

Michael let out a disdainful "Pooh!" Every man wanted to make money. "He may say he doesn't. But perhaps he's afraid he can't."

"He's not interested in business," Ekaterina said. "He's an intellectual."

Michael thought she was being naïve now. What else would keep a man in the Republic but making money? Sometimes he felt that she lived in fantasies, she saw things so oddly. "Anyone with ambition joins the mines here."

There was a silence. Then she said: "Oh, I dare say Howard'll come round." She seemed to be closing the subject.

He did not know why so many of their conversations trailed away like this, as if wounded. The two of them seemed to agree on nothing serious. He felt obscurely that she had no right to do this to him. He sighed sharply, audibly. A woman should bolster a man. But she had refused, in some way, to remain within his orbit. He had the impression that over the past few years she had discovered and compassed him. Then she had withdrawn from what she had found. Not that she didn't respond sometimes—she could still be vivid and soft—but she no longer respected, let alone loved him. He could tell this even in her animation; it was lodged in her eyes—amused perhaps, attentive, but armoured over. He wished even that she was as angry and combative as she used to be. But nothing about her deeply valued him. Unintentionally, in the core of her, was an insult.

It would have been easier to bear if he did not still love her, and sometimes now he wished that he did not. Once or twice, after furious quarrels, he had been afraid that she was going to leave him. The thought touched him with panic.

Cigarette ash fell through his fingers and on to the sheet. He brushed it away. Ekaterina was still awake. He noticed her irregular breathing. He suddenly asked: "Do you think me a fool, Ekaterina?" But in fact he was asking what was wrong, what was wrong with them? Why couldn't she give herself to him? He heard her turn quickly in the bed. Her head came close to his, her hair brushing the side of his face.

"What did I say, Michael?"

"You behave as if I don't understand you."

"I didn't mean to."

No, he thought, perhaps she didn't mean to. Yet at the same time he never felt adequate to her. Without speaking, in her very being, she emphasized things whose lack in him no Greek woman would have noticed. Least of all could he bear the look of abstraction on her face when they had intercourse. No intelligent woman should do that to a man. Didn't she owe him trust? He gave her more freedom than most men gave their women. He even allowed her to continue nursing. Moreover they were among the richest people in the town. Why, then, couldn't she respond properly?

Chapter Twelve

For the first time in his life Howard was enjoying esteem. The townsmen, at first mystified and suspicious, now found it natural that the harmless, pedantic youth should desert so unspeakable a father. He rarely ate in the Seven Brothers Restaurant without somebody coming up to seize his hand or pay for his meal. Out of curiosity people even listened to what he had to say, although they did not understand it, and however cruelly some of them joked behind his back there were other simpler folk who were touched and grateful that he should have abandoned everything—as they put it—for the sake of the town.

Helen was not included in this friendliness. The people despised licentious women. She was a native daughter of Kalepia, and had brought discredit on them. One of these days, the old people said, she would pay the price of prostitution: the devil would ride into her bedroom on a three-legged lion and carry her away.

Howard was growing more relaxed. He aired and developed his views and was pleased by the agreement of everyone around him. Even Philippou became friendly. Three weeks before the day of the St Vichinos pilgrimage, as Howard was walking along the wharf, the fat fisherman came rolling out of the flour mill, seized his arm and petitioned his help. He needed to confide in a "man of principles", he said. If his pig-like eyes had not seemed so serious, Howard would have suspected him of malevolent play-acting. But Philippou turned him away from the dock so that they huddled against the flour-mill wall. Then he set his mouth to Howard's ear and whispered theatrically: "The arms have arrived."

"So it's true there are arms?"

"Yes, it's true." Philippou curled a finger at his lips. "But keep it to yourself. People can't be trusted. In this town there are fifty jackdaws to every owl."

Howard felt flattered by the man's confidence, but also uneasy. He could not envisage his father being shot—it was simply not imaginable—but the thought of these people possessing weapons at all was a nightmare. They might do anything. He said: "I hope the arms will not be used."

"They won't." Philippou's clown face looked regretful. "In any case, they're nothing. Just a few old rifles. Something to make a show. We can only look big and hope for the best." He sighed heavily and stared at the ground in caricature of downtrodden peasantry. The question, he said, was where to hide these arms. He needed the opinion of an educated man, whom they could trust. So what did Howard think?

Howard glanced about him. "Is the law hard on people who keep arms without a licence?"

Philippou unconsciously ran his fingers along his neck. "A little hard, yes." Then he fluttered his hands in deprecation. "But what's the law? You said yourself that it was corrupted." Now the small, inscrutable eyes were fawning into Howard's face. "And of course you're right. The law treads down the weak. That's why we have to be armed in the first place." He lifted a chubby fist. "We must combat the ethic of aggression in modern industrial society!"

Again Howard stared at him in hard suspicion. But the fisherman's face showed no trace of mockery. Howard grimaced—there was something which he did not understand.

They were both silent as a group of women brushed by them: middle-aged women in short skirts and heavy-heeled shoes; they carried wicker shopping-baskets and their heads were covered modestly in black or brown scarves. The last of these was Cat's-Bottom, the wharf prostitute. Philippou pinched her as she passed. "É, Charalambia, I hear you've been going with God-Asleep. How does he pay you?"

She turned a bloated face to his. "He makes more from charity than you do from work."

"But God's-Nod!" he hissed. "That's an insult! Tell me, is he a man or a goat down there?"

She snapped: "He's as good a man as you are *down there*, and the same in brains." She watched him with eyes as small and hard as his; the fat was creasing over them.

Philippou shambled a pace towards her and slid an arm round her shoulders. "My little one." Then he nestled his face against hers, turning a hand through her hair, and said quietly: "Did you hear anything?"

"Nothing more. . . ." She sauntered away.

Philippou went back to Howard, whose nose was wrinkling his spectacles up and down. "That's Cat's-Arse," he said. "A proper bitch." He turned against the wall again, unhitched his straw hat from his belt and tilted it low over his eyes, as if to make himself anonymous. In a lowered voice he said: "Kallis suggested rowing the arms out to the cave on Rat's Point tonight. That's a safe place. Nobody ever goes there."

Howard did not see why he was being asked. He did not know one part of the coast from another. But he said judiciously: "Yes, I would think that a good place."

Philippou eased his stomach over his belt, and stood silent for a moment, staring at his splay feet. His hands were plunged in his pockets and under the hat his forehead contracted with thought. "The problem will be to find somebody to row them out there."

"Either you or Mr Kallis..."

Philippou clicked his tongue. "No, no. Too obvious. Everybody watches us." He placed a hand confidingly on Howard's thin shoulder. "And as for the others, there are so few we can trust. We need somebody responsible, somebody intelligent." He stared into the other man's eyes. Howard felt a lightening in the well of his stomach. "To tell you the truth we've all discussed it together and come to one conclusion." He dropped his hand and said in a small, fluty voice: "You."

Howard blanched. For a moment he wished that he had never expressed an opinion, never confided any thought to these terrifying people. As he looked at Philippou he knew that the fear must shine in his face, and his own voice sounded querulous and small: "I can't."

Silence fell between them. It filled with the lazy sounds of the wharfside at noon: glasses tinkling, the wheezing of a crane. The dry, pleasant smell of flour hung in the air. Philippou said slowly: "I see." Yet he was smiling. Howard did not understand the smile. It appeared to break unwilled from under the surface of his face. He began: "We must all have misjudged you." His voice was paradoxically injured and forlorn. "I thought you meant what you said ... about aggression in society and so on."

Howard took a grip on himself, and rapped out: "Of course I did."

"Well then. . . ."

He must not let himself down, Howard thought. He must work the thing out logically. He only wished he had more time. He said: "Be reasonable now. You can't expect me to hide arms which may kill my own father." He added morosely: "Whatever I may think of him."

For a second he thought that a slight sneer crawled into Philippou's face. But then it had gone and instead the man was grinning and had burst out in disbelief: "You weren't thinking these guns were to be fired, were you?"

Howard said sourly: "They must have ammunition."

Philippou stared at him. His jaw sagged open and his eyes bulged. "Ammunition?" He planted his hands on his hips, threw back his head and exploded with laughter. "Ammunition! Blessed Virgin no! You thought there'd be *ammunition*? Hahaha! Oh Christos! What a devil you are! You think we want to kill somebody? These guns must be fifty years old! Back to the War of Liberation!" His double chin, half shaven, quivered with laughter a foot away from Howard's face. "Oh, that's a good one! Ammunition! You'd have a better chance of buying cannon-balls! Hahaha!"

Howard reluctantly began to laugh too, a laugh of foolish relief. All the muscles of his face were easing back into their accustomed positions. But he was mortified by his own panic, and now Philippou was saying: "Of course if your principles only exist on paper, then there's no use . . ."

"They certainly do not!" he snapped, flushing. "I'll act on anything I've said. I'm perfectly willing to hide your rifles or do anything else which will promote passive resistance. I'm not a coward. . . ."

But before he could finish Philippou had grabbed his hand and was shaking it up and down. "I knew you would, Mr Howard." Now his face appeared to hold nothing but a huge earnestness and respect; it even seemed as if tears had collected in his eyes. "I knew we could trust you. And you'll be safe all right. Nobody would suspect *you*."

Howard did not know what to think. The chill was spreading under his ribs again. He could not tell what risk he was taking. This Philippou seemed to have a whole collection of faces, none of which was his own. And now the fellow was saying in a dark, dramatic voice: "You mustn't leave before midnight. You'll find the arms in two crates under a pile of nets in the back of my fishing-boat—that's the blue skiff. You know Rat's promontory? It's the second to the west. You'll see the cave low down among the rocks. It shouldn't take you more than twenty minutes each way. But don't use the motor. It'll attract attention."

Howard began: "The blue skiff . . . ?"

"Yes, yes." Philippou glanced at his watch. "It's moored opposite the Angira Restaurant. "You must excuse me. I've got to go now. There's a meeting." He seized Howard's hand again and shook it fervently—"I knew we could rely on you"—then vanished into the flour-mill.

Howard made as if to go after him, then stopped, turned round and folded his arms to hide their trembling hands. This fear was ridiculous, he thought. Rifles without ammunition were no more lethal than baseball bats. He stared out to sea, which showed smooth and grey, and tried to think of some reason for refusing his help. But his mind produced none. And he wondered how, if he drew back, he would be able to face himself again. He could not refuse without rescinding everything he had said and thought.

He walked slowly towards the wharf to see where the blue skiff was moored, keeping his hands in his pockets.

Inside the mill Kallis was seated among the men he trusted: fifteen dockers and fishermen. The grain-brushing machines were whimpering around them, and a coat of flour lay like a pall on everything. Alastos, whose knowledge of mining had been useful to Kallis, sat among a pile of unstitched sacks, and Matheopoulos hovered near the grinders. But the old man looked unhappy. He appeared always to be on the point of leaving, as if afraid of hearing something which he did not wish to know.

But among the rest exhilaration had grown. As the day of the pilgrimage had drawn closer, they had felt the spirit of the town rising with them: they were going to win. They were being carried forward on their own enthusiasm. Now, seated together with their cigarettes passing from mouth to mouth, their confidence moved among them like a physical presence.

As soon as Philippou entered, Kallis noticed his smirk, and asked in irritation: "What have you been doing, Antis?"

The fisherman settled himself between two of the dockers, and closed his eyes. "I've been marinating a squid."

Kallis hissed impatiently and continued poring through the file spread across his knees. But when the room fell quiet he looked up and said matter-of-factly, to suppress overexcitement: "The arms arrived safely this morning."

A hushed applause went up. The men listened in silence as he continued, their only movement the passing of the cigarettes like a talisman between them. "The lorry ran into a spot check of security police soon after it left Chakistra. But the rifles got through undetected. I unloaded them early this morning in umarked crates. They're under tarpaulin in one of the boats."

A fisherman rasped out: "You weren't short-changed? Did you get what they promised?"

"Yes, it's all there." Kallis could not keep a note of triumph from his voice. "Twenty repeating rifles. Two thousand rounds of ammunition. Some gelignite. A detonator."

Murmurs of satisfaction broke out. Several men started to laugh with a release of tension. To them the arrival of these weapons was like the advent of a combine harvester among farmers who have watched their fields grow golden and over-ripe. Yet few of them thought of pulling the triggers. They simply imagined the heavy comfort of the barrels in their hands as they marched up the Mountain, the smoothness of the butts against their hips. That was power. With that, nothing would be refused them.

One of the millers said: "But we're not going to leave them in the boat, are we? Where are we going to hide them?"

Kallis stood up. "They'll be hidden tonight in the cave at Rat's Point. I'm relying on you all to keep away. Don't hang around the dock this evening. Marangos'll sniff out trouble like a bloodhound." He stared round at them.

Philippou yawned melodramatically and said: "Marangos has already told things to the police."

At this several of the men broke into low cursing and threats, but nobody was surprised. Alastos asked sharply: "Who told you that?"

"One of the policemen goes with Cat's-Arse." Philippou still lay propped between the dockers with his eyes closed. "He told her that Marangos split weeks back."

Kallis' hands lifted in a calming gesture. "We expected that." Surrounded by practical needs, by the certainty of his own men, he could forget himself. Among them, there could be no thought of failure. "There's nothing Marangos can do. We're the only ones who know where the rifles will be hidden. If we keep silent, we're safe." One or two men glanced uneasily round them, but the faces which they saw seemed as dedicated as their own, and they turned to Kallis again, reassured.

He had picked up the list on his knees and was underscoring names with a pencil. "I want men who can handle these rifles," he said. "They'll spearhead the pilgrimage. Everything may depend on them."

Alastos broke in heavily: "You give those rifles to responsible men, Mr Kallis, not just to anybody."

Kallis said briskly: "Every man will be selected." He looked at the others. "You've all seen military service. But we've only twenty firearms. We can't waste them."

Nearly everyone raised his hand. The clamour of their voices, claiming experience on the Albanian front or in commando regiments, was overridden by Kallis' thrusting questions. "Where did you serve? ... That's too long ago ... your sight is too poor. ..." Within ten minutes eight of them had been assigned rifles, and Kallis was noting down the names of others whose army "certificates of marksmanship" had been noticed hanging on their walls alongside pictures of their family and name-saint.

All this time Matheopoulos had been watching from among the grinders with deepening dismay. His hands kept twitching at his suit, as if fingering its quality, and had run through his hair so often that it flared in a white mist round his head. In the end he walked over to the operating panel and switched off the buttons one by one. The sounds of brushing and grinding purred to an end, and the transparent tubes along the walls fell silent with a tinkle of falling wheat and husk. Then the old man walked to the perimeter of the circle and said in a trembling voice: "I don't understand what you're doing, Mr Kallis. You don't mean to shoot?"

Kallis looked at him with a hint of intolerance. His voice came soothing yet cold: "We don't intend to harm a soul, Mr Matheopoulos. Unless we're fired on, we shall regard this as a pilgrimage."

Matheopoulos had turned pink. "You won't bring those rifles into this mill. I forbid it." His knuckles were white against his lapels. "I thought you'd given up this idea of arms."

Alastos was watching him with sadness and respect. "I used to feel as you do," he said. He wanted to explain. He wanted to explain that there were things worth defending even with violence. "Without arms we'd be laughed at."

Matheopoulos was breathing heavily. He wagged his finger at Alastos. The ridiculous gesture, coupled with the hoarse quaver of his voice, was somehow obscene. "You don't know anything, young man. This isn't even your country." He had to stop for breath. "Even deaths won't end this affair. Blood produces blood here ... it goes on for ever." He peeled off his spectacles and dabbed his fingertips against his eyes. "Don't you know your Bible? 'Thou shalt not kill' ... no, not even for a saint. Let them take the shrine if they want it. God will punish them...."

"Men are God's instruments," said Kallis. "That's what the priest says."

Matheopoulos' head was shaking in its starched collar. "That's all very well...."

Alastos got to his feet and stood beside the old man. The eyes of the others followed them in silence. He said sombrely—his cumbersome mind had gone over and over these things in the past weeks: "Listen. What happens if peaceful people always give in at the thought of bloodshed?" He tried to smile at Matheopoulos. "The world would be trampled under! We'd all be ruled by brutes!" He squeezed the old man's arm. "When people are in the right, they must stand up!"

Matheopoulos pulled away his arm. "Everyone thinks he's in the right." He looked away bitterly.

Again Alastos tried to articulate everything he had thought, talking to the ruffled white head turned away from him and staring at the silenced grinders. "Isn't there anything you'd die for, Mr Matheopoulos? Not your family, say, or your freedom?" His voice was rising in its old, didactic heaviness, and his arms began to flail at his sides. "Every time people let themselves be trodden under, even if their cause is hopeless, they betray their fellow men...."

"Bravo, bravo!" shouted Philippou. He yawned at Alastos.

"I don't know what you're talking about," said Matheopoulos plaintively. He turned from Alastos to Kallis and back. "You and your ideas. How many human beings is an idea worth? You'll see ... his fingers came up to his eyes again. "You'll have bloodshed."

Alastos kicked the ground unhappily. "There's a possibility," he said. He glanced down at the others. "We can't evade that." But it was not a possibility which he could readily envisage.

Kallis said: "The blood will be on the Company's head." Several others murmured agreement.

But Alastos said in his stubborn tone: "On all our heads. On mine too. That's the risk we take. Don't let's start whining." He walked into the centre of them. Sometimes these men, with their open, enthusiastic faces, gave a feeling of irresponsibility, as if they might do anything and blame the Company for it; while at other times he wondered paradoxically if they would not evaporate at the first sign of danger. "If you carry arms you must expect to be shot at. That's how it goes. You take the risk with open eyes."

The men merely puffed their cigarettes, not listening much, and waited for him to end. They trusted him now, but they did not understand him. Besides, there were rumours of his liaison with the Company Secretary's wife; the stories were all over the town.

Matheopoulos had turned his back on them all. He rested with his elbows on the sack chute, his head bent. "The town has got to go on living with these mining people," he said. "Generations of us." But the fishermen and dockers had started arguing about something else among themselves, and nobody was listening to him except Alastos, who came and sat beside him on the sacks of semolina flour. Alastos wondered what sort of future the old man was envisaging. Within a few years, if they failed, there would be no town at all as Matheopoulos had known it.

"We're defending your world," he told the old man gently. "Everything you've grown up with—streets, habits, religion.... In ten years' time this town wouldn't be the one you'd known. It would be like all the other towns in the Republic."

And these towns turned a man's heart to lead. The Capital was a frenzy of nerve-ridden businessmen and jealous factory-workers; they lived in flat-blocks like concrete beehives and died years before old age. Chakistra was an industrial slum; Ambos a dying miners' town; and Nikitari, the Republic's chief port, a pretentious metropolis which pampered the hated tourists all summer and suffered from chronic dock strikes.

But Kalepia preserved the rhythms of the land. Its Mountain was beautiful with trees, and its sea clear. For all its poverty, he could understand why his father had loved it. It was like a deep breath in the panting of the world.

Ekaterina had been right. This pointless fury which people called progress! There was no sign, in any of these other towns, that people were happier or less selfish than in Kalepia.

"I agree, I agree," said Matheopoulos testily. "Ours are not a bad people. That's why this violence is ... is..."

But Alastos was thinking of Ekaterina. He could remember from his childhood the riots in the little district town of Margo, and how the people had plundered the richer houses and butchered two families. He wished she were safe in some other place. Every time they met now, after her nursing rounds, the day of the pilgrimage hung over them with its threat of change. Yet their moments together had become eased and happy. They had talked of the past in mutual forgiveness. Even the discovery of one another's bodies, so long refused, was sometimes a tender and loving game. At other times his fear of losing her had been too strong for him—a fear that Lerides would somehow retrieve her—and he had started to plead with her to settle things. But always she had placed her hand against his mouth and said "Wait." In those moments she had become the woman he did not know. Her facial expression, even the timbre of her voice, appeared different. She had not looked happy, and her gentleness to him afterwards had been frightening, as if she was comforting him.

Beside him the old mill-owner Matheopoulos was still talking intermittently; but he had no coherent ideas. Alastos only listened to him out of respect—but respect for what, precisely, he could not have said.

Chapter Thirteen

The night was cold and very still, such a stillness as sometimes descends upon these coasts at the end of winter, leaving the sea in a glassy calm. To the east, lit by a three-quarter moon, a mass of cloud spread like a violent continent from horizon to horizon.

By this gaunt light, early in the evening, two truckloads of police left the compound at Kalepia and vanished out of sight along the road to Nikitari. But one kilometre farther, where Oldenburg joined them in a limousine, they doubled back westward over a dirt track with their lamps dimmed. The carabiniers were sullen and cold. They sat face to face on the iron benches of the trucks, with their rifle-butts wedged between their boots and their chins withdrawn into their overcoat collars. The sergeant sang a peasant love-song mockingly from behind clenched teeth.

While still half a kilometre inland from Rat's Point they stopped; the trucks were steered off the track and the men moved forward on foot without lights. The winter rains had been so heavy that the mud sometimes rose above their boots and in several gullies they brushed among the meshed roots of pines swept down from the moonlit slopes above. After a while they could hear the sea. The Chief said: "We'll keep to the far side of the promontory as long as we can."

They crested the last rise, with their rifles still slung at their shoulders. Below them wind-blown acacias all stooped in the same direction, as if praying in the sand, and beyond stretched the headland, a finger of dark rocks, pointing at Greece. Oldenburg and the Chief looked eastward, but the lights of Kalepia were still obscured by mountains. Far around them the sea, as if possessed of some profound, interior peace, lay motionless, like beaten silver. Nothing moved on it.

Oldenburg asked: "Did this Marangos give any indication of time?"

"None," said the Chief. "He didn't know."

The men began to clamber down to the coast. They went quietly, although nothing breathed for miles around. The presence of the sea and the immensity of the land—black shoulders of cliff muscling to the shore—imposed a deep quiet. Soon they were groping along the promontory. The water lisped and gurgled at their feet without the breaking of a wave. The Chief ordered them to spread out among the rocks above the cave, while the sergeant entered it, shining a blue lamp into its recesses. The place stank of bats' urine. So long was it since anybody had been there that the dust lay over its floor in a film a centimetre deep, patinated by the feet of birds.

Oldenburg and the Chief sat shivering in their overcoats, and stared over the boulders towards Kalepia. From here the lights of the wharf showed clear across the calm, and seemed closer than they were. The sergeant emerged from the cave, detailed the corporal and another man to watch, and settled himself under a stunted pine tree, where he began to clean his revolver by the light of the moon.

The Chief said: "Marangos'll give us a signal. He'll switch off the jetty lights ten minutes after the boat leaves."

Oldenburg grunted. This man Marangos, he thought, had not trusted the police to act, but had informed the Company too. That was disquieting. He glanced around him. The men's cigarettes glowed fitfully here and there. "Should those men be smoking?"

"No." The Chief relayed an order, and the lights went out. The whole promontory was sunk in darkness.

The hours passed coldly. The silence was so deep that once, when a man dislodged his rifle, it clattered like an explosion among the rocks and set every man's nerves jangling. Hour after hour the jetty lights reflected steadily in the water.

Helen was curled in bed with her knees drawn to her chin, and her back turned to Howard. She was afraid of his leaving. Her people, she said, would only make use of a foreigner—they kept their secrets to themselves. If they had given him an assignment, it must be dangerous.

Howard was angry with her—he did not want his own fear revived—and told her that she was being childishly illogical. His stance was recognized all over the town, he said, and he was trusted. Nobody knew about the arms except Kallis, Philippou and him. He stared petulantly at the curve of her back. If she would only develop her mind instead of her feelings, he said, she might grow to understand something.

Soon after midnight he must have dozed off, because he woke to see the hands of his clock illumined at quarter to two. Helen was asleep, and the lights from the dock, filtered between the wharfside houses, lit the curtained window in a wan rectangle. He slid out of the bed and started to dress, shivering. He put on his heaviest clothes, with waterproof boots and a thick scarf. But the cold now seemed to be inside him, in the centre of his chest. He lifted a corner of the curtain. Outside, framed in the alley, a section of the quay showed deserted. The sea was a black wedge beyond. He trod softly to the door; but his fingers shook so much on the handle that he did not dare open it. He turned and leaned his back against it, warming his cheeks with his hands. The light showed a part of Helen's head buried in the pillow, asleep. He went back, pulled the blankets over her shoulders, and kissed her.

Only a few cats flitted across the street at his tread. The wharf was empty. He found Philippou's boat creaking and slopping against the soft wood of the quay. It smelt of tar, and was filled with nets and tins of paraffin for the lantern at its prow. He stepped gingerly into it. The two crates were there, under the netting. He sat for a moment facing the dock, watching for any movement. But there was none. Every window was curtained, or invisible. He thought: there's nothing to worry about, this place is stone dead after midnight. The oars slipped obediently into their sockets, and he cast off.

In the cabin of the crane, enveloped by shadow, Marangos was smoking. He watched in silence, keeping the glow of the cigarette under the lip of the window, bending down to draw on it. Around his feet the floor was littered with the stubs of a four-hour vigil. For ten minutes more he waited, timing himself by his watch, then he eased himself to the ground and walked towards the customs shed. As the hour had grown late he had begun to wonder if anybody would come, and suspected that the lean, ambitious docker—one of Kallis' chosen few—had informed him wrong. Now he said to himself morosely: clever of them to send Howard—nobody would suspect him. All the same, he thought as he switched off the jetty lights, that wouldn't save Kallis because Howard would be forced to split on him.

The clouds were drifting closer to the moon. Howard was alone on the sea. The harbour beacon had fallen behind him, and he rowed with short strokes. Only once he stopped to examine the crates, but their lids were nailed down hard. As the lights of Kalepia grew small he saw that ahead of him the coast swung in a double loop, of which the farthest headland must be Rat's Point. He decided not to look at it—it seemed too far away—but to keep the land at a level distance to his left.

The risk, he told himself, was over. Nobody would find him now. There was no danger in darkness. People might come to the coast by day, but by night never. It was only its obscurity which turned it ominous. In fact it was empty, and fear of the night was irrational.

He felt more satisfied. How dare anybody suggest he was just a passive thinker! No, he was striking his blow for a new civilization by an act of decision and courage! And he did not do so like these townsmen, in a mindless jealousy, but with the clarity of reason. Most of these people, he remembered, were afraid of the dark, like children; they peopled it with spirits.

He was pulling more strongly at the oars now. He kept his eyes on the fading town lights. The movement of the boat through the water and the splash of the oar-blades no longer sounded lonely, but purposeful. He wanted to sing with their rhythm. Within an hour he would be back in bed, his self-esteem warm inside him. He started to count to the stroke of the oars, watching the moonlight fall from their shafts: "One-two ... in-out ... one-two...."

Ten minutes later he approached the first headland, where the cargo boat had been wrecked a year before. He could see it leaning out of the water like the fragment of a cliff. As he rounded the cape he rested on his oars, and drifted. The moonlight fell full on the flaking paint of the wreck's hull. He noticed the name: "T.S.S.Stavrovouni". Under the water its prow was dimly visible, lit by the moon. It lay aslant sunken rocks, and phosphorous gleams of fish were nibbling at its sides. From the cabin window a piece of cloth—a man's coat, he thought—undulated dreamily.

He fumbled for his oars, jolted one into the sea, and recovered it. The commotion glinted ripples round the rotting stern. He had no command of his hands. Who had been drowned in that wreck? He did not know. He stared again far down at the terrifying coat.

Other things were swaying behind it: dense, green fronds, which moved all together, like hair.

Kallis and Philippou watched through the shutters as Marangos wheeled his bicycle out of the customs shed, mounted it and rode slowly away.

Kallis rubbed his eyes; he had been asleep in Philippou's cottage when the jetty lights had suddenly gone out. He said: "I don't understand what Marangos is up to."

Philippou grimaced. "Nor do I."

They crammed on their overcoats and walked quietly across the dock. The moon was overcast. They looked quickly about them, then climbed into a boat belonging to Philippou's brother. It was hung with netting and bundles of gourds which were used for floats. "If anybody asks us," Philippou said, "we're fishing."

They cleared the harbour arm as a light rain fell, and turned west.

Now that Howard held Rat's Point well in sight, this thin, icy rain had come to mist it away. He wanted to turn back. The sight of the wreck had unnerved him, and the night seemed to be interminable. In their gloves his fingers were stiff with cold, and his whole body seemed uncontrolled and fragile, as if it might start to shudder.

He wrenched harder at the oars. He was afraid of losing his direction. Behind him the rain fell in drifts, like light touching gauze. But after a few minutes he saw the profile of the cape again, with trees twisted on its skyline, and came in closer, looking for the cave. The whole promontory lay motionless, silent. Only the rain faintly hissed over the surface of the sea. He rowed where some bushes created the appearance of an opening, and found the cave by chance. It lay not far above the tideline, smaller than he had expected. All about it the boulders overhung the water and seemed vaguely to threaten. But nothing moved as his boat nudged the shingle. The tip of the headland was indistinguishable in the night.

He grasped the anchor and slid overboard. The water barely reached to his ankles. The rain was thinning away. In a moment he was glad to feel the hard ground under his feet, and to wedge the anchor among the rocks. As he turned back to the boat he thought he heard something move above him, but he grasped the prow and swung the stern of the boat to shore. The crates were slippery with rain. He heaved one out, balancing it on the lip of the boat, and staggered with it through the water. It was then, as he bent and laid it on the ground, his fingers too numb to grasp it properly, that the lights flashed on from all over the slopes above, dazzling and pinning him to the side of the boat. He watched them, stupefied. They began to move. They wavered towards him. He remained frozen, his ankles in the sea and his mouth half open. He was almost too tired for terror. His heart was pounding, but his eyes mesmerized. Now voices were shouting at him in Greek. Men's boots trampled among shrubs and stones, closer. He heard the sound of a rifle's bolt locking, while pebbles and clumps of earth came rolling down the slope towards him, splashed into the sea. The voices sounded violent. Then they were around him, eight or nine of them, indecipherable behind their torchlight—policemen. He thought he was going to faint. Three different rifle barrels were probing his ribs. He retched and was sick on the shore at their feet.

As he stooped there, he wondered fleetingly whether it would be better to seem weak or strong. But when he looked up again he was conscious of a change. The voices had turned quiet. They were murmuring with confusion and surprise. The lights played back and forth over his face. He heard his own name, but nobody spoke to him. Now he began to discern them as individuals. A man with shifty eyes—a sergeant—cursed softly and rammed his revolver back into its holster, which creaked with his every movement.

Then other lights appeared on the slope and suddenly, inexplicably, a voice which he knew demanded: "Who is it?"

The policemen did not answer. They shuffled and murmured, easing their rifles back on their shoulders. Howard heard his father's feet coming, marching over the shingle. The voice repeated irascibly "Who is it?" And the circle of men parted before him in silence.

Howard watched his father's face move into the ring of lights. It was nested unfamiliar between a low cap and high collar. For a second, he thought, it did not recognize him. Then its expression became baffled, and the whole face flinched and tautened. When he tried to speak, the bottom seemed to have fallen out of his voice. It was almost a croak: "Howard."

Howard stared at him for any sign of anger. There was none. He had the impression—although he could not tell in this dimness—that his father had turned very pale. Now another man thrust between them—people were replacing one another like the deepening stages of a nightmare. He recognized the sour face and long, greying moustaches of the police chief. The last time they had met was at one of his father's parties; he had offered the Chief a slice of jellied pork. And now, although the man was grim with his duty, his voice held the faintest apology. He said formally: "Howard Oldenburg?"

One or two of the torches flashed again in his face, as if he might not, after all, be himself. He said weakly: "Yes."

"You realize the possession of illegal arms is a crime against the State."

It was spoken as a fact, not a question. The faces and lights had all gone quiet about him. The men might have been standing before some memorial. Their silence sent a shock of new fear through him. Crime against the State. He had read these words in the newspapers after insurrections, during political trials. They breathed up a cloud of terror.

He wanted to sit down. He wanted to go somewhere warm, somewhere away from the terrifying agitation inside him. He felt thin as paper. The rain must be pouring through him.

The Chief said harshly: "How did you come into possession of these arms?"

Howard's throat had gone dry. How had he? For a moment he could not remember, could not recall anything which had happened before those lights burst like fireworks in his face.

Then his father stepped close and grasped him by the forearm. "Don't answer. You're not obliged to answer any question yet. We'll demand a lawyer first."

Howard stared at him. The Chief seemed to spit. "Mr Oldenburg, this isn't the United States. Your son has committed a capital crime. He will be arrested and interrogated at once."

Oldenburg said: "He's an American citizen, and he'll get protection."

The Chief kicked the crate at his feet. "You don't seem to understand the seriousness, Mr Oldenburg." He rapped at the sergeant: "Get the lids off these crates!"

Howard kept his eye on the chests as the rifle butts thudded on them, but he was conscious only of his father, who still stood beside him. His father's hand was on his arm, and the warmth of it was almost unbearable. He felt the tears burning behind his eyes. His father was afraid for him—he had never seen him afraid before—

but was passing his strength into him, through his hand. By this one motion, this proof of love, he had dissolved everything alien inside his son. Howard looked away into the rain.

The rifle butts were no longer falling on the crates. The corporal had heard something rolling inside, and the men, afraid of dislodging the pins of hand-grenades, were easing their knives under the lid. The Chief came back impatiently and stared at Howard. His hands were on his hips. He started to talk. He still looked angry, but with the self-induced anger used by officials against those who have flouted the system. Only a few of the Chief's words reached Howard at all. "... Utmost gravity ... in the case of those who are willing to uphold the law against their previous associates ... the law may deal more leniently...."

Howard vaguely understood that they were trying to make him betray Kallis. And he found, to his surprise, that a germ of stubbornness remained. He would tell his father, of course, he would tell his father anything now. But he would not talk direct to the police.

His father repeated harshly: "My son is not obliged to answer anything until he's properly represented." His voice came close against Howard's ear: "As soon as we get back I'll ring the Company lawyer."

By now the lids of the crates were easing loose. Oldenburg and Howard became part of a watching circle. Howard had the illusion that his father was physically supporting him. He said thinly: "There's no ammunition."

"Tell that to the crows," said the Chief.

There was an awed hush as the men lifted off the splintered lids. They did so almost with reverence. Everyone felt that he was presiding not only over the end of a town's cause, but over men's deaths. Half a dozen torches were trained into the blackness of the crates. The heads all crammed forward, and as the light shone on the contents, an audible gasp went up.

They were filled with potatoes.

One of the men began to laugh: a nervous falsetto. Oldenburg brushed a hand across his face. With a contemptuous grunt the sergeant flung himself on his knees and delved furiously under the vegetables, but his arms emerged only covered in dirt and cascading potatoes over the sides of the boxes.

"Anathema!" The Chief turned to Howard, blazing. "What the devil is this?"

Howard blurted: "I don't know ... I thought ... thought they were rifles."

The Chief glared at him, as if the naivety of this answer must conceal mockery. But Howard was staring foolishly into the crates, like everybody else. Relief was surging through him. He thought: that Philippou.... He wanted to laugh—he felt slightly hysterical—but he was too weak. And a moment later, noticing that two of the policemen sniggered at him, he was already mortified at what had been done to him, at the whole misery of this endless night. These filthy people. They would joke with your soul.

But the warmth of his father remained. He followed his father with the eyes of a slave.

The Chief barked at the sergeant: "Get the men back to the trucks."

Oldenburg, Howard and the Chief were left alone on the shingle. The rain had cleared and the moon still showed dimly, like a halo discarded in the clouds. The empty boat remained at anchor, forgotten, and the crates stayed where they had been opened, their spilt potatoes mingled with pebbles. The Chief stood with his legs planted apart and his head bent. He lit a cigarette and flicked the match into the sea. Then he demanded in a tone of chilly disappointment: "Who sent you on this chicken's mission?"

Howard said: "That fat fisherman, Antis Philippou. The cynical one. He said they were rifles." He shot a look of remorse at his father. "But harmless ones ... old."

The Chief asked: "And what about Kallis?"

"I don't know anything about Kallis."

The Chief slid one hand under his cap and scratched his scalp. He started to pace up and down. The lines of his face, lit by the cigarette, showed deep and bitter, like scars. Oldenburg said in a voice of unwonted lightness—he was feeling strangely buoyant: "D'you think it's a hoax? Perhaps there aren't any arms. Perhaps they just want to create confidence among the townsmen."

The Chief spat denial. "There are arms all right." His pacing came to a halt in front of Howard again. "What do you know more?"

"Nothing."

Oldenburg said to the Chief in an exasperated tone: "This is a dead-end. There's no law against rowing potatoes about in the night. If the town hears about it, we'll look bigger fools than anyone else."

The Chief did not answer. This had occurred to him long before. He continued pacing up and down, kicking the shingle. Far out to sea, the lights of a freighter were sliding eastward. Momentarily the Chief wondered if Marangos might not be playing with them all, then put the thought from his mind. In the end he said: "We'd better get back to the men." He glanced at Howard. "I don't want any more spoken about this."

Howard followed them along the promontory and up the shore, where the stooped acacias brushed the wind. His father looked at him once with no expression which he could discover. "You'll be coming back with me."

He said: "Yes."

He could hardly force his feet to grip the edges of the blackened gullies where they went. Exhaustion had dimmed even the tumult in him. His father's back was square and familiar in front. When they were alone, he thought, after they had driven home perhaps, he would take his father's hand in his. Wouldn't he? But he had never done such a thing. And he knew that little by little, as they passed each landmark back into town, this resolve would grow unreachably difficult and strange.

Cruising along the shore through the rain, Philippou had asked Kallis: "Which way do we go? To the tombs?"

"You guessed," said Kallis in surprise. "How?"

Philippou giggled, squashing a woollen cap over his ears. "Because it was the opposite direction to what you told the others."

By now they were far enough from the town to use the boat's motor. Philippou steered, keeping his eyes on the shore, while Kallis, as soon as the rain ceased, stripped the tarpaulins from the three long packing-cases in the back of the boat. He struck a match, shielding the light inside the flaps of his coat, and pulled a stick of sealing-wax from his pocket. Methodically he applied it to each side of the lids, stamping it with the flat of a key.

After a while he heard above him a series of throaty gasps, like a dog trying to be sick. He looked up to see Philippou convulsed by secret laughter. The fisherman was holding his stomach as if it would explode, and his eyes were screwed to dots.

"What's up with you?"

"All the saints!" Philippou's shoulders were shaking up and down. His jowls quivered. "I sent somebody on a little errand."

Kallis asked sharply: "Who? Where?"

The fisherman stopped and soothed him with a patting hand. "Now don't be angry. It was a joke between friends." Then he began to curl up again, while the laughter pealed out of him. "Howard Oldenburg ... Oh *Panaghia*! ... I sent him to Rat's Point with some crates of rotten potatoes! Hahahaha! ... You should have seen his face when I asked him.... Hahaha! Shivering like a mimosa...."

"Shut up!" Kallis crouched opposite him. "What in the devil's world have you done? When did you send him?"

"Tonight!" Philippou pulled the boat round with a face of mock seriousness. He had been making straight for shore. "This very night!"

Kallis blazed at him: "You idiot! What if one of the others told the plan to Marangos? What if the police heard?"

"What if they did?" Philippou simpered, then burst into renewed howls of laughter. "Imagine the reception! Oh Christos! Monkeys biting each other's tails!" He slapped Kallis on the back. "Oh God in heaven! ..."

But Kallis had seized the steering handle and was now guiding the boat into a shallow bay, where the ancient tombs stood empty and waiting in the cliffs.

Chapter Fourteen

A week before the pilgrimage, with religious feeling intensifying every hour, rumours of miracles and visions circulated wildly through the town. Many people claimed that the saint had visited them in dreams, others had seen a figure in grey armour walking on the Mountain, and one of the fishermen claimed that for several nights a cross had been inscribed upon the moon.

Every day the church of the tall priest, although barely within the town's limits, was filled with prayer and votive offerings. At the beginning of the week, when the icon of St Vichinos was set upon its stand for veneration, such a forest of candles was planted before it that the great earth-filled bowls could scarcely hold them all.

It was now rumoured that the archimandrite had threatened the priest with excommunication. Long afterwards this was found to be untrue, but meanwhile all the ground floor windows of the archimandrite's residence were smashed. The old man had himself been seated at his desk when a shower of splinters scudded over the floor, followed by stones and excrement.

The hardening between the Old Town and the miners' village was emphasized by the river dividing them. Swollen with storms, it swept down splintered pines and holm-oaks from the inland mountains, and so close did its surface move beneath the town's one bridge that the uprooted trees were trapped there and tangled with the bodies of drowned sheep. Time out of mind the river had carried down a reddish soil every spring to the sea. Local stories told that this was the blood of a god slain and buried in the Mountain; and now, seeing the thick current a darker crimson than in memory, the old people pointed their sticks and said that the Mountain itself was angry.

The miners had grown intolerant of the townspeople. They saw the river too, and aired a joke together that the god in the Mountain was copper. Copper was the Resurrection and the Life. They urinated into the river. Some of the muckers had grown so virulent, accusing the townspeople of ruining their jobs and families, that they had run amok in the streets one evening, overturning carts and shop stalls until the police moved them back.

Generally the police avoided action against their fellow-townsmen; but several of the popular leaders, including Kallis, took to sleeping in friends' houses to foil any attempt at night arrests. It was easy, in any case, to acquire rooms. In anticipation of the pilgrimage notices were appearing all over the streets, and instead of the usual "Rooms for Hire", they read "Rooms Free—Pilgrims Welcome", "Welcome to the Faithful in Christ", or even "Welcome to St Vichinos" as if the saint was present in the house.

Since the priest's speech on the dockside everyone expected that the clash would take place on the near slopes of the Mountain, where the pilgrims' path met the Company's new fence. Already the Company had built too much on the site—a repair and service depot, small offices—to leave it undefended. The picket at the barbed wire entrance had recently doubled in size, and the nearby Nissen huts where the sentries slept were now too small to house them all. Every three days the convoy which left the mines to relieve them looked less like a new shift than a military sortie, the helmeted muckers racing in jeeps over the bridge with batons and lanterns slung at their waists.

Every townsman feared waking up one morning to find that the shrine had been demolished overnight by the Company's bulldozers. It had become a nervous mannerism in Kalepia to glance up at the white dome and murmur "God be thanked!" And now, at any time of the day or night, the sanctuary was occupied by two or three of the stouter householders near the summit, who locked themselves in each evening and slept with clubs or sickles at their sides. So the Mountain remained like a castle whose walls have been captured but whose keep holds out.

Oldenburg was at last beginning to realize the magnitude of the problem. The knowledge that the town was arming itself kept turning uncomfortably in his brain. Lerides, who had felt the position's seriousness and delicacy months before, advised him that the only way to avoid a heavy clash was to win over a faction of the people by a public speech. The two men sat together all through one day and drafted the pith of it with the help of telephone calls to the municipality. Lerides and Oldenburg worked like oil and vinegar. Lerides' flexible intelligence saw all that Oldenburg's mind did not. The one gave finesse, the other stability and direction. They knew that they could never break down those townspeople whose jobs or homes were in jeopardy. Their aim could only be the more modest one of weakening the confidence of the small tradespeople—men who had so far been inundated by the fears of the others. If they held the meeting in the less formal atmosphere of the school hall, they decided, and if Lerides and not Oldenburg were to speak, the memory of the first public meeting might fade.

The talk was arranged on the same day as it was held. So tense was Kalepia's atmosphere that an announcement could be made merely by speaking to a single citizen—and within an hour the whole town knew. Early in the evening the people from the port moved on the hall in a body and occupied the entire centre of its auditorium. Their temper was high. They were not dressed as before in dark suits, but wore their working clothes defiantly: frayed oilskins, sheepskin cloaks, tar-stained windbreakers. They sent up a roar of conversation; while all about them, like the soft plasma round a cell, sat motley groups of other men—clerks, storekeepers, craftsmen—who looked less homogeneous than the rest, murmuring together and playing with their beads.

Sofroniou, seated near the door, noticed many changes since the first meeting. The front row no longer held a line of privileged mining personnel and their families. Not a single woman had entered the hall; only a few of the fishermen's wives were clustered outside waving illiterate placards; and the bankers and officials had barely shown themselves. Of all the Company only Oldenburg, Muller and the Chief Engineer sat in front together, and although the hall was so crowded that the men at the back stood shoulder to shoulder, the chairs to either side of these three were empty, as if they had plague. Sofroniou noticed that Matheopoulos had kept away; and so had Alastos; and the only priest to be seen was the tall primitive who had been making so much trouble with his sermons.

There was silence when Lerides climbed on to the platform, and nobody made an introductory speech. He looked easy and confident in a casual suit. The stage had been hastily cleared during the dress rehearsal of a school play, and the garish sets for Euripides'

Medea were still stacked on either side. Six masks, slung over a screen, leered at the audience, as if to announce that behind appearances existed nothing at all. The crowd was hunched and waiting. It breathed an almost jubilant sureness in itself. Lerides smiled blandly to some point at the back of the hall, rested his brief-case beside his chair, and stepped forward to the edge of the dais. The air was filled with smoke and garlic. The people were so tensed that the tapping of the madman's stick could be heard distinctly against the wall outside.

"People of Kalepia," began Lerides—his tone at once spelt sympathy, reconciliation—"on behalf of the Company let me say that we are all deeply concerned about the town's disapproval of our plans. I'm afraid that we've been guilty of allowing serious misunderstandings to arise, and I want to rectify some of these now."

The silence did not break. Each of his words fell without echo into an infinite well of suspicion.

"As you know," he continued, "the Company adopts the attitude that it is wrong to ignore the world's resources." He cupped one hand in a gesture of reasonableness. "Everything unexploited makes the world poorer, poorer than its potential." He added a little too suavely, too lightly: "If there's copper in the Mountain, then it was placed there by God for a purpose, and we must utilize it."

Sofroniou, staring at him, was not impressed. Was what he said true? Somehow it did not matter. His face was like a wolf's. And now the tall priest, the only one present, called out in his misshapen voice: "You have no right to talk of God, Mr Lerides, in view of what you are doing."

A wave of assent rippled from the centre of the hall and splashed against the stage. "There are differing points of view even on the will of God," said Lerides levelly. "The archimandrite is satisfied. . . ."

"The archimandrite," boomed the priest, "has not even safeguarded the rights of the poor to the olive trees!" His jaw jerked forward with every syllable. "Of the archimandrite I say with St Augustine that the Church is filled with predators!" Again came the fierce ripple, mixed with a heartless laughter. It was becoming clear that many of these flushed faces were merely waiting for a chance to shout their revenge. Cries and watchwords were bounding back and forth along their lines, and now, almost before Lerides' speech had started, the shouting of many other people drowned his voice in demands which succeeded one another like machine-gun bullets. Whenever this bitterness seemed to be waning, the claque of dockers and mill-workers around Kallis would start to shout "Ayios Vichinos!" or "Foreigners away!" so that for a full five minutes Lerides was forced to stand silent and wait. But his only sign of discomfort was the uneasy turning of the gold ring round his finger. His face continued almost courteous. For these men were not his target. His speech was aimed at the tradespeople, whose heckling was less organized, and who sat on the hall's circumference smoking their fusty cigarettes.

After a while Lerides tipped the masks off one of the stage screens and pulled it to the centre of the dais; unrolling some charts from his brief-case, he laid them face downward on the table. Then he waited, in the knowledge that eventually the boundless inquisitiveness of these people would want to hear him. He felt little but contempt for them. If you regarded them as backward children, he thought, you could anticipate all their reactions. While they shouted, his gaze did not register a single face. It was easier to smile at a mob of them than at an individual.

When the clamour was being sustained only by those around Kallis, Lerides managed to interject from time to time in a loud voice: "Are you Greeks?" and this peculiar question evoked an expectant fading of noise. "Our ancestors invented free speech!" he shouted at last, rhetorically. "Have we degenerated?"

Several obscenities answered this, but the crowd seemed slightly shamed, and his speaking voice could now be heard above them. "I want to give you some facts," he said, and quickly poured as much as he could into the brief quiet. "By the end of next year the Company will be employing an extra hundred and twenty men. That's one in twelve of the working population of this town—enough to eat up all our unemployment. During their interim training alone these workers will earn sixteen hundred drachma a week. By the second year..."

Half a dozen men were on their feet. "When have you ever employed people from here unless you had to?" bawled a sullen-looking road-mender. "And you don't have to this time and you know it! The Capital's seething with out-of-work miners from Ambos. You could call up a thousand trained personnel just by farting! Don't think we don't listen to the radio!"

Lerides answered with satin assurance, raising his own voice a fraction: "We will employ as many men from the town as qualify. That is a promise."

"Qualify, yes! We'll qualify as cleaners and labourers! Nothing better than that. Even our docks will be supervised by foreigners and Nikitari men. You're turning us into a slave-town!"

Still nothing showed Lerides' unease except the turning and turning of the gold ring round his finger. Everybody knew that the reason for the men's anxiety was that the workers in the Capital were more reliable than the Kalepiots, who had a reputation for waywardness. But neither the townsmen in their pride, nor Lerides in his tact, could admit so. He had blundered into the darkest of the people's obsessions: their fear of outsiders. All around him now this suspicion and possessiveness, born during centuries of Turkish oppression, had so thickened in the hall as almost to be touched. This way, he knew, they would reject everything, and shrivel back with a childish pride into their own stagnation. They were, he thought, the pettiest people in the Levant.

"The Company wants this town vital and wealthy as much as you do"—he tried to sound confidential, but had to raise his voice—"and our expansion will not only make each of you richer (he spoke the words slowly) but enhance the town through the taxes we'll pay the municipality. . . ."

At the mention of the municipality the people began to hoot and jeer and several minutes elapsed before Lerides was able to say: "I telephoned the councillors today to ask what this money would bring you. The answers were these. First . . ." He softened his voice. The silence fell like an axe. "First, the repair of our town's roads. . . ."

Somebody yelled: "For the Company trucks!"

Lerides at last showed his pique: "All the Company's access routes will skirt the town. The plans can be seen by anybody in the municipal offices." He planted his hands on his hips, checked himself, folded them casually and said: "Secondly, the extension of public washing facilities. . . ."

"Po-po-po!" The fisherman Philippou flopped in his seat with mock acclaim, clapping his hands. "In exchange for our town they give us lavatories!" Again came the hard laughter of people inured to promises.

Lerides was growing angry at their stupidity. Some poison seemed to have crawled into them. After all, there must be many here who'd profit. Didn't they understand where their future was?

Pride, religion—such things could be adapted. But without money people were nothing. Behind his smile he was filled with nausea for them. He went on: "Thirdly, the purchase of new equipment for our hospital. This has been needed for years, especially respiratory apparatus."

Silence. Amazing, he thought, nobody had complained. None of these half-wits had suggested that the hospital would be used by the Company to transplant the brains of Nikitari men into Kalepiot bodies.

"And lastly for the immediate future," he continued, "the municipality is considering a new football pitch." This, he felt, was a potent move; in the last few years football had become a fetish in the Republic.

At the back of the hall somebody said tentatively: "Bravo." It was like the cry of a gull lost in a storm.

The dark mass in the hall centre sat brooding and inarticulate. And now Kallis cried quickly, hotly: "They'll be doubling municipal taxes on all of us for these benefits!"

A vindictive grumble supported him from the hall's centre, died away. Sofroniou, watching them, was shocked by the change in these people. All through the town men he had known for years, rational and temperate men, were starting to talk like Dark Age fanatics. And now, their cigarettes dripping ash through their yellowing fingers, he thought they resembled the worshippers of some malignant god, all staring up through the incense of their own thoughts with their six hundred monkeys' eyes, proof against anything but each other's littleness.

Lerides had walked over to his charts and was pinning them on the screen. He began: "Now whether this fresh mining personnel comes from Kalepia or anywhere else, it is going to constitute a new salaried class in our community. This will benefit everyone." He pointed to the largest of the charts. It was headed: "Annual Income of Shopkeeper, Municipality of Kalepia". "You will see from the diagram that because of this new wealth, and within less than two years, the average gross income of a shop or restaurant, earning, let us say, two hundred thousand drachma per annum, will have increased by fourteen per cent. That is to say that at the end of the year any of you running a shop or a small business should receive..." His fingers slid up and down the columns of figures. The increases were small enough to believe, large enough to seduce.

Kallis realized at once that Lerides was trying to alienate the tradesmen from the labourers. "Mr Lerides"—he lodged his tone between a plaint and a sneer—"you know perfectly well that the families from Ambos will also set up shops, just as the Nikitari men did in the 'thirties. The wealth will be lost."

Lerides jibed: "And since when were Ambos men a match in business for Kalepiots?"

There was some reluctant laughter at this. Lerides' finger resumed its journey up and down the mesmerizing columns of figures. His tone remained matter-of-fact, as if pointing out obvious truths. "An average craftsman ... an average cobbler ..." On the periphery of the hall one or two shopkeepers surreptitiously took out little notebooks and started to make calculations.

Kallis thought: the fools are starting to believe him; he's touching the bourgeois in them. So long had Kallis felt secure in the angry sea of men round about, that this small sign of disaffection jabbed him with disquiet. The thought of failure, darting, momentary, fled through him. Even he was surprised at the thinness of his confidence; the lightest tread cracked it.

"Charts and figures!" he sneered.

Lerides said mildly, almost friendlily: "There's no other method of forecast, Mr Kallis."

The hall was silent.

"Puh!" Kallis spat. "If you work enough with figures they'll stand on their heads for you. But these people aren't the fools you think. Why should you do anything for them when you're trampling on the rest? No, they'll only trust you when they see it." He rested his hand on the shoulder of the man beside him, a blind fisherman whose clothes were in tatters, and exclaimed fervently: "I'll believe you when I see this man fed and clothed as you are!"

A burst of applause exploded from the hall's centre, and went on and on. To Sofroniou it sounded like hounds baying. The scepticism of these people seemed only to have deepened. It stood so thick in the air that you could knead it in your hands, drink it from a glass. It was beyond reason. The whole angry horde, it seemed, was simply awaiting its chance to destroy, like water behind a dyke.

But the chance did not come. Lerides only smiled. When he saw the sentimentalist in Kallis, he despised him; and he sensed weaknesses which could be used. Still affable, he kept his eye on the shopkeepers. All along the perimeter of the hall, he noticed, many men no longer looked him in the face, as if they were afraid of explicit collaboration. It was a sign of weakening. The nucleus of the crowd was growing harder, but the plasma had loosened a little. "The figures I've given you can be deduced by common sense," he said. "I assure you they are accurate. Whatever Mr Kallis may say, I am an accountant. Figures are my business. I would not try to teach him how to manoeuvre a crane."

The tradespeople were now being openly wooed. Kallis felt as if a member of his own family was being seduced. He said: "You don't have a monopoly over figures, Mr Lerides. Any educated man..."

"You must forgive me for saying so," broke in Lerides with exaggerated politeness, "but you are not what I would call an educated man, Mr Kallis."

The result of this remark on Kallis was extraordinary—a noise less like the cry of a man than the breathy, outraged whinny of a horse. He was on his feet. "I not educated! ... Eat your tongue! ... I don't need . . . that smug accent! . . . God protect me!" He crossed himself, choking. "My mind ... my mind is twice what yours is!"

"Then you should discover how to control it," said Lerides with bland calm. "That is another thing that education would have taught you."

Kallis' eyes had assumed their sweating look. His knuckles were grinding on the chair in front of him.

Philippou nearby said: "Keep calm. He's only twisting your tail."

But Kallis did not even hear him. His voice had risen to falsetto and a furious flush lit his cheeks. "You won't stand there for ever!" He was almost screaming, yet the scream was hoarse and thin. "All of you rich! We'll bring all of you down in the end! Only wait!" He smote his fingers into the thickened air. "It'll come. May God quicken the day!"

Lerides said drily, before his words were drowned by the crowd: "So we've reached the truth at last, Mr Kallis."

He was beginning to enjoy himself. He had touched the right nerve, he thought. He was reducing Kallis to the banal pamphleteer that he was. The man looked positively diseased, and although harsh cheering had swollen behind each of his remarks it contained, thought Lerides, the rage of frustration. More important, some of the shopkeepers were openly sneering at the little crane-driver's manner. The noise was now so great that he and Kallis could no longer hear one another, and Kallis pushed through seven lines of chairs to the foot of the platform. His forehead was rumpled by thick veins.

Lerides said condescendingly: "Slowly, slowly, Mr Kallis. Your silliness is only proving my point."

"God break you!" Kallis was thrashing round for anything which might hurt. The water was pouring from his eyes. "Company of fascists! Controlling other people's land and jobs, other people's homes and holy places. You . . ."

The shouting was so loud that Lerides was able to reply scarcely overheard: "And we shall soon control you."

"Me!" Kallis' voice broke. "You can't even control your wife! Sleeping like a prostitute with that ex-foreman!"

Slowly the bawling of demands and questions, the dinning anger, the vindictive cheers, died. The men who had stood up sat down. Nobody had been able to hear anybody but himself and his close neighbours for several minutes, and now Kallis had plunged back to his own seat, his lips trembling, and Lerides was standing a little farther back on the stage, not speaking.

When at last he started to talk again, his voice was different, abstract. He pinned fresh charts to the screen, and touched on pay rises for municipal workers. When his figures were again challenged from the centre of the hall, he did not seem to hear. The tradespeople began to lose interest in these charts. Lerides himself appeared not to believe in them. Now he referred to them almost vaguely, as if they were playthings.

Sofroniou was puzzled. The man was no longer doing his case justice. He would lose any sympathy within seconds, the schoolmaster thought; because an argument was only half believed for what it was, the rest was a matter of how it was dressed. It occurred to Sofroniou that the heavy atmosphere in the hall might be troubling him. But the windows, and even the doors, were already open.

Lerides was now rambling badly. He kept putting his hand to his head, and was reading from notes, tripping over simple words. He pinned up one of the old charts by mistake, took it down again.

Philippou said: "He's put himself to sleep, he's so boring!"

Meanwhile the people watched him distrustfully. They had fallen rather quiet. They wondered what trick he was playing on them now. After a while they started putting questions again, but only received half-answers, as if Lerides did not know or did not care.

Oldenburg started to look grim, drumming his fists on his knees. He wanted to shout at Lerides, or shake him. Muller muttered: "What's got into the man?"

The people's questions sharpened and grew more bellicose. They came from all over the hall. Lerides' vagueness was angering them. His eyes looked dislocated, as if he could not be bothered to see. But the crowd's demands persisted with dogged savagery. One by one the familiar grievances were poured out: all the old fears and jealousies and pieties—the demolition of the shrine, the displacement of families from the dock and from the Mountain, the ruin of the fishermen and of the olive groves of the poor, the use of alien personnel, the disfigurement of the town. The people had now seen the land bulldozed by the Company for rehousing: the valley lost among billows of slag. Their disgust was only tolerable to them because they knew that they would never go there. They would fight.

But Lerides stayed oblivious to them. His voice had glazed. Frequently he would not find the words he wanted, but this did not seem to trouble him. He simply left his sentences unfinished, while he groped through the notes in his hands. Once, frowning remotely, he looked up and said: "There can't be much more to say. . . ." Then he brought a handkerchief to his face, appeared to wipe his eyes and for a minute seemed to forget that anybody else was in the room at all. And at the end, when he was asked what would happen when the Mountain householders refused to move, he replied distantly: "The Company will bulldoze them."

This produced such a howl of defiance that Sofroniou backed out of his side-door and locked it. It seemed impossible that Lerides would not be torn piecemeal. And even after he had climbed down from the platform the fury continued—not the wounded roar of the first meeting, but a strident, arrogant sound, as if the men were already marching.

Chapter Fifteen

Ekaterina lay exhausted on the bed. For an hour she let the storm of his anger break over her. Time after time she thought he was going to strike her, but he never did. Instead he painted a picture of her so grotesque and humiliating that even she could not believe in it. His speaking lapsed into violence, and he said things he knew to be absurd, whatever would give her pain. Then, for another and more horrifying hour, they argued pitilessly, she finding such recesses of bitterness and frustration in herself as she had not known existed. She cast at him her neglected heart, her starved mind, her whole broken life. He who had no imagination, no humanity, no real gentleness at all; he who existed so crudely for himself—he had taken and snapped her in two.

But after a while she noticed that only the shell of him was fighting her. Now, when she spoke, he flinched as if her words were physically striking him. His jaw was working to and fro in an involuntary fever, and he pulled savagely on a succession of cigarettes which he threw away quarter smoked. As her remorse at his misery grew, her own fury petered out. And she began to see herself in his eyes, precious and conceited as she must once have appeared to Julian when they parted: as if she was some gift to the world which the world had tainted. Little by little she felt ashamed. She watched him crumbling in front of her eyes. And at last she began looking for ways to give him her sorrow. She went silent and turned her face away from him on the pillow.

After a long time he came and stood over her. She did not know what to expect. She felt she deserved anything he did to her. But his eyes were pink and dilated. Suddenly he said in a quiet voice: "I know I haven't been good to you."

She stared back at him. The knot in her, fierce and unravellable, was sliding down far inside; she felt a deep relief; no doubt all this hurt and rancour would be resurrected some time; but not now, not tonight. She said: "I expect you've been as good as you were able." But even that sounded cruel and condescending. She added after a little struggle: "Which is more than I've been to you."

A moment later she felt something strike the bed at her side. Michael had knelt forward with his forehead against the mattress. Now he squeezed his fingers among hers, and said in a hoarse whisper: "You've been all right."

She covered her face with her hands. "I've tried." She remembered how true this was, how hard and how long she had tried, and said again more vehemently, with a rage not against him but simply, deeply, against the way things were: "By God I've tried!"

Michael went on gazing at her, his eyes level with hers. His hair was dishevelled and his face dead white. He said: "Did you mean what you said?"

But she could not remember what she had said, she had said so many things.

"That you can never forgive me for destroying your life."

She felt a dulled amazement that he was asking her forgiveness. She was grateful and a little shaken. She passed her fingers through his hair. She thought: it's easier to forgive those you don't love. He was sobbing now. "No, I didn't mean that." He seemed to be imagining that his fury with her had destroyed something—something which had not been there. She wondered fleetingly: why is it he who is pleading with me? But she realized that he was weaker than her, needed her; if she were to leave him he would not survive as a man, only as a husk. She would take away with her the illusion of his strength and self-esteem. She would kill him.

He insisted pathetically: "We can begin again."

He seemed to believe it, she did not ask him why. She closed her eyes. There was no such thing as beginning again. Nothing had changed between them. Only her failure to love him was lodged for ever in the concrete memory of her infidelity.

She noticed now that he did not ask her penitence for this. He seemed to accept it as partly his own doing. But she was grateful and faintly surprised. And now she longed again to love him, to overcome this barrenness between them. She wanted to be herself, warm, whole. She knew it was impossible. She lifted his head off the mattress. He would not look at her. Then she bent her mouth to his lips, which for a long time had not interested her and did not now, and kissed them.

He began to thank her. He sat on the bed, knitting and unknitting his hands with hers and gazing into her face, looking for his restoration. She would stay with him, he implored, they would go away together—they and the child, they would start again?

Yes, yes.

His gratitude was rather terrible. After all, she had nowhere else to go. Her parents were dead. And it flashed on her in a renewed pain that she would never go to Julian. Julian, whose resplendent and foolish world she was not young or good enough to enter—she wrenched her thoughts from him. She refused to let her mind wander down ways they might have taken, in case it was true, and they would have been happy. But this chance of happiness did not strike her as either true or false. It was simply unimaginable. It could not be.

She tried to smile at Michael's warming face. She felt older than him, older than any man, older than the Mountain. She comforted him as she had once comforted Alexia after the child had hit her in a rage. (She longed to hold Alexia again: a child unfurling, the life she had mislaid. . . .) Michael was talking about the future. He must hand in his resignation to Oldenburg, he said; he could not bear to face the townsmen or the Company. They must leave, they must leave at once. Did she think that wise?

Yes, she said. Better to get away. To the Capital, even to relatives in England. The idea darted through her that perhaps she belonged in England; but the word "belong" instantly sounded false.

Oldenburg was already deeply depressed. Not only had the meeting the day before proved a fiasco, but in an interview with the police chief he had elicited no guarantee that reinforcements would be summoned from Nikitari to supervise the pilgrimage. Without them, he knew, the Kalepia police would make no stand against their own people. They would simply vanish to their homes. But the Chief was too proud to call in any other force, and confined himself to vague promises and to toasting the Company in his gaseous whisky.

Yesterday too the archimandrite had announced that the pilgrimage this year would be confined to a procession round the old cathedral; but the notices, pinned by his deacons in the entrance to every public building, had all been torn down within an hour.

And now Lerides wanted to quit. When he picked up the telephone the man sounded so unstable that for a second Oldenburg did not recognize him. And the next moment the Company Secretary was dismissing himself, mouthing pious thanks to the Company for his past good fortune, as if it was a state lottery, and sometimes speaking so incoherently that Oldenburg had to bark at him to repeat himself.

Would the General Manager accept his resignation at the end of the week, he enquired? He had two reliable assistants who would tide the Company over.

Oldenburg reminded him that his assistants were no more than bumptious clerks, and that he himself had constantly complained of them. The Company required his services for a month more.

But Lerides was no longer himself. His plea took on a whining insistence. He and Ekaterina were leaving for the Capital within the week. Their house would be sold later. Their child was already away. He did not expect any courtesy payment. He would clear up certain problems within two days, then leave.

Oldenburg, listening to this gutted voice, began to agree that his departure was best. When he asked Lerides for his assessment of the situation now, he found that the man was no longer talking responsibly. He virtually advised surrender. The interests of the shareholders and employees did not seem to concern him. While before he had insisted that anybody hurt when attacking Company property would have no protection in law, he now temporized with a morbid fear of extremes. In the end Oldenburg accepted his resignation; but as he replaced the receiver he realized that he had lost the only executive in the Company who understood the Greek mind.

For a while he sifted through some supplementary reports from the Mine Geologist, underscoring key points in a thick, black pencil. But to his irritation he found that he could not concentrate on these, and took to pacing his study and occasionally glancing at his watch; he had called a meeting of Company executives for an hour's time. Once he stopped in front of the window—he had not observed the view for years. The wind was ripping dead twigs from the junipers. Beyond them the roofs of the miners' houses looked grey and efficient: built in '67, he remembered, with Company profits. Once in a while, over many years, he had mentally assessed the number of extra men employed since his General Managership, the number of miners' houses built, even how many new cars the men had bought. When he added to this the many hundred thousand tons of ore exported, the Company profits over fourteen years, and average rises in salary, he was used to feeling a sense of irrefutable worth.

Today this feeling did not come. He could not concentrate his mind. For the first time he was not absolutely sure that he was going to succeed, and he turned away abruptly from the window. He even felt—yes—lonely, and it was a bewildering feeling; he had no idea how to cure it.

He sat down in the chair behind his desk, picked up the geologist's report, but pushed it away again. In the next door room Claudia was rearranging the furniture for the meeting. He got up and opened the door. She was smoothing the cushions on the sofa. She glanced at him, stared harder, and asked: "Was that Michael?"

He said brusquely: "He's sacked himself." He watched his wife's face, the self-contained mouth, the eyes which only pretended to look outward. In the last few weeks, with the Company's difficulties mounting and her outlook apparently justified, he had sometines wondered whether she was not laughing at him a little. But she did not seem to be. He studied the back of her head as she laid out the drinks. For his own part, he would have understood such laughter—but then he and she did not seem to see things in the same way at all.

She said: "Surely Michael will help you over the crisis?"

She still said "you" and not "us", he noticed. He poured himself a glass of vodka. "No."

"Oh Frank." She took a step towards him.

"It's better that way," he snapped. He sat down almost aggressively. He did not want her exploiting his weakness. This secret delight of women in their husbands' troubles or illnesses made him angry. And besides, Claudia's consolation would be meaningless. It would speak in that voice which was more like a barrier, and in any case her knowledge of the Company's problems was ridiculously slight. For years she had wilfully withdrawn herself; yet now she looked at him in that half-concerned way as if she hoped to reap some sentimental harvest from his anxiety. He cleared his throat belligerently, but said nothing.

He did not care for looking back, but when he did so he saw that Claudia's enthusiasm—the essence of the woman he had married—

had blurred years ago. Only in his memory it trailed after her like an irritant.

Claudia saw his annoyance. She did not know how to reach him. She went on arranging the drinks for the meeting: Scotch for the Chief Engineer and the Mine Safety Officer, beer for Muller. Perpetually now it seemed to her as if Frank believed in an ideal of himself which was more inhuman than the old reality. Any doubt, any indecision, he considered feeble.

"Michael's lost his head," Frank said. "He'll be better out of the way." Perversely, he now felt depressed by her indifference. He looked again at her back, at the slender calves of her legs. In the back of his mind, half acknowledged, was a feeling that he might not always have done her justice. After all, she was fifteen years younger than him. Perhaps he had expected too much. Perhaps he should have indulged her.

He lifted himself almost painfully from the chair and stood a short way behind her, staring at the floor. He said: "You're pleased about Howard anyway."

She looked surprised, and surprised too that he should be standing behind her like this. "Why did you say that?" She turned to him, with a glass still in her hand.

He said rather harshly: "I don't seem to have done much to please you." It did not sound like a criticism of either of them: just a fact.

She gazed down at the glass. She could think of nothing to answer. From Frank this was a strange acknowledgment, rising as it did out of nothing, and spoken without irritation.

He was still looking at the floor instead of at her. Extraordinarily, he wanted to touch her; or for her to touch him. He began again: "If this mining business goes wrong, you realize we may have to leave?"

"I know."

He was trying to tell her something, but he himself could not articulate it. Something of need, and of regret. Now that his head was bent, she noticed the grey rings under his eyes. He was looking into the future, she thought, and seeing himself unemployed at the age of fifty-seven. And he must be thinking of his personal life too, because after a while he turned his back and said in a stifled voice: "So much . . . sacrifice."

Even while he said this, the voice disturbed him. He steadied himself and calmed, with an effort of will, that movement inside him which seemed faintly to shake the whole structure of his life.

Claudia stared at him, then looked away. She understood that he wanted to say more but could not. It was as if for a second his armour had split apart, and inside was a body as weak and unformed as an infant. Suddenly she touched his arm, but he took her wrist and set the hand aside, although not roughly. "The executives will be here in a minute," he said. "You'd better go and visit Ekaterina, if that's what you want."

After she had gone he looked through his notes for the meeting, but even these did not hold his attention. So he poured himself some whisky and consciously enumerated favourable points: the miners had shown solidly for the Company; Howard had accepted a teaching job in Athens; Helen was out of the way at college ... But there the list stopped.

The next moment Caroline looked in and said excitedly: "Is it true about Michael?"

"He's quit."

She came round the sofa and slipped her arm over his shoulder. "You sound awfully depressed." She was dressed in green trousers which made her look top-heavy. "Does it matter so much? You can find somebody else."

He glanced at her, barely smiling. Her face still showed a trace of summer brownness. Then he stood up and went to open a window, but instead stayed in front of it, looking out at the junipers with his legs planted in their habitual stance, firmly apart. "We've been building this business up for fourteen years now." His voice was colourless. "And a single day could smash it."

Caroline slid round beside him. She felt alarmed. Something was changing. "Nonsense, Daddy."

"It's not nonsense. It's fact. These people are barbarians." He patted her hair abstractedly, the hair which crowned her in confidence. "I'm not saying it'll happen. It won't. I'm only saying it shows how fragile progress is." But what was he really saying? He did not know.

The doorbell rang. Caroline ran out to answer it, waving him goodbye, and a minute later the executives came trooping in. They were on time. They looked embarrassed as they settled into their chairs, opening their files and fingering pens, and drank their whisky in a businesslike way, as if it was on the agenda. Nobody mentioned Lerides, until Muller, who was wiping his greasy hands on the side of the sofa, volunteered: "I suppose Don Juan won't be joining us."

Oldenburg said tersely: "Lerides has resigned. His affair has no bearing on ours. We'll proceed exactly as before." Now that there was work to do, he felt himself again. He ran over basic points already discussed. There was no question of the Company leaving the Mountain undefended on St Vichinos' day. Not only was it ringed by seven thousand dollars' worth of stakes and wire, but a repair station and office had been constructed on the site. To permit the crowds to demolish these would not only be expensive but a fatal error of judgment. Any townsman or pilgrim would then feel free to damage Company property.

When Oldenburg looked round him for confirmation of these views, he was ringed by assenting voices. But he was aware that of the six men present only the rabbit-faced Mine Geologist was a Greek. And now Muller broke in: "I'm in favour of calling in troops. Give these bastards something to think about." He looked round belligerently at the others. "Have you seen the pilgrims this year? Some of them have arrived already, and they look a bloodyminded lot, I can tell you. Carrying staves and knives and Christ-knows-what. Seems like fewer women coming too. Bad sign that."

Oldenburg said impatiently: "I can't call in troops like a district commander. And if the government became alarmed at the situation here it might freeze us altogether. No. Let's not exaggerate the thing." He rapped out: "Keep your heads. All of you."

The Chief Engineer, whose lap was full of scribbled notes, said: "We'll have enough men ourselves if we use them properly."

"Precisely." Oldenburg set his mouth in a way all the others knew. He said: "The basic plan is this. The mines will be closed down the day before St Vichinos' day. At sunrise the morning shift will be driven up to the Mountain as a skeleton garrison." He pointed at Muller. "You'll be in charge of them. It's vital we move early in case of surprise. The afternoon and night shifts will follow in the evening. Those convoys will come under my supervision. They should be across the bridge by eleven that night and at the base of the Mountain ten minutes later. Our land'll be sealed off by midnight."

He paused, but they were all satisfied. The Americans had the heavy faces of third-generation German and Scandinavian stock. They were conscientiously writing down the times in their files.

Oldenburg found himself wondering what Michael would have said.

Only the Mine Safety Officer asked if the men should go round the town or drive through it.

Oldenburg said: "Go round."

Everybody wrote down: "Go round."

Oldenburg said to the Chief Engineer: "I want a thorough check on all transport. We can't afford a drop-out. We'll need every dump truck in the service sheds."

Then Muller broke in: "What about guns? The men are hoping that anyone owning a licensed rifle or shotgun can bring it."

Oldenburg looked up with saturnine displeasure and snapped: "That's out of the question."

"Seems a pity," said Muller. "They're a steady lot of boys. And their morale's at peak."

"Out of the question," Oldenburg repeated. He would not have called the men's mood "morale". It was more like vindictiveness. The miners now thought that the town was wilfully destroying their future. They regarded the townsmen's attitude neither as piety nor self-defence, but as a chronic, deep-seated envy. He stressed again: "We only have to wound one of these people for relations between the town and the mines to be embittered for ever. The men can carry batons. Nothing else. Any miner with a firearm will be dismissed on the spot."

Oldenburg felt confident that his men could hold their own. He was still a little sceptical that the dockers had weapons at all. These childish people loved to surround themselves with an aura of mystery and importance. Very likely they had little more than a few shotguns. The pilgrims, it was true, were a rough lot, but stupid and poor and easily scared. He could remember the pilgrimage thirteen years ago, when his men were first using the six-inch blast hole. The moment they detonated, half these devout peasants had run away while the rest, feeling the earth shake, had shouted that St Vichinos was moving in his grave under the Mountain.

And all this for a saint who had never existed.

Chapter Sixteen

Two days before the Feast of St Vichinos most of the pilgrims had already arrived. They came on foot leading donkeys, or drove horse-carts filled with their baggage and women. At any time of the morning you might look northward and see the dust rising from six or seven tracks over the hills, and the woods below the Mountain were now scattered with makeshift camps. These men marched in loose-fitting boots and baggy trousers, and wore their hair close-cropped. They came from the hill-villages of the inland provinces: places of goat-herding and carob farming, where the snows fell early. Their short, hard, uncomprehending faces were of another type from those of the townsmen. Some said they were Vlachs, others that they descended from an ancient Anatolian stock. But nobody knew. Least of all themselves.

Trailing about the streets of Kalepia, they stared in the shop windows as into El Dorado, accompanied by heavy-breasted women in shapeless gowns and head veils. They did not seem to notice their new popularity. They concentrated on selling their goatskins as they had in other years. They could not read the banners slung across the streets, but many had heard of the threat to the Mountain long before, and some came with ancient rifles, swaggering a little, and others carried pruning-knives in their sashes.

Kallis felt a foreigner with them—they spoke a thick, strongly-aspirated Greek which was hard to understand. Walking to his house from the dockside at evening, he came across three families camped on the streets, and when he looked at them he was uneasy. He could not act on their behalf. They knew nothing of the threat to the town's poor. They were the poor of the country, and compared to them the meanest townsman was sophisticated. Yet they accepted their serfdom without complaint. In fact they rather looked down on the Kalepiots. They were independent of anybody.

When he reached his home Kallis found the popular leaders already assembled there. Philippou was trying to dance on his hands, while the others clapped in unison; and a feeling of jubilation was about. The mill foreman had brought bottles of wine with him and these were passing from mouth to mouth so that half the men's lips and chins dribbled red. Everything was going right for them. The arrival of the pilgrims was like a warming coat around their shoulders, and news of Lerides' humiliation had sent ribald jokes from tongue to tongue.

Kallis was unhappy about this. Watching his men singing and drinking, lit in the fire of their own confidence—men mostly older than himself—he thought how child-like they were. How could they celebrate at such a time? And there was Philippou still upside-down with his shirt-ends over his head and his white stomach mounded above his trousers. The rest had given up clapping and were dancing a *syrtos* round him, their eyes glittering in half-shaven faces. Kallis, leaning in the doorway, felt painfully responsible for them.

But one of the dockers had caught sight of him. The revelry petered out and within a minute the men had sobered and settled round the walls. The room contained no chairs for them; only a bench and an old-fashioned stove. The walls were decorated by shells and sponges pinned on hooks.

Kallis said formally: "Are we all here?"

Philippou burped, his face still crimson from dancing upside-down. "No," he said. "None of us. Not a soul."

But Kallis imposed seriousness on them. When he started assigning individual duties, they sharpened and asked questions and scrutinized his written orders. He outlined the plan for St Vichinos' day. The pilgrimage would move at eight o'clock in the morning from the cathedral square as on other years, he said—it would be impossible to gather the people in strength any earlier. The tall priest would lead it—no other clergy were expected to appear—and the crowd must be kept densely packed, with the women as far behind as possible. He expected that in all they would number some two and a half thousand. When they reached the base of the Mountain the priest would address them briefly, and they would climb the traditional path until they met the barbed-wire gates of the Company's fences. The procession would be headed by the twenty riflemen, giving an impression of more. If the gates were not opened to them a second gang would break them down with wooden clubs, and once the pilgrims were inside the enceinte the miners could not hope to hold them.

Kallis knew that the miners would not carry arms. The Company was playing the crisis in a low key, and it would pay for that. Typical, he thought, of these supercilious people—they could not believe that anyone would seriously challenge them. No doubt they expected to line up in their helmets on the safe side of the fence, and jeer at the pilgrims. And the muckers on night shift would put in a claim for overtime.

One by one his men left. Some of them would spend tomorrow bracing the pilgrims to assemble early the next morning. But others would return to the swelling bustle of the cafés, where the town's secrets were already rising in a fervent roar. That was why Kallis reserved his confidence only for Philippou and for the senior fisherman, a grey-faced, taciturn man whose father had been martyred in the War of Liberation. The fisherman asked Kallis: "When do you want those rifles brought back?"

Kallis lowered his voice. "Late tonight. You often fish by the old necropolis, don't you? Well then, you'll find them in the tomb with the inscribed entrance: buried under the trough of rock at the back. The police won't dare search the boats tomorrow, because the dock will be thick with pilgrims."

The fisherman stood up stiffly and bowed to them with an antique courtesy. Philippou started to make an obscene comment, but checked himself. When the old man reached the door Kallis grasped his hand and said "Go to the good!" He watched him walking very erect down the alley, his white hair flopping about his ears. He turned to Philippou and said: "You shouldn't mock such people."

But Philippou was inspecting a bottle of wine. Kallis stood over the stove and started to tear up old notes and push them into the flames. He had a bundle of petitions sent by almost every faction in the town. He was supposed to have presented them to the municipality, even to the Capital. It was like being an intercessory saint. Except that he had not bothered to hand half of them in, because he knew that for answer there would not be so much as an insulted ripple on those slime-filled pools of bureaucracy. He found a list of

Company personnel and crumpled it in his fist. Most of the names were meaningless. Since the defection of Lerides he had found it harder to concentrate his anger at the Company. Hating Oldenburg was like hating a hammer or a power-drill. So Kallis had found himself thinking less about the Company and more about the townspeople. But he did not want to enter into combat feeling protective; that left too much room for fear. To attack, you must hate.

He wanted it to be a swift and complete operation. At dawn a small party would carry the explosives and detonator down to the bridge. Through the next day the men would take turns on watch, and as the miners tried to cross they would blow the bridge into the river. Its waters were still so swollen that no truck could ford it. The Mountain would be cut clean off from the miners' town, and the pilgrim would overrun their meagre party on the crest. It would be simple, final and bloodless.

Philippou said: "And who's going to lay a charge like that? None of our people can handle explosives."

"That's settled," Kallis said. "I've got Alastos to do it. He's an ex-miner. He could lay them blindfold."

Philippou gurgled rudely: "That Alastos! He'll be blowing a bridge between himself and Mrs Lerides! What a drollery!" He tipped the wine dregs into his mouth, spat them out.

Chapter Seventeen

Ekaterina's suspense had become so acute that when Julian appeared in the doorway she felt only relief. Michael was not in the house. Half the furniture was covered in sheets and the place looked like a morgue. Already, it seemed, a blanket of dust was descending over the shapes which had been her home. She pulled one of the covers from the sofa, and they sat down together, isolated in the desert of a room.

She saw that he looked exhausted. The lines of his face were streaming to the inner corners of his eyes, and knotted between his eyebrows. He asked her in a hoarse voice if she had been hurt or afraid. But she could not remember either of these things: only a great bitterness, now drained, so that it might have happened years ago. Sitting in the clinical room, answering each other's questions nervously, rationally, they appeared to her like two emptied people, ghosts whispering together. When she looked at his face it seemed no longer the face of her lover. It was sick with apprehension. She watched him with deepening alarm and misery, and she realized that he knew of her decision to leave, because he spoke with a sombre tension, as if he pitied himself as much as her.

After a silence he said: "How did your husband find out?" But his jealousy of Lerides was remote and impotent.

"I don't know." She frowned, she had not even asked him. "Does it matter?"

Julian shook his head. He did not care about Lerides. He was afraid only of what Ekaterina was going to say. And now she put out a hand in her quick gesture and laid it on his forearm. "I want you to promise me something before we go. . . ." She faltered. "You knew we were going?"

He was staring at her grimly. The bones of his face thrust out like crags. He said: "Promise what?"

"That you won't get involved in the pilgrimage." Her eyes pleaded with his. "Don't join the people. Keep away." Her fingers tightened on his arm. "Promise me."

Julian did not know how to answer, because at this moment the town's cause was meaningless to him. Kalepia seemed no longer to contain a proper person. Only this one he loved, who sat beside him with her look of smothered tears. And she was leaving.

But he said: "Would you respect me if I went back on the people? What do you expect me to say? We've talked about this enough, haven't we? About the people's rights. Was it all a game?"

She said: "I don't want you not to care. I just want you to keep away."

He got up violently, but did not know what to do with his body. For a while he stood facing the wall. He would not look at her. "Don't ask me that again."

She stared into her lap. "I'm sorry." She knew her plea had been unworthy. But she was becoming afraid for him.

He said: "I'd be betraying your beliefs too."

She said: "Yes."

He felt inside him a terrible hopelessness. He could feel the older woman in full possession of Ekaterina, the woman he had never known. And his heart sank. The battle to win her back to him would be like scaling a mountain which had no summit. He did not know how he could reach her. Some part of her which was sadder, and irreparably different, had already decided. He understood that she was maturer than him. She could accept her own littleness, the limits which life had placed on her fulfilment. While he never could. She was an adult, which was to say, broken. While he was still a child, who dreamt.

He forced himself to say: "You are going away."

She watched his face for the breaking of its discipline. If he so much as touched her, she thought, she would weep. She hid her hands behind her back. She said: "Yes." As she did so, she thought with horror that she was leaving the only person in the world whose love she respected.

Julian asked in the same tone: "It's not because of your duty to the child, is it? Or to Michael?" The Christian name sounded peculiar on his lips. "That wouldn't be enough." He knew that he could break down such duty in the end, if she wanted him. With her he was totally unscrupulous. He would break down the world. Yes, he would make the child his own (she could not have another), and as for Lerides, he could go to the devil.

But she said in a voice pitched hard against any emotion, his or hers: "It couldn't have happened, Julian. We only made a kind of spell together (forgive me)." She thought that something in her must break or cry out. But she went on: "When I'm with you I'm not myself. God knows what myself is. But not this." Yet she longed to believe in the myth they had made. "We couldn't go on. You're a better person than me. . . ."

He interrupted bitterly: "You mean I'm too young."

She got up and stood behind him where he faced the wall, and took his hand. "Thank God for it." Her fingers looked incongruous in his. They reminded him that compared to her he was so homespun that even about his love there must seem something ridiculous. He let her fingers lie over his hand. She was whispering now. "It's not fair. Nothing's fair." She left a silence, but he did not fill it. "I can't change. You can't change me." Then she shook her head almost angrily. "I'm getting maudlin. Do say something."

He said: "You don't love me." The moment he had spoken he remembered Ekaterina as a girl, saying the same, holding the word above him. Days and weeks of "You don't love me", "you can't love me", "how can you say you love me?"

She pretended not to have heard him. She turned her face away. "You'll get over this. You'll marry and have children. I couldn't give you children."

But he dashed away her hand. He could no longer bear such a way of parting. He would turn it into something else, anything else. He shouted: "You're running away, Kat! How can you go on living with this man? It's nonsense! It's impossible!" He forcibly turned her face to his. "Is that it? Do you like to suffer?"

She tried to wrench her head away. "I don't know." Her voice was trembling. "Not like this anyway."

But Julian took a hold on himself. He led her back to the sofa, and sat a little apart from her. Then he said more softly: "Nothing will change for you if you stay with him. You know that. People don't change. Are you prepared for that?"

"I'm going to try."

"And how far will trying get you? One year, two? You've tried already. You've given him enough. There are limits to giving."

He looked hard into her eyes—their extraordinary beauty struck him with sickening force. She said: "I haven't reached those limits."

"But you will," he said, "so why wait to reach them? Why hurt yourself more? Christ knows, Ekaterina, you've done enough." He heard the force of his emotion rising, he could not stop it. "D'you think I'll always be here for you? No, it's not true. I won't. I won't wait like a sick monk until we're old." He did not believe these words as he said them—he felt he would wait for ever—but he went on: "You're twenty-nine and you're throwing away your life."

It was perhaps to deflect her pity from herself, she thought, that there came over her this appalling tenderness and sorrow for him. She knelt with her head on his knees, and clasped his hands to her lips. She would never feel again, she knew, that sensation of youth with him. She was herself now, the disillusioned self which belonged to Michael, the self which he had created. She did not understand, so she could not explain to Julian, how two people can be twisted and welded together in unhappiness. But in some such way she had condemned herself to Michael.

She said: "I'm not throwing away my life. That part of my life is already over." She added with gratitude: "It belonged to you."

But he could not bear this new acceptance of hers, this apparent submission to change and compromise. He noticed the pleading in his voice. It was the noise of defeat. "You and I, we don't belong here, Ekaterina. We're English. We'll make a future over there." Yet even in that instant he could not imagine his future worth sharing. He stood up and went to the window, leaning heavily against the frame, and looked out over the valley. Among the myrtle and eucalyptus trees columns of smoke were rising, where the pilgrims were camped along the river.

His hope was succumbing to pure pain. Very clearly, as in some colourless light, he saw himself an aberration in her life. He could not imagine himself and her together. Not truly. Not if he was honest. And in personal relationships, it seemed, what you could not imagine never came true. He looked round to see Ekaterina wiping her eyes on the dust sheet. She did not know that he was looking at her. He came and stood beside her. She said truculently: "I've wrecked you again."

He understood that this was a question, and took a deep breath as if returning himself to sanity. But he could not answer it. She was trying to be matter-of-fact; there were things which she wanted to ask and she was asking them quickly before her tears or his anger intervened. "I shouldn't have let this happen. How are you going to forgive me?" She spoke it like a challenge.

He said: "I seduced you."

"Then how will you forgive this parting?" Her gaze was steady on him, but her face—the whiteness of skin and blackness of hair—held a look of almost sensual violence. She was pushing him, in as hard a voice as she could use, to the limits of honesty.

He started to bluster. "I'm sorry, Kat. There's nothing to forgive. I'm close to desperation. I'm not accusing you." He noticed he was stuttering. He had never stuttered in his life.

She said tensely, again like a challenge: "But it wasn't worth it."

He opened his hands. People had a mindless way of saying love was always worth it: even if somebody paid with years of humiliation for a few moments' ecstasy.

He asked instead: "Where will you go?"

She said: "To the Capital first. After that, we've no idea."

He watched her with vague wonder. It sometimes seemed as if women could bear far more than men. "What will you do?"

"I don't know, but I'll get a job, start a career. I won't just lie down." She realized that of her whole future—years and years of it must lie ahead—she knew nothing. But she did not think that she could tolerate being unhappy for ever: that self-obsession.

Julian continued to ask about her future, but little by little, as they were speaking, she saw that his face was breaking up. She could not bear this. She would rather he was angry, cruel, even cold. She tried to inject optimism and humour into her voice, but neither sounded. And the next moment she was protecting her own heart by trying to comfort him. She heard the clichés trickling from her mouth. Everything would be all right, she said. Time would cure even this. And you never knew what was going to happen. You planned and planned, but something always took you by surprise. Wasn't it so? Her tears began falling on to the sofa. She ignored them. Just as everything seemed to be going badly, she said, something good would fall out of the sky. You never knew in life. . . .

Suddenly Julian was trying to hold her.

She almost shouted at him: "No! Please! Don't!"

He stared at her, standing up. Then he looked around him as if there might be others in the room and said in an odd, clumsy way: "I suppose I'd better be going." He kissed her very hard, almost angrily, on the mouth, and blundered towards the door. He refused to look round at her, fumbled with the handle.

It was she who cried out "Julian," as he opened it, and heard her own voice pleading, like a girl's. "We won't see one another again."

He did not look back at her, but closed the door, pushed down the stairs and out into the street. He turned like a robot along a footpath and walked with long, fast strides in no particular direction. A sharp wind was blowing off the sea. He passed the mining offices and the explosives dump, then skirted the hills of slag inside whose ring the pit mine had expired. His feet, shod only in canvas shoes, kicked the loose limestone left and right. He was holding his stomach.

In front of him low hills bent up from the plain. The light trickled down from an empty sky. Beyond, the land rose to igneous crags, which darted up through the sandstone and showed a sprinkle of pines. Now he could look down on Kalepia, meaningless town. The thought of it started a sickness in his throat, so that he spat into the rocks. For half an hour he continued tramping over this indifferent earth until he stopped and heard only cicadas, dry, prattling . . . and saw nothing but the steep slope of a bare hill, and a crater whose mouth was stale with grass. He lay down among its rocks. The stubs of the grass against his cheek were a sickly yellow. The year long dead. He turned away his gaze. The decaying colour lay over the whole hillside below, like the flank of a mangy camel. His breath was tired and light against the stones. Around the whitened stems of the thorn bushes, underneath and in between, the cyclamen were growing, and a black file of ants was trickling over the porous rock.

Chapter Eighteen

Kallis' face had broken out in a hot rash, which he kept cooling by twisting first one cheek then the other against the straw pillow. Finally he lay and stared into the darkness, imagining the saint's day in the uncomplicated form of his own plans. He was not exactly afraid, even at this cold hour. But while he had once looked forward to the day as revenge, now that it was approaching he found himself steeled less by hatred than by a protective duty. The feeling was less happy. The people's trust was mounted like a crate upon his back. His head was filled with their voices and pleas, and by the almost infantile faith in some of their faces. Such people, trooping in and out of the flour mill to see him, could not have known how weakly their confidence was based nor how, after they had left him with their troubles and petitions, he sat brooding and doubting.

An hour before dawn Philippou padded into the cottage and shook his shoulder, but by then he had already been awake a long time. For a few minutes more he gazed at the ceiling and one by one, as if putting on a suit of armour, he recited to himself the intentions of the Company, until they had cemented again into his hate. Then he eased himself off the mattress, the flagstones chilling his feet, and thrust on his boots and jacket. Through the window the night sky showed cloudless; no hint of dawn. In the mirror over his basin he saw that the rash was fading out of his face, leaving pink lines as if he had been struck. He started to shave fastidiously.

Philippou, who had been chafing his hands above the stove, came over to him and said tensely: "You mustn't do that—shaving before danger." He drew away Kallis' razor from his cheek. "If you make yourself too smart before such a day, God will take you."

Kallis turned to him sourly. For a moment he did not know if Philippou was joking, then he saw that the fisherman's left cheek was dark and rough; he had only shaved one side of his face. "I didn't know you were religious," he said.

Philippou grimaced. "That's not religion." He went back shivering to the stove. "Put on second-best clothes too. Don't tempt the Powers."

Kallis laughed and went on shaving, while Philippou watched him in silence. The fisherman's oilskins were buttoned to the neck; above them his face looked doughy and drained by the early hour. He was chewing gum. He said: "You heard the Company put a convoy through to the Mountain last night?"

"Yes." Kallis nicked his chin, winced. "Two dump trucks. That can't mean more than forty men. The rest are still on the other side."

He picked the razor-blade from the shaver, went over to the box in the corner of the room and slit the seals along its sides. The old fisherman had done his job. He had carried the detonator and explosives quietly ashore the previous night, as if they were a crate of fish or paraffin oil, while the rifles remained in his boat, anchored off-shore with his son asleep in the stern.

Kallis ran his hands over the contents, then loaded them into two shabby suitcases: detonating cord and blaster in one, gelignite in the other. A moment later Alastos came in, very quietly for so big a man, without knocking. He looked grim and self-contained. He stood in the middle of the room, his hands deep in the pockets of his windcheater, and asked sombrely: "You've got the explosive?"

Kallis said: "It's all there."

Alastos picked the detonator diagram and instructions off the bench, glanced at them and muttered: "That's all right."

When Philippou opened the door the air blew in cold, but windless. Kallis checked his watch: it was quarter past five. He carried the case of gelignite himself, and gave Alastos the other. They squashed straw hats low over their foreheads and set out down the street without talking.

There was still no trace of dawn, and few of the houses showed lights, but the three men skirted the wharf, cutting through alleys friendly to them. The street lamps were still lit, but whenever

Kallis stopped to listen he heard only the howling of the dogs which ran in wild at night to eat the town's garbage. Once Alastos concealed the suitcases in a doorway and walked ahead to inspect the main street, but it was quiet as death. Avoiding the residential suburbs in case of police, they moved into open country. They planned to join the river east of the bridge, where the banks rose steep, and to follow it downstream. They judged their way by the town lights on one side and by the Mountain on the other, only hurrying their pace where the Company's lamps shone over their path. In spite of rain, the ground held firm underfoot, and they walked confidently even where they could not see. Over abandoned terraces thistles squealed against the sides of the suitcases, and as the three neared the river they found themselves pushing through waving fields of asphodel.

Alastos fixed his mind on the bridge. He allowed nothing else to enter it. The screaming of the thistles round his feet echoed a noise far inside him, but he did not listen. By a cold effort of will he turned himself into a machine, adapted only to the business in hand: to preserve a people against an industry. He kept his pace long and slow so as not to outdistance the others.

Kallis said: "We must be nearly there."

They listened for the noise of the river, but could not hear it. Beneath a clump of eucalyptus trees a group of pilgrims lay asleep under goatskins, with their feet all pointed to the embers of their fire. One of the men cradled an old gun, lying with it against his cheek as if it were a woman. But the women's heads were covered by their shawls—they looked like so many corpses—except for a young girl, rolled on to her back and grimacing at the stars. Philippou pulled out his chewing-gum, crept forward and placed it deftly on her teeth. She did not move. He knew that Kallis would be glaring, so walked on without looking at him, and whistled tunelessly between his teeth. A minute later they had reached the river.

It ran higher than any of them could remember it, flowing fast and without sound into the dark. As they followed it downstream, the roots and branches of pines swirled past them, and sometimes they had to wade over flooded terraces. Soon the lights of the mining installations appeared high on their left, and by these they saw the bridge a hundred metres ahead.

Kallis checked his watch and stared behind him. "I think it's dawning." They looked up and saw that the stars were fading and that a white mist was growing up beyond the hills. They settled in a crop of boulders which Kallis had noticed the day before, and opened the suitcases.

"Nobody can see us here," Kallis muttered "and there are enough rocks to hide the detonating cord for ninety metres along the bank."

Alastos said: "There's a crack in the bridge on the nearside pier." He stood the detonator on the ground. "We'll wedge the charge in that."

Kallis asked: "Where's the firing device?"

"It's sealed into the cylinder. All you have to do is press down the handle." Alastos turned the detonator in his hands. "These are efficient things, American."

Kallis looked at him anxiously: "It'll do the job?"

"Yes. Mixture of mercury fulminate and potassium." Alastos settled it back on the ground. "It's not the detonator I'm worried about, it's the explosive. It may not carry a heavy enough charge. That bridge is solid."

Philippou was grinning to himself. "I reckon it'll work," he said. "Did my service with sappers. Blew a pair of fellows to thin air once. One moment they were there. The next they weren't." He pulled his hat more firmly over his face. "Do you believe in the resurrection of the body?"

Kallis said: "You told me you were too blind to do military service."

Philippou took no notice, only went on: "Trouble was, they were our own fellows I blew up. So I told the sergeant, very polite: my mistake, I said. And he decided he'd put them down as deserters, since they'd vanished so completely." Philippou began to heave with laughter.

Kallis did not say anything—some things were better ignored—but kept his gaze on the paling sky. Sometimes Philippou reminded him of men he knew who had worked for Intelligence or the security police. When people asked you what such men were like, you opened your mouth to answer but realized that you did not know. The character they presented to you was not an insight, but a wall.

By now the stars were waning and there was enough light to see their way, without easily being seen. Alastos unclipped the detonating flex and he and Kallis ran crouching along the bank, laying the cord behind rocks and occasionally mounding loose earth and stones over it. The river furled close round the base of the bridge. After he had checked the blasting caps Alastos leant round the pier and pushed the charge high up between the stones. He grimaced as he went back to the boulders—the bridge was massive, built of jointed limestone—but the other man was not looking at him. The lights of the miners' houses were all burning bright, and Kallis was wondering why this was. Yet the three men were too far away to hear anything, so they settled among the rocks while behind them a cold sun rose through the trees.

Philippou was rubbing his hands together with excitement. "Why don't we blow it up now and have done?"

"No." Kallis looked at his watch again. "The later we blast the better. Gives them less time to think. As soon as they get near we'll see the lorries' dust, and detonate before they reach it. So keep your eyes on the track."

It was quarter to seven. Among the trees some of the pilgrims were already stirring. The sunlight hit the dome of the shrine, setting it aglow, and came leaking down the crevices of the Mountain. As on many other mornings, Kallis noted with relief that the sanctuary still stood. He did not believe in the saint, but there was a remote fear of divinity in him—the fear of country people for an avenging God. He had an idea that God, like man, would act only when His own interests were at stake. So, kneeling behind the rocks, his gaze on the empty track, he thought that this God must now be on their side.

But Alastos was not thinking of God at all. God to him was anarchic, unknown. He was remembering Ekaterina's face and reminding himself that his beliefs were hers too. That steeled him, even to violence. She too had loved the town and wanted it to live and keep its spirit. He lay on his stomach, his head in the shade of the rocks, and tried to see into tomorrow. He wondered if men would be killed, and how many, but wondered this in abstract, unable to envisage it.

At seven o'clock, just as the sun touched the top of the bridge above the red river, a spurt of dust showed. Kallis craned his neck over the rocks. "They can't be coming this early." But he kept one hand on the detonator handle.

After a minute a white limousine drew up on the far side of the river and a man got out. He was sifting through some papers in his hand. They could not distinguish his face. He strolled to the bridge and looked down into the river, as if gauging its depth. Now the sun shone full on him and flashed against the miner's helmet at his belt.

"Who's that?" whispered Kallis.

Alastos said: "Muller."

The Mine Superintendent walked half way over the bridge and stood in the alcove at its centre, writing notes. Kallis said through gritted teeth: "They must be going to send the men over now." He cursed. "He's not going to stand there."

But Muller did not move. They could see the hard gloss of his head in the sun. He appeared to be sitting on the stonework behind him. Kallis was starting to sweat. He took his hand off the detonator and wiped his palms on the knees of his trousers. Muller was now perfectly still; he must be reading. Philippou said: "He'd make beautiful thin air."

But Kallis rounded on him tightly: "We're not killing! We wait until he goes!"

"What if he doesn't go?"

Kallis turned away, swearing between his teeth. The sun was shining on the river and had flattened out the shadows from the hills beyond. And now, far away at first, then nearer, a rumbling sounded. Kallis listened, his face white. Winding down the slope in clouds of dust, the lorries were coming. Even from here he could see the mass of silver-helmeted heads inside them. Without thinking, he knelt upright among the boulders, fully visible, as if he would wave Muller away, but the Superintendent was looking at the notes in his hand. He was going to check the lorries as they crossed.

Alastos had been lying flat under the rocks. But now he saw the danger, jumped to his feet and shouted: "Don't blast! I'll get him off!" and galloped like a bear towards the bridge.

Kallis was breathing in gasps. He dashed the back of his hand over his face. The trucks were lurching close now, he could hear their clanking, ten or fifteen of them in a long, dust-plumed convoy. He realized that they were going to cross while Muller remained on the bridge, and that Alastos would be too late. He could not keep his hands from shaking, his whole body shaking from fury and despair, and his voice exploded in an almost soundless hoarseness: "Get off! Get off! Get off!" But Muller had not moved a pace, and Alastos was still fifty metres from him, running and waving his arms, unseen. And now the noise of the lorries drowned everything.

The lead truck was almost at the bridge and Muller still waiting at its centre.

Philippou shouted: "Blow the bastard up!"

Kallis' hands were trembling on the detonator handle. "Move off!" he screamed. "Curse you!" His fingers were dancing on the handle. He was almost crying with frustration. The first lorry had reached the bridge's crest, and stopped. Kallis dug his fingers into the soil in front of him, not trusting them on the detonator, and stared over the rocks in a thickening anguish. A second truck was close behind, and a third. They were all filled with men.

Philippou peered into Kallis' face and asked in a thin, teasing voice, as of a child: "Can't you do it?" Then his own face split and he fell on to his back, convulsed by a laughter which pealed out of him over and over and over. "Did you ever see anything so stupid? He has Muller sitting there like a stuffed partridge and then he can't ... hahahaha! *Kyrie Eleison!* Oh Holy Mother! Hahahaha!" Where his oilskin jacket divided from his trousers a heap of white stomach pulsed under his fingers, with a trickle of pubic hair. "I won't be able to move for a week ... not a month. Oh *Panaghia*! Pour wine on me. Piss on me...."

But Kallis was not hearing him. He was staring at the bridge with a face as pale as chalk. The first lorry was over now, and another very close. Alastos was scrambling up the river bank, bellowing his lungs out, but Muller had not moved. Kallis began to whimper out loud. "Failed ... Failed." For a moment he knelt with his head in his hands. Then, trembling violently, he grasped the detonator handle. The second truck was almost on the bridge. Kallis crossed himself, closed his eyes.

The blast was strangely quiet. But an enormous spiral of dust engulfed the bridge and burst over Alastos as he reached it. For a moment he sank on to his haunches and was coughing uncontrollably; at every breath his throat and lungs thickened with powder, and the cloud was so dense that he could not see five metres ahead of him. He heard the second lorry groan to a halt, and a noise of stones trickling and splashing into the river. He crawled forward. The air was rank with the stench of explosive. Then, tentatively, he stood up. He found himself isolated, as if in a sandstorm. On either side of him men were crying and shouting, but they were all invisible. He heard too the water's lapping underneath him, and knew that the bridge must still be standing. He shouted: "Muller! Muller!"

The noise of the men behind and in front of him was more subdued now. They sounded farther away. He groped forward. He could see the parapet of the bridge beside him; its stones looked loosened, but were still in place. He sensed the river strong and close beneath, and as he looked the blurred shape of a tree branch floated below him, as if through air. He strode forward and shouted into the haze: "Muller!" Then his foot hit something. It was a miner's helmet, the lining torn away.

He advanced a few more paces. He had a sensation that the bridge was swaying in the river's current. The stone was ripped and scattered above where the charge had been laid. Beyond it was spreadeagled a huge, discoloured shape. Muller lay on his back in a spreading stain of blood. It was coagulating in his hair, and his eyes were staring at the sky. Alastos crept forward, leaned over him and put out his hands, shaking, as if to staunch the wound which had opened over half one side of his chest. Then he saw that the whole body, even the eyes, was covered with a film of dust.

He knelt staring at Muller for what seemed a long time. They were alone together in the yellow mist. The only noise was the lisping and grating of water under the bridge. The German's face wore no expression except surprise. Alastos felt for his pulse. He knew at once that this was futile. But his fingers stayed a full minute on the coarse, red wrist, and once he tried to slide his hand under the head to support it—it seemed wrong that it should be lying in the dirt.

But in the end he stepped back and waited for the sun to pierce the haze, while Muller lay in front of him with his mouth open in its look of dismay. Gradually lifting, the dust blurred the bridge and the river and the farther bank together. But by contrast the body at Alastos' feet became defined minute by minute more terribly.

He was shaken by a deep, uncontrollable revulsion. It struck him in waves, filling him with astonishment at all he had said or thought of violence without comprehending it. It was as if only now did he understand the force of death. It was not the clouded eyes nor the split chest which moved him with awe—his hands were already covered in Muller's blood—but the monstrous finality, and the violation and the mystery of it. He did not know who, if anybody, had cared for this man. To him Muller was a brute. But he stooped down and closed the lids over the eyes. He heard himself rasping over and over again "Not right, not right, not right. . . ." He knew that men killed every day, every hour. Yet the words went on stuttering in him, confused by self-horror: "Not right, not right. . . ."

By now the miners from either side of the bridge were crowding through the haze. The sight of Muller's body confused them; they did not associate Alastos with his death. The men in the first lorry had seen two figures running along the river bank after the explosion, and had given chase, but lost them. Now they stared curiously at Muller's corpse, muttering among themselves, and finally lifted it on to their shoulders and carried it back to his limousine. A small crowd of townspeople gathered on the far bank, but the miners drove them away. They were becoming savage. They tolerated Alastos only because he had been first on the scene and appeared agitated. The other lorries had all stopped on the Company's side of the river, and for a while the men debated heatedly as to what they should do. A bellicose foreman was promising them revenge on the morrow. At last one of the drivers ran his truck over the shaken bridge, and the rest followed. So the convoy continued on its way to the Mountain, while Muller's body, humped on the floor of his car, was driven along the main road to the hospital.

Alastos was left alone in mounting alarm. He rested against the bridge's parapet, as Muller had done, and tried to steady himself. He thought: so Kallis has killed Muller. He closed his eyes. Nothing sounded but the river. All theory, all thought had been cleaned from his mind by the mangled shape in the dust, the individual man, defiled, ended for ever. Alastos had no ideas left. He knew only that he had been wrong, and that nothing must stay as it was. To accept things unchanged was to accept this too: a people which killed. Death was accepted here. Even in the Capital the mortality rate for children was frightening; every child had seen the end of sick brothers and sisters, and had kissed a corpse its funeral farewell, while by the country roads the carcasses of cattle lay no more noticed than fleas. He thought: generations must divide such a town as Kalepia from civilization; perhaps no people had yet achieved civilization—but such a place must not stay itself. It must change. It must march. He opened his eyes to the bright sunlight. The bridge was still empty. A circle of flies was crawling round Muller's blood. He was seized by a sense of urgency, yet of nothing to be done. Tomorrow Kalepia was going to celebrate its age-old character. It was going to murder itself.

He went down to the water and washed the blood from his hands. But he felt Muller's death through his throat, his lungs, his stomach. For the first time in years he wanted to pray. Instead he stood up, turned towards the town and began, in shaking strides, to approach it.

Chapter Nineteen

From high on the hillsides, whose eroding earth was dotted only by holm-oaks, Kalepia looked at peace. The sun beat out a lazy sheen on the sea, where a few fishing-boats moved, and above the dock the roar of murmuring men left no sound at all. Heavy with melted snows, the river flowed high between the Old Town and the New, and carried its crimson earth in clouded seams for half a mile out to sea. The wind had fallen. Above the valley vertical pillars of bluish smoke rose, and the inland hills showed the dust-plumes of pilgrims travelling to the coast.

The country looked worn and old. To the east sinews of rock, in some primaeval age, had broken through the cooling crust of the earth, and now rolled uninhabited to the skyline. To the west the dome of St Vichinos shone above the town, and the silver helmets of the miners glinted along the Company's fence. Their patrols were six men strong now, and restless. In this clear light Alastos could pick out the swing of their batons. Even from here they sickened him with their miniature violence. He thought: they must all be madmen over there.

A few hours before, he had returned to the deserted bridge and had ripped out the detonating cord from among its rocks and thrown it into the river. Despising himself, he had thrown in the blaster too, which was covered in his fingerprints. Then he began to walk, hot with frustration. His own powerlessness maddened him. It seemed as if everything had been decided long ago in the days when he had talked of violence, and that nothing could now be changed.

On the way into the town he came up behind a group of pilgrims.

They had the pinched, hard, straight look of fanatics. One of the men had lashed together a cross out of pinewood, which he carried over his shoulders. Alastos blundered past them. The sun was flaming in his eyes. It was past noon and he had not eaten; he was covering the track in trembling strides. He reached the main street, slackened his pace, and crossed the road towards the docks. The lanes were slung with banners and streamers, while many others had broken and hung down from the guttering and balconies, or lay trodden in the street.

The wharfside was thick with people; some of them carried heavy sticks. They stood together in clusters while the coffee-boys scuttled between them dangling their cups from brass trays. From a nearby church the chanting of the liturgy was swollen with unaccustomed voices. The cranes were at a standstill. Two freighters groaned beneath them unattended, their cargo of carrots half-loaded.

Alastos barged into the flour mill, panting vehemently. The hall was deserted. The machines looked as if they had been silent a long time, and from under the casing of the grain-washer the foam had coagulated in mucous clouds. He clanged up the iron stairs and saw a light through the glass door of Matheopoulos' office. The old man was seated alone, writing letters, his pen scratching over the page. A cup of coffee stood at his elbow, but had not been drunk.

He looked up at Alastos with pale-eyed disapproval. He appeared very tired. His face and neck were creased in unhealthy-looking folds, which lapped over his collar and depressed his mouth.

Alastos did not even notice his hostility. He grabbed the old man's hand almost before it had put down the pen, and shook it boisterously. "Mr Matheopoulos, it's good to see you! Thank God there's a sane face here!" Then he sat himself on the desk, dangling his legs, and stared earnestly into the lined face. But Matheopoulos unhooked his gold-rimmed spectacles and looked back with deep distaste. Alastos' shirt was grimed with sweat, his boots worn out and his English twill trousers baggy and torn at the knees.

He was still shouting, although his mouth was near to Matheopoulos' ear. "Things are going from bad to worse!"

The old man lowered his head as if to weather a storm. "That's what happens."

Alastos said: "Somebody had better do something quick, that's all I can say, or there won't be anyone left to do it. Did you hear that Muller's been killed?"

"Yes, I heard."

The palms of Alastos' hands landed on the old man's shoulders. "What are we going to do?"

"Do?" Matheopoulos looked him up and down contemptuously. "What do you mean? You wanted this, didn't you? You and your talk of not being afraid of bloodshed!" He jerked his shoulders, as if ridding himself of something. "There are things more important than life, you said. People shouldn't let themselves be trodden under. People should stand up." He tucked his pen petulantly into his inside pocket. "Well, that's what's happening."

Alastos banged the desk in frustration. "Of course there are things more..." Those words of his seemed centuries old; they belonged to somebody else. "But Muller has been *killed*."

"Life's full of that sort of thing." Matheopoulos was trying to edge his chair away from him. "Violence is all these people know."

Alastos was breathing heavily. He poked his finger vindictively at Matheopoulos. "You call yourself a Christian man! And you accept that!"

"It makes no difference what I accept." Matheopoulos' voice had turned acid. "Or what you refuse to accept."

Alastos fumed. "So you're going to run away from it! You're just going to watch!"

"Yes. And so are you."

"My God I'm not!"

"Then you're a fool," said Matheopoulos; he fingered the watch-chain over his portly stomach, as if he must go. "Because tomorrow there'll be bloodshed."

Alastos' temper broke. He seized Matheopoulos by the lapels of his coat and shook him to and fro. "You just sit there and say 'Tomorrow there'll be bloodshed'! God damn you! God damn you!"

Matheopoulos turned bright pink. He grabbed at his watch, which had jumped out of its pocket, then subsided in the chair. "How dare you, young man!" He wiped his face with a huge, spotted handkerchief. "And you set yourself up as a pacifist!"

"No!"

Alastos himself was wheezing as if the dust of the bridge had entered his lungs. He was surprised to feel a little faint, then remembered that he had eaten nothing. He said grimly: "Look here. There's no time left. If anyone's going to act they'd better act now." He stood over Matheopoulos, bullying him. "This town must still be full of moderates, if only we can find them. They might be able to mediate. Twenty men—twenty determined, respected men—might still do something."

Matheopoulos had caught back his breath. He looked at Alastos bitterly. "You will not find twenty such men in the Republic."

Alastos watched him ease his fingers round his collar, then loosen his tie. The old man's voice sounded different. It was half sneering. "Respected, you say! Who respects anybody?" The words twisted his mouth. "This is the age of disrespect. They say respect is slavery." He refused to look at Alastos, but began to tidy the ruffled papers on his desk. "I don't know. I'm just an old man. But now there's no respect for law or opinion or anything else. They're remaking the world everywhere." He brushed the dust from the desk, as if he was brushing away Alastos too. "And you tell me to do something about them. Well, I've done enough." He added quietly, as if to himself: "Let them get what they deserve."

Alastos at last realized that he was talking to a man who no longer cared. And now Matheopoulous did not want to see him, but was fumbling with his letters. He drew out his reading spectacles again, polished them quickly, and bent the gold hooks behind his ears. "Good-bye, Mr Alastos."

When Alastos emerged on to the dockside again the sun had slipped from its meridian. He should have been teaching in Sofroniou's school half an hour ago, and now his legs carried him automatically in that direction, although the idea of school was ridiculous. As he shouldered his way through the people he caught sight of himself in the side-mirror of a parked lorry; he looked haggard, and his eyes burnt blue through a dust-lined face. He ran his hands through his hair and tried to crush it down. It sprang up. He buttoned his shirt and shook the dust from his trousers.

Sofroniou's school was not far from the bridge. Almost alone among people from the New Town, the miners' children still crossed it unmolested, but returned immediately after their lessons. Most of them, he thought, were likeable pupils, and during the past months they seemed to have grown fond of him. But the trouble with which his teaching had started had rapidly deepened. More and more of the children, generally girls, had complained of sickness and stomach cramps. Their work had deteriorated. On the day of the attack on the archimandrite's residence he had found his blackboard chalked with threatening slogans; and the morning after the muckers had run wild in the town, none of the miners' children had appeared for lessons at all. Often he had arrived to find the classroom in uproar while the loutish Vassos, a farmer's son, fought with the fat Stelios whose father was a miner. And no sooner had the priest's boy recovered from his black eye than a jagged cut appeared on the bridge of his nose. This time Alastos had not asked him how he came by it.

Now, as he was approaching the school, he heard the distant swell of a crowd's voice. It came at him in gusts of talking and crying. He looked at his watch: he was forty minutes late for his class. As he came close the noise grew harsh and staccato. He heard the smack and thud of stones. The hoarse man's voice of Vassos bawled "Unbelievers!" and somebody else was howling with either pain or temper. Alastos emerged opposite the bridge to find his class in two dense ranks which were hacking and screaming at one another under a rain of pebbles. Packed together in a frightened fury, the miners' sons were trying to escape towards the river while the town's children prodded them with sticks. Even as he looked the fat Stelios received a stone full in the face and fell on his knees. Behind him the miners' girls were picking up stones as big as rocks, and a hoyden with blood on her shins ran up and punched another girl in the throat.

Alastos rushed towards them. They were no more than a hundred metres from him, yet seemed far away, as if by the time he reached them there would be nothing left to save. The softness of the ground added to the dreamlike feel of his running. He made no noise. In the scene in front of him the priest's son was tearing at Stelios' head while he knelt on the ground with his fingers in his eyes. Some of the miners' girls were running away.

Alastos burst between the two ranks shouting "Stop! Stop! Stop!" He glared threateningly to either side of him. But the terrible screaming continued and the stones made whistling arcs round his head. In a moment of bewilderment, with his hands fallen to his sides, he realized that they were not even seeing him. They were looking clean through him at one another, and even as he stood there the town's children advanced past either side of him and began jabbing at the legs of the boys opposite. He had a nightmare sense of being invisible. He ran back between them, still shouting. A centimetre from his thigh somebody thrust forward a stick and the girl in front screamed and bit on her hand. He looked round stupefied. Their faces froze his blood. They were no longer those of children. The next moment a stone hit him behind the ear.

Never, never, never, Sofroniou had reminded him, strike the child of a Greek. If you do, his whole family will come at you. But it was too late for such scruples. They were tearing each other to bits—the pupils he had thought he knew; and the blood was trickling down his neck. He hurled himself into them, his sheer weight bowling them over left and right. He kicked the feet of the priest's son from under him and tore and snapped the sticks out of half a dozen hands. He cuffed four or five of the larger boys so hard that they tumbled on the ground, and twisted the ears of the miners' girls until they had dropped their stones. Vassos had so far lost his head that he came at Alastos with his fists and ended running away in tears. And even after the two sides had stopped fighting, they remained glowering at each other in their ranks, only waiting for Alastos to go away. They panted round him like animals. Their eyes were glittering with a strange excitement; their faces scarlet. At one time he had an idea that they were all going to rush at him. Many of them were bleeding or limping. But some still trailed their broken sticks in their hands, and others were eyeing stones on the ground.

Alastos' voice, as he harangued them, sounded exhausted even to him. "What's wrong with you? You've been in the same class as one another for years! Haven't you learnt to be friends?" and so on. But after a while, seeing the deaf fanaticism on their faces, he gave up. The only way to disperse them, he thought, was to dismiss them one by one. He started with Stelios, who was moaning and holding his ribs; a great crystal of a bruise was rising on his forehead. Alastos pushed him towards the bridge. "You go home now. Get some ointment. And stop blubbering. It's your own fault." He picked out the dark miner's daughter, whose green and white uniform was spattered with somebody else's blood, and told her to accompany him.

The others filtered away in groups. Some of the miners' sons rounded defiantly on the bridge, but the town children only jeered and turned their backs. Alastos bellowed at them to get out of his sight. With a deepening horror he walked over the ground where they had fought, and picked up a brooch, a pen-knife and a watch with a broken strap. He pulled a leaf from the mulberry tree by the bridge, where Caroline and he used to kiss, and wiped the dried blood off his neck. Then he made his way to the school. He could not imagine what he would teach or say to these children after tomorrow. He had nothing left with which to command them, except his size.

He found the classrooms empty; the teachers had sent the elder pupils home. The strip-lights still glowed in the passages, but the only sound came from the far side of the courtyard, where infants were chanting in the nursery school. He wanted to find Sofroniou. But he would not trouble the old man with the children's behaviour. Tomorrow was more important. He had an idea that in a moment the Company and the Old Town must start to feel afraid of one another. Then they would want to talk, and there would be nobody left to talk through.

Alastos noticed how unsteady his own footfalls sounded, reverberating in the corridors. As he turned a corner, he came face to face with Caroline. They could not avoid one another. She taught in the nursery-school at different hours from the rest and although he had seen her at a distance, they had not spoken. Now she backed against the wall as if he must want to pass. He hesitated.

"Hullo." He noticed her sky-blue blouse. Somehow you always noticed what Caroline was wearing.

"Hullo," she said. "How are you?"

"Me? Pretty filthy."

Caroline was looking embarrassed. Her hand kept coming up to her hair. She said: "I thought I heard a noise out there. Did you hear it?"

"Yes," he said ruefully. "It was my class. Fighting."

"Oh. These children have got so out of hand recently. Mine have been naughty too."

"Have they?"

She said with an uneasy brightness: "Let's hope their parents aren't as bad tomorrow."

Alastos failed to smile; he was not focusing her well. "There's a danger," he said.

She fingered her golden hair. It looked unreal to him, like a brittle halo. "It'll be the town's fault if anything happens. Daddy's already spoken to every one of the miners that they're not to fight unless they're attacked. Every single one! That's not bad in a company of over three hundred."

Alastos said: "No. That's good." He nodded at her a little vaguely, yet a little nervously, and made as if to go. "I'm looking for Sofroniou. Do you know where he is?"

"Yes, he's in his classroom. Most of his pupils didn't turn up today." She came closer to him. "Are you feeling all right?"

"Me? Yes, I'm O.K."

Caroline nodded briskly. They walked away from one another. But when she reached the corner of the corridor, he heard her stop. She returned to him a little paler and said: "I was sorry to hear about Ekaterina, Julian. You must have been awfully upset."

Alastos said: "Yes."

He made for Sofroniou's classroom. The sky was darkening. The west wing of the school barely showed a light. He thrust through the double wooden doors, which were painted with slogans, and peered into the headmaster's lecture-room. Sofroniou was seated high at his desk, just as Alastos had found him almost a year before on his return to Kalepia. He resembled, for some reason, a judge. And as before, Alastos walked clumsily to the foot of the dais and stood beneath it like a defendant, before the old man recognized him. Sofroniou eventually peered down and said: "You look as if you've been somewhere."

"I've been ... walking."

Sofroniou made no move to descend from the platform. He was correcting exercise books with angry flickers of a silver pencil. The waning light, sickly orange, lit his wisps of hair in a faint, harmless fire. Alastos said: "I've got to talk to you."

Sofroniou sighed.

"You know everyone in this town," Alastos said to him. "Why don't we try to find some men in public positions—town councillors, civil servants—and get them to act as mediators? It might just work."

Sofroniou clicked his tongue in disparagement, while his pencil continued to dart over the exercise book. "If that was going to work it would have happened months ago."

Alastos started to stride up and down under the dais. He could not get near Sofroniou while he sat up there. As a pupil it was always forbidden to mount the platform. But he raised his voice rudely. "You've always stood for moderation. You must know people who feel the same. Where are they all?" He stopped his marching and stared hard up at Sofroniou.

The old teacher had laid down his pencil. "They've locked up their houses and gone away," he said, his voice turned plaintive. "That's what sane men are doing here. Yes, all over town. Haven't you seen the northern suburbs? ... Locked and gone away."

Alastos burst out: "God damn them!"

Sofroniou was bobbing backwards and forwards. "I don't see what you think they could do," he said. "No one can do anything any more."

"There must be an answer!"

"Why?" asked Sofroniou in his shaking voice. "Why must there?" He stared at his ex-pupil, and thought: has he not learnt anything? But no, he was like the poor archimandrite, always looking for the answers instead of criticizing the questions. No doubt, thought Sofroniou, you could forge many solutions in the mind—the brain, after all, was an ordering instrument—but out in the world, where things happened, it didn't work.

Alastos was shouting: "Let's at least show ourselves! Make it known the whole place isn't insane!"

Sofroniou's alarm sharpened. He said plaintively: "That's for the police to do. It's not our job ... you leave it to the police." Far in the back of his mind he was wondering why Alastos found these people so much worth saving. Couldn't he see them? If he was honest, he would acknowledge that they were little more than a mob. Any person of culture and intelligence had bolted himself in his home.

Alastos looked as if he might mount the forbidden platform. "Police! They're just a lot of townsmen in uniform! They won't lift a finger!" He glared at his old master. "It's we who have to do something! Me! You!"

"I?" Sofroniou was squirming his hands along the rim of the desk, as if he was playing a piano. "I go out there? What are you trying to say?" The sun had slanted down from his face and picked out the isolated hairs on his neck; he looked scraggy and pink, like a baby bird. The neck, Alastos thought, asked to be strangled. "No.... My wife is frail. We're going away this evening. To my home village ... it's not very far. My granddaughter is having her first child." He was not looking at his ex-pupil's face. "In any case, I dare say nothing much will happen here. No bloodshed, I dare say...."

Slowly, as Alastos listened, the anger left him and instead a cold depression began spreading through his body. He could feel it physically, sinking down from his head and leaking along all his veins, so that he suddenly wanted to sit down. His feet were very heavy. He noticed them caked in mud. He said colourlessly: "There's been bloodshed already."

"Yes," Sofroniou said. "I heard."

Alastos turned to one of the desks behind him and sat heavily. Why was Sofroniou not standing by him? The schoolmaster had always seemed so humane; and he understood more than anybody. Yet he was going away. He did not seem to care.

Sofroniou saw the disappointment in Alastos' face, and feeling ill at ease, came down from his desk and sat in the one beside him. It was sad, he thought, to see Alastos. He, who had wanted so much to happen, was now merely trying to prevent anything from happening. Sofroniou put a hand on his shoulder and said: "You shouldn't upset yourself about things you can't change." He picked a bag of sugared almonds out of his pocket and offered them, as to a child. "There's a saying in this country—do you remember?—that you can't alter mules or Kalepiots." Alastos, who was ravenous, plunged his hand into the bag and took three sugared almonds while Sofroniou was talking. The old man was starting to ramble: "You yourself haven't changed a jot since you were a child ... no, not a jot. And as for me ..." he laughed with fluting self-mockery, "did I ever tell you that I wanted to be a painter?" Alastos did not answer; his mouth was full of sugared almonds, and Sofroniou's mind seemed to be wandering. "But everything I painted turned the same. Yes, it was as if everything was already done. And I was trivial." He was sitting back with a dreamy look. "I didn't know I was trivial until I began to paint. Now I know. And I don't paint any more."

By the time he had finished this anecdote he had forgotten what it was intended to prove. Alastos, in any case, had not been listening, and now looked up from licking his fingers and said: "So you won't be here tomorrow?"

"No, I won't," said Sofroniou, "and I don't think you should be either." He shook Alastos' shoulder. "Why don't you come with my wife and me? My village is in the valley behind the Mountain, a charming place. We'll spend a quiet day." He stared enquiringly into the other man's face, but Alastos was not answering. Sofroniou went on: "Did I tell you that I'm about to become a great-grandfather? It's a strange thought."

Julian wanted to sleep. He would have liked to have gone with Sofroniou into that valley, and seen his village. "I can't," he said. "All the same, thanks." He stood up unsteadily. "I'd better be getting back home. I haven't had a meal all day."

Sofroniou called after him in his querulous voice: "Don't you go doing anything silly tomorrow. It wouldn't do at all if ... no, it wouldn't ... just stay indoors."

Alastos did not reply. He said good-bye curtly. He was angry with Sofroniou for making him despise him. He pushed through the wooden doors. The sun had set a moment before. He watched its afterglow shrink into the roofs. For a few minutes the sky showed porcelain blue, then the night fell. On either side of the river the town was awake and watching itself. The lights of the Mining Company were already blazing all over the hill.

He started to walk, following the river through the eucalyptus groves in spite of memory. Above him the torches of the miners' patrols moved along the Mountain fence, and two arc lamps, attached to a mobile generator, cast the shadow of the barbed wire gates half way down the slope. All along the valley and the base of the Mountain the pilgrims' fires flickered among the trees; they appeared like the camp of a besieging army.

Alastos walked towards them by the river. He was feeling close to despair. High above him something exploded softly; he remembered that the town set off fireworks on St Vichinos' eve. And soon they broke open the sky with a pathetic, transient glitter. From his childhood he remembered them like jewels, impossibly beautiful; but now they seemed nothing.

Chapter Twenty

That night Alastos' sleep was troubled by dreams of Ekaterina, and of the fiasco at the bridge. Twice he woke up clutching the sides of the bed and groaning for help. But he was so tired that it was eight o'clock in the morning before he woke again. The second his eyes were open the day ahead filled him with foreboding. He sat up, as if to some well-defined task. But there was no such task, he knew. There was only his inability to stay still.

He might have dressed and run at once into the town, but he had noticed his appearance the previous night and in the quietness before sleep had thought that it was small wonder people had not listened to him. So this morning, even with little time, he shaved carefully and brushed down his angry hair; he thought of carrying one of his father's heavy sticks with him, but decided against that.

Zena had been padding noiselessly about the house in the hope that he would not wake until the crisis on the Mountain was over, but now, intercepting him in the passage, she realized by his face that it was useless trying to prevent him going, and only delayed him another minute by calling from the kitchen: "You won't go without eating again. No, you won't." She pushed a pair of apples into one trouser pocket, a packet of bread and olives into the other. "You can get a good view from the edge of the northern suburbs. Don't go looking for better."

He cupped her heavy, troubled face in his hands, and kissed it absently. "Don't you worry."

The brightness of the day and the clarity of the sky were good omens, he told himself as he walked into the street. He saw at once that on the Mountain crest, small as models, but vivid and menacing, the miners were massed three deep behind the gate, and scattered in platoons all along the fence's perimeter. He thought: the whole Company must be there.

He made straight for the dock, running in long, easy strides. Through all the residential suburbs he did not see a soul. Only a few guard dogs roamed the barren little gardens. Iron shutters were clamped over most windows, and padlocks showed on half the gates. For a quarter of an hour's running the thud of his feet was the only sound.

As he reached the main street he thought that here at least must be some life. But no, nothing. A light wind was lifting the rubbish about the pavements, and cats prowled over the tarmac. The shops were bolted. On either side of the street the cars were parked in silence head to tail.

Alastos turned down an alley towards the wharf. He did not know why he was still running, because he could not think of anything he might achieve. As Matheopoulos had said, a man could only watch, and hope to see nothing happen. Yet this senseless drumming of his feet continued. He could not stay still and watch people die. The banners above the deserted lanes gave the feeling of a carnival long over. "Keep off our Home", "St Vichinos intercede for us", "Give back our Holy Ground". Their cries already looked redundant.

Even the dock was silent. The wind brought a bright sea tossing against the harbour arm, and the quay was strewn with the country people's rubbish: vegetable peel, chicken feathers, rope, wood-shavings. Alastos leaned against the customs shed, catching his breath. On the Mountain the ranks of miners had not moved, and nothing showed along the pilgrims' path below. A medley of jeeps and dump trucks cluttered the summit near the shrine, with several of the executives' cars, and two bulldozers stood among the threatened houses.

He walked in the direction which he supposed the pilgrims to have followed. In the cathedral square he found some women and children settled among their baggage and kindling fires on the flagstones. Inside the cathedral only three widows had obeyed the archimandrite's call, and were gossiping on chairs against the pillars.

The only other person in the building was a novice who stood by an icon of St Vichinos, hoping to sell candles. He was nervous and deferential. "The archimandrite is not well," he whispered. "One of the deacons will celebrate the Eucharist."

Alastos gazed round the darkened building, where he had tramped so furiously a year before. Above him the great Christ still lifted his hand in an empty blessing—the God of his childhood's awe—while from the iconostasis the saints stared through a hundred eyes, and canvassed for his worship with their painted scrolls and swords. They were no longer terrible to him, nor right, nor wrong. They were merely the comfort of people afraid—a buffer state against oblivion.

He asked the novice: "Which way did the pilgrimage go?"

The young man did not know. But as Alastos left the cathedral there broke from the outskirts a sound which froze his veins. It was inexpressibly savage. It moved over half the northern suburbs and must be rising from an enormous crowd. Its shouts resolved into no one cry, but its mood was intent and united.

He went through the lanes towards it. It was growing all the time. Above the men's deep cries sounded the hysterical ululation of women. When he emerged from the houses he saw what seemed to be the entire town and pilgrimage spread at the foot of the Mountain. There could not be less than three thousand people. In the shallow wadi below the path they were jammed shoulder to shoulder, and a thicket of crucifixes, lashed together from pinewood, jostled above them. On this crowd's circumference showed the bright scarves of wives and daughters, but its core was thick and dark with men, whose staves mingled with the crosses. The priest had just finished addressing them. He was still standing on a rock. The congregation's bellowing rolled about him, but he looked preoccupied, as if he was listening to something else. Below him his son, Alastos' pupil, held the censer and processional cross, and some twelve-year-old schoolgirls, absurdly precious in white and blue cardigans, were clutching psalm-sheets.

Alastos pushed his way round the crowd's edges, in a deafening noise, until he was standing close to the priest. He saw with a pang that this man, of whom he had heard so much, had administered the last rites to his father. Beneath him the upturned faces were nothing now but a sea of mouths and eyes. It was as if some contagion had raged through them. In their lifted hands the staves and crosses clacked obscenely together and their cries, he thought—clamouring for their saint's revenge—must be striking at the miners' hearts on the Mountain above.

For a moment Alastos imagined that these were only the country people, and that the town had locked itself away. Then, one by one, he recognized men he knew—tradesmen, restaurateurs. Sometimes their expressions were so changed that at a distance he was unsure of their identity. But he was starting to panic. Minute by minute, before his eyes, the crowd was transforming itself, by the intoxication of its own voice, into something more ghastly than the character of any man who composed it. Yet he could not tear his gaze from them. They were primitives, a horrible truth of men. But they were the ghosts, still, of kindly people whom he remembered. It was as if the everyday faces were corroding before his eyes, were being melted down, and sliding into the furnace. He noticed the old fisherman from the delegation, the mill foreman, God-Asleep the beggar—and there must be many others. He watched their features in horror as they were consumed.

The priest still stood in front, holding his icon of the saint. The men were hustling to kiss it, and some knelt at his feet and set their lips to his hands. Quiet and aloof, he seemed already to have achieved his end.

Alastos looked for Kallis or Philippou, but in this crush he could not see them. Nobody was organizing the crowd—it was beyond control. Whatever rifles it might own were lost in the congestion, but several men with wooden clubs were thrusting their way into the vanguard near the base of the path. And now that the congregation was about to move, the noise had coalesced into a fanatic shout, curdled by the screams of the women: "Ayios Vichinos! Ayios Vichinos! Ayios Vichinos! Ayios Vichinos!"

But that cry, Alastos thought, had little to do with the saint. In this Republic politics, religion and basic human desires were inseparably mixed. You only had to look into these men's faces to see that they did not want the Mountain for God's sake. Nobody wanted anything for God. Nobody knew Him. Alastos was not even sure that they wanted the Mountain at all. Their cries seemed to be for nothing so simple or accessible.

The schoolgirls were assembling on the path. They brushed timidly together. Two of them were from his own form. Despite their pretty frocks they could be as ugly as their parents, he knew. Yet he felt anxious for them; no child should lead a pilgrimage like this. He was stricken by his utter helplessness. They turned to face the Mountain, opened their psalm-sheets and in thin, clear voices started to sing.

"Let God arise, let his enemies be scattered: let them also that hate him flee before him.

"As smoke is driven away, so drive them away: as wax melteth before the fire, so let the wicked perish at the presence of God. . . ."

Now the priest, with his son behind him, hoisted the icon high on its pole, and began to climb. Alastos watched him in momentary fascination; for he carried his singleness of purpose like a glittering axe, something of a predatory and alarming innocence. He seemed both more and less than a man. The mass of pilgrims shuddered and jostled, then slowly, four or five abreast, began to mount the path behind him.

Alastos started to run. He overtook the vanguard by clambering over boulders, and where the path coiled up steeper slopes he climbed direct, sometimes on hands and knees. His palms grew bloody with thorns. The scrape and thud of his boots drowned any other noise for him, and soon the people were far below. Five minutes later, pouring sweat, he came within hailing distance of the Company's fence. He could see the silver-helmeted phalanxes drawn up behind it, but nobody answered his shouting. He came close until he was almost touching the wire, and bellowed: "Where's Oldenburg?"

But the ranks did not answer and scarcely moved. Their faces, in the shadow cast by their helmets, were indecipherable to him. They might have been so many machines. He shouted again. One or two lazily swung their batons, and he saw another wipe his neck with the sleeve of his overalls. Several of them held rifles. But his question fell dead among them: it was as if they had never heard of Oldenburg.

He began to claw his way along the fence, and as he did so a foreman strode up on the far side and said: "What the hell are you doing?" His face was red and ferocious under the tin hat.

Alastos said: "I want Oldenburg." He settled his hands on his hips, and tried to arrange his thoughts. He must talk to the General Manager. He must pretend something. Anything was better than what was about to happen. He said: "The pilgrims have gone crazy. They're on their way up. You won't stop them unless you want to kill. If you open the gates . . ."

"Puh! You think we'd let them in here?" The man spat through the wire at Alastos' feet. "You must be off your head!"

Alastos watched him shamble back to his men. The people had all turned like that, he thought. There was no way to reach them.

But something in him still would not give up. He cursed softly and continued to climb up the fence's perimeter. In front of each group of muckers he paused and asked for Oldenburg, but the men simply stood and stared at him, as if they saw nothing beyond the circle of their wire. They had been ordered to silence. In one group he recognized his old shovel-operator and shouted to him with relief: "Hey! Lambros! Have you seen Oldenburg?" But the man only shifted a little among his fellows, as if some spark of memory discomfited him a moment.

Alastos could now physically feel his fear. It was high and cold in his chest. He wondered whether there was anybody sane left in the world. A while ago the world had seemed full of ordinary people. But now this plague had spread among mankind, compared to which the pettiness and hypocrisy of the old ways were a golden age.

He looked behind him where the ground sloped gently to the barbed-wire gates, and saw that the miners were still waiting. The pilgrims must have climbed close under the lip of the Mountain, because they were out of sight. A total silence covered the slope. Nothing moved. You could hear the hushing of the waves along the coast two kilometres away, falling on the headland under the ancient tombs. A pair of partridge, startled, circled back to rest with a whistling of wings, and down in Kalepia the howling of the dogs had died away.

Alastos could think of nothing to do. Quite near him, on a spur of the hill, he saw a goatherd whose animals were grazing on thorns. He lumbered over to the youth, pleased at finding a proper human being, and sat exhausted on the ground beside him. He offered him one of the apples from his pocket. The goatherd inspected this and nodded his thanks. He looked poor as a Turk, Alastos thought, and his sheepskin coat barely covered his shoulders. Even his goats were scrawny and few. He asked Alastos: "Who are you with?"

"I'm on my own." Alastos pulled the packet of bread and olives from his other pocket and offered this to the youth too. "I can't eat much." He had an idea that such things would cumber his running, although where he would run he did not know. He bit methodically into the other apple.

Suddenly the pilgrimage was in sight, moving up the path two hundred metres from the Company's gates. The priest walked before it, holding the icon, with his son a pace behind, and the people were marching almost in silence so that even from far away the girls' singing, husky now, penetrated up the Mountain.

"I will bring my people again from the depths of the sea...."

Alastos looked down at them, mesmerized. One moment the schoolgirls were still following the priest, the next they were faltering in their tracks and being absorbed by the mass of pilgrims swelling over the slope. But the priest moved on as impassively as in a liturgical procession; behind him his son still swung the censer in little blue puffs of fragrance; and behind them again the host of people was brimming like a great storm over the lip of the Mountain.

Alastos was on his feet, choking with suspense. He saw that within the fence Oldenburg's limousine had spiralled down from the Mountain's crest and had stopped at the entrance. He waited, praying for the gates to open. But nothing happened. His breath came short. His fists began clanging at his sides, and in the heavy simplicity of his mind he thought that if he only reached the gates he might effect something. He wrenched the rest of his food out of his pocket, his last week's pay packet too, and crammed them into the goatherd's hand. Then he shouted "Good year to you!" and charged down the boundary of the wire. Nothing any longer motivated him, nothing constructive. Only the terror of violence. His boots crashed among the stones so that the miners posted along the fence saw him coming from a long way away and yelled derisively.

A minute later he arrived breathless and shouting for Oldenburg. He looked like a brigand. The perspiration was glistening on his neck, and his jaw was set in a half bullying way. "Mr Oldenburg! If you don't let these people in they'll kill you all! Tell them you'll let them in!"

Oldenburg stepped against the wire and looked at him sternly. "Calm yourself down, Alastos." All the same, Alastos thought, he did not look calm himself; his complexion was like dirty snow; the people must have shaken him. "Nobody's moving us." He was tugging on gauntlets. "Any man who breaks through the wire is trespassing. By the law of this country he can be shot on sight."

Alastos turned his back on the gates. He thought: I must talk to the people. He had an idea that all about him men were starting to forget human speech.

The pilgrims were spread wide in front of him now—thousands there seemed—and their shouting had become a confused, staccato roar. They were running forward over the low scrub, so many that their ranks looked solid. They carried their staves upright, and he saw the gleam of a rifle. Not fifty metres from him the priest was advancing like a god, with the golden icon high over his head.

Alastos halted, his heart pounding. The mass before him showed no face to talk with. Its chanting and crying were indecipherable; he could not even distinguish the name of a saint or of a cause. He wanted to retreat on the barbed wire and on the miners behind him, but they seemed not to be men at all. And now the pilgrims were almost on him. He stepped back and felt the wire bite into his shoulders. He tried to cry out something. But there was nobody he recognized, either in front or behind.

On the thorny knoll, smoking a stale cigarette end, the goatherd wanted to go on gazing—you did not often see a man die—but he was afraid of stray bullets, and set out after his animals, which had wandered half way across the opposite valley. Examining the bread in his hands, he was unsure if to eat it might not bring bad luck, and dropped it behind him. But when he opened the crumpled envelope, he stopped dead and hissed through his teeth in astonishment. Two thousand, two hundred drachma! He looked around him guiltily. But the fellow had certainly given away the money, and would scarcely need it now. He must have been a madman to have gone running between the combatants like that. Any shepherd could have told him that you should not go between two pastures which are not yours.

The goatherd counted the notes again. With this he could buy a transistor radio! You could get all the popular music from the Capital on that, and the news, and programmes about every manner of thing. That was how people got educated, found jobs, earned more money. He stuffed the notes carefully into the back of his boots as he descended into the valley. Yes, he thought, there might be no end to it. A whole new world would unfold. . . .